Cops and Killers. Mounties and Madmen.
The critics rave about the novels of Michael Slade

"Michael Slade's thrillers are overrun with psycho killers who pose grisly mysteries for the RCMP. The depiction of cutting-edge investigative work has won Slade fans among the police. His devotion to delivering kick packs quite a wallop."
—*The Globe and Mail*

"Slade knows what he's writing about. He knows psychos inside and out. The bad guys are real monsters . . . Profound knowledge of the insane criminal gives a Slade book its credibility."
—*The Toronto Star*

"Slade specializes in the defense of insanity. Which explains his ability to explore sick minds so convincingly."
—*The Montreal Gazette*

"There are psycho-thrillers and there are psycho-thrillers, but the ones to watch are those by that Vancouver father-daughter team, Jay and Rebecca Clarke. Writing under the pseudonym "Michael Slade," this high-powered writerly duo have produced the latest in a series of acclaimed thrillers—from HEADHUNTER to GHOUL to BURNT BONES and HANGMAN, to name but a few. The team has just returned with another loaded mystery, DEATH'S DOOR . . . You might want to take a deep breath before starting this seemingly baffling case . . ."
—*The Ottawa Citizen*

"Literary bungy-jumping with Agatha Christie's bastard son."
—*The Georgia Straight*

"Riveting crime/horror novels. The courtroom honed Slade's story-telling ability. He writes a heart-stopping thriller."
—*The Edmonton Journal*

"Bloody, violent, and extreme: what a good yarn! Slade walks a fine line between fiction and reality. It is very difficult not to believe his fictional world is absolutely real. As a Crown prosecutor, I deal with cases that are investigated by the Serious Crimes Unit within the Royal Canadian Mounted Police. I now intend to look in their Directory under the letter X." —*The Vancouver Sun*

"Will raise hackles, eyebrows, and blood pressure everywhere . . . Gives you real shock value for the money."
—Robert Bloch, author of *Psycho*

"Would make de Sade wince." —*Kirkus Reviews*

"Slade runs a three-ring circus of suspense." —*Booklist*

"The kind of roller coaster fright fans can't wait to ride."
—*West Coast Review of Books*

"Well written, very well researched. A gripper."
—*London Daily Mail*

"Very interesting supernatural police procedurals." —*Playboy*

"Fast-paced action . . . full of spooky, weird stuff . . . twists and turns, and sudden shocks." —*Montreal Gazette*

"The most chilling murder-suspense-horror-cop-procedural prose ever to stain paper." —*Calgary Herald*

"Macabre." —*London Daily Telegraph*

"Who knows what evil lurks in the hearts of men and women? Michael Slade knows." —*North Shore News*

"The literary equivalent of a very loud scream . . . packs shocks around every corner." —*Peterborough Evening Telegraph*

"Those who like Stephen King or going to the Saturday night horror show will thrive on Slade." —*Macon Beacon*

"A heart stopper." —*Washington Monthly*

"Fast-paced, gritty action." —*Science Fiction Chronicle*

" Chilling . . . suspenseful, quirky, complex, and never dull."
—*Rave Reviews*

"There is no safety for a reader in a Michael Slade book."
—*Vancouver* Magazine

"Delves into the the criminal mind far past the limits usually expected." —*Ocala Star-Banner*

"A thin line separates crime and horror, and in Michael Slade's thrillers the demarcation vanishes all together." —*Time Out*

"Slade has crawled the ancient sewers of London, studied modern crime tech, and gone backstage with Iron Maiden. A master."
—*Toronto Sunday Sun*

"Awesome . . . A *tour-de force* . . . brilliant, shocking, and bizarre. I am still lost in admiration. Does for the mind what a roller coaster does for the body." —*Australian Magazine*

Also by Michael Slade

The Special X Psycho-Thrillers

Headhunter
Ghoul
Cutthroat
Ripper
Evil Eye
Primal Scream
Burnt Bones
Hangman

DEATH'S DOOR

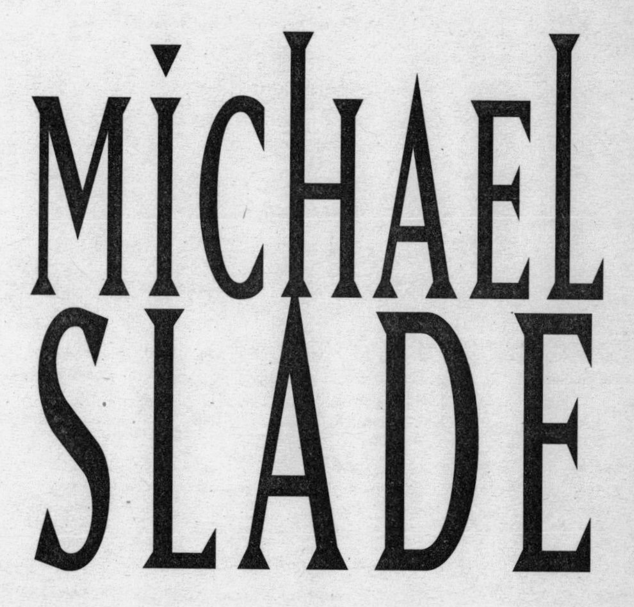

SIGNET
Published by the Penguin Group
Penguin Putnam Inc., 375 Hudson Street, New York, New York 10014, U.S.A.
Penguin Books Ltd, 80 Strand, London WC2R 0RL, England
Penguin Books Australia Ltd, 250 Camberwell Road, Camberwell, Victoria 3124, Australia
Penguin Books Canada Ltd, 10 Alcorn Avenue, Toronto, Ontario, Canada M4V 3B2
Penguin Books (NZ) Ltd, cnr Rosedale and Airborne Roads, Albany, Auckland 1310,
New Zealand

Penguin Books Ltd, Registered Offices:
Harmondsworth, Middlesex, England

First published in Viking by Penguin Books Canada Ltd., 2001

First published in this edition, June 2002
2 4 6 8 10 9 7 5 3 1

Printed in Canada

NATIONAL LIBRARY OF CANADA CATALOGUING IN PUBLICATION DATA

Slade, Michael
Death's door / Michael Slade.

ISBN 0-451-41060-2

I. Title.

PS8587.L35D42 2002 C813'.54 C2002-901225-2
PR9199.3.S5515D42 2002

PUBLISHER'S NOTE

This is a work of fiction. Names, characters, places, and incidents either are the product of the author's imagination or are used fictitiously, and any resemblance to actual persons, living or dead, events, or locales is entirely coincidental.

For
Eric the Webmaster
"The game is afoot, Watson!"

When first my way to fair I took
Few pence in purse had I,
And long I used to stand and look
At things I could not buy.

Now times are altered: if I care
To buy a thing, I can;
The pence are here, and here's the fair,
But where's the lost young man?

—A. E. Housman, *Last Poems*

You have only a few years in which to
live really, perfectly, and fully.
When your youth goes, your beauty will
go with it, and then you will suddenly
discover that there are no triumphs
left for you.

—Oscar Wilde, *The Picture of Dorian Gray*

THERMAL LANCE

Richmond-upon-Thames, England
March 20

Undertakers they could have been, the two men who gingerly maneuvered the casket out the front door of the stately manor overlooking the Thames River from Richmond Hill. Dressed in workmen's overalls, caps, gloves and boots, they eased the dolly conveying the casket down the ramp over the manor's steps to the open rear door of the hearse.

"Easy does it, Andy," said the foreman. "On the count of three. One, two, *three.*"

Both heavy-set movers pushed, sliding the casket off the dolly and into the death wagon. The foreman secured the back. A butler fetched the dolly. With the corpse now ready for transport, the movers climbed into the cab of the hearse.

Undertakers they could have been.

But they weren't.

Four men armed with handguns watched the casket being loaded. Shaded by dark sunglasses and peaked hats, the suspicious eyes of the security guards were on the lookout for poachers after more than rabbits or deer. In posture and stance, all had the bearing of ex-military men, an impression enhanced by their crisp, blue uniforms.

"All clear?" asked one.

"All clear," confirmed the others.

Two by two, the wary guards got into their escort cars. With one car positioned in front of the hearse, the second tailing behind, the convoy drove away from the eighteenth-century manor. Unknown to those in the procession, a surreptitious watcher tracked them through binoculars from a nearby hill and radioed the fact that they were on the move ahead to Stopwatch.

Though the body in the casket had been a welcome guest at their estate for years, the lord and lady standing on the balcony of the manor were too aristocratically proud to come down to bid farewell to her. He didn't look like a lord, this sallow fellow with the comb-over and the potbelly, but then they rarely do. She looked like a lady, but then they always do, upper-crust women who marry for status and fritter away their lives hosting snobbish high teas.

To mark this bittersweet event, the butler served them gin.

"Dearly Departed," Lord Ridding said, and raised his glass in a toast.

Lady Ridding smiled at the pun.

"*Dear* is right, my dear."

Lord Ridding, as a peer of the realm, owned a seat in the House of Lords. So had every Lord Ridding who'd ruled this enclave since the 1600s. Upriver was Hampton Court, the favorite country palace of King Henry VIII, said to be haunted by the ghosts of two of his many wives. Downriver was Kew Palace, designed for the early Hanoverian kings and later home to the world-renowned Royal Botanic Gardens. Lesser lords and ladies had flocked to out-of-town estates along the stretch of river in between, which was now strung with waterside inns and boathouse promenades. Urban sprawl from obese London was gobbling up the greenery and would soon cannibalize those of the gentry still clinging to a bygone past, many of whom could no longer afford to hold back the advance of time. Lord Ridding had lost a bundle as a "name" with Lloyd's of London, so he too was now on their endangered species list. That's why—"Dearly Departed"—today's parting had to be. To keep from going bankrupt, he was selling off the most valuable relic on his estate.

Sleeping Beauty.

The corpse in the casket.

The wide carriageway from the Georgian brick manor to the tree-lined riverside drive, beloved by landscape painters for centuries for its panoramic view over the valley to the Twickenham bank, led the convoy around the terraced grounds. There, come lazy summer, picnics would be consumed on the soft lawn in the walled rose garden, and polo would be played on the field just this side of the gate.

"Phew," snorted Andy. "So that's how the other half lives."

He was riding shotgun in the bulletproof hearse.

"Pardon me, your ladyship," said the foreman as he raised an ample cheek off the driver's seat and blew a hearty fart.

"Was that for Lady Ridding or the mummy in back?"

"Neither," said the foreman. "That was for me."

"Just my luck the windows are sealed."

The foreman's name was Berk, and Berk was addicted to beer. Tapped off the wood or off the gas, he chugged pint after pint down his gullet—the first of the day with a pub lunch at noon and the last of the night at closing time.

Berk could tell you the history of every major pub in London. That research was recorded in his flesh, for his face was flushed, his chins were numerous and his beer paunch put Lord Ridding's potbelly to shame. Between gaseous toots, he would relate how the inns to the west of London had been haunts for daring eighteenth-century highwaymen.

The byway that passed in front of the gate to Lord Ridding's estate ran parallel to the main road, close by the river. Between the trunks of budding trees, Berk and Andy caught glimpses of sculls being rowed on the Thames. Quaint English villages dotted the bank. A traffic accident was blocking the route where it cut through the village ahead. Two cars with bashed fenders were angled across the Tarmac. One of the drivers was on a mobile phone, relaying information. He didn't seem as angry as one might expect.

"They're turning," cautioned Andy.

"Aye," replied Berk.

The escort car was detouring into a one-lane alley that led to the parallel riverside road. The hearse did likewise, followed by the rearguard. This alley divided the pub from the adjacent warehouse. The brick walls to either side lacked doors and windows. The pub was in the shape of an L angled around its Thames-front courtyard, where patrons would have been welcomed in coaching times. The short leg of the L ran along the alley, and as the escort vanguard thumped over flat metal doors set in the cobblestones, a sensor tripped a red traffic light to stop them from shooting out onto the riverside road.

All three vehicles idled, waiting for the light controlling cross-traffic to change.

"Crooked House," said Berk. "That's what it was called."

"What was?" Andy asked.

"The pub beside us."

"Why? The walls are crooked?"

"Aye," said Berk. "And this same pub is where Heath hid out."

"Ned Heath? The highwayman?"

Berk bobbed his head.

"I thought he waylaid coaches at Putney and Wimbledon?"

"He did," said the foreman. "But after Ned shot and killed a Bow Street runner, this is where he fled to hide from the law."

"A crook in the house?"

"Aye. Crooked House. Before the name was changed to the Highwayman."

Andy sniffed the air.

"You smell something burning?"

"Probably off the river. Diesel fuel."

Beads of perspiration popped out on Andy's brow.

"Heath hanged here?"

"Aye," said Berk. "The cops nabbed him in this pub in 1793. He laughed as he climbed the steps to the gallows, then waved to the mob before he went down with a rose between his teeth. His mom had always said he'd die with his boots on, so Ned kicked them off before he hanged."

"Cheeky bugger."

"That was darling Ned. His corpse hung in chains at the crossroads until it rotted."

Trickles of sweat ran down between the pimples on Andy's face. "Christ, it's getting hot."

"Aye," said Berk. "Turn off the heater."

"I'd kill for a pint," Andy said as he reached for the knob.

Berk crooked a thumb at the wall of the pub beside them. "If only *this* Highwayman would waylay our coach, mate."

Highwaymen as bold as Ned Heath can still be found in Europe. Stopwatch was the code name of the best of the best. Split-second timing was his trademark, and so the name. Had he been heisting in 1963, Britain's Great Train Robbery would have been just his style. It wasn't only the money that motivated him, however; it was the thrill he got from pulling off the perfect job. Stopwatch saw himself as an artist akin to a Swiss watchmaker, and clients paid a suitable sum for his skill.

The man who'd hired him for this job was a regular client. All transactions were via the Internet. This proposal had come by e-mail, and once he had determined its feasibility, this highwayman had sent back his contract price. The money got transferred from one to the other through shady Asian banks, half on agreement and half on delivery. The two crooks had never met, and never would, for both were professionals of the highest rank.

The loot this client desired was the mummy in the casket. Stealing the casket from the estate was too big a risk, since the manor's security system was state of the art. Waylaying it en route to London was dangerous too, but Stopwatch—as always—had conceived an audacious plan. The byway past Lord Ridding's gate was the only road. The safest, shortest route for the convoy to take was in this direction. Standard procedure for such a convoy encountering an obstacle, like an accident blocking the way, was to detour, not stop. By arranging the accident where he had, the mastermind had ensured that the convoy would detour down this alley, and would be forced to brake to a halt at this traffic light.

And right above the thermal lance.

"The loot's in the alley. They fell for it."

Those words, phoned to him by one of the drivers in the bogus accident, were received by the audio plug in Stopwatch's ear.

"The loot's in place."

Time to act.

It was dark and dank in the cellar of the pub. In days of yore, when beer was shipped to the Crooked House by boats on the Thames, the kegs were unloaded dockside and lugged underground by means of a tunnel beneath the river road. These days, beer was trucked from local breweries by lorry and unloaded directly into the cellar through the metal drop doors set in the alleyway's cobblestones. The doors under the idling hearse were released, exposing the vehicle's undercarriage and flooding the subterranean passageway with light. Sporting a fireproof Nomex suit like the kind race drivers wear, his head encased in a welder's helmet, the highwayman aimed an acetylene torch at a spot beneath Berk's seat. Heating the metal until it glowed red hot, he swapped the torch for the lance a henchman held.

A thermal lance is an awesome tool. What Stopwatch took in both gloved hands resembled a flamethrower from the Second World War. It consisted of a six-foot-long magnesium tube, which he raised up through the doors so its top end was against the spot heated by the torch. A handpiece with a trigger was attached to the base of the tube. The trigger controlled how much oxygen was released from a portable tank. When the highwayman pulled the trigger, raw oxygen shot down the 3/8-inch hollow tube and was ignited by the red-hot metal on the undercarriage of the hearse. At 8,000°F, the blast of a thermal lance will slice through a foot of cold steel in seconds.

The undercarriage of this hearse was nowhere near as thick.

Inside the cab of the vehicle, Andy was turning to ask Berk if he thought the engine was overheating when the blast from the lance burst up through the floor and the driver's seat, coring the foreman from his buttocks to the top of his skull. The human body, we are told in anatomy class, is mostly made up of water. Berk's bloated body was largely made up of beer, his water content greater than most, and at this searing temperature, that water turned to steam. The steam expanded with violent force, literally blowing Berk apart.

In that harsh moment before the heat hit him, Andy saw the foreman's eyes explode from their sockets an instant before Berk's skull mimicked the big bang. His chest tore open from the slam of sudden evaporation, spewing forth organs and cracked ribs in a splash of scarlet gore. So hot was the heat that marrow frying in his bones burst them, fracturing his skeleton while his flesh ignited in flames. Charred and melted, all that would remain of Berk was a bone-spiked mess of mush on the smoldering seat.

Huugghh!

Andy's gasp of shock was what did him in. For what he inhaled with that sharp intake were superheated gases that caused his throat to constrict and go into spasm, clogging his airway and strangling him to death. Unable to raise the alarm, he thrashed about in the hearse while tinted glass and the divider between the cab and the casket space hid the drama from the escort guards in front and behind.

Meanwhile, Stopwatch used the lance to vaporize a large access hole to the casket space farther back along the rear undercarriage. Aided by burly henchmen, he reached up into the hearse, and once they got a grip on the cargo coveted by his anonymous client, they extracted the casket from the vehicle and hauled it down to a dolly positioned in the cellar below.

Everything about this heist was carried out with exact precision, from inside information acquired for a pile of money. Stopwatch knew the dimensions of each vehicle in the triple-car convoy, and he knew that this hearse would be the same armor-plated tank hired for sensitive funerals with terrorist potential. That's how he had calculated where it would idle in the alley, and why he had secured the lance to gut its underbelly.

Tick . . . tick . . . tick . . .

Around the highwayman's neck hung his trademark stopwatch, an Interpol legend.

Tick . . . tick . . . tick . . .

It counted off precious seconds.

What determined how long it would take for the gas tank to blow from this smoldering heat was a simple law of physics.

Tick . . . tick . . . tick . . .

Make every second count.

While Stopwatch shut the overhead doors to protect the cellar from the imminent blast and gathered up the tools of his trade, the torch and the lance, his henchmen trundled the casket through banks of beer barrels to escape by the river tunnel.

Tick . . . tick . . . tick . . .

Up in the alley, smoke began to billow out of the hearse.

"Something's wrong," the rear escort radioed to the vanguard.

Tick . . . tick . . . tick . . .

"Let's check it out."

With guns in their fists, the four guards scrambled out of their cars.

Running along the tunnel beneath the guards' feet, burdened by all the equipment slung over his shoulders, Stopwatch glanced down at the luminous dial bouncing on his chest.

Tick . . . tick . . .

Time's up.

BOOOOOOMMMMMMM! The hearse blew above.

Even down below, concussion from the explosion blasting the drop doors flattened Stopwatch to his hands and knees, loosening the bricks of the tunnel and raining a hail of powdered mortar down on the fugitive highwayman.

Above ground, a broiling fireball surged along the alley, damning every living thing in its path to the flames of hell on earth. The screams of the guards shrieked in the scorching heat of the narrow passage.

Pandemonium reigned as the heisted loot was loaded onto a getaway boat moored by the tunnel's open end. Groups of frantic villagers tried to save possessions from the flames, too preoccupied to notice the heist taking place beneath their noses. While the sirens of emergency vehicles wailed from all directions, Stopwatch stood astern to enjoy his handiwork as the boat chugged downriver.

It would be days before the cops figured out what had happened.

Not a trace of evidence would survive this blast.

By tonight, Stopwatch would be safely back home in Zurich, and the mummy in the casket would be in the cargo hold of an Air Canada flight to Vancouver from nearby Heathrow Airport.

Stopwatch grinned.

Good-bye, Sleeping Beauty.

WOLF-DOG

Galiano Island, British Columbia

Oww! Oww! Owwhoo-oo-oo . . .

The howl of the rabid wolf-dog sent chills up and down their spines. Armed with Colt AR-15s, the current long arms of the force, semi-automatic rifles with thirty rounds of .223 Remingtons to a clip, the three stalking Mounties crept through the moonlit woods. The point man of this triangle was Insp. Bob George, Ghost Keeper, if you preferred his Native name. A full-blooded Plains Cree from Duck Lake, Saskatchewan, born in a one-room shack on the local reserve, Ghost Keeper had honed his tracking skills when he was sent out alone as a boy to survive in northern wilds on a spirit quest. Flanking him as backup was Sgt. Ed "Mad Dog" Rabidowski. The Mad Dog was the son of a Yukon trapper raised in the Arctic, and he could take out the eye of a squirrel with a .22 at one hundred feet before he was six.

Oww! Oww! Owwhoo-oo-oo . . .

They were getting close.

The Mountie in command held the lowest rank of the three. The Outer Gulf Islands detachment of the Mounted Police, a small force of only four men, patrolled the islands clustered off the coast of Vancouver. As officer-in-charge of that detachment, it was Corp. Nick Craven's jurisdiction, and therefore he was head of this hunt. It had been a month since the beast's first kill on Saturna Island, where it had torn Rod Stewart apart. Rod was the strutting cock in Senator Healey's henhouse, and the senator himself had witnessed the crime.

"It's a wolf, I tell you," the politician had told Nick over the phone.

"A wolf, Senator?" was the Mountie's reply.

"I know my dogs. It was no bow-wow. If it wasn't a wolf, it was a wolf-dog."

"Describe it."

"Huge! With bloody fangs."

So Nick had boated across the sound from Otter Bay on Pender Island to Saturna, a trip that had more to do with smoothing the senator's ruffled tail feathers than it did with gathering up those torn from Rod Stewart. A pissed-off politician must be appeased, so Nick had done his best to hunt down the elusive "wolf." But in the end, the Mountie had failed to get his man, or whatever had done Rod in.

An unsolved case.

One for the cold file.

The case, however, had heated up a few weeks later, when two sheep, a deer and the Dalai Llama had suffered the same slaughter on Mayne Island. Not the Dalai Lama, the exiled chief monk of Tibet, but a real llama, with wool and long ears, from South America. Again, the beast that had been witnessed at the scene was described as a wolf-dog.

Nick figured the canine killer had crossed from Saturna to Mayne by way of narrow Boat Passage at Winter Cove. The elusive predator was island hopping.

"Bad news, Corporal."

This call had come in from the vet, two days after the detachment's search on Mayne had failed to turn up the animal.

"How bad, Doc?"

"Real bad," said the vet, sighing. "I ran rabies tests on the animals killed. In each case, saliva slathered into the wounds proved hydrophobic."

"A *rabid* dog?"

"Afraid so. You'd better find it."

The hunt was well under way the day before on Mayne when a hysterical call came in to 911.

"Help me! Jesus! Someone *help!*"

A child was screaming in the background at the top of its lungs.

"It's biting my boy! It's killing my dog!"

The emergency dispatcher could hear a vicious dog fight raging in the background.

"Are you on a cell?"

"Yes!" cried the woman.

"Where?" asked the operator at 911.

"Oh, God! It's a *wolf!* Foaming at the mouth!"

"Where are you?"

"At home on Galiano! The thing is in our yard! My son is on his trike! He's standing on the seat! Our dog is trying to protect him! Do something! *Please* help! I only have a broom!"

The dispatcher heard a clatter at the end of the line as the woman dropped the phone.

Crying!

Shrieking!

Yelping!

"Get back!" yelled the mother.

The operator was sweating. There was no help to send.

The Galiano constable was currently off island, on the other side of Active Pass, where all four members of the detachment were out hunting for this beast on Mayne. It had somehow traversed the strait at slack tide to reach Galiano.

"Mommy!" wailed the boy.

The operator felt sick. Her hand was shaking as she punched in the numbers for Nick's cellphone.

The battle was over by the time the cops responded to the emergency at the waterfront farm. The mother had managed to haul her son off the seat of his tricycle as the family pet sacrificed itself to give her the opportunity to get the boy into the house. The Mounties had found them cowering behind the kitchen door, the boy in need of immediate medical attention for his chewed leg, the mother in need of a sedative to calm her down. Left to die from its wounds by the rabid wolf-dog, a panting collie lay on the ground beside the child's trike. The doctor treating the family had moved them away from the yard so Nick could put the animal down with a shot from his service pistol.

Bam! The blast pierced the island silence. The collie lay still.

Nick's eyes followed the bloody paw prints left by the rabid monster across the yard and into the bush beyond. Of all the Gulf Islands under his protection, Galiano was the worst to have a crisis like this. Because most of the land was thick forest controlled by a lumber company, hunting this beast in the bush would be taxing, and the cops tasked with the job were transplanted city boys.

It was time for the specialists.

So Nick had called Special X.

The helicopter from Vancouver had set down in the yard. Before he'd naively abandoned HQ for what had turned out to be anything but a laid-back country lifestyle, Nick had worked with Ghost Keeper and the Mad Dog. Both men were dressed in the bush uniform of the Mounted Police, blue baseball caps with the RCMP bison-head crest on front, blue shirts under blue fleece vests under blue waist-length patrol jackets, and blue combat pants with yellow side stripes and large cargo pockets tucked into heavy-duty black boots. Armed with assault rifles and force carryalls stuffed with tracking equipment, they climbed down through the swirling dust blown up by the chopper's rotors and could have been fresh troops arriving to fight a jungle war.

The Mad Dog read Nick's mind, and he sniffed the island air.

"I love the smell of napalm in the morning," Ed said, mimicking Robert Duvall in *Apocalypse Now.*

Ghost Keeper swept his sharp eyes around the yard as a bald eagle circled overhead. Without assistance, he picked up the animal's trail.

"Okay. Let's do it," he said.

With the Cree tracker in the lead, the marksman and the corporal flanking him from behind, the hunters had spent the day advancing north through the woods. Darkness fell at 6:45 p.m., so the men had strapped night-vision goggles over their eyes and continued on through a green world iridescently lit by starlight magnified thirty thousand times. It was now after midnight and into the first day of spring, the landscape an eerie shimmer under the fat face of the moon. The cops were closing in on the rabid howl of their prey when—

Oww! Oww! Owwhoo-oo-oo . . .

There was the feasting demon. The hunters had come across the beast as it ripped apart the flesh from its meal—the body of a naked human rotting in the green salal close to the bush trail. Half wolf, half dog, the 150-pound creature from hell heard the call of the wild, a call that told it that these men were its worst enemy, and that it was dead if it didn't kill them first.

The monster attacked.

With the precision of a British colonial regiment going into action—for that was the model upon which the Mounted Police was based—Ghost Keeper retreated a few steps so the Mad Dog, the marksman of the group, could assume the point position.

Ears erect and aimed at Mad Dog Rabidowski, its bloody forehead wrinkled over blazing red eyes, its lips peeled back in a vicious snarl that bared two-inch fangs dangling shreds of meat, the wolf-dog leaped over the half-eaten horror and rushed toward the sergeant in a straight-for-the-jugular onslaught.

The Mad Dog had barely a moment to cock the gun in his hands. Because he had been trailing Ghost Keeper on this hunt, Ed had lugged his AR-15 on an empty chamber. Trip with a loaded chamber and the gun might have gone off, shooting the Cree in the back. The swiftness with which their quarry mounted an all-out blitzkrieg caught Ed by surprise, and in his haste to release the safety and tug back on the T-shaped cocking handle attached to the bolt, the Colt jammed. The cartridge failed to slip cleanly from the clip and caught in the bend between the magazine and the firing chamber.

A second later, the wolf-dog was in the air.

It seemed to Rabidowski as if time had slowed down to a crawl. By the gleam of the watching moon, he could almost count the teeth going for his throat. The matted monster was eager to sink those razor-sharp rippers in him, and here they came in a stream of slathering saliva and frothing foam. The animal's jaws cocked sideways for a better chomp, then the huge paws hit the cop's chest as blood spewed everywhere. The Mountie tumbled back on the ground with the monster on top of him, and he gazed up at those savage eyes glaring down at his. Suddenly, the red gleam behind them began to fade.

The bullet fired by Ghost Keeper from behind and to the side had whizzed over Ed's shoulder to catch the wolf-dog in mid-leap, drilling it through the brain just inches shy of the sergeant's throat. A sudden jerk in the wrong direction and it would have been the man, not the monster, who was dead. But if Ghost Keeper hadn't taken the shot, Ed would have been dead for sure.

A calculated risk.

Decided in a split second.

No way did Nick have the confidence to take a shot like that.

With the butt stock in his armpit and the trigger grip in his hand, Ghost Keeper closed in to stand over the supine sergeant.

"Y'okay?"

"I think so."

"You weren't bitten?"

"No."

"Good."

"I owe you one. Holy shit, Tonto. That was a *hell* of a shot."

"We aim to please, *kemosabe*."

"And I'm damn pleased with your aim."

As Ghost Keeper hoisted the mangy monster from the Mad Dog's chest, then offered him a hand to pull him to his feet, Nick was on the radio to the pilot up in the chopper.

"We've got a body down here. I'll guide you in. Shine some light down through the trees."

One hunt had led to another.

It would be a long night.

ETERNAL SPRING

West Vancouver, British Columbia

Can a bird wolf-whistle?

Binky could.

The green-winged macaw sat on a perch in the huge aviary-cum-solarium he shared with a West African gray parrot named Gabby. The gilded beams of the morning sun on this first day of spring ignited the multiple colors in the feathers of both birds, and twirled rainbows from the dangling prisms that danced with the solar rays. As Binky and Gabby eyed Gill, the woman eyed her naked contours in a full-length mirror.

"Srrit . . . srreeew!" from Binky.

"Hot mama!" Gabby said.

"Behave yourselves, boys," she chided the birds, an empty admonition if ever there was one, for it was Gill who'd trained them to admire her new shape.

"Ruffle my feathers, baby!"

"Where's the Viagra!" squawked Binky.

Gill turned from the mirror to pout for the wolves like Brigitte Bardot in full male-meltdown mode in *And God Created Woman.* In her case, however, God was really Dr. David Denning and the UltraPulse CO_2 laser he had used to rejuvenate her face and reshape her body. Gill was on the downside of forty, but she looked as young as she had in her heyday again.

Life owed her this, she figured.

With eyes as green as everglades and tussled hair as auburn as maple leaves in late autumn, Gill Macbeth was a good-looking woman, handsome, not pretty. Her mom was the first female pathologist in the Commonwealth, a role model who had inspired her daughter to aspire to a similar height, which decades of dedicated work had seen Gill achieve. The cost to her as a successful woman was the onerous price so many feminists had borne: a family life put on hold for the sake of her career. Suddenly, she had found herself trying to rewind a rundown biological clock, and though she'd snuck under the wire to start a family with Nick Craven, she had lost her last crack at motherhood to a bombed ship and a cold dunk in a cruel, aborting sea.

Middle age, with no kids.

That was Gill's future.

That was Gill's *now*.

"Hooters! Hehehe!" said Binky.

"Shake that booty for Daddy!" added Gabby.

"Cool your jets, boys. Or I'll wash your beaks out with soap."

"Hubba-hubba!"

"Ooh-la-la! *If you want this birdy . . .* " Binky Stewart began, strutting along his perch while crooning the chorus from "Da Ya Think I'm Sexy?"

"Ah, Binks. A disco classic," said Gill, laughing.

At forty plus, thanks to the skill of Dr. Denning, Gill was taking one last stab at playing a Barbie doll. Was this how Gloria Steinem felt in that Playboy Bunny suit?

Hmm, Gill thought. I'd look good in one of those. Naughty me.

Youth is wasted on the young, according to a hoary proverb. Time is, time was and time is past. Time and tide wait for no man. Take time when time comes, lest time steal away. It is too late to call back yesterday. There's no turning back the hands of time . . .

But Gill had done just that.

Dr. David Denning was one of the best-kept secrets in Hollywood. Tinseltown is a meat-grinder that chews through female stars. When the camera stops loving you, baby, your days at the top are numbered. Perhaps it was because he was such an odd-looking fellow himself, with simian features and a short, squat physique, that the doctor was such an artist with a scalpel and a laser. Hollywood goddesses who wished to have "work done" with skill and discretion snuck north "on holiday" to his surgical clinic in Vancouver. The name of Denning's clinic was Eternal Spring, and the rumor whispered by those rich enough to afford such rejuvenation was that the name alluded to the Fountain of Youth.

Denning was a wizard.

And Gill could afford him.

If the legacy from her mother was a drive to accomplish anything she desired, the legacy from Gill's father was money to burn. She had inherited his string of top Caribbean hotels, and by splitting the profits with on-site managers, leaving them to run the day-to-day business, Gill was free to enjoy life as an independent woman of means, pursuing the same career as her mom.

Through sacrifice, Gill had worked her way to the top, and by letting youth slip away while she struggled up the ladder, she was now the best forensic pathologist on the West Coast. The problem, when Gill looked back, was that her memories of the good times were almost all related to death, and not to romance, red-hot passion and other youthful joys. So while there were those who would heap scorn on her decision to go under the plastic surgeon's knife—those who made up the let's-grow-old-gracefully crowd—Gill had set her mind on fighting age tooth and nail.

Could she recapture what she'd let slip away?

Affairs of the heart?

Torrid flings?

Bites from the forbidden apple?

Like a menopausal male with a new red sports car, Gill had a sleek chassis she was dying to take out for a spin.

Vroooom!

Vroooom!

Vroooooooooom!

Here's lookin' at you, kid.

The younger woman winked at herself.

Spring was in the air when Gill stepped out of her front door to return to work at the VGH morgue, her first day back since the surgery. Her house was a West Coast modern of cedar and glass that crowned Sentinel Hill at the edge of West Vancouver, the most affluent community in Canada. The daffodils were yellow and the plum blossoms pink, and the view from her yard as she crossed to her car was a 360-degree vista of natural splendor. With the north shore mountains' snow-capped, sun-splashed peaks at her back, Gill paused for a moment to take in the panorama at her feet—the harbor, the city, the river, the delta—stretching south to the border Canada shared with the States.

Spring was in the air.

Spring was in her step.

Her BMW shone like new in the glare of the morning sun. When she climbed in behind the wheel and turned on the ignition, the tune that greeted Gill from the radio was Dusty Springfield's "A Brand New Me." On the drive down to the harbor to cross Lions Gate Bridge to Stanley Park, an exuberant Gill Macbeth sang along. The song ended long before she reached the hospital beyond False Creek, but she couldn't get the catchy melody out of her head. So that's what the happy woman was humming when she strolled into Vancouver General Hospital's morgue to find Corp. Nick Craven waiting for her with the half-eaten cadaver from Galiano Island.

Some things never change.

"Wow!" said Nick. "What happened to you?"

"Don't know what you mean."

"Bullshit, Gill. You look ten years younger than I do."

In his mid-thirties, Nick was five years younger than Gill.

"Must be the light."

"What's brighter than a morgue?"

"Must be your eyes."

"I had 'em checked last month." A light went on, and he snapped the fingers of his good hand. "Of course, Denning. That's why you sent me to him. I thought you knew the doc from medical circles or teaching at UBC. Truth is, you know him because you planned to go under the knife!"

"Good detective."

"You look great."

"From what I can see, he did every bit as fine a job on you."

The corporal tapped his prosthetic ear and held up his mechanical hand, so state of the art that they both looked like real skin. By maneuvering his shoulder muscles, he opened and closed the fingers. His original hand and ear had been hacked off by a psycho named Mephisto, who had kidnapped Nick and cut him up to force Special X to find the Highland Hoard.

But that was another story.

The secret behind burnt bones.

"You know I appreciate it."

"Yes," said Gill. She shrugged as if to tell him it was no big thing. But it was a big thing, the guilt she felt, for had she not broken his heart by breaking up with him, he would not have left Special X to command a small detachment policing rural islands, and thus wouldn't have been the Mountie grabbed by Mephisto. Patching him up was the least she could do.

"Denning's out of my league. This sort of device is expensive. Where would I be if you hadn't come to my rescue?"

"That's what money is for. To spend," Gill said. "If it can make you whole again, then it's well spent. If it can make me young again, then I'll bankroll the Fountain of Youth."

"I'll drink to that."

"So what have you brought me today?"

This fifty-foot-square dissecting theater of off-white tiles over a stone terrazzo floor was where Nick and Gill had first met. Butchered flesh, you might say, was what they had in common. The mortuary was equipped with six autopsy stations, each unit fixed to the floor with its own sink, garburetor, scales and water supply.

There was an isolation chamber for decomposing remains, so that's where the morgue attendant—having X-rayed the body for objects lodged in its tissue—had wheeled the gurney, locking it feet to sink into that dissecting unit.

Soft classical music came from the stereo. Chopin or something romantic, which seemed out of place. It would have been more fitting, from Nick's point of view, to have "I Love the Dead" by Alice Cooper blaring from the speakers. Perhaps that was why he and Gill had not worked out. Except in bed.

He told her about the previous night's hunt for the rabid wolf-dog, and how Ghost Keeper's aim had saved the Mad Dog from the jaws of death. "Who'd have guessed Ed and the Cree would ever be friends? Rabidowski was a racist bred in the bone."

"That's the cure," said Gill. "Respect earned one-on-one. Did I ever tell you about my trip down the Yangtze River?"

"No," said Nick.

"Come on. I'll tell you while I change."

She led him from the mortuary to her office, where she closed the door and began to shed her clothes. Gill had never been one to shy away from nakedness in Nick's presence. The first night she had taken him home to her mansion on the hill, she had stripped to lure him into the hot tub out on the rainy deck. But that's when they were flirting as a prelude to seduction, and that's not what was taking place here.

Gill hung her suit jacket on a hanger and brushed away the wrinkles. Was that a subconscious metaphor for what Denning had done to her skin? Then she unbuttoned her blouse and shucked it too.

"The Yangtze River flows through central China. A permanent dam was going to flood the Three Gorges, so I booked a river cruise to climb the twin peaks of Feng Du before they drowned. The mountains rise like a pair of breasts on the bank of the river. Strung from tip to tip is a suspension bridge."

"I've got the picture," Nick said.

Gill wasn't wearing a bra.

"Two sisters and their husbands were also on the boat. It soon became evident that one of the men loathed the Chinese. He was a sickly redneck who was falling apart. Lung problems. Stomach problems. A walking pharmacy. He had licked the Big C, to quote John Wayne, and had been roped into going to China by his wife and in-laws. That kind of bigot is cancer on a trip. He made no bones of the fact that he had no use for 'Chinks.'"

"The old Rabidowski."

"Right," said Gill, unzipping her skirt to step out of it. Now down to her panties, she hung the skirt next to her jacket, and Nick found himself staring at the figure of a woman in her twenties. A perfect hourglass with most of the sands of time yet to flow.

"The boat docked at Feng Du, and we went ashore to see the Ghost City. A Taoist temple, it dates back more than nineteen hundred years. It's believed that Feng Du is the place where all people's ghosts go after death. We scaled one peak by climbing hundreds of steps, and along the way, we had to pass superstitious rituals to see what would happen to our ghosts once we died. One test was to climb thirty-three stairs in one breath. Another was to stand on one foot on a slippery rock for thirty seconds. The tests were to prove to the Jade Emperor that we were good people, so the Lord of Heaven would allow our ghosts to cross the gold bridge to positions of nobility in our future incarnations. If we failed a test, that meant our ghosts were destined for the Hall of the King of Hell. Those evildoers would be tortured in the afterlife, and be reborn as animal subspecies."

"Did you pass the tests?"

"Yes," said Gill. "So I crossed the suspension bridge to the heavenly peak to get a taste of what was in store for my ghost."

"And the bigot?"

"He failed miserably. His lung condition caused him to run out of breath and his foot slipped off the rock into a shallow pool. At the top of the peak were grisly models of his afterlife, scenes of the most horrific butchery you can imagine. You should have heard his rant when we got back to the boat. A diatribe rife with disparaging comments about China and its backward culture. The upshot was that he stomped off to his cabin and loudly slammed the door."

Nick was sorry to see Gill pull on hospital greens and a plastic apron of the same color that reached down to her ankles. As she tugged the top on over her head, the Mountie was treated to an uplifting, stare-all-you-want peep show before the curtain fell.

"Next morning, I was eating breakfast on the boat when I was joined at my table by the bigot's in-laws. Had I heard what happened during the night? they asked. No, I said.

"Around three, the bigot had suffered an all-out wheezing fit. Choking to death, he fell out of bed and lay gasping on the floor. When I'm on vacation, I keep it a secret that I'm a doctor, so I don't have everyone coming to me to cure their ailments. While I slept on, the bigot's wife dashed to the bridge for help, and the doctor who responded to treat the man at Death's door was a traditional Chinese herbalist."

Nick guffawed. "The redneck must have thought he *was* in hell."

"So there's the bigot, collapsed on the floor and gurgling his last gasp. Hovering over him is Confucius, with his Fu Manchu mustache, and in his hand is a piece of torn newspaper folded around some powder. The doctor doesn't speak a word of English, so he has to force the powder down the bigot's throat.

"While I'm hearing this over breakfast, in comes the patient. The first thing he tells us after he takes a seat is that he hasn't felt this alive in years. He shows us a prescription in Chinese script, and for the rest of our stay in China, he utters not another prejudiced word about 'Chinks.' The last glimpse I had of him was in Hong Kong, where he was taking suitcases full of the herbal remedy back to San Francisco."

"One-on-one," said Nick.

"The cure for bigotry. The Mad Dog was a racist until that confrontation up north. The standoff between the Mounted and Natives over sacred land. Remember when Chandler sent those two into the woods on dogsleds to stop that weapons shipment? Well, something happened to Ed on that hunt, and whatever it was, it tore the blinders from his eyes. The Mad Dog experienced an epiphany, and thanks to Ghost Keeper, he no longer views aboriginals as aliens."

"Can I tell you something?"

"Shoot," said Gill.

"Whatever you paid Denning, you sure did get your money's worth."

It was exactly what she wanted to hear.

Before they went in to dissect the body, Gill gave Nick Vicks VapoRub to dab under his nose to kill the stench, as well as a surgeon's mask to place over his breathing holes.

"Royal Jubilee's the morgue that should have this cadaver, Nick."

"I asked the coroner to send it to you."

"How sweet."

"You *are* the best, Gill."

Sweet was hardly the word for the chewed-up female on the stainless-steel gurney. Not only had she offered a meal to hungry animals in the bush, but her body had been rotting for several weeks. Nick was puzzled by the fact that the corpse had not been found earlier by Galiano hikers using the trail. It was a common enough exercise track, and the stench of death was so overpowering that it was hard to miss.

"I doubt she died from natural causes," he said. "We didn't find a stitch of clothing with the remains. It's too early for nymphs in the woods."

"No," agreed Gill. "It's foul play."

The pathologist stood in the angle of the L-shaped station, a small recorder gripped in one double-gloved hand, taping comments while she scanned the corpse from head to foot with a powerful light. When it illuminated the raw tissue where the breasts had been, the sight of the missing glands caused Nick to wince. As he blinked, a memory flashed before his mind's eye.

Post-traumatic stress.

Nick's shadow sat slumped against the dungeon wall where it met the floor, the collar around his neck on a two-foot leash. One wrist was cuffed in a similar way. His other arm angled out and was lashed securely across a log section, a bracket at his elbow and a clamp locking that hand. Donella's shadow loomed statuesque above the chopping block; the claymore grasped in both hands was held high over her head.

Another silhouette.

Moving across the wall.

Then Mephisto appeared in the flesh before Nick's cowering form.

His black hair was slicked back with every strand in place. His sunken eyes were black pits like those of a skull. His Vandyke beard narrowed to a perfect V, his mouth a slash of sadistic cruelty.

"Do it!" he ordered.

The sword came down.

And Nick might have gasped aloud from the phantom pain had Gill not pulled him back to reality.

"Here," she said. "See these margins where both breasts were removed? Had animals chewed them off, we'd see jagged, irregular edges from their teeth. Instead, the skin ends at sharp lines."

"Her tits were cut off with a knife?"

"Or a similar blade," said Gill. "So the animal responsible is of the *human* kind."

COFFIN CHEATER

Richmond, British Columbia

Cargo handlers call it a hurem.

Hurem, for "*hu*man *rem*ains."

The coffin lowered from the hold of the Air Canada flight from London Heathrow was put into a tub cart for transport to the airline's cargo shed. The bonded warehouse was next to the hanger that serviced Air Canada's planes on the West Coast. The Canada Customs office sat out front, on Miller Road. Separated from each other by parking lots, the three box-like buildings had roofs as flat as the runways beyond.

One after another, jets took off or landed.

The din was deafening.

The hearse was parked in the lot between the cargo building and Canada Customs. Not only was the vehicle a glossy black, suitable for mourning, but the windows were all of smoked glass so that no gawkers could see inside. The Undertaker who was driving was dressed in funeral duds. The door swung open so he could climb out. A black shoe and a black pant leg emerged first, a black glove and a black jacket sleeve next, followed by a black peaked cap and black-lensed shades. Short black hair framed pasty skin. Beneath his jaw lurked a shadow of dark beard.

The Undertaker crossed to the cargo office.

The woman behind the counter glanced up as he came in the

door. From the uneasy look that pinched her face, you'd think the hearse was for her. Something about the body collector gave her the creeps. Coldly unemotional, he seemed dead himself.

"I'm here for the body." His tone was flat.

"Flight?" asked the clerk. She grabbed a sheaf of papers from a box.

"The plane from London. It just landed."

Leafing through the air waybills until she came to the hurem—014 LHR 35450257—the cargo clerk gave the Undertaker the documents he required and breathed a sigh of relief when the door closed behind him. A well-endowed woman, she didn't trust men in shades. She was sure their hidden eyes were ogling her.

With this guy, that felt like necrophilia.

She crossed herself.

From the cargo office, the Undertaker made his way across the lot from the parked hearse to Canada Customs in the squat blue building in front. There, he entered a door next to the Runway Café, passed a wall of locked mailboxes, then walked toward the service desk, a purple counter decorated with a tiny red-and-white Canadian flag.

The customs inspector was East Indian. As he was handed the cargo documents by the Undertaker, the inspector was reminded of Tommy Lee Jones in *Men in Black*. The only thing missing, the inspector mused, was a gun—which, in fact, wasn't missing at all. The Undertaker carried a .22 Remington semi-automatic pistol armed with standard-velocity hollow-points and equipped with a silencer; it was slung in the shoulder holster under his jacket.

Ready if needed.

The document with the airline waybill was a death certificate from Britain. A body cannot be brought into Canada within six months of the time of death if the cause was cholera, or in the case of plague, unless the death certificate states the body is free of insects infected with disease. For AIDS, anthrax, viral hemorrhagic fevers and hepatitis B, the corpse must be embalmed and sealed in a hermetically secure container. The inspector checked the certificate to ensure that the man in the coffin had not died from anything communicable, then told the Undertaker to wait.

Meanwhile, the cargo runner at the wheel of the tub cart had trundled the hurem from the plane to the cargo shed. "Shed" was hardly the word for the big bonded warehouse with the yellow line painted on the floor to divide it in half. The office side (or public side) was in Canada; the runway side (or air side) wasn't in the country. Cargo on the air side of the line was in legal limbo until customs cleared it.

Cargo like the hurem.

The Canada Customs van parked on the Tarmac at the air-side door to the shed used a portable X-ray machine to search for contraband. Cargo handlers fed the coffin into the rear of the van so customs inspectors wearing earmuffs to block the booming din of the jets could take a look inside. The woman manning the X-ray screen held up her hand as a signal to her partner that smuggling was afoot. The male inspector joined her to get a gander at the treasure buried in the coffin. Each pulled back one ear guard so they could talk.

"We got a coffin cheater."

"Yep," said the man.

"The eyes aren't human."

"Nor is the tongue."

"It looks like a bird's."

"Bizarre, huh?"

"Perhaps we got the Birdman of Alcatraz here."

"The skeleton's human."

"What do you make of the heart?"

"Some kind of bug?"

"I'd say a beetle."

"And what's that weird thing on the belly?"

"One way to find out," said the woman, recording the mutant finds on film.

The X-ray van was required for other customs work, so cargo handlers returned the coffin to the cart, then, under the direction of the male inspector, trundled the hurem into the shed. Away from the roar of jet engines, the inspector swapped his earmuffs for a cell-phone to alert the office.

The East Indian behind the counter with the small Canadian flag crooked an index finger to summon the man in black. As the Undertaker approached the official, he was stalked by a muscled customs enforcer. The trio met at the counter over the cargo documents. The Undertaker noticed by the ink pad the Cleared stamp, which had not been used on his waybill.

"Your cargo will be inspected. Go with Tad."

"Is there a problem?"

"We'll see," said the official.

"Where am I going?"

"To Richmond General."

"The hospital? Why?"

"To open the coffin. We don't check human remains in the cargo shed."

Tad could have been Karloff as Frankenstein's monster. The hand that seized the documents was as huge as King Kong's. The customs enforcer accompanied the Undertaker to the hearse. The loading bays beside the cargo office were raised for trucks, so the Undertaker drove around the side to door 31 to load the coffin.

Inside the door and across the threshold were rail tracks used to guide a towering pallet mover. The cargo cart bumped over both tracks in reverse so the coffin could be transferred. Once the hurem was secured in back of the hearse, Tad and Cliff, the male X-ray inspector, got into the front of the car, a tight squeeze with three of them on the bench seat. The Undertaker unbuttoned his jacket for access to the gun and drove off.

The Fraser River thunders west to meet the Pacific Ocean at Vancouver. The north arm of the river borders the city's southern flank. Sandwiched between the north arm and the Fraser's main channel are the flat, fertile islands of the river delta: Sea Island to the west and Lulu Island to the southeast, divided by the middle arm of the Fraser. Vancouver's southern suburb is an island city: Richmond.

From Air Canada Cargo, the hearse headed east on Miller Road, away from the airport out on Sea Island and toward the hospital on the other side of the middle arm on Lulu Island. The road ran parallel to the seaward runway, on which screaming jets arrived and departed.

"You see this?" Cliff asked, pulling a pamphlet from his shirt pocket. The X-ray inspector was squeezed in the middle, so extricating the brochure was no small feat.

"What's that?" Tad asked, feigning interest.

"A promo piece on the airport's expansion. Twelve million passengers a year now. And that's gonna double before long."

The hulk grunted. "Job security. Think of all the smugglers in that horde."

They passed a park-and-ride lot, then a few catering kitchens on the runway side. A budding chestnut tree flashed by on the grassy median.

"Hard to believe it all began with a biplane, eh? A Curtiss pusher, back in 1910. Folks in their Sunday best used to ride the tram here to Minoru Park. That racetrack was named for King Ed's thoroughbred. March 25, the stands were packed when a pilot named Hamilton buzzed the spectators at fifty-five miles an hour. That was the first flight west of Winnipeg."

The hulk yawned. History bored him. Tad's passion was wrestling on UPN. Imagine what the World Wrestling Federation could have done to spice up that flight. Top-heavy babes in skimpy undies dancing on one wing while Black Mask and the Enforcer tussled on the other. Cable fees would have reaped millions.

A cluster of dinky houses approached on the right, three hundred tiny homes dating from the Second World War, built to shelter aircraft workers at Boeing's Sea Island plant. As the hearse curved around them onto Russ Baker Way and traversed the flatlands at the inland end of the seaward runway, heading for the bridge that spanned the middle arm across to Richmond General Hospital on Lulu Island, Cliff waved his pamphlet and prattled on.

"That's Burkeville. It's named for Stanley Burke, who was Boeing's president when the company town was built. They held a competition to name the town. His name won. Big surprise. Lose your job, you lost your home and you were off to war."

Tad wondered if this guy would ever shut up.

Cliff's nose was back in the brochure, rooting for facts.

The rumble of an approaching jet meant help was on the way. Glancing left, past Cliff and the Undertaker at the wheel, Tad caught sight of a sure means to squelch the historian's dull ramble: a giant 747 dropping from the sky.

"I'll bet you don't know how Lulu Island got its name—"

The scream of the jet passing overhead drowned out Cliff's sentence. Tad turned his eyes right to watch it land. Wheels down and nose up to hit the Tarmac, first the shadow of the plane, then the plane itself roared in over the helipad beside the hearse. The jet stream caught a wind catcher mounted on a flagpole a moment before the window next to Tad turned red, except for a silhouette on the glass shaped like his head. Framed in the distance by his sudden outline was the airport and its control tower.

Whap! It felt like a wasp sting on the back of his neck.

In pain, Tad turned to find Cliff's face a mess of blood. A .22 had drilled a hole through the short man's brow before striking the nape of the hulk's neck with its almost-spent force. Cliff too had turned his head to watch the jet land, and that's when the driver had pulled his gun.

The gun that now faced Tad over the bloody mask of Cliff's face.

The gun with a silencer on its muzzle.

The .22 fired with a sound like clapping hands. It punched a third eye in Tad's face. Because Tad's skull was thicker than Cliff's, the standard-velocity hollow-point careered around inside his head, turning his brain to mush before it lodged in what was left of the pulpy mass.

The dark, unbroken windows of the hearse kept their secret as the Undertaker drove across Dinsmore Bridge, boats on the Fraser to either side. He skirted Richmond General on his cruise through town but didn't stop at the hospital's morgue. At Highway 99, the hearse with the mummy in the coffin in back—the mummy Stopwatch had shipped from England—angled south, heading for the Massey Tunnel under the Fraser's main channel, a short distance north of Canada's border with the United States.

WRECK BEACH

Vancouver

The cliffs of Point Grey have witnessed many great treks. After a wild canoe trip down the canyoned river that now bears his name, on July 2, 1808, Simon Fraser finally reached the Pacific on the riverbank below. But no sooner did he land at the Native village of Musqueam, where he'd spotted a mammoth cedar house fifteen hundred feet long and ninety feet wide, than hostile Natives emerged from the thickets "howling like so many wolves and brandishing their war clubs." His trek over, Fraser barely escaped upriver with his life.

The Great Trek of 1922 was a march by twelve hundred angry students along a dirt trail that led through the forest from Vancouver out to the point. They trekked to demand that the government build a university, and stood forming the human letters "UBC" for newspaper photographs. Their legacy is the most spectacular campus in Canada—the University of British Columbia—which crowns the clifftop of the high peninsula. From here, on a clear day, you *can* see forever. Over the harbor to the mountains. Over the ocean to the islands. Over the river to Washington State.

Today, a lesser great trek was under way. Its prize wasn't as lofty, but who cares? The students had spring fever and wished to mess around, so down the cliff they trekked for privacy.

"Almost time for the Wiener Man," said Gwen.

"At your service, baby."

"Not *you,*" she said, laughing.

"What better name for a wiener man than Rod?" he asked.

"You see that Austin Powers film with a spaceship shaped like a cock and balls?"

"*That's* what you study in fine arts?"

"Of course," said Gwen. *"Citizen Kane. Lawrence of Arabia. The Spy Who Shagged Me."*

"I'm switching from history."

"Film's more fun. Remember the edit sequence in the second Powers flick?"

"I didn't see the movie. I must have been reading Shirer or *Mein Kampf* instead."

Thirty-five thousand students populated the campus above, but here, in the last stand of urban forest saved from the ax, Rod and Gwen were as alone as Adam and Eve in Eden. So taxing was the climb down from the clifftop to the log booms floating in the junction of river and sea below at Wreck Beach that, even though logging has always been the core industry of British Columbia, the timber that towers on Point Grey today—red cedar, Sitka spruce and Douglas fir—predates its sighting by Captain Vancouver on the ship *Discovery* in 1792.

Down . . .

Down . . .

Down they went . . .

Through the primal woods.

"*The Spy Who Shagged Me* is a spoof of James Bond films," explained Gwen. "The spaceship blasts off to plant an earth-destroying laser on the moon. The flying penis is witnessed by people on the ground, one of whom says, 'It looks like a—' to his friends. The editor makes a jump cut to another group, where someone yells, 'Woody,' and guess who turns around?"

"Woody Woodpecker?"

"Woody Harrelson, Rod. But actually, your guess works better than the bartender from *Cheers.*"

"I get it. Genital jokes."

"Then someone else says, 'It looks like a—' to his friends, and the editor makes another jump cut to an actor calling, 'Willie.'"

"Let me guess," Rod said. "Willie Nelson appears onscreen?"

"Good, huh?" Gwen said.

"Yeah," he agreed.

"If *I* had been the editor, the next jump cut would have been from someone saying, 'It looks like a—' to *you,* Rod. And you'd be seen standing on Wreck Beach as buck naked as the Wiener Man."

With a quick zip, Gwen undid his fly. Then she ran down the steep path, two steps at a time.

Down . . .

Down . . .

Down he chased her . . .

Out onto Wreck Beach.

In summer, the wide-open sandy stretch at the foot of these sandstone cliffs would become—as it had been since the early seventies—a secluded haven for nudists. The clothed and the naked, the voyeur and the exhibitionist would mill about, peeking and preening under the bright blast of the sun. The tribal community would collect in a cluster of totem-like pilings raised at the water's edge, stringing hammocks and tents and clotheslines and volleyball nets. They'd pluck guitars and smoke pot and enjoy picnic food, or dine out by wandering over to the Wiener Man.

"Good advertising."

"What is?" Rod asked, catching up to Gwen.

"The Wiener Man selling hot dogs in the nude."

"Not to me. Would put me off my food."

"You're homophobic."

"You have penis envy."

"Besides, don't the two of you have something in common?"

"The Wiener Man and me?"

"Yes," said Gwen. "He sports a Viking helmet to serve customers from his barbecue."

"I don't get it. What's in common?"

"You're both horny," Gwen said, and ran off again.

The nymph was chased by the satyr toward the mouth of the Fraser. To their left, a chunk of the sandstone cliff had broken away, exposing a swath of beige in the wall of green. Dead trees lay broken on the sand below. To their right, the freshwater-and-salt-sea mix flowed across the strait toward the humps and dips of Vancouver Island. The only clouds in the sky were above that land mass on the horizon. Ahead, penned in by the north arm breakwater and jetty, lay the log-booming grounds of the river. Beyond that, across the Fraser to the southeast, spread the airport on Sea Island, where the Undertaker had just shot Cliff and Tod.

Gwen stopped running.

Rod grabbed her.

"Friday?" Gwen said, pointing to the sand. A set of boot tracks emerged from the smooth shore seaward of the high-tide mark.

"No, Ms. Crusoe. Friday went barefoot."

"The prints are from the sea."

"He must have anchored a boat, then waded ashore. See the tracks over there where he doubled back to the water? The sea erased his footprints below the tide mark."

"Why'd he come ashore?"

"Who cares?" said Rod.

"What's that over there?"

"Where?"

"By the lagoon."

The ocean arced around the sand dune on which they stood to form a shallow waterway between them and the cliff. As Gwen followed the mysterious footprints toward the lagoon, a flock of Canada geese skimmed in to land near what she'd spotted.

The prints led to a naked body dumped on the sand. So emaciated was her corpse that the dead woman was no more than skin and bones. She looked like a mummy.

X IS FOR EXTERNAL

Vancouver

Special X had a squad room unlike any in the movies, dissimilar to any bullpen in 99.9 percent of the cop shops around the world. Ours is an age of institutional drab, when—unlike the glories of architecture past—pennies are pinched on designing and furnishing public buildings. No one, politicians think, deserves cheap as much as those who break the law, so to flaunt contempt for them, police stations are made as mundane and banal as possible. That cops have to work there too is but a fitting punishment for having chosen such a shitty job. If cops were deserving, wouldn't they be politicians on the gravy train?

Go take a look at where politicians work.

No expense is spared.

Your common bullpen, however, is full of cops in shirtsleeves, packing pistols in shoulder holsters slung under their armpits or fastened to their belts, penned at desks bunched together like cattle in a corral. Whoever is in command has an office in the corner, not much bigger than a toilet cubicle. Sprucing up the walls like portraits in a gallery are the black-and-white mugs on wanted posters. The coffee's bad, the unsolved files are many, and most of those working them know exactly how much time they must put in until they can retire.

But not Special X.

Historically, the Tudor building at Heather Street and 33rd Avenue was to accommodate the Langara School for Boys. Instead, it was purchased by the Mounties in 1921 as a barracks for two hundred horsemen. Four stables were added for 140 horses, and ever since, the striking Tudor throwback to that artistic era has been known as the Heather Stables.

Today, the Heather Stables house Special X.

Chief Superintendent Robert DeClercq loathed politicians and the pork barrel around which they wallowed. He considered it his duty to rub their noses in it. Why should they greet heads of state at lavish affairs with tuxedos, gowns, champagne and caviar, while he, as head of Special X, the Special External Section of the Mounted Police, was relegated to greeting foreign chiefs of police in surroundings designed to make them feel as if they were slumming?

What hypocrites.

It's amazing what you can do with a small budget and a lot of history. The Mounties date from 1873, the heyday of the British colonial empire. Early detachments were furnished with what were now antiques, so DeClercq had rummaged through storage rooms from coast to coast, commandeering treasures from Queen Victoria's realm. Charles Russell and other great artists of the Wild West were lured by the myth of the Mounted to capture the force on canvas. Those paintings were also gathered by DeClercq.

The result?

Voilà.

A vast expanse of green lawn fronted the beamed façade of the Tudor building, instilling the impression that Shakespeare might have resided here. Preconceptions of *other* squad rooms vanished at the door. The thoroughly modern Mounties who worked with state-of-the-art computers and high-tech forensic gizmos on the ground floor did so in an environment that embraced their frontier traditions. Mannequins displayed those changes made to the classic red-serge uniform over time: from the pillbox hat to the white pith helmet to the wide-brim Stetson. On the walls hung an impressive array of weapons: the Adams, Enfield, Colt and Smith & Wesson side arms; the rifles carried in a sling attached to the pommel of the

California stock saddle; the cavalry swords of officers; and the Maxim machine gun, acquired in 1898 to police miners climbing the White Pass during the Yukon Gold Rush. The cops who worked in uniform at the antique desks in this museum drank a choice of three blends of fresh-ground Starbucks coffee.

It's the little things, DeClercq knew, that foster morale.

And morale solves cases.

Facing the front entrance, a wide staircase angled up to the second floor. Hung sequentially on both sides of the stairs were the paintings collected by DeClercq. A visitor passed pictures of a long line of redcoats on the grueling march West in 1874 to capture Fort Whoop-Up from whisky traders. Of Superintendent James Walsh laying down the law to Sitting Bull after Custer's last stand, which induced American newspapers to dub Bub Walsh "Sitting Bull's Boss." Of *The Siege of Fort Pitt* and *The Fight at Duck Lake* during the Second Riel Rebellion, when the Métis and Cree were crushed by the Mounties to end the last war cry. Of *Beyond the Law* by Franz Johnston, one of the Group of Seven: the Arctic manhunt ending with the fugitive lying dead in the snow, a Mountie in snowshoes and his dog set against the northern lights. Of *The* St. Roch *in the Ice,* the RCMP ship that conquered the Northwest Passage to extend Canada's sovereignty to the North Pole.

Image after image.

Triumph after triumph.

Before you reached DeClercq's door on the right at the top of the stairs, you knew these were the barracks of history's best police force.

Or at least its most photogenic.

DeClercq was on the phone long distance with Katt when Ghost Keeper and Zinc Chandler entered. The two inspectors gave DeClercq space to finish the call, for both understood how the absence of his surrogate daughter had torn a hole of loneliness in the fabric of his life. Ghost Keeper wandered across to the bank of windows looking out at Queen Elizabeth Park and picked out the signs of spring budding in the afternoon sun. Zinc Chandler busied himself by pinning up X-ray photos on the Strategy Wall, for when DeClercq worked a case he worked it visually.

"The rain in Spain falls mainly on the plain, I'm told," Katt was saying to DeClercq.

"Oh? By whom?"

"Professor Higgins."

"From *My Fair Lady?*"

"No, from school. He's my new English teacher. My *English* English teacher."

"What happened to Mr. Burns?"

"He left suddenly. It's all very hush-hush, but we suspect he got caught in bed with one of his students."

"It's midnight in London. Why are you still up?"

"We just got in from the theater." Katt pronounced it *thee-ah-tah.*

"Oh? What did you see?"

"*Pygmalion.* By Bernard Shaw."

"That explains Higgins. So what's your teacher's real name?"

"Higgins," said Katt. "Isn't that cool? I'm the only student in class with a North American guttersnipe nasal drawl, and a *real* Professor Higgins is trying to turn me into his fair lady."

"Is it working?"

"You tell me. The rhine in spine falls minely on the pline."

"What's that?"

"My cockney accent. Before I got cultured. Didn't you see the movie?"

"You sound more like an Australian to me."

"Take a pisser, Bob."

"Now *that's* my guttersnipe."

"By the time Higgins is finished, I'll sound like a toff."

"Now don't go fetching his slippers. Remember Mr. Burns."

"That's a different story."

"Huh?"

"I'm living *Pygmalion,* not *Lolita.*"

With that exit line, Katt blew him a kiss over the phone and was gone. Cradling the receiver, DeClercq sat at his desk for a moment, gazing at her picture. He was a man in his fifties, lean and wiry in build, with dark hair graying at the temples and even darker, brooding eyes. To those who knew his story, the photos displayed on his well-organized desk said it all.

His first wife, Kate, was photographed acting on Broadway in Ibsen's *Rosmersholme,* the picture snapped a half-hour before he conned his way backstage to meet the alluring siren. Later, Kate was shot to death in their Montreal home, the victim of a revenge attack for the takedown DeClercq led in Quebec's October Crisis.

His daughter, Jane, was photographed at play in a pile of autumn leaves, the youngster's head thrown back in a laugh with sunlight dappling her curls. The thugs who'd gunned down his wife had also kidnapped his child. Before he could rescue little Jane from a cabin in the woods, the killers had broken her neck.

Loneliness had driven him from that haunted house. Loneliness had followed him to the West Coast. Loneliness was a prison from which he thought he would never escape. And then—do you believe in magic?—Genevieve freed him.

Her body tanned in contrast to the pale bikini she wore, her hand holding a large conch shell to her ear, his second wife was photographed on a beach in Western Samoa during their honeymoon. Then—*bang!*—Genny was dead too, cut down by a ricocheting slug from the Headhunter's gun.

That well of loneliness seemed bottomless, all the deeper since he had previously plunged into despair over Kate and Jane. He swore to himself he would never again get close to another human being, would never foist the jinx of his love on anyone, but then Katt came along . . .

"Something wrong, Chief?" Ghost Keeper asked.

DeClercq glanced up from Katt's photo to find both inspectors watching him.

"No," he said. "Just having a senior moment."

"Don't wander too far. We need your brain focused on this."

The Cree pointed to the X-ray photos that Chandler had pinned up.

Three Victorian library tables joined in the shape of a horseshoe served as DeClercq's desk. The chair nestled in the crook of the U was an antique from the early days of the force, high-backed with a barley-sugar frame and the bison-head crest of the Mounties carved as a crown. The chief pushed back from the desk, then turned to face the picture on the wall behind.

Sydney Hall's *Last Great Council of the West* was painted for the London *Graphic* in 1881 to capture a tour of Canada's Northwest by the Marquis of Lorne. The pith-helmeted governor general sat in regal arrogance under an awning erected at Blackfoot Crossing. He was guarded by the Mounted Police, their hands on their swords, while at his feet squatted feathered Indians. The tour, complete with a French chef and six servants, had been mounted to commemorate the fact that with Treaty 6, signed at Fort Carleton on August 23, 1876—about a month after they had helped the Sioux annihilate the Americans at Custer's last stand—the Cree had surrendered what is today Saskatchewan and part of Alberta.

"Does the picture offend you?" DeClercq had once asked Ghost Keeper.

"Not if it's accurate. I'm not offended by truth. You can't rewrite the history of the past. But you can write the history of the future."

Promoting the Cree to give him that chance was one of the best decisions DeClercq had ever made.

"So what have we got?" he said, joining both men at the Strategy Wall.

No toilet cubicle, DeClercq's corner office was an airy, high-vaulted loft. The two walls without windows were sheathed floor to ceiling with corkboard on which a number of collages were arrayed. The Special External Section investigated cases with links to other nations, so studying the array was like taking a trip around the world.

The Cree had been on duty for thirty-two hours. He had worked his regular shift yesterday, before spending all night stalking the wolf-dog and combing the site of the Galiano body. Then he had put in his regular shift at HQ, and now he was briefing DeClercq on the murders in the delta. To look at him—black hair, bronze skin, wide cheekbones and hawkish eyes—was to see a hefty man still as sharp as when he came on duty. Ghost Keeper's stamina impressed DeClercq. The Cree made no concession to who he was, and having come straight to HQ from the bush hunt, he had worked the day in a buckskin shirt with spirit designs embroidered by his mother in a colorful rainbow of beads.

"An hour ago, Delta police pulled a sunken hearse out of the Fraser. Someone had pushed it off the end of a dock. Inside, officers found the bodies of two Canada Customs inspectors. Both had been shot in the head with a small caliber gun."

"Sounds professional."

"Yeah. All the marks of a hit. Low-velocity slugs pin-balling around in the skull."

"Anyone see the sinking?"

"No, the dock's an old one out on River Road."

"Who found the hearse?"

"Two boys playing hooky from school. Tom and Huck were fishing off the dock when they spotted the ass end of the vehicle in the water."

"In the muddy Fraser?"

"The bank must be shallow there."

DeClercq scanned the X-ray photos on the Strategy Wall. "Smuggling, huh?"

The Cree nodded. "Must be jewels. Who would shoot two customs men to keep a dead body?"

"Air Canada flew a coffin in from London Heathrow today," said Chandler. "These X-rays were shot at the cargo shed. An undertaker arrived to fetch the deceased in the hearse. Customs told him they were going to search the coffin. He left the airport with two inspectors to drive to Richmond morgue. They didn't make it. Instead, the hearse vanished into thin air."

"Into muddy water."

"Whatever," Chandler said.

If Katt was living *Pygmalion,* DeClercq felt as if he was witnessing *The Picture of Dorian Gray.* In Oscar Wilde's novel, no matter what Gray does to his physical and moral self, it doesn't show on him. He retains the youth and beauty of spring. Hidden away in a locked room at the top of Gray's house, however, his portrait reflects every mark of decay. In this re-enactment, Ghost Keeper was Gray. And the role of Ghost Keeper's picture was played by Zinc Chandler. Where Ghost Keeper looked healthy and alert, physically and mentally, Chandler was a mess.

A bullet to the head in Hong Kong and the Ripper's knife in his back on Deadman's Island, off Canada's West Coast, had sapped Zinc Chandler physically. But even more debilitating was a series of tragedies in his personal life. DeClercq knew only too well what that could do to your psyche, and he saw the signs of an on-coming breakdown displayed on the world-weary canvas of Chandler's face. His natural steel gray hair—responsible for his given name—was shaggy and in need of a cut. His gray eyes were bloodshot and glazed from insomnia. The hollowness of his angular features testified to the worry that he was burning out, for Zinc's way of coping with grief was to work, work, work.

Something *had* to be done.

DeClercq was going to get tough.

"This undertaker?" he said. "Do we have a photo of him?"

"Customs security cameras are being checked as we speak. It won't be good," said the Cree. "The suspect wore a peaked cap and shades. The verbal we got is 'He looks like a ghoul.'"

"Employer?"

"Sort of. The funeral home is real. But it's gone into receivership. The assets are frozen. One of those assets was the hearse. It was stolen this morning from the shut-down mortuary."

"Slick."

"Yeah. This guy knows what he's doing."

"Coffin?"

"Missing from the back of the hearse. Transferred to a boat at the dock is my bet."

"The boat could be just about anywhere by now. Up the river. In the islands. Out to sea. Maybe it's south of the border in the States."

"Lots of boats. Can't check 'em all."

DeClercq locked eyes with Ghost Keeper. "You look beat," he said. "Gather in the loose ends and go get some sleep." A flick of his gaze toward Chandler asked the Cree to read his mind. That comment applies to him, not you, was the telepathic message. So perceptive was Ghost Keeper that he required no more. A quick blink of his eyes: message received.

"Zinc—" began DeClercq as the door shut behind the inspector.

"I'm okay, Chief." Heading him off at the pass.

"No, you're not. You may be kidding yourself, but you're not kidding me. You can't kid a kidder, and the photos on my desk prove I'm adept at the game. A tragedy like yours exacts a heavy toll. Others have the option of burying themselves in overwork. You don't. Sleep and four caps of Dilantin a day are your defenses against an epileptic fit, and overwork is robbing you of sleep. What you need is a rest in the tropics. I'm looking for an assignment to send you there."

"Do I have a choice?"

"Yes," said DeClercq. "You can accept my advice as your friend and go willingly, or you can force me as your boss to order you onto a plane."

"I prefer the South Pacific to the Caribbean," Chandler said with the slightest touch of a grin.

"I'll see what I can do."

That messy business over, the Mounties returned to work. For minutes, DeClercq silently studied the X-rays on the Strategy Wall, noting the shape and position of each jewel hidden on the corpse. A pair of round stones the size of quarters were stuffed in the eye sockets. A sliver of what seemed to be metal covered the tongue. A jewel cut in the shape of a bug of some sort was placed over the heart. And a brooch of irregular design seemed to be slipping off the abdomen.

"Our best lead is these jewels," said DeClercq. "I wonder why they're scattered about the corpse. Does that not increase the odds of detection at this end? If they were hidden in a single cavity, it would take only a moment to open the coffin, find the jewels and spirit them away."

"Instead, he took the corpse."

"Why?" asked DeClercq.

"The hearse was hot. He had to ditch it fast. The undertaker transferred the coffin to a boat so he could do a thorough search somewhere safe. The jewels must be worth a lot to warrant such risk."

"An emerald or a ruby the size of the stones we see stuffed in both eyes could be worth millions, depending on quality."

"And the bug?"

"Depends," said DeClercq. "If it's a single cut stone, it depends what it is. Same with the brooch on the belly. Content counts."

"So what's the plan?"

"We work it from both ends. Let Ghost Keeper have the trail in Canada and you take Britain. Precious stones attract a history. Someone owns them, buys them, steals them, offers them for sale. The coffin came in from London, so the history of the smuggled contraband may lie there. Who was that Scotland Yard detective you worked with on the Ghoul case?"

"Hilary Rand. She's a commander now."

"Before going to a travel agent for South Pacific brochures, send Rand these X-rays and ask if they match any stolen jewels."

PORN KING

Vancouver

The picture framed on the wall beside the one-way mirror in Wolfe Capp's office was a reproduction of the "femicide" cover from the June 1978 issue of *Hustler* magazine. Sleek with body oil, the legs and buttocks of a female protruded gracefully from the top of a manual meat grinder. Head first, the woman was being processed through the machine. Accumulating on a plate on a table under the spout of the grinder, her head and upper body emerged as a mound of ground beef. A sign resembling a meat-packaging stamp announced, "Last All-Meat Issue—Grade 'A' Pink." On the far side of the one-way glass, a naked sixteen-year-old girl vamped at her reflection in the mirror while, unseen on this side, the porn king and the plastic surgeon discussed her.

"How big does she want them?"

"Who cares?" said Capp. "My client's a tit man, and he wants 'em *huge*."

"I don't know," replied the doctor. "This girl's underage. What if she squeals? That could mean jail."

"She won't squeal, Fletcher. She's dying to break into the trade. You should have seen her eyes light up when I said I'd buy her a new rack."

"Tits make the woman."

"Not in my videos. It's a woodsman who makes her. Again and again and again . . ."

Dr. Ryland Fletcher laughed. "Okay, how much do I pocket if I pump her up?"

"Ten grand, and you can fuck any porn queen in my stable."

"Fifteen, and they'll be so big this budding babe will fall on her face."

"Twelve."

"Thirteen."

"That's your lucky number."

The porn king and the plastic surgeon shook hands to seal their deal in flesh as the girl on the far side of the glass pinched her nipples and tugged her breasts out to wannabe size.

Twice the size of Hollywood.

Ten billion dollars a year.

That was the monetary pull in Wolfe Capp's line of work.

Money, money, money.

A bountiful pornocopia spewing forth green.

Back in 1970, Capp was a student in pre-law when a girlfriend broke his heart. To mend the wound, Capp ran away to the Caribbean, where he boozed himself from one island to the next, ending up, down and out, on a beach in Barbados. In those days, Larry's Nitery was in full swing, and if you were a "swinger" out with the boys for a fling in Bridgetown, Larry's was the sort of dive where you could howl.

Imagine a bed in the center of a room. Chairs lined the walls on all four sides. Seated on those chairs were mostly button-down corporate types who wouldn't be caught dead in a place like this back home. But when you're on vacation, you can let it all hang out, so here they would wait on plastic chairs for the show to begin as black women in white underwear serve them bottled beer. Though well into the evening, the air was usually hot and stuffy from baking all day under the merciless sun. With no air conditioning, this room was rank from human sweat, partially masked by the cheap perfume slathered on Larry's "girls."

Larry's Nitery was known far and wide. The rumor was that Larry put on private shows, and he would sate your most perverse desire for a price. A woman and a donkey? That can be arranged. Buggery may be against the law in your state, but if you want to watch two guys get it on for you, Larry's palm was the one to grease. Rumors like those were whispered as a couple in evening attire were shown to the last two chairs, and the usher padlocked the door. These latecomers were definitely out of place. They were gussied up like a husband and wife who expect a Las Vegas show.

Rustle, rustle.

The businessmen squirmed.

They didn't like a woman dressed like one of their wives in this room. Not when they're here to wallow in taboo denied at home.

The crack of a whip caused the voyeurs to jump in their seats. A secret door burst open and two cowering black women scrambled into the room. Like those serving, they wore skimpy white. The man who tailed them cracking the whip was Larry himself, a black, rotund bowling ball of a slave master. He looked like a blues man out of New Orleans. Behind him stood a tall, skinny black man wearing a codpiece of white cotton.

"Diane!" Larry shouted.

A crack of the whip.

"Marta!" Larry shouted.

Another whip crack.

"On the bed. The two of you. These gentlemen want a show."

Obediently, both women scampered aboard, followed by the male in the bulging codpiece. Then, just as the show was getting under way, a voice as harsh as the whip snapped in the foul air. "I thought we were going nightclubbing, George?"

George cringed in his plastic chair. "It said 'nitery' in the ad, dear."

The Las Vegas–style matron bounded from her seat to storm in disgust out of Larry's Nitery, but the door was padlocked and guarded by the usher. For years, the cops had tried to shut down this moral blight on the island landscape, dragging the entrepreneur into court several times. The current state of the case was that Larry was banned from his own club, so that's why the door was locked.

He would sneak in for each show by way of an underground tunnel from the building across the street. Larry's Nitery had little time left, and Larry was squeezing out every last cent.

"Let me out!" the irate woman demanded.

The guard stood his ground.

Used to getting her way with milquetoast George, the fuming woman slapped the guard's face.

On reflex, the guard slapped her back.

"Call the police, George!"

The woman dropped to her knees, blood running from her mouth.

"You're through!" she screamed, pointing a finger at Larry.

The scowl on Larry's face attested to the probable truth in her statement, and his eyes grew dark from calculating how much this woman would cost him.

Like a deer caught in the headlights, George was afraid to move. But move he did when two ruffians grabbed him and his cursing wife and hauled them unceremoniously out through the secret door.

"What a bitch!"

The voice is next to Capp.

"How *dare* that woman spoil our fun."

The man sitting next to Capp could have been an executive in any corporation. He and the man next to him might have spent the day playing golf or tennis, for they had the powerbroker look of those who wheel and deal while they enjoy themselves. A merger that cuts a thousand jobs, a layoff of dozens of underlings to trim the bottom line—for these two that would have been all in a day's work. Benign on the surface and ruthless beneath, these men had millions of clones on the prowl in every city where money counts.

"How much have you got in cash?"

"On me?"

"In your wallet."

"Two grand, I think."

"I've got three. That makes five large. It should be enough to prompt Larry to put on a private show. The bitch and the whip. It's time they met."

"You're kidding?"

"Dare me. No one spoils *my* fun."

Larry looked none too pleased as he cleared his club of patrons, a necessary precaution against a visit from the cops. Parting with each refund seemed to hurt him as much as parting with a pound of his own flesh, until he was approached by the businessman whose seat was next to Capp's.

Words were exchanged.

A wad of green switched hands.

The businessman summoned his buddy from where he was still seated, and the three men disappeared into the darkness beyond the secret door.

The last thing Capp saw as he got up to leave was the grin of satisfaction on Larry's face. A moment ago, the woman pointing her finger at him was a money loser. Now the skin on her back is worth five grand.

Imagine that.

Supply and demand.

New York City, 1976

The poster outside the theater caught Wolfe Capp's attention as the young Canadian corporate lawyer passed through Times Square. He was in the metropolis to hand-deliver prospectus documents for the senior partners in the firm. His flight home was six hours away, so he had time to kill.

The poster featured a naked young woman whose head lolled back. Her picture had been cut into four pieces with the mammoth pair of bloody scissors displayed beside her body. Flowing from her neck, breasts and abdominal area were floods of blood gushing from the cuts made by the scissors. *Snuff* was the title of the film. Three blurbs on the poster lured the curious in: "The picture they said could NEVER be shown . . ." "The film that could be made only in South America . . . where life is CHEAP!" "The *bloodiest* thing that *ever* happened in front of a camera!"

Hook, line and sinker, Capp took the bait.

Paying his blood money, he joined the men already seated in the darkness within. As the film advanced, he heard soft sighs and satisfied groans from the leering profiles around him. The climax of *Snuff* depicted a man ripping the uterus out of a woman and holding it up as a trophy while he ejaculated. Jack the Ripper performed the same perversion on his victims, and when the lights came on to expose the perverts surrounding Capp, he saw to his delight that half of them were Wall Street businessmen.

A protest was in full blossom when Capp slunk out of the theater. Hundreds of women and dozens of men were picketing the movie with handwritten signs.

One sign was a quote attributed to Aldous Huxley: "The higher and more advanced the civilization, the more perverted the sex."

Femicide: the misogynist killing of women by males for sexual gratification.

Capp read deeper in the psychology text, until he came to this quote by Henry Havelock Ellis, the pioneer of S&M, in *Studies in the Psychology of Sex:*

> Every normal man in matters of sex, when we examine him carefully enough, is found to show some abnormal elements, and the abnormal man is merely manifesting in a disordered or extravagant shape some phase of the normal man. Normal and abnormal, taken in the mass, can all be plotted as variations of different degree on the same curve. [Every man] is connected by links, each in itself small, with Jack the Ripper. We all possess within us, in a more or less developed form, the germs of atrocities.

Reading deeper, he found support in this quote from Carl Jung, in *Psychological Types:*

The dammed-up instinct-forces in civilized man are immensely more destructive, and hence more dangerous, than the instincts of the primitive, who in a modest degree is constantly living his negative instincts. Consequently no war of the historical past can rival a war between civilized nations in its colossal scale of horror.

Ellis, again:

There is no finer task in life than to let a little light and sunshine into those parts of it which have so long been shut up to fester in darkness.

Jung, again:

The spirit of our time believes itself superior to its own psychology.

Hmmm, thought Capp.

Supply and demand.

He recalled the businessmen in Larry's Nitery.

He recalled the businessmen watching *Snuff.*

Men with money.

Men addicted to power.

And of all the types of power one human being can wield over another, the ultimate is the power over life and death.

Imagine *that* market.

Money, money, money . . .

But how do you bring together such a subterranean supply and demand?

This was, of course, *before* the Internet.

Wolfe Capp was in trouble now. A sure-thing investment in the Orient had gone wrong when Japan took a nose dive in the markets.

The money Capp had fronted was from his trust account, "borrowed" from a client whose closing was weeks away. Now the money was gone, those weeks had passed and Capp lacked the wherewithal to complete his client's deal. Fiddling with a trust account was grounds for disbarment, followed by four years or more in jail. The chance he might be gang-raped in the shower scared him, and what with the rate of HIV in prison . . .

"I could be serving a *death* sentence," Capp told his livid client.

The old man looked him over. "Yep," he said. "A pretty boy like you is gonna end up a shish kebab on a lotta spikes. And you know what, Wolfe? I'd pay to have that filmed."

"Would you, Bud?"

"Bet your ass."

"So how much would you pay to see her *done?*"

"What does that mean?"

"'Done' means whatever it takes to wipe the slate clean."

They were in Capp's office. The door was shut. The old man leaned forward in one of the client chairs. His hard eyes narrowed. "Spell it out."

The lawyer leaned forward, tête-à-tête, in conspiracy.

"Let's face it, Bud. You're in deep shit too. You downloaded your porn collection at work. In that collection is some exotic stuff. *Deep Sheep. Swastika Snatch. Kneeling for Daddy.* That temp your company hired while your secretary was sick is a nosy little hacker who's got the goods on you. She's made you an offer you can't refuse. Either you buy her a hair salon franchise or she'll accuse you of sexual harassment and use the porn collection she copied to prove her allegation. Zero tolerance is the company policy in such matters. Your wife is an Orthodox Jew. And your daughter is the apple of your eye."

"Bloodsucking bitch!"

"That she is," Wolfe agreed. "And now, Bud, you're in a double bind. I've lost the money you gave me to buy her off. You can report me, but what good will that do? Long before you're reimbursed from the law society fund, you'll be unemployed, in divorce court and estranged from your beloved daughter. Besides, even if you did complete the deal, who's to say the little vampire won't come back for more?"

The old man nodded. "Get to the point."

"She's fucking with your head. Why not fuck with hers? Forget about the money I lost and sending me to jail, and I'll give you the jewel in the crown of your porn collection."

Snatching her was easy. He got her off the street. He parked the stolen box truck near her basement suite and waylaid her as she came home from a dance club late at night. He drove the truck way out of town and down a logging road until he found the perfect place that was hell and gone. There, beneath a moonless sky, he braked to a halt and got in back with her.

Still in her dance dress, a sexy, clinging sheath, the woman came out of a chloroform stupor to find herself the terrified star in a "fem-jep" video. She was lashed at her ankles and wrists to the legs and arms of a chair. The chair was fastened upright to the floor of the box, and every backdrop around her was draped with black plastic sheets. Lights and videocams were mounted to focus on the chair. They were run by juice from one of two generators. Wires from the second battery snaked to the chair, then rose to electrodes taped to the nubile young blackmailer's temples.

"Fem-jep" is porn jargon for female in jeopardy. Part of her jeopardy in this black box was the electric chair. The other part was Woody Bone.

Woody Bone was a play on words. "Wood" is a word staple in the porn trade. Erecting a boner on demand is "the getting or copping of wood." Keeping it hard for the length of the shoot is "the wielding of wood." A "woodsman" involved in "woodwork" who can't keep it up has "difficulties with wood" if he stops the shoot before he can "bring it all home."

The woodsman in this video was Wolfe Capp himself. To keep from being recognized should his artwork escape into the marketplace, he stripped and painted his naked flesh black with a white skeleton superimposed over his own. Woody Bone was able to cop wood on his own demand, and as he approached the switch that would control this shock therapy, the woman tied to the electric chair let out a scream. From different angles, five video cameras recorded what went on in the box as scream after scream echoed through the woods. The stars above shone down on Hollywood North as a new star was born and another snuffed out.

The body dumped from the box truck before it drove away was soon devoured by black bears that crunched the bones for marrow. By dawn, the truck was back where it had been stolen from, empty of equipment and stripped of the plastic that caught the blood. The deal for the hair salon franchise was canceled at eight, then Capp spent the rest of the day editing his videotapes. The following afternoon saw Bud back in the lawyer's office, where he was given a private screening of the director's cut. So ecstatic was the businessman with the result that he offered his hand immediately to forgo the debt owed to him from the trust-account fraud.

Skull Fucker is the title of that video. Bud keeps it locked away in a secret place, and when his wife is at synagogue and his daughter is out on a date, he cops wood and wields it by hand in the privacy of his den as he watches that bloodsucking bitch scream for mercy and forgiveness with each shock Woody Bone delivers.

Watching it again . . .

And again . . .

And again . . .

If the old economy was an old boys' club, the new economy is a network. As the World Wide Web spread near and far, it linked those of like mind together. The Spider's Web was one of those links. It joined connoisseurs of fem-jep to Wolfe Capp. Wolfe no longer practiced corporate law. He was too busy catering to other corporate needs. From his underground studio in Vancouver, made-to-order porn was shipped around the world.

Most of it was benign stuff. Like the nightly show at Larry's

Nitery, it was as staged as wrestling on TV. A businessman in Tokyo or Berlin would script a fem-jep fantasy and send it by e-mail to the Spider's Web. Back would come the cost of filming it, and if the vicarious woodsman responded with a bank transfer, he would get a password that let him view Wolfe's gallery of available porn queens.

That's how Dr. Ryland Fletcher had linked up with the porn king.

Externally, Fletcher was a man of self-confidence. A swimmer all his life, his body was buff and trim. His physique was complemented by an array of designer suits with red suspenders: a statement that said, "I'm one of those doctors in it for money, not my patients' health." His features were good-looking, if a mite too feminine, and that was the aspect that gave him difficulties with wood. Internally, his masculinity required a boost, and what made Fletcher cop wood was the reassurance fantasy of sexy porn queens craving *his* cock.

As they did in the videos he had ordered from the Spider's Web.

That, of course, was back when he was a practicing plastic surgeon in Hollywood South.

The *real* Hollywood.

Tinseltown.

But what Fletcher didn't know as he and Wolfe Capp stood this side of the one-way mirror that looked in on the adolescent wannabe porn queen was that the Spider's Web was a front for Snuff Lib. Sure, there was cash to be made from the benign stuff, but spread around the world was an elite network of well-heeled powermongers who could, and would, pay dearly to have their malignancy fulfilled.

These were the clients of Woody Bone.

The same way that rumor spread that Larry's Nitery would—for a suitable price—put on a private depths-of-debauchery show, so it was whispered among the elite that Snuff Lib would free the demons in those whom money and power had corrupted to the bone.

And one of those so corrupted was a televangelist in Houston, Texas, who had spent a lifetime praising the Lord on national TV and begging his faithful following to keep that money flowing in so he could maintain his crusade against the Devil's work. And the vilest threat of the Evil One (he had come to realize in the thoughts that tormented him while reading *Hustler* at home) came from the perky, budding boobs on the teenage sluts in his congregation. Remember that other pious reverend caught with his pants down in a car when the Devil made him seek out a hooker to polish the holy knob? Well, if this holy roller didn't fight back, the same fate could happen to him, except it would be a million times worse because the wanton titties that drove him mad were all jailbait.

So that's why he had diverted money sent in to the Lord's ministry to Snuff Lib. And why, when Dr. Ryland Fletcher had asked if he could *personally* be the woodsman in the third fantasy he had ordered on the Spider's Web, Wolfe Capp had invited the plastic surgeon to come to his Vancouver studio to discuss a quid pro quo offer of mutual benefit. The deal they had just sealed with a handshake would see the recently disgraced surgeon turn the teenaged girl on the other side of the glass into a lascivious mockery of adolescent chastity. But Fletcher had no inkling of what would happen then, for this girl was destined to become Woody Bone's next starlet snuff. And when, a week or two from now, the televangelist sat at home grinding his meat as he devoured the latest issue of *Hustler,* and suddenly the Devil came to lead him into temptation with one of the sluts the Evil One had insidiously inserted into his congregation, the man of God would be armed and up to the task of scaring even the Devil back to hell.

Pop *Meat Grinder* into the VCR and that would take care of that.

What Fletcher didn't realize was that the femicide cover from the June 1978 issue of *Hustler* framed on the wall beside the one-way mirror wasn't hanging there for decoration.

Instead, it was a shooting script.

Literally.

THE HITCHCOCK SYNDROME

Vancouver

"Was that not the solicitor general who passed me on the stairs?"

DeClercq turned from the Strategy Wall to find Dr. Gill Macbeth standing at the door. If she had one, she could have been her *own* daughter. He blinked, but this younger Gill didn't age.

"Good God! Show me the way to the Fountain of Youth."

"First day of spring."

"So I see."

"*Was* that who I thought it was?"

"Yes, the penny-pincher."

"He seemed none too happy."

"He's grinding his molars to dust."

"Oh? Why?"

"Because that political cheapskate hoped he could nail me for corruption."

"Ah," said Gill. "The new decor?"

"I *loathe* politicians."

"So I hear."

"I consider it my sacred duty as an officer and a gentleman to undermine those pigs at the trough whenever I can. That tightwad has cut the force's budget to the bone, so I took it upon myself to redecorate Special X."

"It looks like a million bucks."

"It does," said DeClercq. "And that no doubt is what the solicitor general heard. He's doing everything he can to cripple morale, so the only explanation that occurred to him was that I was taking graft or stealing money seized from drug busts."

"So what did you say to him?"

"I thanked him for the paint."

It was the last act of a glorious day, the setting sun now casting light that shone like gold polish on the crown of Queen Elizabeth Park topping Little Mountain. As she walked from the door to gaze out of the eastern windows at the uplifting rites of spring, Gill passed square after square of northern dazzle that silhouetted her uplifted figure. Watching her made the chief feel as if he were rejuvenated too.

"I brought you this," Gill said, waving a ViCLAS booklet in her hand. The Violent Crime Linkage Analysis System is the computer database gathered and worked by Special X to alert cops to the presence of serial killers preying on Canadians. The 168 questions in the booklet are crafted to isolate patterns in individual crimes. Program the answers into a computer and ViCLAS searches the database for similar patterns in previous homicides.

"The corpse from Galiano?"

"Yes," said Gill. "I thought it might help if I answered the questions on mutilation."

"Did you find a signature?"

The pathologist nodded. "The breasts were cut off *surgically*. Unless I'm mistaken, the person responsible has done mastectomies."

"A cancer surgeon?"

"Possibly. Or a plastic surgeon who knows his way around breast reconstruction."

"A mad doctor?"

"They aren't just in the movies."

Gill passed him the booklet and followed the chief over to his desk. While he added her work to the ViCLAS in-box, the pathologist scanned the four photographs on the leather surface. "How's Katt?" she asked, picking up the headshot of the teenager. Sleeping on top of her head in the photo was a tiny kitten.

"Katt's Katt," said DeClercq, which said it all.

"How'd she do this?"

"*The Cat in the Hat?* The day she got Catnip, Katt took Dr. Seuss literally. When she removed her hat, there the kitten was, sound asleep."

"I hear Katt's in London?"

"Just spoke to her on the phone."

"What's she doing?"

"Going to finishing school. I believe Katt sees it as her *My Fair Lady* phase."

Gill burst out laughing. "Hope springs eternal. I suspect she'll finish that finishing school long before it finishes her."

"Probably."

"What's the name of the school?"

"Hogwarts," he said jokingly.

"How long is Katt in Britain?"

"For the school year."

"Your house must seem lonely."

"She left the cat behind. Those two were like peas in a pod when she was here, so Catnip cries all night if I don't let him sleep with me."

"Miss her?"

"Terribly. I hate dining alone."

"Okay," said Gill. "Tonight you dine with me. I have a new figure to celebrate, and you sent that cheap politician packing. Grab your coat. I'm taking you home with me."

Which, of course, was the *real* reason she had dropped by.

"Srrit . . . srreeew!"

"Va-va-va-voom!"

"Classy chassis, lassie."

"Foxy lady! Who's your birdy?"

The Dirty Duo welcomed Gill as she and the Mountie came in the front door. The parrot and the macaw hopped about on their perches.

DeClercq shook his head sadly as Macbeth punched off the burglar alarm. "It must be galling to you as a feminist to hear such sexist remarks."

"The only thing more galling to a confident woman is when she reaches that age when attractive men are no longer attracted to her. 'Femininity' is a major aspect of modern feminism. The daughters of feminists rejected that asexual we're-all-just-human-beings political crap in favor of Madonna and the Spice Girls. Titillation is where it's at."

Nonetheless, she closed the door to the aviary.

"Fancy a drink?"

"Sure. What have you got?"

"Everything but rum."

"I thought you were raised in Barbados?"

"I was. The rum capital of the world. That's why I don't touch the stuff."

"Overimbibed, eh?"

"No," said Gill. "I saw it being made."

"I can't imagine what could be distasteful in the process."

"Sugar cane is the major cash crop of the island. When I was a little girl, my dad took me to a mill. The cane was piled in huge mounds near the grinding wheels, which were giant horizontal corkscrews revolving at the base of a wide slanted chute. A clutching machine would pick up large clumps of cane and swivel to release the load into the chute, where the stalks would roll toward the grinding wheels. As the cane went tumbling down, I saw rats by the hundreds scurrying this way and that on the sugar stalks, until they too were ground up by the corkscrews. The mash of sugar and rat juice was flushed with water to make molasses, and that molasses went to the rum distillery."

"I'll have water," said DeClercq.

"Water's distasteful too. Fish *fuck* in it," said Gill with a sly wink.

Her sexy emphasis caused his throat to go dry. Her youthful look kept transporting him back to his own youth, and he felt like he did that first time he got blown by Estelle Lefleur at a film-noir festival in Quebec. They were sitting in his car at the drive-in theater, trying to keep off the windows the mist that kept fogging up the image of *The Postman Always Rings Twice,* when—*ziiiip*—down went his fly in her skilled fingers, and Estelle murmured in the dark, "Fill me in if I miss anything important."

"I'll have Scotch," he said.

"Single malt or blended?"

"Single malt," he said.

"Which brand?" she asked.

"You're kidding?"

"Call my bluff."

"Bowmore," he said.

"A connoisseur's choice."

"And a lucky guess?"

"No," said Gill, sliding back the hardwood doors of her built-in liquor cabinet to reveal her collection of every brand of Scotch available in the province. "I have the odds covered."

"You certainly do."

"Let's eat," she said like a spider might to the fly caught in its web.

"You keep yourself in shape."

"I try," he said.

"Doing what?"

"Fencing. Every other morning."

"Fencing? At what time?"

"Six-thirty sharp. The master is an old Hungarian who's a stickler for punctuality."

"Here's a stickler," she said, passing her guest a fondue fork from the butcher block in the middle of the kitchen, where they stood in chefs' aprons putting the final touches to beef bourguignon. "It's sharp. Show me your punctuality, Zorro."

DeClercq withdrew from the butcher block to assume the classic fencer's position, weight balanced between flexed legs with feet at right angles, the hand without the sword crooked in the air for counterbalance. "En garde." Feint, thrust, parry, then a lightning-fast lunge, and when he stepped back to reassume the original stance, a cube of punctured beef was skewered on the fork.

"Touché, Sir Loin," Gill said, clapping. "Good exercise."

"The only comparable workout is ballet."

"You do that?"

"No." He laughed.

"Too bad." Gill sighed. "I love to watch men in those skin-tight pants."

"Sexist."

"I confess." She plucked the cube off the fondue fork and returned it to the meal they were about to eat in the candlelit dining room.

Cognac and coffee by a crackling fire followed the romantic meal. It was cold on the peak of Sentinel Hill after the sun went down. The lights of Vancouver in the blackness beyond sparkled like solar debris. Mahler—the Adagietto for Strings from the Fifth Symphony—set the mood while DeClercq scanned Macbeth's video library.

"Hitchcock," he said. "Another collection? I'll bet you have every one of his films."

"Guilty," Gill confessed.

"How'd you get so obsessive?"

"A collection isn't a collection to me until it's complete. How dull a person's life must be if she or he doesn't collect something."

"I collected bottle caps as a kid. The big thrill was a trip to the States. They had all these soda brands we didn't have."

"What'd you do with them?"

"Nailed them to a board. By the time I stopped, I had hundreds."

"Bet you can't guess what Hitchcock collected."

"That's easy," said the chief. "Hitch collected blondes."

The Hitchcock videos were shelved sequentially. As Gill jumped her finger from box to box, they took turns identifying his ice queens.

"*The 39 Steps.* Madeleine Carroll."

"*Spellbound.* Ingrid Bergman."

"*Rear Window.* Grace Kelly."

"*The Man Who Knew Too Much.* Doris Day."

"*The Wrong Man.* Vera Miles."

"*Vertigo.* Kim Novak."

"*North by Northwest.* Eva Marie Saint."

"What's the red divider for?" DeClercq asked. It was slotted in between the director's earlier films and *Psycho.*

"You're the detective."

"It looks like a bloody slash. The divider stands for *Psycho*'s shower scene?"

Macbeth raised her snifter in a toast to him. "It marks what I believe to be the most remarkable turning point in the history of film. Here you have a tubby man who was a psychological mess. Isolated as a boy, lonely as an adolescent and virtually closeted with his mother until he was twenty-seven, Hitchcock lived a repressed mind warp of sexual frustration."

"Like Norman Bates," commented DeClercq.

The pathologist nodded. "Lurking behind that bulk of obesity and that ugly, chinless mug was a yearner who was forever denied consummation with the sex goddesses that leading men enjoyed. His consolation prize was fantasy. 'The perfect "woman of mystery" is one who is blonde, subtle and Nordic,' Hitchcock maintained. Coolness and beauty combined was his fantasy, so Hitch satisfied his repressed lust vicariously by exerting complete control over every nuance of the screen personas of his various ice queens."

"He couldn't respond to a woman until he reshaped her to correspond with his fantasy," the Mountie said. "In doing so, Hitchcock made their movie careers, then seethed as they spurned him one after another for other men. Bergman went to Italy to live with Rossellini. And Kelly left to marry the prince of Monaco. As for Miles, she got pregnant. And when Audrey Hepburn—though not blonde—backed out on Hitch and *No Bail for the Judge*—"

"His rage exploded with *Psycho,*" said Macbeth as she pretended to hurl her cognac snifter at the massive fireplace.

"The same psychology motivates anger retaliatory rapists," said DeClercq. "Seething with rage at women in general, or at specific women in the past whom they feel have used and abused them, they turn to sexual fantasies of rape as a means of vicarious punishment and to gain control over the past."

"The shower scene in *Psycho* is rape with a knife. Plunge . . . plunge . . . plunge . . . relentlessly in and out. The shocking cinematic effect is that it tears apart the Blonde, who had been treated with obsessive reverence in all of the previous films."

"What Hitchcock did to Janet Leigh was a fantasy. What he did to Tippi Hedren in *The Birds* was worse. The final attack saw her trapped in a room full of ravens, gulls and crows that were scripted to tear at her until she collapsed in a state of shock. Day in, day out, for a whole week, she was subjected to swooping assaults by actual terrified birds. The pecks were real from diving beaks tied to her by elastic bands, and when one almost took her eye out at the end of the week, she suffered an unscripted nervous breakdown. The rumor persists that Hitch shot that last day without film."

Back to Macbeth: "By the time we get to *Frenzy,* the strangulation-rape of the Blonde shows Hitchcock's anger unrestrained by repression. The strangling of women had popped up in seventeen of his films, and now it was shot lovingly in every detail. Hitchcock demanded a close-up of the dead woman's tongue dripping saliva, but he eventually bowed to pressure to cut that shot."

"The red divider," said DeClercq. "I've changed my opinion. It slashes like a bloody cut between *North by Northwest* and *Psycho* because that's the great divide that bisects Hitchcock's work. It marks the point where he turns murderously on the fantasy blondes whom he had created."

"The Hitchcock Syndrome," said Macbeth. "We sound like a pair of film critics."

"That we do," Robert agreed.

"It's good to talk to someone who goes *behind* the screen."

"As interesting as the movie itself is the auteur who filmed it."

"The same with music."

"And with novels."

"The artist *is* the art," mused Gill. "Mind if I ask you a question? It puzzles me. Why do you insist on keeping me at bay? We read the same books. We watch the same films. We listen to the same music. And there's no woman in your life. I've asked around," she added, a subtle smirk on her face.

"Do you believe in jinxes?"

"No," Gill said.

"I'm jinxed."

"Bullshit."

"Maybe. And maybe not. But it's like believing in God. Better to err on the side of caution than blithely to thumb your nose at fate. The agnostic is wiser than the atheist."

"I'm not afraid."

"I am. Never again will I endure the agony I went through with the deaths of Kate, Jane and Genny. Women who get close to me die."

"Katt broke the spell."

"I almost lost her too. If the Mad Dog had missed that shot in the bush, she'd be gone."

"But he didn't. Your luck has changed."

"You think?"

"I *know,*" Gill replied. Draining her snifter of cognac, she then set it down on the mantel. "It's hot in here," she said, raising her hand to the top button of her blouse. "Would it not be wonderful to be young again? Is youth not wasted on the young, as they say?" Releasing the button exposed lace in the wider and deeper V, the bra cut low on the tight flesh of her now youthful breasts. "Remember the thrill in making love with a young woman, before sex became jaded by all the baggage it later took on?" Gill shucked off her blouse and shed her bra. "You can go back, Robert. You can go back with *me.*" Her hand eased his free hand toward her breast. "Close your eyes. Be young again in *me.* Remember the first time you copped a feel that felt like that? The first time you got to first base with a chance of sliding home?"

He felt her breath on his cheek.

Her lips nibbled his ear.

It *was* hot in here.

He *did* feel young again.

It was like Jane Austen wrote.

The *expectation* of happy events was worth swapping for happiness itself.

"The way I see it, you have a choice to make. Who are you going to sleep with?" Gill's seductive whisper asked his ear. "Catnip or me?"

THE SECOND DEATH

Vancouver
March 21

Whistling the infectious "Colonel Bogey March" from *The Bridge on the River Kwai,* the chief bounded up the stairs to his office the following morning. Zinc Chandler turned from the Strategy Wall, on which he was pinning several CAT scans photo-faxed from London of the same jewels exposed yesterday by the Canada Customs X-rays.

"You're chipper," said the inspector, greeting his boss. "I can't remember *ever* hearing whistling out of you."

"It's the second day of spring. The sun is in the sky. It's great to be alive."

"Uh-huh," said Chandler.

"What does 'uh-huh' mean?"

"It means that's the whistle of a man just out of bed after spending the night frolicking with all twelve yearly centerfolds from *Playboy.*"

"Surely that's illegal?"

"Uh-huh," said Zinc, cracking the first smile he had cracked in a long, long while.

"You can't seem to stop your detector from trying to detect clues."

"There's no need to detect when a villain exposes himself like you."

"Really?"

"Who's the best month?"

"Miss May," said DeClercq.

The morning sun blazed like the jewel in the crown of Queen Elizabeth Park. So dazzling were the rays that streamed into his office that DeClercq could focus his eyes on the Strategy Wall only once they'd adjusted to the glare.

"The Yard came through?"

"Yep, with a match. The jewels in these CAT scans went missing in London yesterday."

"Are they valuable?"

"Yes," said the inspector. "But *how* valuable no one knows."

"Why?" asked the chief.

"Because they haven't been seen for three thousand years. Not since the mummy was embalmed and bandaged in Egypt at the time of the pharaohs."

Egypt.

The mere mention of that exotic word was enough to transport DeClercq back to the last surviving wonder of the ancient world. Travel abroad just once in your life and Egypt *must* be your goal. Katt had yet to leave B.C. when she moved in with him (her kidnapping in Boston as a newborn didn't count), so Robert's first move to bond with the teen, when he still thought she was an orphan and her natural mother had yet to surface, was a trip to Cairo.

Fifteen million people milling in a cloud of dust, mixing and melding Africa, Europe, Arabia and Asia into a sprawling, throbbing, chaotic collision of conflicted cultures. The midday heat of Cairo closed in around the cab as they drove through the honking, hooting melee of crowded streets. Donkey carts trundled watermelons past modern skyscrapers. Minarets and muezzin called Muslims to mosques for prayer. Cloverleaf intersections swirled vehicular traffic about. Men in *gelabias* and turbans tugged stray camels into medieval bazaars where vendors puffed smoke from hookah pipes and flogged their wares. Then—*bang!*—the taxi rammed another vehicle, crunching its fender like a crushed soda can.

"Uh-oh," Katt said. "We'll be here for hours."

"Why?" asked the Mountie.

"All that insurance stuff."

"Stuff like that means little here. You're in the Middle East. Watch and learn."

The drivers jumped from their vehicles like a pair of trench soldiers on opposite sides in the First World War. The rat-a-tat-tat of their guttural outbursts was accompanied by fists shaking in the air, but no punches landed. Then both got back into their bashed-up cars and lurched away.

Insurance stuff.

Middle East style.

Traffic lightened and dust thickened on the broad, tree-lined boulevard that forsook Cairo on the Nile for Giza at the edge of the desert. Through a haze of smoke from the Cleopatra Milds their sweaty driver chain-smoked, and through the bug-squashed windshield beyond the fake-fur dashboard under hypnotically swinging worry beads, Katt squinted to scan the horizon for—

"The pyramids!" she enthused.

Yes, there they were. Jutting up from the sandy landscape ahead, three tiny triangles that grew rapidly in size as the rattletrap cab drew near, until they parked at the Mena House Hotel beside the colossal man-made mountains of stone. Eyes wide, mouth open, Katt climbed out of the car and, for the first time in her life, was at a loss for words, standing awestruck on the anvil of the Giza plateau while the hammer of the blazing sun pounded down on her.

Two and a half million stones.

Two and a half tons each.

One hundred thousand men (according to Herodotus) toiling for twenty years.

That's what it took to build the Great Pyramid of Cheops, just one of the three pyramids that still stand today.

Four thousand five hundred years.

The lifespan of civilization.

"Wow!" said Katt.

"Wow, indeed." DeClercq stood beside her, taking in her wonder.

"How high is it?"

"Five hundred feet."

"Why's the top missing?"

"No one knows. Some believe the apex of the Great Pyramid was capped with solid gold."

"Why the bumpy sides?"

"That we know. All three pyramids were originally encased in polished white limestone. Like the crown of Khafre." He pointed to the smooth peak of that lesser pyramid sharing the plateau. "When the Arabs conquered Egypt in the name of Islam in the seventh century, they stripped the ancient pyramids of their casing stones to build the mosques of Cairo. And by removing the casing, they exposed those steps up the side."

Two hundred and one layers of stone stacked one upon another made up the Great Pyramid. The layers shrank in width as they rose. Removing the slanted angles of the limestone casing had revealed the indented substructure of square stone blocks. Without the smoothing skin, the blocks formed a stairway to the sun.

Like most Canadians, DeClercq used American money for travel. Certainly in the Third World. Katt fished a dollar from the spending allowance in the pocket of her jeans and studied the back of the bill.

"It's destiny, Bob."

"What is?"

"That we climb." She glanced back up at the flat top of the Great Pyramid.

"Impossible."

"Why?"

"Two reasons," he said. "One, it's illegal. And two, see those guards with machine guns standing at the four corners of the base?"

"In God We Trust," said Katt. Her finger touched the slogan printed on the bill behind Washington's back and slid over to the topless pyramid on the Great Seal of the United States, where a disembodied eye peered at her from the peak.

"The symbol is Masonic."

"Money talks," said Katt. "And this dollar is telling me that there is something mystical to see up there."

Late the following morning, DeClercq awoke to find Katt gone from their suite in the Mena House Hotel. The note she had left on the pillow of her rumpled bed read "Climbing the Stairway to Heaven."

Oh no, he thought.

Fetching the pair of binoculars from his carryall, he wrenched the drapes back from the windows that overlooked the pyramids and their guardian Sphinx. Focusing on a tiny figure nearing the summit, he watched as Katt conquered the last few blocks.

Her pose atop the pyramid reminded him of Rocky on top of those steps in the film.

Utter triumph.

He envied her.

The historian in him recalled what Napoleon Bonaparte said to his French troops before they crushed the Mamelukes in 1798 at the Battle of the Nile: "Soldiers, consider that from the summit of these pyramids, forty centuries look down upon you."

Katt too was looking down.

He wondered what she saw.

Sweat was dripping off her when she staggered into the room.

"What a workout! I'm pooped, Bob."

"You could have been killed."

"How sweet. You sound like a parent."

"How'd you do it?"

"What?"

"Get around the guard? I take it you gave him plenty of those dollar bills."

"Never underestimate the power of an awesome pair of boobs. I recruited the looks of a tourist with a set out to here"—Katt stretched both arms full-length in front of her—"and after undoing the top two buttons of her blouse, she sashayed over to ask one guard for a cigarette."

"You set a honey trap?"

"Yes," said Katt proudly. "When she gazed up at the pyramids, he gazed down her neckline, and that gave me sufficient time to sneak around behind him and start my climb."

"Very clever."

"I have a criminal mind."

"Where'd you get that idea?"

"From the pyramids," said Katt, pointing out the window at the triangular mounds. "Do they not look to you like huge breasts? I think I've discovered the true meaning of pyramid power."

From the pyramids of Giza, they journeyed upriver to the ancient capital of Thebes, across the Nile from the Valley of the Kings, where Howard Carter discovered the tomb of Tutankhamen in 1922. As they strolled among the ruins on the east bank of the river, the surrogate dad and daughter talked about Death's door.

Egypt, DeClercq explained to Katt, was, from about 3100 B.C. on, ruled by thirty dynasties of pharaohs. It was during the fourth dynasty of the Old Kingdom (2700 B.C. to 2200 B.C.) that the pyramids of Giza were built as lasting tombs for Kings Khufu, Khafre and Menkaure, known as Cheops, Chephren and Mycerinus to Herodotus, the great Greek historian who toured Egypt in the fifth century B.C.

"A tomb with a view," said Katt teasingly. "Oh, sorry, I forgot. You haven't seen the Wonder—capital *W*—that I have."

To understand *why* those tombs were built, DeClercq continued, requires a grasp of how Egyptians viewed the afterlife. The death of the body did not mean an end to life if you had prepared properly to save your soul. An Egyptian's soul had three spirits—the Ba, the Ka and the Akh—which were set free the moment the body died. The Ba—your personality—could visit the land of the living as a ghost. The Ka—your spirit of life—could not leave the tomb.

Molded by the creator god Khnum at your moment of conception, the Ka was an exact physical and emotional replica of you. It was imprisoned in your living heart, and was expelled at your moment of death. To preserve your earthly memory, it had to remain with your corpse. The Akh—your immortality—embarked on a perilous journey far to the west, until it reached the door to the afterlife.

"Death's door," Katt said.

"And we've reached it."

"This looks heavy."

"Judgment Day. The Akh is in the court of Osiris, the king of the dead, where the spirit must justify its life on earth."

"I'd rather face St. Peter."

They were standing in front of a wall mural carved in stone. The jackal-headed god Anubis was weighing the heart of the deceased against a feather that symbolized truth and justice. The scribe of the gods, ibis-headed Thoth, recorded the result in his scroll. Seated on his throne, King Osiris watched. Crouching beside the heart on the scales lurked a mutant monster with the head of a crocodile, foreparts of a lion and hindquarters of a hippopotamus.

"He looks mean," said Katt. "Why's he there?"

"That's Ammit. Eater of the Dead. Only the true in heart pass the feather test. The hearts of those who fail the weighing are fed to him, and their spirits are doomed to haunt the living as evil dead."

"Do you think I'd pass?"

"Definitely not. Those who climb pyramids without permission are sinful souls."

"What if your heart was lighter than a feather?"

"You were granted a plot of land in the Field of Reeds."

"Egypt's heaven?"

"The kingdom of Osiris. The Field of Reeds was a glorious place. A parallel world to that of the living, except that it was ruled by the king of the dead. All the bad stuff in life was gone. No more floods, famines, pests, diseases. All the good stuff was magnified many times. There, you were restored to health and vigor, reunited with deceased loved ones and surrounded by servants to sate your whims. You could spend eternity eating, drinking and fooling around."

"Sounds like you could die happily ever after."

"Well, there was a hitch."

"Oh, pooh," said Katt.

"If you could live again, you could die again. To an Egyptian, the Second Death was the worst thing that could happen to your spirit. Perishing in the land of the dead was a permanent obliteration from which you couldn't return. The Second Death was caused by loss of all memory of you by the living, and that was caused by the destruction of your corpse. To survive, the Ka residing in your tomb had to be able to return to what was once its physical host. Because your Ka was an exact replica of you, it could recognize only its own form. So if the corpse you left behind decayed beyond recognition, that spirit of your soul would perish too. And if one spirit died, that destroyed all the others, so the death of the Ka ensured the deaths of the Ba and the Akh. If the living forgot you, you would die the deadly Second Death among the dead, and *that* made it imperative that your corpse survive in a recognizable form. To stop decay, Egyptian embalmers had to—"

"Turn you into a mummy," finished Katt.

"An Egyptian mummy?" said DeClercq, returning to the here and now of his discussion with Zinc Chandler in his office at Special X. "It could be we're after more than jewel thieves. Were the Canada Customs officers shot during an *antiquities* heist?"

SUCKED DRY

Vancouver

"You look like the cat that ate the canary."

"I do?" said Gill.

"You do," said Nick. "Whoever fell prey to your sleek new form last night, his feathers are stuck to your satisfied lips."

"You make me sound like a femme fatale."

"Heaven forbid!" said Nick, recalling the striptease she did for him yesterday.

"I'm hurt that you didn't fly back to the islands to jump into bed with Jenna. As a pinup, it seems I'm a failure."

"How do you know I didn't spend the night at some brothel?"

Gill smiled. "I feel better. So what keeps you in town?"

"Two things. I've come for your autopsy report on the Galiano corpse munched by the wolf-dog. Then I'm off to see Dr. Denning about my prosthetic hand."

"Trouble?"

"No. Just a follow-up."

"Now I'm *really* hurt."

Nick rolled his eyes. "Why?" he asked.

"The reason you *should* be here is to see if I'll strip for you again."

"You're evil, Gill."

"Meow!" she said.

As they were flirting for old times' sake outside the entrance to the morgue at the VGH, the door at the end of the hall swung open to admit Dr. David Denning. Like the White Rabbit from *Alice in Wonderland,* the plastic surgeon flustered toward them as if he were late, late, late for a very important date. The sleuth in Nick told him that something had happened on Denning's way here, throwing his tight schedule off for the day. When he spied the Mountie, the surgeon's pace suddenly slowed. By examining Nick here instead of in his office later, the hurried, harried doctor could cancel that appointment.

"Dr. Frankenstein is coming to see his monster," whispered the corporal.

"Don't think of yourself that way, Nick."

"The monster I meant is *you.*"

"Now I'm really, *really* hurt," Gill said with a playful pout.

"You hurt easily. For a sexual predator."

"What a cad! You should thank me. By asking David here to give me a surgeon's opinion on the breasts cut off your Galiano corpse, I've saved you the trouble of going to his office."

"What about that striptease?"

"Hop on your boat and go ask Jenna," Gill purred.

"Assholes rule the streets these days," the plastic surgeon blurted out as he approached the pair kibitzing by the door to the morgue. "No wonder road rage is epidemic. Yesterday, I finally got my Jag back from the body shop after some moron dinged it in some parking lot. The first time I take it out is to drive here, and some shithead shouting on a cellphone rear-ends me on the way."

"How much damage?" asked Nick.

"That's not the point," fumed Denning. "A Jag is a Jag. My *perfect* automobile. I keep it in immaculate shape to please *me.* If I had caused the dent, that would be bad enough. But what boils my blood is these stupid assholes ruining *my* beautiful things."

Perfectionism, Nick thought. That's what you want in a surgeon. If you make the hard decision to go under the knife, it's assuring to know the knife-wielder is a picky, finicky, details man. Vanity is what drives most patients to plastic surgeons, and what they desire is a miracle of flawless perfection. The skills of a plastic surgeon are blatantly on display, so Dr. Denning's work had taken him to the top.

Picky . . .

Finicky . . .

High-strung . . .

And a sculptor in flesh on a par with Michelangelo in marble.

How ironic, Nick thought, that someone obsessed with perfection should be so *im*perfect himself. Short, squat, and simian-featured, Dr. David Denning was no Michelangelo's *David.* How telling that a doctor who went into plastic surgery to make other people beautiful was in such desperate need of some of that altered beauty himself. It was like the old axiom about walking into a barbershop: always go to the barber with the worst haircut, because you know he didn't cut his own hair. Similarly, it would appear from seeing Denning in the flesh, the best plastic surgeons are ironically the ugliest people.

"You did a beautiful job on Gill," Nick complimented him, which had the effect of calming down Denning's road rage.

"She was beautiful to start with. I merely turned back the hands of time."

"Merely?" said Gill. "You have rejuvenated me *and* my life."

"And you made me whole again," added Nick. "I'd feel like half a man if not for you."

"The hand's fine?"

"Yes."

Denning took a look.

"And the ear?"

"Great."

The surgeon examined that too.

Nick held up both the fleshy hand he was born with and the artificial prosthesis. "If I get these hands—both mine and yours—on the genitals of the guy responsible for my amputations, we'll see how good you are at sewing back on his ripped-off cock and balls."

The surgeon nodded. "You'll find this prosthesis a perfect tool for that."

Nick closed the mechanical fingers into a clamping vise-grip.

Gill Macbeth had asked David Denning to attend at the morgue to give her a second opinion on the wounds suffered by two dead women: the breastless remains chewed by the wolf-dog on Galiano Island and the desiccated, mummy-like corpse cast away on Wreck Beach. While both doctors were changing into autopsy greens in Gill's office, she pointed to her reflection in the mirror. "I wish I could look like this forever," Gill said, sighing.

"Dora Gray?" said Denning. "Dorian Gray's twin sister?"

"I'm like the man in that Housman poem. Now that I've got where I'm going, I find my youth's slipped away."

"You sound like an ideal candidate for the next stage."

"Oh? What's that?"

"The Panacea Clinic."

"I've never heard of it."

"That's because it's new. Over the past month, I've been referring post-op patients there. Patients who, given a second spring, want to hold onto it without becoming plastic-surgery junkies."

"What goes on there?"

"Metabolic therapy. Graham battles the enemy where aging begins: free-radical damage to our bodies' cells."

"Graham?"

"Graham Worlock. He's the director of the Panacea Clinic. If you want to meet him, drop by Eternal Spring tomorrow afternoon at closing time. The three of us can share a bottle of wine."

While both doctors were changing in Gill's office, another troop of Mounties arrived to watch the postmortem slated for that morning. Nick tagged along as the group entered the butchers' theater, where a morgue attendant was wheeling in the Wreck Beach corpse on a hospital gurney.

"What in hell have you got there?" Craven asked Corp. Rick

Scarlett of the University detachment, the RCMP office that polices Point Grey. "An Egyptian mummy?"

"You never know what you'll find below the campus cliffs."

"*That* washed ashore?"

"Nope, it was carried. Someone hit the beach in a boat and left ol' skin and bones for us, then departed by way of English Bay."

"Sounds like a psycho's setup."

"Yeah," Scarlett agreed. "Bet it makes you wish you were still with Special X."

Athletic and lean, with short brown hair, an Errol Flynn mustache and strip-Gill-naked eyes, Rick Scarlett was one of the retrograde men of the force. In this era when females, ethnics and those with university degrees were climbing the ranks fast, the sort of throwback the Mounted had recruited in its first one hundred years was doomed to follow the dodo bird along the narrowing path toward species extinction.

Homo macho copus. RIP.

"Fuck me!" Scarlett gasped. "What happened to Gill?"

Deep in conversation, the doctors had emerged from the office to cross the terrazzo floor to the isolation chamber. "Knockers up, baby," Scarlett murmured to himself as he ogled Gill, then after she and the plastic surgeon shut the door behind them to examine the decomposing remains from Galiano Island, he took Nick aside and said, "Time to eat your gun, son. No sooner do you stop banging her than she does *that* to you."

Nick contemplated lowering his prosthetic hand and clamping its vise-grip on the corporal's *cojones.*

Scarlett whistled mutedly. "Who did the uplift on Gill?"

"The doc who's with her. His name's Denning."

"Man, there's got to be a lot of dough in what he does. All those baby boomers raised to believe they're the beautiful people. My old man used to say there are only *two* secure jobs: the food industry and undertaking. 'Cause everyone's gotta eat, and everyone's gonna die. What he overlooked is everyone's gonna age, and when it comes to looking younger, the boomers will pay through the nose. If you want to know how many are going under the knife, count the number of ads for docs doing plastic surgery in the Yellow Pages."

"'Here's *lookin'* at you, kid.'"

Scarlett frowned. Humphrey Bogart's toast to Ingrid Bergman in *Casablanca* went over his head. It also went over Nick's, though he didn't know it. Nick thought the toast referred to beauty, when in fact it came from being able to see a fellow drinker through the glass bottom of a drinking mug.

"Who did the work on you?"

"The same guy who worked on Gill," Nick replied.

"With a doc like him and a pocketful of Viagra, I'll be banging chicks well into my eighties."

"I'm sure your sensitive personality is seductive enough."

"You figure? Since you're out of the picture, I'm gonna go after Gill."

"Lucky her," Nick said dryly.

"Whadda you care? Rumor is you're banging a chick named Jenna Bond. I'm far too sensitive a guy to crack the joke myself, but you must hear a lot of yuks about her and Dr. No."

"Dr. Who?"

"No," said Scarlett with a wink, "that's another guy. Dr. Who's a British twit obsessed with phone booths."

"So who's No?"

"You know."

"No, I don't," Nick said, fielding the ball.

"No's No."

"Then who's Who?"

"Who's not No."

"Then who's No?"

"The thug with those mechanical hands in the first Bond film. *Dr. No.* He gets a grip on our hero and tries to squeeze the juice out of him."

"How?" said Nick. "Like this?" And down scooped the prosthetic hand.

While this poor man's version of the classic Abbott and Costello "Who's on First?" routine was playing out in the main autopsy room of the morgue, Dr. Denning examined the chest of the decomposing body Nick had stumbled across on Galiano Island the night of the wolf-dog hunt.

"Has she been identified?"

"No," said Gill. "The face is too far gone for anyone to recognize. Fingerprints and dental charts are in the works."

"You're right about these incisions. This bilateral mastectomy has a professional signature. Not only did the surgeon remove subcutaneous tissue, but the pectoralis muscles of the chest wall were included in the procedure."

"Any sign of breast reconstruction?"

"No," said Denning.

"What do you make of that?"

"She might have died during the removal operation. There'd be no reason to reconstruct."

"The body was found rotting in the Galiano Island woods. There's no hospital or surgery on the island."

"Strange," said Denning.

"Yes," said Gill. "I can think of two reasons that might account for that mystery. One, the operation was done outside regular channels. Whoever performed the mastectomy did it underground."

"A disqualified surgeon?"

"Without hospital privileges."

"And two?" said Denning.

"The body was dumped *after* it was released by a hospital. The woman died, like you said, during the procedure, and her body was later released to her family for burial or cremation. For some reason, it didn't go into the ground or the furnace. Instead, it ran afoul of an unscrupulous undertaker."

"Jeez! I almost pissed myself!" Scarlett exclaimed.

"You asked for that by talking dirty about Jenna and Gill."

"Talk about dirty! That was underhanded! You went straight for the family jewels!"

"Aren't you lucky I didn't clamp on?"

"Christ! I coulda dropped dead from fright!"

"Every man has his Achilles' heel. Your heel sits at the top of your legs," said Nick.

The door to the isolation chamber opened, and out came Macbeth and Denning. Having X-rayed the Wreck Beach remains to detect any foreign objects lodged in the desiccated flesh, the attendant was locking the gurney feet to sink into one of the six dissecting stations. Nearby stood a big bandsaw for cutting through bones and three refrigerators flanked by clear plastic bins filled with formaldehyde for fixing specimens. As Beethoven's *Pathétique* played from the stereo speakers, the doctors approached the gurney to see what Gill's day had in store. With Nick tailing, Scarlett crossed to meet them.

"Where was *this* body found?" Denning asked.

"Wreck Beach," Scarlett replied.

"Identified?"

"Nope. Who's gonna recognize Mommy as a mummy? We call her Skin and Bones."

"Am I mistaken," Macbeth asked, pointing to the corpse, "or are those cuts also professionally made?"

"You're not mistaken," Denning replied. "They're cannula slits."

"Would you translate that into English so I can understand too," Scarlett said.

"Here . . . here . . . here . . ." Denning pointed to several half-inch-long cuts puncturing the skin. "There must be hundreds of them covering the body."

"For what reason?"

"Lipoplasty."

"Huh?" said Scarlett.

"Liposuction," Gill explained. "'Lipo' means fat; 'suction,' surely you know."

"You're telling me this mummy was *sucked* dry?"

"Fat removal," Denning said, "goes back one hundred years. The original technique was to cut out chunks of fat. In the 1970s, a

French surgeon developed a better method. He cut small slits through the skin to insert an instrument called a cannula. A cannula is a blunt-tipped, hollow metal tube with one or more openings along the side close to the tip. Suction is applied to the other end to draw fat globules into the tube and along a pliable hose to the pump's canister."

"I saw that movie," Scarlett enthused. "*Fight Club,* with Brad Pitt. The fat from liposuction was used to make soap."

"It's an *art,* Corporal. We call it liposculpture."

"Pardon me, Doc. I thought you were sucking Twinkie saddlebags out of fatties."

"I'm listening," Nick said. "Please go on."

"The human body develops a limited number of fat cells by the end of puberty. The cells are like containers that fill with fat. They swell and shrink as the body gains and loses weight, but the number of cells remains the same. A plastic surgeon uses the cannula to tunnel directly into the fatty layer between skin and muscle, then he works the instrument back and forth in a crisscross pattern to break down the tissue, sucking out fat cells as the tool pumps."

"Sounds like you fuck the fat away," Scarlett said, and laughed.

No one laughed with him.

"The network of tunnels and spaces creates a sponge-like effect in the layer of fat. The fullness, firmness and size of the tissue is reduced. When the spaces collapse, the layer shrinks to tighten the skin above to the muscles beneath. The object, however, is not to remove all the fat. That would result in one large cavity, which would indeed cause greater shrinkage, but the irregular collapse of the skin would also deform the patient."

"Is that what happened here?" Nick asked.

"Yes and no," said Denning. "Two recent refinements advanced lipoplasty. The first was developed in the U.S. in 1987. Called tumescent liposculpture, it's the technique I currently use. 'Tumescent' means 'to swell,' and that's what we do. The surgeon fills fatty areas with many liters of a blended solution of local anesthetic, adrenaline and salt water. The anesthetic allows the patient to remain awake, while the adrenalin constricts blood vessels to staunch bleeding. We can suction out eight pounds of fat at a time."

"The other advance?"

"UAL," said Denning. "Ultrasonic-assisted liposuction. Invented in Italy and Israel, UAL uses ultrasonic energy to liquefy the fat before suction is applied."

"Sounds like a blow job," Scarlett said, and cackled again.

Nick found those who laugh at their own jokes *very* irritating. And he wondered about those whose every comment seemed to focus on sex.

"So?" he asked. "What do we have here?"

"A perversion of liposculpture," Denning replied. "Some monster used ultrasonic waves to liquefy her fat. Then he slathered her skin with something to counter the caustic effects of a tumescent solution he'd injected to break down her muscle tissue. Then he went to work with a scalpel and a suction tube, shrinking her subcutaneous flesh down to skin and bone."

"Was she conscious?"

"Probably at first. The trauma of the procedure likely killed her along the way."

"A sadist," concluded Gill. "With this many cuts, I get the feeling he enjoyed his work."

"So?" said Nick. "Who are we looking for? A mad plastic surgeon with a cannula?"

"Maybe," Gill replied. "Or is this the work of a mad undertaker skilled with a trocar?"

HEART SCARAB

Vancouver

"*Antiquity* thieves?" said Chandler, echoing DeClercq's comment a moment ago as they stood at the Strategy Wall in his office at Special X and compared the images of the jewels in the Canada Customs X-rays to the CAT scans sent from London, which Zinc had just pinned up on the corkboard.

"You saying 'mummy' took me back to Katt's and my trip to Egypt. After we saw the pyramids, we journeyed up the Nile to the Valley of the Kings. What I was told there should have clued me in to what was in the coffin hijacked yesterday."

"How so?" asked Chandler.

DeClercq described the journey . . .

Initially, only the pharaohs of the Old Kingdom could have an afterlife. The pyramids were built as permanent resting places for their mummies and their Kas. There, sealed up deep within the stones of the royal burial chambers, hid a fabulous wealth of worldly goods for use in the land of the dead.

In ancient Egypt, you *could* take it with you.

The Middle Kingdom—from 2000 B.C. on—saw power decentralize up the Nile, where Death's door swung open to admit provincial dignitaries to the Field of Reeds. By the time of the New Kingdom—beginning around 1600 B.C. with the eighteenth dynasty—the afterlife was open to every Egyptian, and consequently the embalmer's art was at its height.

The pyramid of the New Kingdom was a communal one. Above a gorge gouged deep into the rocky desert across the Nile to the west of Thebes, nature provided a 1,650-foot-high, ready-made pyramid of rock, into the cliffs of which the pharaohs burrowed their tombs. Like those who built the pyramids at Giza, they experimented with ways to thwart grave robbers—hidden doors, false chambers, backfilled passages—but to no avail. Sacrilegious thieves had stripped every tomb of wealth by 1000 B.C., except for the burial chamber of an overlooked boy-king nicknamed Tut.

All the ghouls left were the mummies.

And soon, they too were gone.

"Stop the car," Katt said as they headed west to the Valley of the Kings. Metal squealed on metal as the brakes without brake pads finally brought the cab to a halt. Climbing out into the glare, Katt hurried back to plant her feet on both sides of the sharp dividing line where the fertile soil of the Black Land, irrigated by the flooding of the Nile, met the Red Land of the desert that stretched across the Sahara. Without water, life is snuffed out, so the desert was seen by New Kingdom Egyptians as the land of the dead, and they honeycombed the yellow cliffs with tombs.

"Take a photo, Bob. It's not every day you get to have one foot in the grave."

A little baksheesh goes a long way. No sooner were they out of the cab in the Valley of the Kings than the usual horde of dragomans were upon them like vultures. The one they chose to guide them around the royal tombs was a disreputable-looking rascal in a dirty turban who flashed a sinister smile of crooked teeth and a grease-smudged birth certificate that seemed to prove he was a genuine el-Rassul.

"You know this name?" he asked.

"Yes," said DeClercq. "El-Rassul found the tomb that hid the royal mummies."

The man's smile grew wider. "*You* are wise man. Special for *you.*" He rubbed his grubby fingers together. "Not for *any* tourist peoples."

"Ten dollars," offered DeClercq.

The rogue was visibly hurt. He thumped his fist on his chest. "*I* am el-Rassul."

"Twenty," countered DeClercq.

"Fifty," wheedled the scoundrel. "For that, you get full Monty, friend."

"Twenty now. Twenty later. I won't go higher than forty."

"Deal," said el-Rassul as the smile spread almost wider than his mouth could accommodate. In this Battle of El Alamein, there was little doubt who this desert fox thought was Montgomery and who was Rommel.

The baksheesh passed hands and the tour got under way. The dragoman led them in and out of the pharaohs' rock-cut mausoleums, the long-looted burial chambers covered with wall paintings from the Book of the Dead, the saga that warned the soul what to expect on its trip to the afterlife.

Tomb robbers, the guide said with pride, were truly brave men. The penalty for those caught was a horrible death by impalement on a stake. Success, however, meant the wealth of a king, for hidden in the bandages wrapped around a mummy were precious jewels and amulets to protect its soul. Easy to steal, portable and simple to recycle, they were the lure that drew robbers to the necropolis.

King Tut, el-Rassul informed them at the entrance to his tomb, had 150 jewels and amulets wrapped up with his mummy. Tut escaped the attention of the robbers only because his small tomb was buried under tons of rubble that had been excavated to reveal the prodigious grave of Rameses IV above him.

The day was getting on when the dragoman suggested they walk from the Valley of the Kings to the mortuary temple of Queen Hatchepsut, built into the eastern cliff face at Deir el-Bahari.

Behind the monument to Egypt's only female pharaoh wound a

path the dragoman used to guide his clients up the cliff. The year was 1871, he said during the climb. Ahmed el-Rassul of nearby Qurna village came up here to search for a lost goat and stumbled instead across the hidden entrance to an unknown tomb. He ran home to tell his brothers, Hussein and Mohammed, who helped him drop a dead donkey down the shaft. The stench from that and tales of evil ghosts kept other robbers away while the el-Rassuls grew rich by selling antiquities stolen from the tomb to black-market dealers.

Ten years later, Ahmed and Hussein were grabbed by suspicious officials. Daud Pasha, the vicious governor, had them tortured by beating the soles of their feet so hard with clubs that Hussein was left with a permanent limp. Though neither man betrayed the location of the tomb, their guide said sourly, Mohammed betrayed his brothers as a result of a family quarrel. In exchange for money and immunity from prison, he led authorities . . .

"Here!" said the dragoman, pointing dramatically at the shaft that hid the tomb in his tale.

They stood at the rim of the pit, staring into the wormhole that burrowed back in time.

"The full Monty," DeClercq agreed.

Not only did he give el-Rassul the twenty promised to him, but the Mountie added ten to top the deal up to what the dragoman had tried to wheedle.

The smile grew wider than the Cheshire cat's.

The tomb was that of Pinodjem II. It had remained undisturbed for three thousand years, until the el-Rassuls raided his resting place of valuables. But also found in the tomb was a cache of mummies with no riches to steal. That's because they had lost everything by 1000 B.C. to the ancient robbers who cleaned out all but one pharaoh's tomb. The Theban priests of Amen had gathered up the defiled royal mummies, rewrapping those stripped of bandages to get at their amulets and jewels, and hid the remains of some of Egypt's greatest pharaohs here for safekeeping.

"Seti I, Rameses II, Tuthmosis III . . ."

The dragoman pulled a crinkled photograph from his dusty robes.

"Mummies stolen by Cairo. El-Rassuls find them," he protested. His scowl decried the fact that the cache was taken from *his* pocket.

Doing their best to sympathize with the descendant of tomb scavengers, the tourists perused the black-and-white photo he waved under their noses.

"Tuthmosis III," said el-Rassul.

The photograph had been shot in the late 1800s. Crudely wrapped, the mummy caught by the camera was braced with two oars and a small broom lashed with ropes to hold it together. A hole was ripped in the bandages on the left side of the chest.

"Who did that?" asked Katt.

"Ahmed el-Rassul," the dragoman answered matter-of-factly.

"Why?"

"For amulet. But amulet gone. Stolen before mummy rewrapped by priests."

"How did Ahmed know where to look?"

"Heart scarab," said el-Rassul.

From that desecrated Valley of the Kings, DeClercq and Katt returned to bustling Cairo at the delta of the Nile. The mummy room in the Cairo Museum was cursed by gloom as they walked amid the unwrapped remains of Seti I, Rameses II and Tuthmosis III. Seti's broken-off head was well-preserved; he looked like a man asleep, rather than one dead for millennia. Rameses the Great was in top condition too, his eyebrows still thick and white, his eyes small and close together, his nose long, thin and hooked like a hawk's beak. Tuthmosis III, Egypt's greatest warrior-king, was as small in stature as Napoleon Bonaparte. When it was unwrapped after el-Rassul's photo was taken, that mummy was found to be missing its genitals.

How far the mighty had fallen.

Viewing the pharaohs with them was an Egyptologist from London. Inquisitive Katt pumped her for the inside scoop on how to make a mummy, a literal expression that captured the process.

Years of digging for relics under a brutal sun and smoking cigarettes that sucked her dry within had withered and wrinkled the archeologist to an extreme beyond the mummies.

"The word 'mummy,'" she said, "is not Egyptian. It derives from the Arabic word *'mummiya,'* meaning tar or bitumen. Mummies were usually coated with a black, glossy resin, so Egypt's first visitors wrongly assumed the ancients preserved their dead by dipping the bodies in pitch.

"The first mummies were made by nature. The human body rots because by weight it is 75 percent water. Suck out the water and it will desiccate instead of decompose. Fertile land is scarce in Egypt, so long before the pharaohs, those who worked it used the sand of the adjoining desert as a graveyard. The sand absorbed the water, drying each corpse, so what the wind exposed in shallow graves were bodies that even centuries later retained their lifelike form.

"Embalming developed because the rich switched to using tombs. Without sand, another way to desiccate the flesh was needed. By the advent of the New Kingdom, the embalmer's art was fifteen centuries old. The technique of mummification was never put into writing. From father to son, the trade passed down in secret. Experimenters did their best to perfect the process, which reached a peak in the century before 1000 B.C."

"The secret's lost?" said Katt.

"Not exactly. We can learn a lot from the mummies we have found. But it's like the missing link in human evolution. An Egyptian mortician might have perfected the technique, but we have yet to uncover the perfect mummy he produced."

"So what *do* we know?" asked Katt.

The mummy-like woman spread her arms to encompass the pharaohs on display. "By analyzing them, the facts we've gleaned are these: Shortly after death and before decomposition set in, the body was taken to the Ibu, the Place of Purification. Stripped of clothes, the body was cleaned with Nile water to symbolize rebirth. I find the word 'pure' a misnomer for such a charnel house. Imagine the heat. Imagine the stink. Imagine the flies. Compounded by the need to wait a few days before delivering the bodies of dead women."

"How sexist," fumed Katt.

"No, a precaution. Undertakers were known to rape fresh female remains."

The teen turned to DeClercq. "If I go before you, see that I'm cremated."

"From there, the corpse was moved to the House of Mummification, the Per-Nefer. There, it was laid out on four blocks on a wooden table. The embalmer removed the brain by shoving a chisel up one nostril to break the nose bone, using a hook to pull out most of the gray matter, then scooping out the rest with a long spoon. The skull was infused with water to decompose any clinging flesh, and the head was flushed by propping it up so brain mush could drain out through the nose."

"Yuck," said Katt.

"Next, the abdomen was cleared of organs. Rituals were enacted as the embalmers worked. The abdomen was slashed on the left side from the hip bone to the pubic area by a mortician called the ripper."

Katt winced. She had nearly been slashed to death on Deadman's Island by a psycho who thought he was Jack the Ripper reincarnated.

"The ripper was forced to retreat from the corpse by fellow morticians who hurled curses and stones at him. After the abdomen was emptied of everything but the kidneys, the diaphragm was cut to pull out the lungs. It was essential, however, that the heart remained in place. Egyptians thought the heart was the center of the intellect and the emotions."

"Home of the Ka," said Katt.

"Yes," said the animate mummy. "The most important organ. A heart removed by mistake was immediately stitched back in.

"Next, the near-empty shell was washed and placed on a sloping board. Inside and out, the body was packed with powdered natron. Natron, a rock salt embalmers got from the desert beside the Nile, works like a sponge to draw moisture out of flesh. We know it as a combination of washing and baking sodas.

"It took forty days for the corpse to dry. During that period, the guts from the body cavity were washed, dried, wrapped with linen and stored in Canopic jars. A jar for the stomach. A jar for the lungs. A jar for the liver. A jar for the intestines. The embalmers of later dynasties stuffed the organs back into the abdomen or placed them between the legs."

"Why?" asked Katt.

"It was vital that the *entire* corpse be preserved for two reasons. First, because any missing parts would be missing for eternity. And second, because the Ka had to be able to—"

"Recognize the body," said Katt.

The woman turned to DeClercq. "You have an Egyptologist in the making here."

"She climbed the Great Pyramid."

"That explains it. The world is forever different once you've seen it from up there."

"Amen," said Katt.

"The dried mummy was lighter in weight and darker in color. Next, it was sent to the Wabet, the House of Purification. The Wabet was where morticians patched up the mummy. In effect, it was plastic surgery for the dead. The open abdomen was stuffed with linen, sawdust or dried lichen. Then the cut was sewn shut and healed by a magic amulet called the gold eye of Horus, which was glued to the skin on the left side of the mummy's belly with molten resin.

"The toughest job was restoring the shrunken face and body to lifelike fullness. The same way that modern plastic surgeons use implants to improve the appearance of living patients, so the embalmers made tiny cuts and shoved linen padding under the skin wherever needed. As is done with prosthetics now, it was common to replace damaged limbs or unsightly features."

"Like what?" said Katt.

"You name it. I've seen everything from enlarged penises and false eyebrows to hair weaves and bedsores covered by leather patches."

"Really?"

"King Tut's penis was prepared so it was erect in death."

"What about the eyes?"

"Nothing could save them, so embalmers pushed the eyeballs

down into their sockets and substituted semi-precious stones so the dead could see again. After the nose and ears were plugged with wax or linen, the face was painted red if male and yellow if female. Finally, the entire body was covered with molten resin to protect it from moisture.

"*Voilà,*" she said, sweeping her arm to encompass the pharaohs in Cairo Museum's mummy room. "The result is what we see here."

"And the bandages?"

"Long gone, I'm afraid. The wrapping of the mummy was the last act in the embalming process. The bandages held the body together, so the wrapping took time and a lot of cloth. Ten to fifteen days and up to a mile and a half of linen. Only royal mummies were bound with the arms crossed over the chest, like Boris Karloff in that classic horror movie. Ordinary women were bandaged with their hands beside their thighs, and ordinary men with their hands cupped over their crotches.

"Spells were spoken as each body part was wrapped with linen. Jewels and protective amulets were hidden within the bandage layers. The form, location and function of each charm was decreed by tradition. Seventy days after death, the mummy was complete and ready to be sealed in its tomb for eternity.

"Eternity, of course, lasted the blink of an eye. Those who breached the pharaohs' tombs ran straight to the royal mummies, tearing the bandages apart to get at the amulets and jewels. Stripped of their original wrappings, the desecrated mummies hidden by the priests of Amen in the tomb behind Queen Hatchepsut's mortuary temple were rewrapped three thousand years ago. When they came to Cairo in 1881, they were stripped again in a series of public 'unrollings' before they finally ended up here, on naked display."

Katt gazed at the pathetic remains of the pharaoh in front of her. The head, the arms, the legs, the feet had all been snapped off by tomb robbers millennia ago. The well-preserved head was prematurely bald. The face, small and thin, had a high-bridged nose, a low forehead and buckteeth.

"Tuthmosis III," she said, reading the display's name card.

"The first royal mummy to be unrolled."

"We saw a photo of him rewrapped in the Valley of the Kings. A hole was ripped through the bandages above his heart."

"Know why?"

"For the heart scarab."

"Even modern thieves know what to steal and where to find it. The heart was the home of the Ka. The heart was the center of the intellect and the emotions. The heart was of vital importance in the afterlife, so of all the mummy's organs, it received the best protection. The scarab was sacred to ancient Egyptians, so the amulet wrapped in the bandages to protect the precious heart was sure to be the most valuable treasure in the wrapping around the mummy. The heart scarab was a jewel carved into the likeness of that sacred beetle."

"Wake up, Bob!"

DeClercq awoke with a start and found Katt shaking him. "What's wrong?" he said, sitting bolt upright in bed.

"Nothing. There's a full moon." She tugged him by his pajama sleeve.

"What time is it?"

"Dunno. Middle of the night."

"You woke me up for a *moon* report?"

"You bet. Come see."

She dragged him out of his warm bed and across the floor to the windows. The curtains were already thrown back on the moonscape beyond. How eerie it was to catch the pyramids in this light. Each square block ascending toward the lunar disk was a checkerboard step of silver and black. The Great Pyramid was a gigantic stone staircase to the stars.

"Ready?" Katt asked.

"For what?" he replied.

"It's our last day in Egypt. We're back where we started. If you don't climb the Great Pyramid with me, you'll regret it for the rest of your life."

"Now?" he said.

"Yeah. No guards. And you're too old to climb it in the blazing sun."

"Thanks."

"You're welcome. I love you, Pa."

"One slip of the foot, and it would be *bump, bump, bump* all the way down."

"'In God We Trust.'"

"He's failed me before, Katt."

"Going . . . going . . ."

"Okay!"

"Let's be gone."

Never was he so thankful for having lunged so much with a foil. There's no better exercise for leg muscles than fencing, yet by the time he neared the top of the climb, his legs felt like Jell-O. Each block met him at chest height and required a push-up to conquer its sides, then a knee-up to reach its flat, followed by a leg stretch to face the next block. By the time DeClercq had repeated that 201 times, his calf muscles trembled in spasm, his heart, pounding in his rib cage, neared cardiac arrest and sweat ran off him in rivulets to join the Nile. Gasping for breath as his fingers clawed the nooks and crannies to hoist him up on top of the final block of the southeast corner, he crumpled down in the layer of desert dust beside Katt.

"Hello, Sir Edmund."

"Hello, Sherpa Norgay."

Side by side, in silence, they huddled together in the moonlight at the top of the ancient world. Time itself, it was said, feared the pyramids. Why became evident with the first rays of dawn, when the solar boat of the sun god Ra sailed over the eastern horizon to enlighten the new day. For here, they could literally take in the beginning. Not only was the Great Pyramid raised at the birth of civilization, but in forty-five hundred years it had yet to be equaled in scale.

He was awed.

He was humbled.

He saw the world like God.

For thousands of miles, the Sahara stretched far to the west. To the east, the Nile, the backbone of Egypt, curved its blue course. So high were they that even the pyramid of Khafre, with its limestone cap in place, was dwarfed beneath them. The Sphinx, so towering when seen from the sand, was nothing more than a tiny kitten with its back turned when seen from up here. As human beings swarmed to Giza to greet the sun god, they were as insignificant in size as ants.

The land of the pharaohs.

As seen from a pharaoh's tomb.

For whatever else the pyramids were, they were the sanctuaries of mummified kings. Outside, what developed was the most potent and enduring civilization the world has ever known, while deep in the heart of this eternal triangle, supposedly protected by the oppressive weight of millions of tons of stone, locked away in the utter blackness of infinite night, with not a peep to disturb its long sleep, lay the preserved body of the mummified pharaoh.

If not for the greed of the living, the king would still be asleep.

For if time feared the pyramids, time also feared the mummy.

The time machine used to transport Chandler back to Egypt with DeClercq for a recap of that journey with Katt returned to the here and now of this office at Special X. "I should have caught it," the chief said, moving from X-ray to X-ray across the Strategy Wall. "If there had been an overall shot of the body, I might have made the connection. The head would have thrown me. I knew about the eyes being replaced by semi-precious stones. What I don't get is the tongue."

"According to the fax that arrived with the CAT scans sent from London by Commander Rand, the tongue of a mummy was sometimes covered with a sliver of gold," said Zinc.

"The eye of Horus on the belly would have fooled me too. It's an outline of the amulet that doesn't show the eye. But the heart scarab"—DeClercq tapped the beetle clearly visible in the chest X-ray—"should have twigged my memory. Piece them together and those clues form a jigsaw picture of an Egyptian mummy."

"Remember what you told me? The maxim of being a good cop? 'If you hear the thunder of hoof beats, think horses, not zebras.' A coffin arrives from Britain with jewels inside. The 'horse' of that scenario has to be that the body is being used as a 'mule' to smuggle jewels. The far-out 'zebra' would be that the jewels are wrapped in the bandages of a mummy."

"One question begs another," said DeClercq. "If the loot heisted with the coffin was meant to be the jewels, why didn't whoever shipped the contraband from Britain do what those tomb robbers did in ancient Egypt—extract the valuables and throw the mummy away? It would have been easier to smuggle in the jewels alone."

"Because the loot wasn't the jewels. It was the mummy," replied Chandler.

"There are lots of mummies available," said DeClercq. "So what's so unique about this one that it motivates multiple murder?"

THE UNDERTAKER

Ebbtide Island, Washington State

The mummy lay naked on a table in the Mummy Room, buried as deep in the rock of the overhead bluff as an Egyptian pharaoh within the stones of his pyramid. The three-thousand-year-old bandages lay discarded on the floor, where they had been dropped during the excitement of the unrolling of Sleeping Beauty's swathing late last night. The heart scarab from the wrappings lay on a nearby counter, but the jeweled eyes, the gilded tongue and the gold eye of Horus glued to the abdomen were undisturbed. This morning, the Undertaker was alone in the subterranean labyrinth with the mummified woman, so he felt free to run his hands caressingly around the curves of her smooth skin.

I *love* the dead, he thought.

He had loved the dead for as long as he could remember. Standing at Death's Door with his dad was his earliest recollection. The door was at the far end of a long, dark hall in their Midwest home. "Mommy loved you with all her heart," whispered his crying dad before he swung open the door to the mortuary beyond. The only embalming room in town, it was sandwiched between their creaky old house and the funeral home on Main Street in front. His dad was the undertaker who served the town, in the same way his father and granddad had before him. Framed by the door, his mom lay dead on the embalming slab, a white sheet draped up to her throat, her scrubbed face more serene than any faced in life. "Kiss Mommy good-bye," whispered his sobbing dad, ushering him in to plant a hesitant peck on the cold flesh of his mother's cheek before he was led up to bed and tucked in for the night.

Minutes later, he crept downstairs and tiptoed back along the hall to Death's Door. The door was ajar. His father wasn't in the mortuary. Compelled to kiss his mother one more time, he inched toward her dead body on the slab, then had to hide when he heard his father's footsteps out in the hall. Why, he didn't know, but hide he did. Entering, his dad locked Death's Door from the inside before he took off his clothes and, pulling the sheet away, climbed up onto the slab and stretched out on top of his naked mom. "Don't leave me, Joan," he begged as he spread her lifeless legs and, while his son watched transfixed from his hiding place, blubbered, "Let me love you one more time."

Years later, he would learn that his dad had embalmed his mom; the undertaker refused to let another mortician see his wife naked. If he watched that occur, he had no recollection, for his next memory was of waking up to find his father gone, leaving him alone with Mom behind Death's Door. No longer naked on the slab, his mom lay dead in an open hardwood coffin on the floor. Primly clothed in her Sunday best, she wore the same starched dress she wore to church for Easter service. Her face was now colored with makeup.

How he longed to cuddle with her one more time on the far side of the threshold between life and death.

One foot . . .

The other foot . . .

And then he was in.

And instantly he knew this was the life for him.

Life in death.

The Undertaker was born.

His next recollection was his dad shaking him. He awoke from a contented sleep to find himself stretched out alongside Mommy in her polished coffin. His head rested dreamily between the soft mounds of her breasts, the fabric covering her nipples soaked from his attempts to suckle the milk of death.

"Come," said his dad.

So he left her behind.

But to this day, he wished Mommy had been mummified, so he could sleep the contended sleep he had slept with her in that coffin, and could wake up dreamily each morning with her mummy in bed beside him.

They wore black for mourning to her funeral. His dad wore black to serve the townspeople as their undertaker. The undertaker's son wore black in respect for his mom, then black for the rest of his life because darkness suited him.

After school, if someone had died in town, he would creep through Death's Door to watch his dad work. Apprenticed to the family trade during puberty, his training began with him washing the bodies before each was embalmed. If the corpse was female, an added thrill lay in store for him, for when he touched her nipple, a shiver wormed down his spine to his groin.

Eventually, his dad taught him how to use an undertaker's trocar and suction pump. A sharp, foot-long metal tube with a half-inch diameter, a trocar was used to puncture and collapse internal organs so the body wouldn't bloat during an open-casket service. The pump sucked the corpse dry of stagnant blood so the vascular system could be infused with "mummy juice," the foul-smelling embalming fluid that kept decay at bay until the remains were buried or cremated. By then, his father was drinking heavily with a local boozing buddy: the town's oldest doctor. More and more, his dad let him do most of the work, until it was the Undertaker alone who walked through Death's Door.

The Undertaker.

Him.

Bonnie Stuart was the most popular girl at school. A cheerleader, she was going with the quarterback of the football team. The Undertaker would sit in the stands and watch Bonnie bounce as—"Rah! Rah! Rah!"—she led the fans in a cheer to boost the jocks. The town was shocked when Bonnie drowned one night at Lonesome Lake, the casualty of a boat party awash with tequila. Counselors came to the school the next day to help the students cope, but the Undertaker could hardly wait for class to let out. When it did, he ran home to Death's Door.

A bottle on the floor, his dad had passed out on the couch. *Creak, creak, creak.* The old house welcomed him home. His heart was beating wildly as he tiptoed down the hall, Death's Door beckoning him at the far end. The hinges squeaked as he eased it open, and there she lay, in all her beauty, on the embalming slab.

He closed the door.

He locked it.

And now they were alone.

Lovingly, he cut the clothes from her cold body, pausing to relish every erotic tingle of anticipation before—*snip!*—he yanked off her bra. Bonnie's breasts were the most perfect he had ever seen. Her pert, puckered nipples mesmerized him. His eyes locked on them as he stripped her body of its remaining clothes, and when he washed her cool skin to prepare her for embalming, the moment his hand touched the tip of her nearest breast he felt that familiar shiver snake down his spine.

"I love you, Bonnie," he whispered.

His other hand reached for the trocar.

He pricked the sharp point into her abdomen.

Closing his eyes, he bent forward to kiss her nipple.

Then he rammed the trocar into Bonnie as hard as he could, and cried, "I'm coming, Mommy!" as he shot off in his pants and almost passed out from the ecstasy of life in death. But that's when Bonnie jackknifed forward on the slanted slab, spewing a fountain of lung water at him as he was hurled back, before she grabbed the trocar and let out a scream to wake the dead.

His dad's drinking buddy had signed the death certificate.

Instantly, his love for Bonnie died. How could he love the dead if she was still alive? She had no right to be on this side of Death's Door. To right that wrong, he had to undertake her death himself, so up off the floor he came to grab screaming Bonnie by her mouth and nose, pushing her back against the slanted slab, where he stared deep into her eyes until life snuffed out.

Yes, he loved the dead.

But he loved *death* better.

The Undertaker knew he had found his life's undertaking.

Taking life.

Bonnie's funeral was a weepy, hanky-wringing affair. The top of the casket was open so her friends could say good-bye, and there she lay before them in her cheerleader's sweater, the quarterback's all-star ring on a chain around her neck so it nestled between the soft mounds of her perfect breasts.

Little did the jock know that death had jilted him.

For after Bonnie's "second death" in the mortuary, she had spent that night in the Undertaker's arms.

And little did the mourners know that the perfect breasts beneath the sweater weren't perfect any more.

They were an illusion.

Falsies, folks.

For Bonnie's perfect nipples were still behind Death's Door, secreted away in a jar of formaldehyde.

There were now hundreds of nipples in his nipple collection. He no longer embalmed bodies for a living, nor did he hire himself out on the World Wide Web—$20,000 a death, anyone snuffed and no questions asked.

Why so cheap?

Because he *loved* his work.

Death, however, had taken a twist of fate. The Undertaker's hobby was mummification. Mummifying the nipples in his nipple collection. It was a passion he had pursued on the Net. Clicking here, clicking there, you know how it is. Posting here and chatting there until he made the connection.

The connection that had lured him here to work for the Director.

A *shared* interest.

The nipples of the mummy were perfectly preserved. Fingering them sent that familiar shiver down his spine, and he wondered what it would be like to make trocar love with a beauty who had died three thousand years ago.

That thought was interrupted by footsteps on the stone stairs that descended from the mansion on the bluff. He turned as the Director entered the Mummy Room.

"Busy?"

"Admiring."

"She takes your breath away."

"That she does," said the Undertaker.

"How goes the other woman?" The Director glanced toward the surgery next door.

"I think he's finished."

"Where would he dump her?"

"Orcas Island," said the Undertaker.

"I want you to dump her on Lopez Island instead."

"Now?"

"No, tomorrow. This afternoon I have a major undertaking for you."

"Who?"

"Wolfe Capp. He has the progeric girl."

THE LONG SLEEP

Vancouver and London, England

"Commander Rand."

"Hilary. It's Zinc Chandler. We're on a speakerphone. With me is Chief Superintendent Robert DeClercq."

In his mind's eye, Zinc pictured the Scotland Yard cop with whom he had hunted the Ghoul through the sewers of London years ago. A tall, thin woman, much tougher than she looked, Rand had gone through the sexist hell in the Metropolitan Police. But taking down the Ghoul had slain the testosterone-breathing dragon and dissolved the glass ceiling above her head. Zinc's memory of her, of course, had frozen the woman's image in time. Given a choice between how she looked in his mind and the present reality, Rand would have had no trouble choosing.

Memory by others does for us what Hollywood films do for flesh-and-blood stars.

Capture the moment.

"Commander," said DeClercq.

"Gentlemen," said Rand. "I was surprised to receive your X-rays of the jewels in the coffin. Until they came through on the photo-fax, we thought we were dealing with Islamic terrorists. Perhaps you heard about our recent bombing in Richmond-upon-Thames? Yesterday morning, a hearse blew up on the outskirts of London. The explosion occurred to the west, near Heathrow Airport. The hearse was transporting a mummy into central London for scientific tests when it was waylaid through the ruse of a false detour. The hearse exploded in a ball of flames, vaporizing the two men in the front cab and—everyone thought—the mummy riding in back. Four men in two escort cars were also killed, as were two unlucky passersby."

"Why Islamic terrorists?" asked DeClercq.

"An Arabic voice anonymously called the Met to claim that the blast was a blow struck to liberate Egypt in the name of Islam. There's no more logic in that than in most terrorist acts, but given the recent attacks on tourists in Egypt by fundamentalists with the same goal, and the fact that the call was made before the explosion was widely reported, we thought it wise initially to investigate that political motive."

"Another ruse?" said Chandler.

"Yes," Rand replied. "Which became patently evident when your X-rays were received. Since then, we have picked up tips from snouts in the underworld that Sleeping Beauty was snatched in a heist planned and executed by Stopwatch."

"Stopwatch!" said DeClercq. "He's the best there is."

"Lord knows how much someone paid to have that highwayman steal the mummy. The hearse was detoured into a trap, and Stopwatch used a thermal lance to burrow up through the undercarriage to pull out the casket."

"Burrowed from where?" asked Chandler.

"The cellar of a pub. He released the flat doors of a well in the road used to lower beer kegs. A tunnel from the cellar led to the Thames, where a boat sped the hijackers and their loot away from a petrol-fumes explosion ignited by smoldering heat."

"The bomb?" said DeClercq.

"Or so we thought. Meanwhile, the mummy was switched with a legitimate body being shipped home for burial in Vancouver. That coffin left Heathrow as cargo on an Air Canada flight while we were being led astray by the anonymous call. Until we heard from you, we assumed the mummy was incinerated."

"Very slick, and utterly ruthless," Chandler said. "Eight people died to steal a *dead* body."

"That's Stopwatch," the commander replied.

"Any sign of him?"

"No, and there won't be. He's as bloody elusive as the Scarlet Pimpernel."

"What about the switch?"

"Nothing yet. The legitimate body was scheduled to be shipped on that flight. Given the time frame, it's likely the switch occurred along the route from the mortuary to Heathrow. The driver involved didn't report for work today."

"A payoff?"

"No doubt a handsome one. But it won't lead to Stopwatch. They never do."

"What about the body?"

"The legitimate one? By now, I'm sure it's been destroyed. Along with the mummy's casket. One way or another, Stopwatch never leaves a clue to follow."

"The situation here is no more encouraging," Chandler said. "The funeral home that was to pick up the coffin was called off. Supposedly, the airline phoned to say the deceased had missed the flight and would be flying in on the next plane. Instead, another mystery man posing as an undertaker with a hearse stolen from a mortuary in receivership arrived to claim the cargo."

"Description?"

"Yes, and a photo. Caught by the security camera in the customs office."

"ID?"

"No. He might as well have been masked. Peaked hat. Sunglasses. And he wore gloves."

"What does he look like?"

"A ghoul," said Zinc.

"Déjà vu," sighed the commander.

"The paperwork seemed in order, but who knows? Documents is checking that. When the X-rays caught the jewels, customs ordered the coffin searched at a hospital morgue. En route, the hearse vanished into thin air. Later, it was found submerged off a dock in the Fraser River. Inside were two dead customs men, but no coffin. From that dock, the trail sinks into the sea. Assuming the mummy was transferred to a boat, it could still be in Canada, or it was smuggled into the States or is on a ship sailing across the Pacific."

"Your end was as slick and as ruthless as ours."

"This heist was professional all the way."

"Why Vancouver?" Rand asked.

"That's the big question."

"Another ruse?"

"Possibly. But it's a long flight from London to Vancouver, and if you got a break over there, we'd be waiting at customs for the mystery man here. So someone must have thought it worth the risk to chance that flight."

"A local buyer?"

"Odds are," DeClercq interjected. "Which begs another question. Of what interest to a local buyer would your mummy be?"

"Of the same interest as it is to you and me. And to everyone else currently alive on earth."

"Which is?"

"That specific mummy—Sleeping Beauty—may provide an Egyptian map to the Fountain of Youth."

As DeClercq listened to Rand's account of the history of the mummy, the historian in him recalled snippets of what he had researched before taking Katt to Egypt.

The first Egyptian mummy acquired by the British Museum was originally purchased as a souvenir in 1722. "Mummy fever," however, did not take hold until Napoleon invaded Egypt almost eighty years later, for his 1798 Nile campaign. As souvenirs, he and Josephine procured a pair of matching mummy heads: a male for him and a female for her. Soon the Louvre had quite a collection of intact mummies, and after the Rosetta stone enabled Jean François Champollion to decipher the lost language of Egyptian hieroglyphics in 1822, Europeans became obsessed with the exotic Nile.

Mummies were *in.*

Yet early Egyptologists had no interest in mummies. Their archeological quest centered on art, artifacts and papyri. The dead were trampled underfoot when a non-pharaonic tomb was breached, victims of the rush to search for buried treasure.

But all that changed when Thomas Cook sent his first boatload of tourists down the Nile in 1840. Luxor, the site of ancient Thebes, across the water from the Valley of the Kings, was soon full of the grand hotels of a thriving holiday resort. Atop the must-see list of every tourist was a visit to the west-bank necropolis of the pharaohs, where archeologists daily laid bare for all to see the secrets surrounding the last remaining wonder of the world. It was the experience of a lifetime to behold, and how better to remember it—and shock the uninitiated back home—than to return with a genuine mummy as a souvenir.

The mummy became the popular aspect of Egyptology.

The people's choice.

A mummy wasn't human—it was a specimen. Preserved forever in its dusty wrappings, it didn't look anything like the dead of European nations. Specimens were bought, sold, displayed or discarded by owners every day, and the fact that this trade was illegal only added to the thrill. The "mummy pits" around Thebes were always full. If necessary, dishonest dealers imported specimens from other tombs. As demand increased, the price went up, until the cost of owning a mummy made it a luxury. With that came prestige.

"Lord Ridding went to Egypt in 1873, when Egyptology was the height of European fashion. He bought the mummy in question," said Commander Rand, "and brought the souvenir back to his Georgian estate in Richmond-upon-Thames."

"Where did he buy it?" asked DeClercq.

"Near the Valley of the Kings. From one of the lesser tombs."

"Was it ever unrolled?"

"No, it remained wrapped. From then until it was CAT-scanned a few months ago, the mummy leaned on display in its open sarcophagus at one corner of his lordship's study. Ridding would usher Victorian ladies in for a shudder before dinner, then regale them with exploits from his seat at the head of the table."

"The mummy remained intact?"

"Yes," said Rand. "Whoever embalmed Sleeping Beauty certainly knew his art. Ironically, the next Lord Ridding to inherit that title was a friend of Lord Carnarvon."

"*The* Lord Carnarvon? The patron who financed Howard Carter's hunt for Tutankhamen's tomb?"

"None other. The finding of Tut's tomb intact in 1922 ignited an even greater passion for all things Egyptian. From furniture to cosmetics to hats to clothes to confections: the rage of the moment was to prove that you had 'Nile style.' Tutankhamen appeared on jewelry fashioned by Cartier and by Van Cleef and Arpels. Needless to say, the mummy in Lord Ridding's study was back in vogue."

"Ridding?" said DeClercq. "That name rings a bell."

"The death of Lord Ridding, after that of Carnarvon, helped create the notorious myth of the curse of the mummy's tomb."

"And now *this?*"

"The stolen mummy had nothing to do with the curse that befell the current Lord Ridding. Just bad investments. He lost a fortune in the recent debacle of Lloyd's of London, and had to make up his losses soon or lose the estate in Richmond. So he put the mummy in the study on the market."

"What's it worth?" asked Chandler.

"That depends," said Rand. "Before it could be auctioned or sold, it had to be assessed. In the heyday of mummy sales in Egypt during the 1800s, not only were mummy pits 'salted' with specimens brought from other tombs, but enterprising businessmen established mummy factories to transform the recently deceased into authentic-looking mummies for sale to gullible Europeans. You know the story of Burke and Hare? The infamous Edinburgh bodysnatchers? Back when autopsies were against the law, except for dissecting the corpses of hanged murderers, the two supplied Dr. Knox with a steady stream of subjects. Knox thought grave-robbing was the source. But in fact, it was murder."

"The same happened in Egypt?"

"Yes," said Rand. "Rumors were rife of recently vanished

Europeans being recognized as 'ancient' mummies offered for sale on the black market."

"Caveat emptor," said DeClercq.

"Buyer beware," said Rand. "So the mummy from Lord Ridding's study was subjected to a CAT scan."

"That was a few months ago, you said?"

"Yes, and the results of the scan shocked everyone. X-rays offer a horizontal, two-dimensional view of the *hard tissues* within the wrapped body. That's what we see in the customs photos you faxed to me: bones and jewels. A CAT scan—computerized axial tomography—offers a vertical slice through the mummy. When the slices are manipulated by a computer, the result is a three-dimensional image of the whole body, including the *soft tissues.* That's what we see in the images I faxed to you: flesh and jewels."

DeClercq rose from his chair near the speakerphone and crossed to the London faxes pinned to the Strategy Wall. "I'm looking at them," he called across the room.

"What shocked those assessing Lord Ridding's mummy was that the soft tissues—*both skin and flesh*—were perfectly preserved. That's when it got the name Sleeping Beauty. It had the perfection of sleep, not the desiccation of death."

"The mummy's a fake?" said Chandler.

"No," replied Rand. "The bandages wrapping it were genuine and not disturbed. Radiocarbon dating put them at 1000 B.C., near the end of the New Kingdom, at the height of mummification."

"Which means?"

"You tell me."

"Lord Ridding's mummy," replied DeClercq, "offers the epitome of Egyptian embalming art."

The Mountie's memory shot back to the conversation he and Katt had had with the living mummy in the Mummy Room of Egypt's Cairo Museum.

"By the advent of the New Kingdom," the wrinkled Egyptologist from Britain had explained, *"the embalmer's art was fifteen centuries old. The technique of mummification was never put into writing. From father to son, the trade passed down in secret. Experimenters did their*

best to perfect the process, which reached a peak in the century before 1000 B.C."

"The secret's lost?" Katt had said.

"Not exactly. We can learn a lot from the mummies we have found. But it's like the missing link in human evolution. An Egyptian mortician might have perfected the technique, but we have yet to uncover the perfect mummy he produced."

DeClercq's mind returned to the present.

"The perfect mummy," he commented.

"Which Lord Ridding planned to sell to the highest bidder," said Rand. "He and Lady Ridding had a pet name for their mummy, Dearly Departed. Dear, as in high-priced, expensive, excessive."

"Was the mummy sold?"

"A sale was contingent."

"Contingent on what?"

"Various tests in London. The CAT scan of the mummy and the radiocarbon dating of its wrappings weren't invasive. Endoscopy was the next process. An endoscope is a long, narrow fiber-optic tube with a miniature camera at its point. Inserted into a mummy through a natural orifice or a small cut in the skin, it can be worked into position to study the soft tissues and take samples as required. Though invasive, the test is non-destructive. It extracts mummy DNA."

"The mummy was on its way to those tests when Stopwatch stole it?"

"Yes," said Rand.

"So now his client has the embalmer's secret?"

"Exclusively."

"How secret was the secret?" Chandler asked.

"News had yet to hit the media. Nothing was conclusive. But there were hints on the Internet. Leaks that sprang because Lord Ridding was seeking the highest bid."

"You said a sale was contingent?"

"Yes, on the tests."

"A sale to whom?"

"A pharmaceutical company with a major cosmetics line. If the embalming process did unlock the secret of how to stop human skin and flesh from aging, it would be worth billions."

Chandler whistled.

"Dearly Departed indeed," said DeClercq.

Freaks

Vancouver

There was a time not long ago when every circus and carnival had its sideshow of freaks. Back then, political correctness concerned itself only with the etiquette of using the right fork for the right appetizer at a state banquet. Freaks of nature have always piqued the obsessive curiosity in us. DNA is programmed to keep the gene pool "clean," so xenophobia—fear of the outsider—is hard-wired into the illogical limbic tissue at the core of our brains. Physical deformity. Grotesquery. There is no culture in which incest is not against the law, and if you want to see why—and many people do—then "Step right up, buy a ticket and come on in, folks."

Welcome to the freak show, Wolfe Capp thought.

The freaks of the pornographer's youth were on show at the PNE. The one common experience of every kid who grew up in Vancouver in the twentieth century, the Pacific National Exhibition marked summer's end. Indelibly burned into Capp's boyhood memories, the freak show lurked on the midway year after year, promising him a horrifying glimpse at the genetic oddities of this perverse world. The freak show was no longer an attraction at the PNE, but it was still a major part of Capp's adulthood. Now, the *mental* oddities were out in number, and their global carnival was *sexually* perverted. And what tied the freakiest of the freaks to Wolfe was the World Wide Web.

Ain't the Internet grand?

Late this afternoon, with the tip of an expensive cigar pulsing red in the dark of his Yaletown office, the pornographer sat on the edge of his desk facing a flickering screen. The TV screen, fed by a VCR, surmounted a wheeled table, which was rolled in front of the *Hustler* meat-grinder cover on the wall. The tape playing in the video recorder was one of the most controversial films ever made: Tod Browning's black-and-white feature *Freaks,* from 1932.

Wolfe was doing research for Woody Bone's next snuff, looking for an angle that he could suggest to the well-heeled client known to him only as the Director. The angle he was trying to work out was a creative way to snuff the progeric girl caged in the adjoining room. On the desk beside him, near the stiletto he used as a letter opener, lay several movie guides. *Freak Show* was the title Wolfe would suggest to the Director, the freakiest of the Internet freaks who commissioned made-to-order videos on-line from Snuff Lib.

Flicker, flicker . . .

Following his huge success with *Dracula,* featuring Bela Lugosi, in 1931, Browning turned to his youth for the subject of his next film. As a boy, he had run away to join the circus, and from that insider knowledge came the bizarre idea to populate his next picture with *real* circus freaks. Daisy and Violet, the Siamese twins. Johnny Eck, the half boy, and Olga, the bearded lady. The Pinheads—Schlitzie, Zip, Pip and Jennie Lee—a quartet with deformed faces. Randian, the human torso, without arms and legs, who nonetheless could light a cigarette by himself. The half-man/half-woman, Joseph/Josephine, a hermaphrodite with both sexual organs. Hans and Frieda, the carnival midgets. And Pete, the living skeleton . . .

Who, thought Wolfe, would have made a good Woody Bone.

Flicker, flicker . . .

The plot played out onscreen.

No wonder MGM execs were horrified by the film that Browning delivered.

And why the censor banned *Freaks* for thirty years.

Hans, the midget, needs a "normal" woman to feel "big." He falls in love with Cleopatra, the beautiful trapeze artist . . . and a conniving slut. She wants the midget's inheritance so she can run away with her love, the muscleman Hercules. Cleopatra marries Hans. At the wedding feast, the freaks embrace her—"We accept you, we accept you"—even though they are as wary of outsiders as we are of them. Cleopatra sees the feast as a farce, and lets them know their honor is an insult to her. Then she sets about poisoning Hans.

Venus, the lovely seal trainer, is Hercules's former girlfriend. The strongman tries to rape her, but the freaks intervene. And now—as the film cranked up to its climax in a driving rainstorm darkened by the dead of night—the pornographer sat forward to steal ideas for the snuff film ordered by the anonymous Director.

Flicker, flicker . . .

Slithering or crawling through the mucky mud, the massed freaks go after the connivers, herding them like cattle toward the slaughterhouse. The freaks close in with dripping knives, the human torso clenching his in his teeth. With Hercules dead, Cleopatra tries to escape, but she is no match for the mutilating blades. As Wolfe's fingers caressed the stiletto on his desk, he watched the freaks carve the woman up into the human chicken, so she could spend her remaining days as just another freak in the freak show.

The TV screen went black. Wolfe pushed himself away from the edge of his desk and approached the one-way window into the next room, where yesterday the wannabe star had admired herself in the mirror and today the frightened kidnapped child afflicted with progeria—the aging disease—cowered in her cage.

A buzzer buzzed.

The security door.

"Yes?" said Wolfe into the intercom.

"It's Fletcher. The job is done."

False Creek has always collected the scum of Vancouver. Actually a shallow arm of the Pacific that extends into the core of the city, it was a Native fishing ground before the Royal Navy nosed its bow into the virgin tidal basin in 1859. In 1887, the railway arrived, and workers relocated from Yale, in the heartland of the province, quickly built their shantytown on its north shore. Yaletown squatted close to the Canadian Pacific Railway's roundhouse and shunting yards. Soon the inlet was surrounded by polluting industries: sawmills, shipyards, breweries, stables, slaughterhouses, soap makers, tanneries, feed mills, a cooperage, a crematory and a creamery. The area was rough and badly lit. The year the railway arrived, police found two murder victims and a knee-high boot still shoeing someone's severed leg and foot. Garbage was dumped on the eastern flats. Raw sewage drained directly into the water. The creek was crammed with log booms and overrun by greasy wharves teeming with rats. The shore was fouled by sawdust from smoke-belching mills and slimed with sludge and offal from the stinking industries. Economic downturns brought squatters to the creek, where their clapboard shacks were known as the jungle. Far and wide, False Creek was dubbed "the filthy ditch."

And so it was for one hundred years.

Most of that was cleared away for Expo 86. Then the entire north shore was flipped to a Hong Kong billionaire for redevelopment. Touted as a glittering showcase for sophisticated urban living in a world-class city, Yaletown was given a facelift by landscape architects, and now—like the painted whores who stroll its streets at night—it is all gussied up for the new millennium. The false fronts of the refurbished warehouses north of the creek house fancy lawyers, trendy restaurants and overpriced furniture stores, international "import-export" firms that keep secret what they do and, in the case of this building on Hamilton Street, one of the production companies and film studios of Hollywood North.

Don't let it fool you.

The past lingers here.

Yes, the sandblasted red brick and striped green awnings on multi-paned windows look brand new, but the soil beneath the feet of the man pushing the security buzzer leaks historic toxins, one of the studios within is still a slaughterhouse and the film producer now opening the door to admit Dr. Ryland Fletcher personifies all the scum produced in Yaletown's seedy past.

"You get 'em?"

"Yep."

"Both Capp and the unknown male?"

"Capp opening the door and the U/M when he turned around."

"Good, let's send what we've got to HQ."

The cops on stakeout behind the window of the second-story room across the street from Wolfe Capp's lair were operatives with Special O, the Special Observation unit of the Mounted Police. The Watchers, as they were known, were the surreptitious eyes of the force. The cop who had snapped the digital pictures through a 600-millimetre telephoto lens affixed to a state-of-the-art Nikon camera downloaded the images from the memory card into a computer, then e-mailed them by wireless modem to Special X, where the JPEG file was opened by another computer and printed to photo quality through an Epson imager.

Meanwhile, the second cop played the digital recording caught by the pin mike hidden near Capp's security door. "It's Fletcher. The job is done," said the unknown male.

That too was transferred electronically to Special X, where it and both JPEG prints were added to the growing Interpol file on the Spider's Web.

And Snuff Lib.

Wolfe closed the security door behind Fletcher and punched in the "open sesame" code. With their footsteps echoing through the maze of deserted halls, the plastic surgeon and the pornographer made their way to the office in which they had first met yesterday. The smell of cigar smoke in the air was pungent, and beside a video system on a rolling stand, curtains had been pulled across the one-way window into the next room, through which they had spied on the wannabe porn queen.

The same teen in the before-and-after Polaroids in Fletcher's hand.

"Big enough?"

"Holy cow! My client *will* be titillated."

"I'd say she's a prime candidate for breast *reduction* surgery."

"Tits make the woman."

"That's my line. It still makes me nervous. Pumping this kid up to pneumatic overload."

"They're just *air?*"

"That's a figure of speech."

"And what a figure. I oughta film her in 3-D."

"That could be dangerous."

"Yeah? How come?"

"If your client sits too close to the screen, she might poke out his eyes."

The porn king snickered. "This should calm your nerves." On the surface of his desk beside the Italian stiletto lay a fat envelope encircled with a rubber band. Wolfe tossed the payoff underhand to the renegade plastic surgeon.

"Should I count it?" Fletcher asked.

"No, that's fifteen large."

"I thought we shook on thirteen?"

"The extra deuce is a tip."

"The tip we agreed upon is my pick from the porn queens in your stable."

"That too," Capp said, handing Fletcher a book of photos from a shelf beside his desk. The doctor leafed through it with a connoisseur's eye. Each double page was a spread devoted to a different porn queen. In this case the word "spread" was a double entendre, for along with each headshot and full-frontal nudie was a crotch shot taken close enough to steam up the lens.

"Her," said Fletcher, handing back the book.

"A good choice."

"If she fucks as hot as she looks. You know the scenario? And my predilection?"

"Don't forget I shot two fantasy flicks for you. The double feature you ordered through the Spider's Web from L.A. If you want to do her here, that can be arranged. Isn't that why you came to Hollywood North? To wield your own wood?"

"I want to up the ante. To catch her unawares. At home. At night. In her own bed."

The porn king shrugged. "The customer's always right. But after you blow 'em, Fletcher, you'll wish you had her on video to blow 'em again and again."

"If so, I'll pay you cash from this envelope to film me crowning another queen from your stable."

"No need for that. We'll figure something out. The extra deuce is an advance for *future* work. In my trade, there's an ongoing need for a discreet professional skilled with a surgeon's knife."

"Good. I need the work."

"How was the facility? Up to snuff?"

"It used to be a vet's office?"

"Recently retired. I rent the surgery room from him."

"It does the job."

Wolfe checked his watch. Fletcher did likewise.

"Mind if I ask some questions?"

"Shoot," said the surgeon.

"Where'd you go to med school?"

"UCLA."

"What'd you do after that?"

"Worked for a biotech firm in California."

"Research?"

"Yes."

"Into what?"

"The effect of free radicals on cells."

"Sounds political. The mess left behind by terrorists released from prison?"

The surgeon chuckled. "Free radicals are created as a by-product of metabolism when cells convert oxygen into energy. The damage they do to our body cells is why we age."

"Genetics?"

The geneticist nodded. "We were trying to develop a way to slow the aging process."

"Why'd you leave?"

"Money. And my sexual predilection. There was more opportunity for both in *practical* cures."

"In plastic surgery?"

"The gold mine of L.A."

"Where'd you work? Hollywood?"

"No, downtown."

"A good practice?"

"Uh-huh."

"So what went wrong?"

"My predilection got the better of me."

"Ah," said Capp, winking.

"I did a lot of work for the hard-core industry. You know my dark side, my lust for porn stars. Two of them accused me of rape. Criminal charges failed, but allegations of sexual impropriety stuck. I was stripped of my license for malpractice."

"So you went underground?"

"And here I am. Have scalpel, will travel. Call me Paladin."

Wolfe consulted his watch. "I have an appointment."

"So do I."

"Here's where she lives." Capp scribbled the porn queen's address on a scrap of paper and passed it to Ryland Fletcher. "Will you do her tonight?"

"No. I've got something on."

"Tomorrow?"

"Likely."

"I'll make sure she's home."

As Fletcher left "the Wolfe's lair"—the code name Special X had given this operation—the Special O cops staked out in the room across the street snapped more pictures.

"I wonder who this Fletcher is?"

"ViCLAS will check him."

"I wish we had a cover team."

"Dream on, kid."

"The fucking bean-counters in Ottawa are crippling us. Can't the solicitor general see that?"

"He's too busy."

"Doing what?"

"Downloading porn to his private collection."

The Watchers watched the U/M turn the next corner. Fletcher was in a hurry. He didn't want to be late. The renegade plastic surgeon was off to meet another employer. The appointment was at the most upscale restaurant in downtown Vancouver. A meeting with the director of the Panacea Clinic.

Wolfe Capp's appointment was with the Undertaker, a moneyman dispatched by the pornographer's biggest client, the nameless Director. That's why the building was deserted this afternoon. In the past, such dealings were all through the Internet. The Director was a mainstay of Snuff Lib, and to date he had commissioned five video performances by Woody Bone. Whoever the Director was, he was one sick fuck, for each snuff film degenerated from the last, forcing Capp to plumb the darkest recesses of his own perverted mind. But nothing had been as warped as what he wanted done with the freak in the cage, so Wolfe had quoted him an astronomical fee to scare him away from his diabolical request. Instead, the Director had e-mailed back, "Let's do the deal in cash."

Half a million bucks!

Woody's retirement fund.

Whoever the Director was, money was no obstacle.

With this deal, the porn king had sold his soul to the Devil.

In less than half an hour, he'd meet the Director's moneyman. It would be interesting to see if the Undertaker—a good underworld name for a Snuff Lib aficionado's henchman, Wolfe thought—had horns and hoofs and a tail.

The front door was Wolfe Capp's front to the world. The Spider's Web did business through that door. Dr. Ryland Fletcher was a client on the Web—until today, his fantasy was *acted* out—so even though he had done the tit job on the upcoming "star" of the snuff film *Meat Grinder,* ordered by the Houston televangelist, filming of which would have to wait until the bruising and swelling from her breast-enhancement surgery had passed, Fletcher had come and gone by Wolfe's front door. This, however, was Yaletown, which predated civic planning, so these old buildings had tunnels that burrowed to hell and gone, some of which were not recorded on any map. The "filthy ditch" of Yaletown had also been a smuggler's cove.

The tunnel into this building was the best-kept secret in town. The only rats to scurry in and out were the vermin of Snuff Lib. The secret passage opened off an underground parking lot, which itself was security-controlled. A camera at the mouth of the ramp caught whoever drove up. Only Wolfe knew the punch-in code that released the gate, and anyone he didn't recognize had to know a password. The password for the Director's Undertaker was "progeria," and if his imminent unknown guest voiced that password into the intercom, Wolfe would grant him access to the lot and release the hidden door that plugged the tunnel. That door was a section of the concrete wall that swung open on a pivot and whispered shut behind visitors. As the Undertaker moved along the tunnel, he would pass through a hidden metal detector, and if he set that off, he would secretly be X-rayed for weapons. A final door, a final camera, a final punch-in code and they would meet face to face.

If entry was hard, escape was easy. A series of beams this side of the doors said "open sesame," releasing and locking them one after another as rats vacated the building. The system was designed so the porn king could flee if there was a raid, by either police or underworld competitors. Such a raid would come by the front door, so a breach of that entrance by force automatically sealed every door between the intruders and Wolfe's internal domain, allowing him to pass like grease through a goose along the underground tunnel. Each laser beam that was cut as he fled from the building would pop open the next barrier to freedom.

The TV screen in Capp's office was bright again. To pass time as he waited for the Undertaker to arrive, the porn king played another video in the VCR. It had been surreptitiously shot at the vet's office to record Fletcher operating on the wannabe porn queen, enhancing her teenage "titties" to the humongous size ordered by the televangelist from Texas.

There was dramatic irony in this upcoming snuff. The teen was a runaway from Cow Plop, Alberta, or some hick town like that, where her fundamentalist father thumped the Holy Bible. She had escaped from his rhetoric and moral repression to become a porn star on the freewheeling West Coast. To keep from being traced, she had told no one back home where she was going, and soon—except for a video hidden deep in the heart of Texas—she would vanish from the face of the earth.

Ya gotta love it, thought Wolfe.

The porn king was contemplating incorporating footage of Fletcher's tit-job operation in the Texan's snuff film—or would the televangelist resent having his fantasy visually constructed in front of his eyes?—when a buzz from the squawk box on Wolfe's desk told him the Undertaker was here. A van at the gate to the parking lot had cut though the outside beam.

"Password?"

"Progeria."

The porn king let him in.

The man driving the black van *looked* like a sick fuck. From what Wolfe could see on the closed-circuit monitor fed by an external camera staring in through the windshield, the Undertaker had pasty white skin, so pale he could be a vampire who never saw the sun. In keeping with the Transylvanian metaphor, his short black hair was slicked back like Bela Lugosi's. A shadow of beard darkened his chin. Black-lensed shades hid his eyes, even though it was now growing dark outside. Everything he wore was black on black on black. A black leather biker's jacket over a black shirt, above black jeans and black motorcycle boots. What he looks like, Wolfe thought, is Satan's disciple.

This ghoul was *definitely* going through the X-ray machine.

The gate clattered shut and the van parked in the lot. The slab swung open on its pivot to expose the tunnel, and out climbed the driver with an attaché case. The case was big enough for half a million bucks, Wolfe duly noted.

Upon entering the tunnel, Capp's visitor set off the metal detector. That was to be expected. All those zippers and chains. Nothing suspect was caught by the X-rays, however, so given the past business of five snuff films, with a sixth in the works that fit the Director's psyche, Capp concluded that the Undertaker came in peace. Consequently, the porn king let him into the office.

Part of the office floor dropped away to open a trap door. The pit below was spiked with steel fangs. The drop operated like a gallows scaffold, sending those who might threaten Wolfe from the space in front of his desk to their death by impalement on the bed of nails below. The spikes moved aside as stairs slid into place, and up came his visitor like a zombie rising from the grave.

This man was a complete horror show.

"Good security."

"It works," said Wolfe.

"Similar bells and whistles guard our place."

"Is that the money?"

The Undertaker nodded. Laying the attaché case flat on the desk, he flicked both catches and lifted the lid. The case was stuffed with piles of used bills, each pack tied with an elastic band. Wolfe figured the cash was drug money collected by a biker gang. Gangs these days functioned like corporations, so the Undertaker was akin to a moneyman on Wall Street, except his power suit was black leather.

"Where's the freak?"

"Next door."

"Have any trouble?"

"None I couldn't handle. Finding her was hard. Kids prematurely aged by progeria are scarce. Snatching her was harder. That took finesse. You read about the cops back East grilling her mom?"

"They think she killed her?"

"Brilliant, huh? We've got the kid here while the cops think Mom snuffed her own daughter to save the freak from suffering the misery of her aging condition."

"Wicked."

"You're dealing with a pro."

"So let's see her."

"Sure," said Wolfe.

The porn king turned from the cash on his desk to lead the ghoul around the hole in the floor to the curtains. When he drew them back to open the glass eye on the next room, Wolfe saw their reflections on the window pane, his in front and the sick fuck's behind his shoulder. What flashed through his mind as he stared at the progeric girl in the cage was something Fletcher said: "We were trying to develop a way to slow the aging process." Given how gerontophobic it was to commission a video in which Woody Bone snuffs a child afflicted with the aging disease, Wolfe wondered if the Director would be interested in meeting the geneticist turned plastic surgeon, but that thought vanished in a sudden spray of blood.

His blood, on the glass bearing his reflection; it spurted from a hole in his throat. A hole caused by the point of the stiletto, now in the sick fuck's grasp and being stabbed through his neck from the nape at the base of his skull.

The point withdrew as the Undertaker seized him by the hair, then reappeared with another splash of blood, punching through a little to the left of the first hole.

Punch, punch, punch, the point punctured a line of holes across his Adam's apple as if it was a sewing machine stitching him up.

Wolfe's last thought?

It was probably this: even Woody Bone, the king of snuff porn, should be wary of spiders on the World Wide Web.

X IS FOR EXTREME

Vancouver

An unsuitable job for a woman?

Not any more.

There wasn't a sexual perversion that passed through the warped psyches of the spiders of Snuff Lib that S/Sgt. Christine Wozney of ViCLAS didn't encounter at work. Question 112 of the crime analysis report that Gill Macbeth had filled out on the breastless Galiano Island remains said it all:

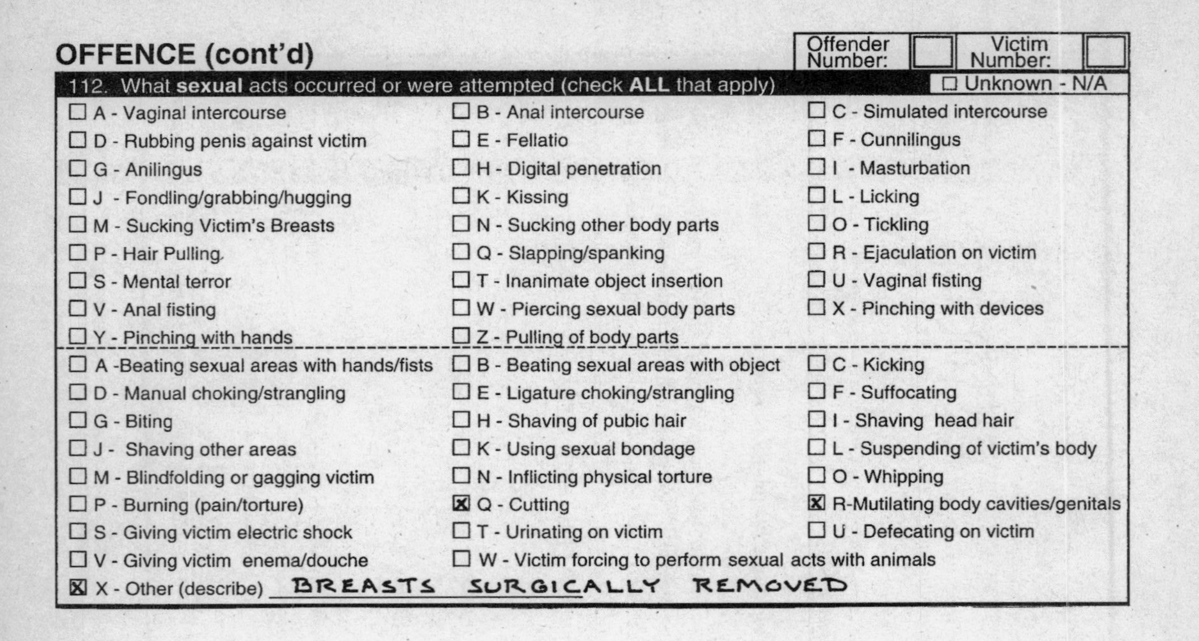

OFFENCE (cont'd)

Offender Number: ☐ Victim Number: ☐

112. What **sexual** acts occurred or were attempted (check **ALL** that apply) ☐ Unknown - N/A

☐ A - Vaginal intercourse	☐ B - Anal intercourse	☐ C - Simulated intercourse
☐ D - Rubbing penis against victim	☐ E - Fellatio	☐ F - Cunnilingus
☐ G - Anilingus	☐ H - Digital penetration	☐ I - Masturbation
☐ J - Fondling/grabbing/hugging	☐ K - Kissing	☐ L - Licking
☐ M - Sucking Victim's Breasts	☐ N - Sucking other body parts	☐ O - Tickling
☐ P - Hair Pulling	☐ Q - Slapping/spanking	☐ R - Ejaculation on victim
☐ S - Mental terror	☐ T - Inanimate object insertion	☐ U - Vaginal fisting
☐ V - Anal fisting	☐ W - Piercing sexual body parts	☐ X - Pinching with devices
☐ Y - Pinching with hands	☐ Z - Pulling of body parts	
☐ A -Beating sexual areas with hands/fists	☐ B - Beating sexual areas with object	☐ C - Kicking
☐ D - Manual choking/strangling	☐ E - Ligature choking/strangling	☐ F - Suffocating
☐ G - Biting	☐ H - Shaving of pubic hair	☐ I - Shaving head hair
☐ J - Shaving other areas	☐ K - Using sexual bondage	☐ L - Suspending of victim's body
☐ M - Blindfolding or gagging victim	☐ N - Inflicting physical torture	☐ O - Whipping
☐ P - Burning (pain/torture)	☒ Q - Cutting	☒ R-Mutilating body cavities/genitals
☐ S - Giving victim electric shock	☐ T - Urinating on victim	☐ U - Defecating on victim
☐ V - Giving victim enema/douche	☐ W - Victim forcing to perform sexual acts with animals	

☒ X - Other (describe) BREASTS SURGICALLY REMOVED

If there were any doubts in the matter, questions 113 and 114 of the report Gill had filled out on the Wreck Beach "mummy" laid them to rest:

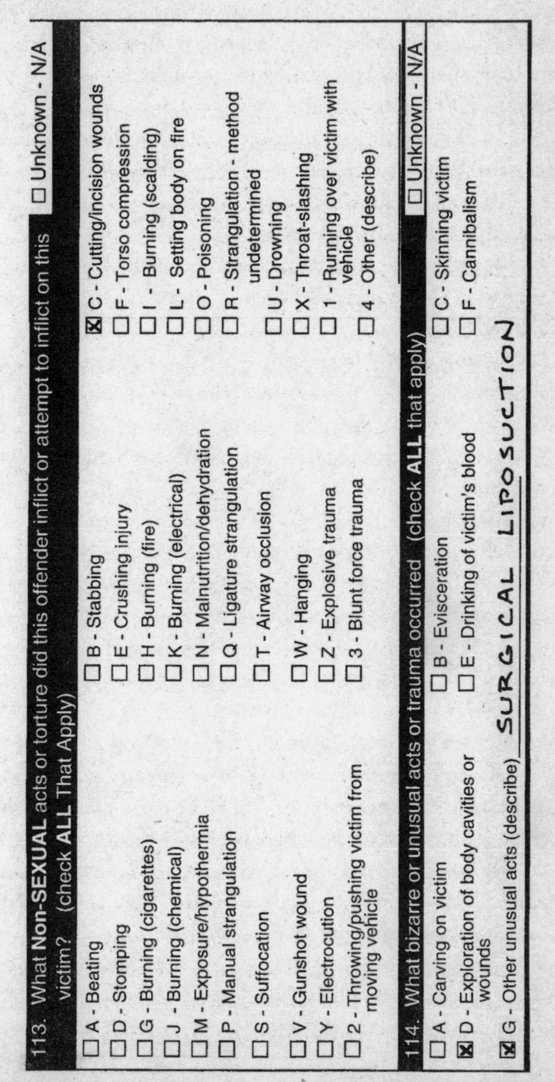

113. What **Non-SEXUAL** acts or torture did this offender inflict or attempt to inflict on this victim? (check **ALL** That Apply) ☐ Unknown - N/A

☐ A - Beating	☐ B - Stabbing	☒ C - Cutting/incision wounds
☐ D - Stomping	☐ E - Crushing injury	☐ F - Torso compression
☐ G - Burning (cigarettes)	☐ H - Burning (fire)	☐ I - Burning (scalding)
☐ J - Burning (chemical)	☐ K - Burning (electrical)	☐ L - Setting body on fire
☐ M - Exposure/hypothermia	☐ N - Malnutrition/dehydration	☐ O - Poisoning
☐ P - Manual strangulation	☐ Q - Ligature strangulation	☐ R - Strangulation - method undetermined
☐ S - Suffocation	☐ T - Airway occlusion	☐ U - Drowning
☐ V - Gunshot wound	☐ W - Hanging	☐ X - Throat-slashing
☐ Y - Electrocution	☐ Z - Explosive trauma	☐ 1 - Running over victim with vehicle
☐ 2 - Throwing/pushing victim from moving vehicle	☐ 3 - Blunt force trauma	☐ 4 - Other (describe)

114. What bizarre or unusual acts or trauma occurred (check **ALL** that apply) ☐ Unknown - N/A

☐ A - Carving on victim	☐ B - Evisceration	☐ C - Skinning victim
☒ D - Exploration of body cavities or wounds	☐ E - Drinking of victim's blood	☐ F - Cannibalism

☒ G - Other unusual acts (describe) SURGICAL LIPOSUCTION

Chris had seen it all.

In the flesh.

Late in the afternoon, she sat in her office in the basement of Special X, checking the two reports against each other and the central ViCLAS database. ViCLAS worked out of a clutch of offices at the foot of the stairs down from the front doors of the Tudor building at HQ. Mounted on the wall of that staircase was the huge bison head that is central to the Mounties' regimental crest, and next door to Chris's office was the officers' mess, where preparations were under way for a function tonight. She could hear the clinking of bottles as the bar was restocked.

The Mounties began recruiting women in 1974. Training takes six months at Depot division barracks in Regina, Saskatchewan, so that's where Chris joined the second co-ed troop in 1976. Eight females among twenty-four men, some of whom resented women for breaching a hundred-year-old exclusively male bastion. Those on the front line took the hard knocks that paved the way for those who followed, and during physical combat, the hard knocks hurled at Chris were *real*.

Important lesson.

No matter what Hollywood says about kung fu women in sexy outfits being the equal of any man intent on throwing his weight at them, the truth is that size counts. One on one with macho hulks, Chris lost every tussle. So she learned that if you can't depend on size and you can't shoot people, a female cop's defensive strength is to *talk* her way out. Brains over brawn.

But then there was the hazing.

Winter and spring were Chris's training seasons. In Saskatchewan, that meant bitter cold. The right marker—the drill sergeant—told the troop members what to wear for what occasion, and a favorite trick was to screw the eight women around by messing with the dress code. The men would show up dressed properly for what they had to do, and the women would show up in garb that threatened their health. That was the environment in which she was trained, and from that "putting women in their place" experience, Chris learned fast where the power base was. Men controlled the Mounted, and would throughout her career. She would spend years on the outside looking in, so if she was to survive and climb the ranks, she would need a survival mechanism to put herself ahead of male opponents.

Chris became a chameleon—and still was one. Put her near green, and green became her color. The result was that people—good and bad—opened up to her. And from that opening, she developed her *confessional* skills, every cop's stock in trade.

A year on general duty in North Vancouver, then four years out in Maple Ridge, gave Chris the opportunity to cultivate informants and to hone her skill at detecting shades of gray where others saw only black and white. The next eleven years were spent in plainclothes, working sex assaults in Burnaby, Vancouver's nearest suburb. Her ease at getting the truth from people was noticed, and that got her promoted to the last old boys' club: Serious Crime. That unit investigated the heaviest homicides around the province.

The first forty-eight hours after a murder are the most important, and Serious Crime cops work around the clock. The terrain is deadly and changes by the minute, so a chameleon will quickly overload and burn out. Added to that was the fact that Chris was back where she started, in the midst of a male powerhouse that ran on a high-octane mix of adrenaline and testosterone.

But then DeClercq came knocking on her door. He lured Chris to Special X to tango with this computer. In the blink of an eye, she grasped the awesome potential of this new tool and knew it would catapult her to the front line against the serious crimes of the future.

ViCLAS upped and bit her.

The birth of a cyber cop.

Actually, Chris owed her job to *two* men: Robert DeClercq and Clifford Olson. DeClercq was chief of the psycho-hunters at Special X and Olson was the psychopath who sexually assaulted and killed eleven kids in B.C.

So let's go back.

On November 19, 1980, twelve-year-old Christine Weller disappeared from her home in Surrey, near Vancouver. On Christmas Day, her body was found in the woods, mutilated with multiple stab wounds. On April 16, 1981, thirteen-year-old Colleen Daignault vanished in the same suburb. Less than a week later, on April 21, sixteen-year-old Daryn Johnsrude was abducted from a shopping mall, and on May 2, he was found dead with his skull shattered from bludgeoning. Then, on May 19, sixteen-year-old Sandra Wolfsteiner went missing while thumbing a ride in another local suburb.

Olson was arrested for drunk driving on May 26. With him in his car was a fifteen-year-old girl. A career criminal with more than ninety arrests for crimes ranging from fraud to armed robbery and sexual assault, he was known as a vicious homosexual rapist in prison. One of the Mounties investigating his latest arrest thought Olson was responsible for Johnsrude's murder, but for some inexplicable reason, his suspicion was ignored and Olson was released.

On June 21, thirteen-year-old Ada Court never made it home from a babysitting job. On July 2, nine-year-old Simon Partington vanished while riding his bike to a friend's house. Five days later, on July 7, Olson was arrested on suspicion of sexual assault. In his car on that occasion was a sixteen-year-old girl. Again, an astute Mountie fingered him as a suspect in the Ada Court case, and yet again, that suspicion fell through the cracks.

Olson was back on the streets.

Two days later, on July 9, fourteen-year-old Judy Kozma vanished too. The rising toll of young bodies and missing children was generating public alarm and media pressure. The final week of July saw the turning point. Fifteen-year-old Ray King Jr. went missing on July 23. Two days later, Judy Kozma's naked body was found near Lake Weaver. Nineteen stab wounds mutilated her diminutive corpse. That same day, July 25, eighteen-year-old Sigrun Arnd vanished while hitchhiking near Vancouver. Then, on July 27, fifteen-year-old Terri-Lyn Carson was abducted, and three days later, on July 30, seventeen-year-old Louise Chartrand was snatched on her way to work.

Finally, at the end of July 1981, the Mounted Police conceded that the cases might be linked, and RCMP headquarters in Vancouver took direct control of the investigation. Special O—the

Watchers—was put on Olson's tail. Two weeks after the Mounties launched a coordinated effort, Olson picked up two female hitch-hikers on Vancouver Island and led them into the bush for a drink. Fearing their quarry was about to kill again, Special O moved in and took him down. A search of Olson's van turned up an address book in which Judy Kozma had written her name. A bizarre deal was struck to solidify the case. In what the media would later call a "cash for corpses" scam, authorities agreed to pay Olson $10,000 a body for information about the known murders and directions to the unknown disposal sites.

In his confession, Olson described his M.O. He would offer a job with good pay to the kids he picked up, then slip them a Mickey Finn spiked with chloral hydrate to render them helpless for his sexual assaults. The girls were stabbed. The boys were bludgeoned to death. He used a sixteen-ounce Stanley stainless-steel hammer to crush their skulls. Olson was Maxwell Silverhammer in his fantasy, and like the killer in the Beatles' song, would—*Bang! Bang!*—bring his silver hammer down upon his victims' heads until he was—*Clang! Clang!*—sure that they were dead. In one instance, he used the hammer to pound nails into the brain of a boy who was still alive.

Olson was paid the cash. The bodies were recovered. On January 11, 1982, he pleaded guilty to eleven counts of first-degree murder. The judge sentenced him to eleven life terms, with a recommendation that he never be paroled.

Serial killing—the big time—had come to Canada.

The fallout from that notorious case tarnished the Mounties. For a number of reasons—overlapping jurisdictions, turf wars, staff transfers, personality clashes, lack of coordination, fouled lines of communication—a serial killer had preyed unchecked for nine months on the kids of Vancouver. When they finally got it together and began to hunt for links, it took less than two weeks for the beleaguered Mounties to get their man.

Links.

That was the key.

The lesson the Mounties learned was summed up by an expert at serial killing. According to Ted Bundy, the slayer of more than thirty women around the United States in a stretch of five years, "Jurisdictional boundaries and the inability of law enforcement agencies to communicate with each other allow transient killers to avoid identification and capture." The same applied to Olson, even in such a small space. What was needed, obviously, was a system to collect, collate and compare violent crimes. And because Olson was a Vancouver monster, the West Coast became the driving force to create that system.

It began simply with Mounties reading files.

America was in the midst of a serial-murder epidemic. DeSalvo, Manson, Corona, Berkowitz, Gacy, Buono and Bianchi, Bundy, Williams, Lucas, Ng, Ramirez—the big names were household words, but several hundred more lurked in the FBI's files. To combat this malignant onslaught from serial killers, the Bureau developed two hunting tools. Psychological profiling would later be made famous by *The Silence of the Lambs,* but what really interested the Mounties was the other development. VICAP—the Violent Criminal Apprehension Program—the FBI's automated case-linking system.

"Link" was the new buzzword.

The first Canadian attempt to adapt VICAP failed dismally. It was called the Major Crime File. By 1990, eight hundred cases had been fed into the database, but the MCF had failed to score a single "hit," linking a crime with a past M.O.

Insp. Eric Chan and S/Sgt. Rusty Lewis were veterans of the Headhunter case. The Headhunter was a Vancouver serial predator who followed close on the heels of Olson's rampage. The Mounties were computerized by Chan, and 1990 saw him return to the West Coast from ten months of training at the FBI's Behavioral Science Unit in Quantico, Virginia. The inspector became the first qualified psychological profiler in the RCMP.

After the Headhunter was taken down by DeClercq's squad, Rusty Lewis was eventually posted to the North Vancouver detachment to investigate sex crimes. Like Chris Wozney, he almost burned out, and he reached the point where he couldn't face another child-victim interview. So Lewis transferred to Major Crime to read files, and he studied psychology and computer programming at night. He quickly reached the conclusion that not only was the RCMP's Major Crime File flawed, but so was the FBI's VICAP system.

VICAP was restricted to homicides. A sexual homicide, however, is basically nothing more than a fatal sexual assault. Most serial killers are driven by sexual fantasies, so how can cops effectively link relevant cases unless sexual assaults are also fed in?

A better rat-trap was required.

And Rusty Lewis would build it.

The Iowa State Sex Crimes Analysis System had the best linking questions for sex assaults, so Chan put Lewis in touch with the Iowans. Rusty would use the homicide questions from VICAP to maintain alignment with the FBI's system. He would add the Iowa sex questions to feed in what was missing. And then, to make the Mounties' system state of the art, he would add something new to the cyber mix.

Behavioral questions.

Psychological profiling is founded on this fact: the crimes of serial predators are fantasy-based and -driven. Something psychological upsets the psycho. That motive is scripted into a sexual fantasy, which he plays over and over in his mind, until he feels compelled to act it out in real life. The victim is a stand-in for what upsets him, and as such is called a "victim-type." Because reality *never* lives up to the perfection of fantasy, the psycho is driven to repeat the crime in an attempt to get it right. His ritual becomes his "signature," so profilers work back from the behavior captured in the crime scene to unearth the fantasy that motivates him.

In effect, they're mindhunters.

Fantasy-driven predators may change their methods and locations, but their ritualistic behavior remains the same. To quote Inspector Chan: "The fantasy ritual will continue over time and space. The guy who rapes out of anger when he's twenty-five will rape out of anger when he's forty." The victim, the offender, the M.O. of the crime and any forensics—those were the focus of the American systems. What Lewis sought to do by adding behavioral questions was use the signature of each crime to forge a link to the serial predator.

Heady stuff.

Again, Chan directed him to the United States. This time to HITS, the Washington State Homicide Investigation Tracking System, where a pioneer in the field of computer linkage had created "Hanfland's Rules" to assess the utility of any feed-in question.

How available is the info?

How reliable is the info?

How useful is the info?

Guided by Chan, Lewis used those rules to develop his behavioral questions, then hunkered down for five years to put in more than three thousand hours of voluntary overtime to build his prototype, redoing and rewriting what had gone before. The result was MaCROS—the Major Crime Organizational System—and when it scored a hit right off the bat, headquarters picked up the ball and ran with it to expand the West Coast initiative into a national system. That system made two more improvements on VICAP by developing a central database, not a fragmented one as in the States, and by using codes—not English—to store information. Consequently, it functions in every country, regardless of language.

ViCLAS was launched in September 1996. The Violent Crime Linkage Analysis System was an international hit, and soon it became the gold standard of linkage systems. Build a better rat-trap and the world will beat a path to your door. Not only was ViCLAS adopted by Britain, Australia and several European countries, but it was also preferred by some American states—led by Tennessee and Indiana.

The big question: How would the Bureau react?

The first indication came from the Harvard University consultant to VICAP. He said the Canadians have "done to automated case linkage what the Japanese did with assembly-line auto production. They have taken a good American idea and transformed it into the best in the world." So the FBI accepted ViCLAS as "the Cadillac of linkage systems" and retooled VICAP along similar lines, so each is now portable across the border.

Today, when a murder or sex assault occurs, the investigator fills out 168 questions like the ones Gill had answered. After the information is fed into the central ViCLAS database, a powerful search engine compares the crime with every other crime reported in Canada over the past thirty years to spot links that will reveal the presence of a serial predator.

Thanks to Clifford Olson, ViCLAS reads minds. And ViCLAS never forgets.

It's a brave new world down here in the basement of this Tudor building.

How do you hunt a serial killer in the twenty-first century?

Ask Special X.

"Working late? Quitting time was four."

Wozney turned from her computer to the open door, where Chief Superintendent DeClercq leaned against the jamb.

"How long have you been standing there?"

"Not long. I was hoping I'd see you rub your nose."

"Did I?" she asked.

"No," said DeClercq. "Of all the personal idiosyncrasies of those in Special X, that's the one I most like to see. It usually means a bad guy is off to jail."

"Well, maybe I should start rubbing."

"A hit?" he asked.

"Big time!" Chris replied.

Lean, savvy, energetic and intense, Wozney was a crackerjack at her job. The chameleon was still evident in this newborn cyber cop. Her blonde hair was cropped close for easy management. Her favorite color was basic black, and on the job she invariably wore black slacks. Less than a minute could see her change into a rumple-haired chick as tough as any on the mean streets, dressed down to the black of a Goth queen with the mouth of a trucker to match.

Then—*presto!*—Chris could turn her looks back to class. A stroke or two of a brush, and it became a good-hair day. Add a colorful top, and the basic black rose to chic level, augmented by her effervescent sense of humor.

An interesting person.

DeClercq's kind of cop.

"I've been analyzing the two reports you sent down," said Chris. "The form Gill Macbeth filled out after her autopsy on the decomposing body that Nick Craven stumbled upon in the Galiano woods. The woman eaten by the wolf-dog, with—to quote Gill's report—'breasts surgically removed.' And the form she completed on the desiccated remains that Rick Scarlett found dumped on Wreck Beach. The woman turned into a mummy by—Gill's words again—'surgical liposuction.'"

"We seem to be up to our ears in mummies this week," said the chief, sighing.

"So I hear," said Wozney. "But that's a tenuous link. One's a real mummy from Egypt. The desiccated Wreck Beach remains just look like a mummy."

"I agree," said DeClercq. "It's a stretch."

"The obvious link between the remains dumped on Galiano Island and those on Wreck Beach is the word 'surgical.' Surgical cutting is the signature common to both crimes."

"You found a series?" asked DeClercq.

"Yes, three hits. ViCLAS used the word 'surgical' to link those mutilated bodies to a third corpse discovered at Cowichan, on Vancouver Island."

"Discovered when?"

"Last Friday," Wozney replied. "It too was found onshore. And it didn't wash in with the tide."

"Dumped from a boat?"

"Or carried to the beach. The shoreline is rocky. No footprints to track."

"Female?" asked DeClercq.

The cyber cop nodded. "And found naked like the rest. This time the cuts were to her face."

"What forged the link?"

"The autopsy report. The pathologist on the island commented, 'A scalpel could be the weapon.' In light of the surgical link between the other victims, 'scalpel' was one of the words I put to the ViCLAS database."

"And scored a hit."

"A home run, it seems. Someone else in the office had entered the Cowichan data only an hour before."

A tube of lipstick lay on Chris's desk. She picked it up, uncapped it, then applied the subtle shade to her lips with the precise instinct of a blind artist. Whenever she was ruminating, Chris colored her lips. That was the only makeup she wore.

"Here's what I'm thinking," she said. "The eyelids, the ears and the nose of the Cowichan victim were cut off. Not only is it possible a scalpel was used, but those mutilations—I've done some checking—run counter to plastic surgery techniques. To blepharoplasty: eyelid surgery. To otoplasty: ear sculpture. To rhinoplasty: a nose job. Such mutilations run parallel to those of the other victims. The breast removal was counter to breast enhancement, and the desiccated remains were lipoplasty taken to the extreme."

"That's the signature?"

"Uh-huh," said Chris. "I'd like to see what Rusty makes of it."

"When's he back?"

"Tomorrow. He's doing a psych profile up in Kamloops."

"Good work, Chris."

"There's more," said Wozney. "Why have none of these women been identified? Rapid ID has failed to put a name to *any* of them. They match no missing-person report in our databank."

"Strange," said DeClercq. "That's against the odds."

"For some reason, no one misses them. Is that because they don't *want* to be missed?"

"Why want that?"

"Why indeed? And something else puzzles me. The corpse found rotting in the Galiano woods—if it decomposed near a popular footpath, how come no one caught the stench?"

"Your theory?"

"Maybe it was moved. The bodies dumped onshore were meant to be found. Did the killer have second thoughts about Galiano and move the body to a better location for discovery?"

"Keep going, Chris."

"The dump sites run parallel to the U.S. border. The killer might be working *both* sides of the line. Now that our systems speak to each other, I'll query HITS in Seattle and VICAP in Quantico."

"Working late? Quitting time was four."

Wozney cupped an ear. "Is there an echo in this room?" she asked DeClercq.

"Am I interrupting?"

"Not at all," replied Chris, swiveling her chair around to face Zinc Chandler at the door.

"Hello, beautiful."

"Hello, handsome."

"How come I don't get a greeting like that?" asked DeClercq.

"Hello, beautiful," Chandler replied.

"Not you. *Her.*"

"Caution," said Chris. "I've had my knuckles rapped by the brass more than once for comments I've made."

"If the day comes when I won't let you speak your mind, rap *my* knuckles," said DeClercq.

"Okay, handsome."

"That's better," said the chief.

The cyber cop extended her hand toward the inspector. "I assume that's a gift for me?"

Chandler passed her the photos and said, "Special O is watching a porn king named Wolfe Capp for us. A televangelist cracked in Houston, Texas, yesterday. Between religious rants about the Devil making him do it, he begged forgiveness for ordering a snuff video through the Internet. The video was to be made to order by Snuff Lib, a link connected with a site called the Spider's Web. The Spider's Web is spun by Wolfe Capp, from a base—as near as we can tell—in the Yaletown building being watched by O. This fellow was seen leaving the building earlier today. See if you can get a line on him, Chris. A bug planted by the door caught his name as Fletcher."

CURSE OF THE MUMMY

West Vancouver

Outside, the relentless sea crashed in angry waves against the shore. Spray spewed up from the rocks and then fell like silver rain upon the beach knoll. The crests of the breakers were silver too, as was the swath of moonlight dappled across English Bay to sparkling Point Grey. The black hole to the left was the urban forest of Stanley Park, from which the span of Lions Gate Bridge crossed to the North Shore. The shore grew darker as it spread west from the lights of Sentinel Hill, topped by Gill's home, to the solitary beacon of Lighthouse Park. As the beacon turned to cut the night with guiding light, it slashed across the beach knoll slick with sea rain, overlooked by the windows of DeClercq's waterfront hideaway. Atop the knoll were a driftwood chair and an antique sundial. With each sweep, the beam caught words etched around the dial, warning those who'd consulted it through the centuries, "The Time Is Later Than You Think."

Sound advice.

If the light out there was cold and stark, the glow from the blazing hearth in here was bronze and warm. Flanking the fireplace were a pair of overstuffed chairs, estate auction relics from Katt's Sherlockian days. The Holmes chair was hers ("I'm more flamboyant"); the Watson chair was his ("You're staid and dependable"). Tonight, as always, Robert sat in the wing-backed chair to the right of the hearth, nursing his Scotch in a cut-glass tumbler, with Napoleon, his German shepherd, asleep on the rug at his feet. With Catnip lolling in her lap as she sipped an aperitif from the crystal in her fingers, Gill graced the Holmes chair. To set the mood for romance, the soft strains of the second movement from Mozart's *Clarinet Concerto* tiptoed around the cozy room.

"A mummy?" said Gill.

"Believe it or not."

"Who would kill eight people to steal a mummy?"

"*Why* is the question. Why equals who."

"Okay. Why?"

"To obtain the secret of the Fountain of Youth."

"You're kidding?"

"No," said Robert. "I'm dead serious. Sleeping Beauty—that's the mummy—is *perfectly* preserved. Whoever the Egyptian embalmer was who prepared her remains for the afterlife, he mastered how to prevent the skin and flesh from aging."

"Wow!" said Gill. "*I* might kill for that. Seeing how I just went under the knife to recapture youth, imagine the effect that motive might have on a psychopath."

"Or a sane person. That secret would be worth billions to any drug or cosmetics company. Entire nations have waged war with far less economic incentive than that."

"Do you think it's a corporation?"

"I don't know. The mummy was snatched while it was being transported to London for tests to seal a deal. Perhaps an outbid competitor hired the highwaymen. Or maybe the winner saw theft as a means to get the secret much cheaper."

"So why ship the mummy here?" Gill asked. "That's taking a hell of a risk with something so precious."

"I agree. That's the puzzle."

"And if someone is going to chance the risk, why not minimize it? A DNA test, a chemical test or any test whatsoever would require just a piece of the mummy. So why take the unnecessary risk of shipping the whole body?"

"Perhaps the entire mummy is the motive."

"I don't follow."

"It could be that the mummy *itself* is medicine. There's a time-honored history of that."

"You're the historian. Educate me," said Gill. "And while you're at it . . . " She wiggled her glass.

Robert turned to fetch the bottle of Pineau des Charantes from the reading table beside the Watson chair. When he turned back toward his guest, he found Gill leaning forward with her glass held out, ostensibly so she wouldn't disturb the cat in her lap. The firelight on Gill's rejuvenated face burnished her with the illusion of youthful innocence. The firelight down her gaping blouse was another matter, and the shadow between her bronze breasts seemed to plummet endlessly.

Gill winked playfully as he refreshed her aperitif.

"The Greeks were the first to prescribe *mummia* as medicine. The first century A.D. saw it recommended as a general cure-all for ailments like nausea, vertigo and paralysis. The wonder drug was created by mixing ground-up mummy powder with herbs and ingesting it with water. When boiled, mummy oil was skimmed off to apply as an ointment to wounds, sores and bruises. By the 1500s, *mummia* was being exported to Europe by the ton. King Francis I of France mixed his with rhubarb. Catherine de Medici sent her own chaplain to Egypt to ensure that her medicine cabinet would be amply stocked. As late as the twentieth century, Thebans were still applying mummy powder and butter to bruises."

"But the mummy was flown *here*. Not to Egypt."

"So?"

"So there goes your mummy-as-medicine motive."

"No," said Robert. "Flown here strengthens it."

Gill rolled her eyes skeptically. "*This* I've got to hear."

"If there's one thing you learn in my business, it's never to dismiss a motive as illogical. Psychos are fantasy-driven, and no fantasy is beyond the human mind. Ed Gein killed and flayed women so he could don their skins, in the hope that his female attire would turn him into his mother. Jeffrey Dahmer drilled holes in the heads of his victims to pour in acid, in the hope that they would serve him as zombies in the next life. From such motives, real-life murders spawned. And that's just the state of Wisconsin."

"I'm waiting," said Gill.

"Vancouver is the gateway for heroin from Asia. Our ties to Hong Kong facilitate the traffic. Chinatown is full of traditional Chinese drug stores. The guiding principle is 'You are what you eat,' so if you want a penis as stiff as rhino horn, you ingest medicine made from the horn of that beast. So great is Asia's demand for such virility that rhinoceroses are on the verge of extinction."

"Chinese Viagra."

"For fantasy-driven studs."

"Hmm," said Gill, "I see where you're going. If Sleeping Beauty has stopped the hands of time, then ingesting 'medicine' made from that mummy will keep the eater from aging."

"Our heroin comes from the Golden Triangle. What if you were a Vancouver importer who wished to impress a 'traditional' drug supplier? How much goodwill would you obtain by supplying him with the means to rejuvenate his body? Murder is nothing to Hong Kong triads, so that explains eight deaths. The supply route both ways is through Vancouver, so that explains the risky flight. And since the mummy itself is the drug, that explains why the entire body arrived." Robert drained his glass. "Do you believe in curses?" he inquired, pouring himself another dram of Scotch.

"No," said Gill.

"The Curse of the Mummy?"

"Is that a *duppy* film?"

"Duppy?" he said.

"A Caribbean term. When I was a girl in Barbados, horror movies were *duppy* films."

"What's a *duppy?*"

"A ghost," said Gill.

The log on the hearth spit sparks up the flue. Gases seeping from the bark danced like fiery spirits.

"According to Scotland Yard, the stolen mummy is cursed. I did some research on the Internet. Anyone with a taste for *duppy* films, as you call them," said DeClercq, "knows how vengeful an Egyptian mummy can be. The curse of the despoiled mummy, the reanimation of the evil mummy, the jinx of the defiled tomb—all are staples of Hollywood. The facts behind those films, however, go much further back.

"The Egyptians used magic in their funeral ceremonies to ensure that the mummy would be reborn in the afterlife. The most important ritual was the Opening of the Mouth. The rite was performed in the doorway of the tomb."

"At Death's door?" said Gill.

"Yes, the last good-bye. The mummy was propped upright in the doorway while the high priest donned the jackal-headed mask of Anubis, the god who weighed the heart. Other priests touched the mouth of the mummy with sacred objects and recited spells so the deceased could see, hear, speak, taste and touch in the afterlife. Having effectively restored the mummy to life, the funeral party then sealed it in the tomb for what was supposed to be eternity.

"In the seventh century A.D., the Arabs arrived. The old word for Egypt was *'keme'*—the black land—which referred to the fertile strip along the Nile. *'Al keme'* became the Arabic term for the Egyptian mysteries they encountered, and from those words we get—"

"Alchemy," said Gill.

"The belief that by correctly applying magic potions and spells, an alchemist can change the properties of matter."

"Turn lead into gold."

"Or animate the dead."

"Like Mickey Mouse did to those slave brooms in *The Sorcerer's Apprentice.*"

The log on the hearth popped as a knot in the wood exploded. The burst brought to life the cat dozing in Gill's lap. Catnip leaped away into the shadows for safety.

"The belief that mummies could be restored to life grew out of the paintings Arabs found on the walls of defiled tombs. Particularly images of the Opening of the Mouth ritual. In the case of mummies, reanimation was easy to accept. Not only did the long-dead continue to inhabit the world of the living, but their lifelike preservation made it seem as if they were suspended in time.

"Would those empowered by such magic allow robbers to ransack their tombs without fear? No, said the Arabs. They would wreak vengeance on anyone who dared, and that gave birth to the Curse of the Mummy in Arabic books."

The music from the speakers switched to Beethoven's *Moonlight Sonata.*

"What kind of music do mummies like best?" Gill asked, giggling.

"Do I want to know?"

"Wrap music," she replied.

It was Robert's turn to roll his eyes.

"Subsequent discoveries established the curse. After Champollion decoded Egyptian hieroglyphics in 1822, the tomb inscriptions could be read. 'As for any person who would enter this tomb unclean or do something evil to it,' warned one, 'there will be a judgment against him by the Great God.' And there was evidence the curse was carried out. In Rikka cemetery, the roof of an ancient stone-cut burial chamber collapsed at the foot of shaft 124. Modern excavators found two flattened skeletons inside. The bones of one were those of the original occupant, a mummy crushed in its coffin when the roof caved in. But there were also a pair of arm bones on the lid and a jumble of bones on the floor. They belonged to a would-be thief who was squashed by the rockfall as he reached out to strip the mummy. Intact, though badly damaged, the mummy still had its jewels."

Gill had curled up in the Holmes chair like a little girl being read a bedtime story. Her hiked-up skirt revealed garters down her thighs. That too spoke volumes. This *was* a bedtime story.

"What's fascinating," said the Mountie, "is how the Curse of the Mummy jumped from fiction to fact. In the nineteenth century, Gothic writers were quick to pounce on plots involving Egyptian curses. The mid-1800s saw Edgar Allen Poe publish 'Some Words with a Mummy,' about a scientist who resurrects a mummy with electricity. After *Dracula,* Bram Stoker wrote *The Jewel of the Seven Stars,* the tale of an Egyptian queen whose unwrapping and reanimation has horrific results. And apart from the canon of Sherlock

Holmes, Sir Arthur Conan Doyle wrote 'The Ring of Thoth' and 'Lot No. 249,' which qualified him as an expert on ancient Egyptian curses."

"Then came Tut?" said Gill.

"You know the facts?"

"Just the basics. Fill me in on the details."

Setting his glass of Scotch aside, DeClercq reached for the poker and stoked the fire before adding another log. The shadows on the walls lurched like the resurrected dead as the disturbed flames jerked on the hearth.

"Lord Carnarvon was plagued by ill health. On his doctor's orders to get away from cold, wet English winters, he went to Egypt in 1903. At first merely a means to kill time, Egyptology soon became his passion. Having the money for an expedition but lacking the training, he teamed up in 1908 with Howard Carter. Against all odds and the evidence found so far, Carter believed that the intact tomb of the boy-king Tutankhamen remained to be discovered. Finally, in 1915, the two obtained permission to dig in the Valley of the Kings.

"By 1921, the project was a bust, so Carnarvon and Carter agreed the next season would be their last. Carnarvon was at home in Britain when he received a cable from Carter. 'At last have made a wonderful discovery in Valley,' it read. 'A magnificent tomb with seals intact; recovered same for your arrival; congratulations.' 'Propose arrive Alexandria 20th,' Carnarvon telegraphed in reply, before setting sail for Egypt with his daughter, Lady Evelyn, and a fellow mummy enthusiast, Lord Ridding."

"Ridding?" said Gill.

DeClercq nodded. "The son of the Lord Ridding who bought the mummy that was stolen, and the grandfather of the current Lord Ridding, from whom it was heisted."

"The plot thickens."

"It jells around the curse. What Carter had found on November 4, 1922, were sixteen stone steps that led down to a sealed doorway. Etched on the seal was the name the two men had searched for more than ten years to find: Tutankhamen. At last, on November 26, the party broke in. Carter burrowed a small hole and peered inside. At first, he could see nothing. The hot air escaping from the burial chamber caused the candle flames to flicker. Then, as his eyes grew accustomed to the light, details within emerged slowly from the mist. Strange animals, statues and everywhere the glint of gold. Carnarvon, standing behind him, couldn't stand the suspense. 'Can you see anything?' he asked. 'Yes,' answered Carter. 'Wonderful things.'"

Macbeth laughed. "You'd think you were there."

"I wish I was," Robert replied. "We live in humdrum times, bled dry of *real* adventure. The closest we get to adventure is renting Indiana Jones movies."

"I'm still waiting for the *duppy.*"

"It's coming," he said. "What they had found, of course, was the greatest archeological discovery of the century. Soon Carter, Carnarvon, Ridding and Lady Evelyn were inside, surrounded by the only surviving treasure of the pharaohs. The effect was exactly what you would expect. The world's press flocked to the Valley of the Kings, with every reporter jockeying for a scoop.

"In hindsight, Lord Carnarvon made a mistake. He had spent tens of thousands of pounds on finding Tutankhamen, and here was a chance to recoup his investment. Consequently, he signed an exclusive deal with the *Times,* and that relegated every other paper to scrounging copy from gossip and speculation. The irony is that Carnarvon himself was about to become a sensation.

"Carter was left to the task of clearing the tomb. Exhausted by all the excitement, Carnarvon sailed south to Aswan, to rest beside the Nile. Somewhere along the way, a mosquito bit him on the cheek. Then, while he was shaving, his razor cut off the scab. Since ill health brought him to Egypt in the first place, the cut became infected and fever set in. That forced Carnarvon to travel to Cairo for medical attention, but blood poisoning led to pneumonia.

"Marie Corelli was a British Gothic novelist. In March 1923, she wrote a letter to the *Times.* In her possession was an ancient Arabic text that warned, 'Death comes on swift wings to he who disturbs the tomb of the pharaoh.' She suggested that the mosquito bite might have been caused by the hand of Tut, and predicted dire consequences for all those who had entered his tomb. 'I cannot but think some risks are run by breaking into the last rest of a king of Egypt whose tomb is specifically and solemnly guarded, and robbing him of his possessions.' Shortly after the letter was printed, Lord Carnarvon died."

"Her publisher must have been ecstatic," said Gill.

"No doubt," Robert agreed. "Carnarvon's death on April 4 made headlines around the world. All those reporters he had thwarted now had a juicy story that Carnarvon couldn't squelch. The Curse of the Mummy sold newspapers by the ton.

"Fortuitously, the lights of Cairo had all gone out around the time Carnarvon died. The *Daily Express* linked that to the curse. He had left his three-legged fox terrier, Susie, behind in Britain. At the instant of her master's death, she sat bolt upright and howled. In later versions, Susie keeled over and died. But best of all was Sir Arthur Conan Doyle's take on the curse.

"Doyle had lost his beloved son in the First World War. He spent his latter years as a spiritualist, trying to contact his son by paranormal means. When news of Carnarvon's death reached England, Doyle was being interviewed by the *Times*. The reporter mentioned the letter Marie Corelli had sent to that paper, and Doyle agreed that Carnarvon's death might be the revenge of the pharaoh. Sherlock Holmes was the height of rationality. With that being the opinion of the creator of the great detective, from that point on the Curse of the Mummy transformed into believable *fact*."

"I love it," said Gill. "Is there more?"

"In a feeding frenzy, reporters began digging into the past. There was quite a history of indignities to mummies. Mark Twain, in *Innocents Abroad,* wrote about watching Egyptian stokers shovel mummies by the spadeful into the fireboxes of locomotives. 'Damn these plebeians,' one engineer was overheard to shout. 'They don't burn worth a cent. Pass out a king.' Others were crushed for artists and turned into 'mummy brown' oil paint."

"Maybe the Curse of the Mummy explains why Van Gogh cut off his ear?"

"Augustus Stanwood was an American paper manufacturer from

Maine. He struck a deal to import tons of linen mummy wrappings to be turned into paper. They were too discolored to become white paper as he had planned, so they were turned into the brown paper that is used to wrap food. A cholera epidemic broke out shortly after, and it was attributed to Stanwood's wrappings."

"Maine?" said Gill. "There's food for Stephen King."

"It's rumored that the British Museum had a mummy with a curse upon it. The museum sold the piece to an American institution ten years before Tut. Guess how they shipped it?"

"On the *Titanic?*"

"Right. And then there's the story of Carter's canary. Expecting a lonely dig in the Valley of the Kings, the archeologist arrived with the bird in a gilded cage. The workers at the site had never heard a canary sing, so its presence was said to be a lucky omen. When Tut's tomb was discovered weeks later, the diggers dubbed it 'the Tomb of the Golden Bird.' After Carter left to meet Lord Carnarvon, a cobra squeezed through the bars of the cage and ate the canary. Not only had good luck turned bad, but the royal headdress found in Tut's tomb bore a snake exactly like the one that had silenced the bird."

"The *duppy,*" said Gill.

"What happened to Lord Ridding was the strangest event of all. It seems Lord Carnarvon was excavating in 1909 when he found a hollow wooden statue of a black cat. Hidden inside the statue was a cat mummy. Cats, of course, were worshiped in ancient Egypt, and it was through that mummy that the lords became friends. Both Carnarvon and Ridding had inherited seats in the House of Lords. That's where they discovered their shared passion for Egypt.

"The Egyptian cat-headed goddess was Bast of Bubastis. If a cat died, the household took it to Bubastis for mummification, and the whole family went into mourning, shaving off their eyebrows. Cat cults grew in popularity, and soon people flocked to the Bubastis temple to select a sacred cat. The priest would kill the animal by breaking its neck, and the mummified cat would be stored for worship. That's the story Lord Carnarvon told Lord Ridding, and from that tale developed the friendship that saw the two aristocrats sail to Egypt to help Howard Carter break into Tut's tomb.

"When Carnarvon died, he willed the statue to Ridding."

"Uh-oh," said Gill.

"Ridding took it home to his estate at Richmond-upon-Thames. It sat on a table near his bed. One night, he awoke to moonlight streaming in through the open French windows. He watched the beam creep toward the black figure of the cat, then must have dozed off again, for he awoke with a jerk in the dead of night to the noise of a loud crack, like a pistol shot. The wooden cat had split in two to expose the cat mummy, the bandages of which were torn around its broken neck. At that instant, Ridding's own cat sprang onto the bed, and before its master could cover his face, the beast clawed out his eyes."

"Crack!" popped the fire.

"Jesus!" Gill cursed, and her hand flew up to protect her eyes as Catnip leaped into her lap.

It took at least a minute for Gill to catch her breath. Robert could see her heart beating fast beneath her youthful skin.

"Do you believe in curses now?" he asked. "After his cat blinded him, Lord Ridding sure did. He threw himself off the roof of his Georgian manor the following month and splattered his brains all over the steps that led to the front door. On the desk in his study lay a note. 'There is a curse on me,' it read. While driving to the cemetery to bury him, the undertaker hit and killed a six-year-old boy."

"What about Howard Carter? When did he die?"

"In 1939. At age sixty-four."

"And Lady Evelyn?"

"Not till 1980."

"Well, there you have it. Coincidence. If there was a curse, they'd have succumbed too."

"Not according to Sir Arthur Conan Doyle. His famous response to that argument was, 'It is nonsense to say that because "elementals"'—his term for your *duppies*—'do not harm everybody, therefore they do not exist. One might as well say that because bulldogs do not bite everybody, therefore bulldogs do not exist.'"

"So Tut cursed Ridding?"

"That's what the papers said. His death within a year of the death of Lord Carnarvon proved the Curse of the Mummy. The irony is that it didn't settle the matter. The open question is: *Which* mummy cursed Ridding? Was it Tutankhamen? Or was it Sleeping Beauty?

"Since 1873, the female mummy had leaned on display in its open sarcophagus in one corner of the Riddings' study. When it was removed recently from its stone container for the CAT scan, Egyptian writing was revealed beneath."

"A curse?" said Gill.

"In hieroglyphics. 'Death to those who disturb my sleep.'"

"Wait till the media get hold of that."

"No doubt they'll blame the eight deaths so far on the Curse of the Mummy."

"Cursed may be those who handle her. But not the rest of us," said Gill.

"Oh? Why's that?"

"If Sleeping Beauty does unlock the secret of age, disturbing her will be a *blessing,* not a curse."

Gill stood and walked toward the bathroom along the hall to the east, beyond the library that Katt had usurped as her bedroom. Robert sat waiting like faithful Watson for Gill to return, while thoughts rolled like shunted boxcars through his mind.

There was nothing like romance to make you feel young. Here he was, in his fifties, supposedly over the hill, about to bed a forty-year-old woman, who had regressed to her twenties.

The best of both worlds.

His reverie was interrupted by footsteps from the hall. Gill wasn't wearing shoes; the steps were those of bare feet. The light from the hall shone on the wall above the hearth, where Gill's shadow appeared as she approached. Something was wrong. Her movements were stilted. And as her outline loomed larger over the mantel, he realized her hair was gone and her round head was bald.

Leaning left, Robert peered around the back of his chair.

Lurching toward him was an Egyptian mummy. She was wrapped in toilet tissue from head to foot, and from indications beneath, she had shed all her clothes. The end of one roll dragged behind her on the floor, and Catnip was playing with it to Gill's detriment.

DeClercq recalled what he had read about public unrollings in the nineteenth century:

Lord Londesborough
At Home
Monday, 10th June 1850
144 Piccadilly
A Mummy from Thebes to be unrolled at half-past Two

That sort of thing.

Well, this was an "unrolling" he would thoroughly enjoy.

Ah, it's great to be young again!

Vancouver

Directly across English Bay from Robert's home, the western tip of Point Grey sparkled beneath the moon. At the foot of those cliffs was Wreck Beach, where the liposuctioned "mummy" found by the students with spring fever had been dumped ashore by boat. The point ran east to the ocean inlet of False Creek, which marked the beginning of downtown Vancouver. Kits Point jutted out into the bay as the west bank of the creek, a small peninsula dotted with street lamps and house lights. One of those lanterns marked Zinc Chandler's home, where the troubled Mountie sat alone in the flickering gloom of a TV screen, his nine-millimeter Smith & Wesson semi-automatic pistol before him on a knee-high coffee table.

As he watched *The Mummy,* Zinc field-stripped the gun.

In happier times, back when Alexis Hunt was still in this world and not the afterlife—if there really *was* life after death—he and she would settle in each Tuesday night with a double feature of movies to critique. To qualify, the films had to be connected, by theme, director, actor or locale. In the final session the Tuesday critics had together, it was the 1957 and 1997 versions of *Twelve Angry Men.* Why he had rented two films of *The Mummy* tonight puzzled Zinc, for he had sworn to himself that that tradition had died with Alex. But here he sat, in this desolate room that she had once lit up, with the remnants of takeout Chinese food at his feet and his mind screaming for relief from the pain that radiated out from the scar the bullet and surgery had left in his brain.

With each beat of his heart, the pain got worse.

The black-and-white film in the VCR was the 1932 version of *The Mummy.* Boris Karloff starred as Imhotep. The video cassette lying on the table beside the dismantled gun was the 1999 remake with Brendan Fraser. As Zinc sprayed the barrel and slide with G96 oil and cleaned the weapon with a toothbrush, a bore brush and a soft cloth, he glanced every so often at the screen to catch a snippet of the Tutankhamen-inspired plot.

The plot was this: A team of archeologists finds the long-forgotten tomb of Imhotep, an ancient Egyptian high priest who was buried alive with his organs intact for stealing the Scroll of Thoth. His hope was that the scroll would revive his beloved Princess Ankh-es-en-Amon from the dead. By reading the scroll aloud three thousand years later, one of the archeologists resurrects Imhotep's mummy. It lurches around and drives the fool insane. Ten years later, his death-like face severely wrinkled, Imhotep reappears as an Egyptologist. He leads an expedition to the tomb of his long-lost love. When attempts to resurrect the dead princess fail, Imhotep turns his attention toward the heroine of the film, whom he sees as the reincarnated spirit of his love. If he kills the woman and revives her body with the Scroll of Thoth, will he and the princess be reunited in the afterlife?

I wonder? Zinc thought.

Suddenly, the pain in his head, as excruciating as it was, was no match for the ache in his heart. As he watched the mummy yearn to be reunited with the lover death had stolen from him, Zinc lost his focus on the screen and instead saw Alex Hunt beckoning from beyond.

Another jolt of pain.

Release me, he thought.

Holding the gun's slide upside down, Zinc inserted the barrel and dropped it into place. The Mountie grasped the frame in his other hand, turned the slide right side up to align the rails, then pushed it back to the rear. Releasing the slide and racking it to check the action, he shoved a full mag into the grip, then racked it once more to insert a cartridge from the clip into the firing chamber.

His physical pain and the pain from longing for Alex were almost too much to bear.

Zinc was in the grip of the curse of *The Mummy* . . .

GERONTOPHOBIA

Ebbtide Island

The juxtaposition of the two was astonishing. The mummy on the table in the Mummy Room had been dead for three thousand years, yet the flesh exposed by the "unrolling" of ancient bandages was still juvenescent in appearance. The progeric girl locked in one of the side-by-side cells built into the wall of the Mummy Room was only six years old, but she was as crooked and as crinkled as a seventy-year-old crone. Three men stood in the space between the table and the cell, marveling at the reversal of the norm in both cases.

"Any trouble?" the Director asked.

The Undertaker shook his head. "Piece of cake. Capp took all the risk in snatching her."

"That's the way I work. Why chance getting caught if you can pay others to risk the odds?"

"I crave risk."

"That's why I pay you."

"In which case, I got stiffed on this undertaking. Killing Capp was easy. He turned his back on me. And kidnapping the kid from his office was a snooze. I carried her to the van, drove her to the dock and got her aboard hidden in a duffel bag. The dock was a stone's throw away on False Creek. From there, it was just a matter of time to cruise across the border to here."

"What's your point?"

"I'm bored," said the Undertaker. "Other guys get danger pay, so I should get the reverse."

"Boredom pay?"

The hired killer smirked. Which was about as close to humor as he ever got.

The child caged behind the bars was still knocked out by whatever sedative the Doctor had supplied to the Undertaker. Prematurely bald, she had a spider's web of blue veins clearly visible through the scalp of her egg-shaped head. Relative to the size of her skull, the girl's miniature face seemed pinched in on itself. The eyes behind the closed lids bulged like those of a fish. Her eyebrows and eyelashes had fallen off. The nose was small and beak-like, and the ears had no lobes. Her tiny mouth was flanked by sagging jowls, and when it opened to take in shallow breaths, the teeth exposed were crowded and malformed. Arthritis and osteoporosis had deformed her bones, and the wrinkled skin covering them was worn out by age. The net effect was that of a grandmother reduced to the size of a dwarf.

"Progeria," said the Doctor. "An aging disease. From the Greek for 'prematurely old.' Children afflicted by it suffer the usual complications of the elderly—heart disease, stroke, cancer and Alzheimer's and Parkinson's diseases. They age at least seven times faster than normal. Their average life expectancy is twelve years."

"How rare is it?" asked the Undertaker.

"It's estimated that progeria affects one in eight million newborns."

"And the cause?"

"A single mutant gene."

"Which does what?" asked the hired killer.

"Normal cell aging is the result of damage caused by free radicals. Free radicals are created when cells convert oxygen into energy. Normal amounts of free radicals help rid the body of toxins, but they also harm cell membranes and DNA. That harm results in the normal aging, and eventual death, of those cells."

The Undertaker nodded at the girl in the cage. "So what happened to her?"

"Healthy cells produce antioxidant enzymes that attack damaging free radicals to keep them under control. Those antioxidant enzymes are regulated by a single gene. In children afflicted by progeria, the mutant gene fails to regulate properly, so their level of antioxidant enzymes is abnormally low. Consequently, free radicals age them at an accelerated rate."

"As a freak of nature, what use is she to us?"

"The freak and the mummy are different keys to the same baffling lock. In alternate ways, both hold the answer to the mystery of why we age. What is it about Sleeping Beauty that kept her perpetually young? Is it in her genes? Is she too a freak of nature? Was Sleeping Beauty blessed in life by the flip side of the genetic curse that afflicts the progeric freak in this cage? Did Sleeping Beauty's body cells sip from a Fountain of Youth unique to her genetic code, an oasis of replenishing antioxidant enzymes that internally thwarted the damaging aging effects of free radicals? If so, find that mutant gene and we *own* the Fountain of Youth. Or is the secret of her perpetual beauty to be found in this particular Egyptian embalmer's mortuary art? Cosmetic manufacturers market creams and other flawed panaceas to help human flesh reduce the inevitable ravages of time. But did the ancient alchemist who embalmed Sleeping Beauty chance upon a formula that stopped the degeneration of flesh dead in its tracks? And if that preservative did in death what we see before us in this mummy, imagine what it might accomplish in life."

"I want that secret," the Director said, "to rejuvenate myself. King Canute tried to turn back the tide of time. Where he failed, I will succeed in staying forever young."

The Doctor turned from the mummy to focus on the freak in the cage. "Progeria is a disease that mimics normal aging but occurs at a very fast pace. Use a monkey as a model to study why and how we age and it will take forty years. Use this progeric child and it will take only three months. Unlock the molecular mechanism underlying progeria and we will unlock the molecular secret that regulates how fast normal humans age."

"Can that be done?" asked the Undertaker. "Can you isolate the gene that did *this* to her?"

"Is there any doubt?" the Doctor replied. "The answer to that is as close as the evening news. Scientists have now cracked our genetic code. Since 1990, researchers worldwide have contributed to the Human Genome Project, the map of a complete set of human DNA, isolating the individual genes that program us as a species, including the genes that determine how long each of us will live.

"For instance," explained the Doctor, "we've found a gene called INDY, I-N-D-Y. That acronym stands for 'I'm Not Dead Yet' and is taken from the movie *Monty Python and the Holy Grail,* in which a plague victim cries out, "I'm not dead yet," while being hauled off for burial. Humans share the INDY gene with fruit flies. By tinkering with it so the gene spawns mutations, geneticists have been able to double the age of fruit flies so that they can live the equivalent of a 150-year human lifespan."

"No shit," said the Undertaker.

"The point I'm making," the Doctor said, "is that science is on the cusp of a brave new world. Every sword unsheathed by geneticists will have *two* cutting edges. Genes can be switched on and turned off. We hear about the marvels of 'expressing' good genes. Genes are expressed when they ship their coded messages through the body by way of protein molecules to guide an individual's growth, health and behavior. But it is also possible to express bad genes, and what we *don't* hear about from the Human Genome Project is the monstrous horrors that will result if something goes wrong."

"Like the freak in the cage?" said the Undertaker, staring hard at the progeric girl.

"Exactly," said the Doctor.

"So how will you find the gene?"

"I'll use a computer. The Human Genome Project has identified about 120 genes that help repair DNA damage from the wear and tear of metabolic processes. It's all in a database. Earlier research into progeria homed in on Chromosome 1. Those are called landmarks. Once a chromosome region is implicated in a certain disease that way, the DNA code for that region can quickly be searched on the computer database, yielding a list of genes for further testing."

"You can do that?"

"Any research student can. What I need for further testing is this child with progeria and a normal subject—a human guinea pig of the same age to experiment on. A gene jockey at UBC bagged the Nobel Prize in chemistry for his gene-editing technique. Using it, we can alter genes the way a writer alters the words in a sentence to give it new meaning. We can rewrite the language of life. From start to finish, it used to take about a week to engineer a mutant gene and get it producing whatever chemicals were expressed by its new code. Now there are gene machines that do it in mere hours. They churn out genes like bank machines turn out money. You punch in some instructions, then sit back while the machines produce the desired genes. Now that you've brought me the mutant kid, I should with a little tinkering be able to engineer a Franken-gene."

"A gene that resets the rate at which we age?" said the Undertaker.

"Yes," confirmed the Doctor.

"Will it work?"

"Why not?" said the geneticist turned plastic surgeon. "The Flavr Savr tomato doesn't rot on the way to market. Why? Because the gene responsible for making tomatoes go mushy has been blocked by an 'antisense' gene. Plants have been engineered to emit light using a gene borrowed from luminescing bacteria in the sea. We'll soon have self-lighting Christmas trees. Human genes have been stitched into goats in Scotland so that along with their milk they produce scarce human proteins. A fish lab in West Vancouver is raising salmon that mature ten times faster than normal. Engineering a Franken-gene to alter the rate of production of antioxident enzymes in our body cells so free radicals will kill us off at a different life expectancy than we experience now is no more difficult to do."

"Will this girl do?" asked the Undertaker.

"Yes," said the Doctor, glancing at the empty cell beside her cage. "But like I said, if I'm to experiment with adenovirus gene transfers, I'll need an *expendable* subject for my herontic tests."

"The normal girl?"

"Right. One that's six years old."

The Director smiled. A wicked, sadistic grin. "No problem, Doc. I know the perfect candidate."

THE PANACEA CLINIC

Ebbtide Island

How much horror can one mind take?

In the half-timbered houses of late-medieval Britain, it was usual to find a hook affixed to one side of the large, open stone fireplace. If a man's wife indulged in scolding him, he would call for the town jailer to bring the "branks" and lock the shrew's head up in that "scold's bridle." The branks would be chained to the hook beside the hearth, and there she would sit in forced silence until she promised to behave better in the future.

The naked woman strapped to the chair in the Plastic Surgery Room, next to the Mummy Room, was wearing a branks. Akin to a catcher's mask in a baseball game, the scold's bridle was an iron framework imprisoning her head. Like all such devices, it had a metal plate that was forced into her mouth to act as a gag, making speech impossible. The plate in this branks was a cruel piece of work, for it had several spikes that pierced the woman's tongue. Facing the chair was a full-length mirror, and what she saw reflected in it made her scream. The screaming was muffled to a mewling by the vicious bridle, so all that gushed from her gaping lips was blood from her impaled tongue. The blood enhanced the horror she saw in the mocking mirror, as it ran red down the artificially extended cleavage between her breasts.

The horror . . .

The horror . . .

She teetered on the brink.

So hysterical was the actress facing this monster she had become that she failed to notice the men entering the surgery. Then suddenly, the Doctor appeared at the corner of her eye as he squatted down to glare in at her through the bars of the branks.

"Comfy?" he asked.

The woman screamed again.

"Satisfied?" he asked.

The scream came out as a gurgle.

"I'll bet you wish you could take back the words that brought you to this."

The bridle was fastened to the back of the chair and cinched about her head so tightly that she couldn't nod. In addition, a garrote encircled her throat, both ends of the metal collar threading through a hole in the upright back, where they were attached to a weighted lever affixed to its rear. The chair was of the type Spanish conquistadors had used to assassinate Atahualpa, the Incas' ruler, and Spain kept it in use to execute criminals until 1963. An iron spike could be placed behind the neck, so that when the collar was tightened around the condemned's throat by the executioner's pulling on the lever, the point would skewer between the vertebrae to rupture the spinal cord.

In this case, however, that would be too quick.

"You're ugly," said the Doctor. "Look at you. No man in his right mind would think you attractive. As far as I'm concerned, you're fit for the slag heap."

Look the woman did, for she couldn't turn away, and above the back of the chair, reflected in the mirror, she saw the Undertaker looming over her. Slowly, ever so slowly, the garrote began to constrict, and the Doctor glared intently to catch every nuance of her suffering. He could be Hitchcock filming *Frenzy*.

The slow strangulation flushed her face. Her breathing deepened, labored, then she struggled to suck in breath. Lack of oxygen turned her skin cyanotic blue, and as her terrified eyes bugged out of her head, red spots caused by bursting vessels bloodshot the whites. The petechiae spread to her skin, dotting her engorged face like smallpox. The clench of the ligature would have forced her tongue to protrude out between her teeth were it not for the spiked bridle of the branks. Instead, her tongue bloated behind her purple lips, hemorrhaging even more blood down her chin, while red frothed from her nose and trickled from her ears. A death rattle gargled in her throat as her body thrashed convulsively against the bonds, though it soon subsided to involuntary twitches. Then the Plastic Surgery Room was filled with a foul stench as the woman's bladder and bowels let go. The gaze of the Doctor, however, stayed locked on her until the last sign of life flickered and died.

"Serves you right," he snarled, "for what you did to me."

Silence ensued.

The interval lengthened.

Finally, the Director said, "Forget about her. Another Tinseltown beauty is waiting for you upstairs."

The Doctor had departed to scale the stone steps ascending from the Mummy Room deep down in the bedrock of the cliff to the Panacea Clinic crowning the bluff overhead. That left the Director and the Undertaker alone with the body in the Plastic Surgery Room.

"May I have her nipples?"

"As many as you like. The Doc's through with her, and she has no use for them now."

The Undertaker fetched a scalpel from a tray of instruments and did a little surgery of his own.

"You said you were bored. You said you craved risk. What I have in mind will cure your ennui."

"You want me to dump her?"

"For a start."

"Tonight?" asked the hired killer.

"Just before dawn."

"The Doc picked Orcas Island."

"He would. That's near."

"But you want her dumped on Lopez Island instead?"

"Location is *crucial,*" said the Director. "As it was with the other five dumps."

"The cop's that good?"

"He's a mathematician. He uses mathematical probability to stalk serial killers."

"Does that work?"

"On lesser men. But in me, the cyber cops have met their match."

"Okay, where's the spot?"

"Let's get a map."

They returned to the Mummy Room next door. The progeric girl was still unconscious in her prison. While the Director flattened a nautical chart of the Pacific Northwest on the counter that ran along one wall, the Undertaker set the harvested nipples down beside the heart scarab they found during the unrolling of the mummy now stretched out on the central table.

"Here," said the Director, planting a finger on the shore of one of the San Juan Islands.

The area covered by the chart was a smuggler's paradise. Islands by the hundreds dotted the liquid border between Canada and the States. San Juan County, south of the line, was the most northwestern county in continental America. With 175 named islands, rocks and reefs visible at high tide, and 600 more that emerged as the tide ebbed, the county had 375 miles of saltwater shoreline. Wool, booze, drugs, illegal immigrants and even an Egyptian mummy were easy to sneak across, as the history of the Northwest proved conclusively. It was the ideal hideout for what the Director had planned.

"After you dump her, cruise up Rosario Strait."

His finger slid up the waterway from Lopez Island in the south to Orcas Island in the north. Orcas was shaped like an inverted U. Beside the tip of the inland prong, his finger came to a halt.

"Here, you'll see a farm that slopes up from the sea. That's where you'll find her," the Director said, nodding his head meaningfully at the empty cage.

"The six-year-old?"

"Uh-huh."

"The Doc's guinea pig."

Independent interests in mummification expressed through a link forged on the World Wide Web had brought them together. The Director was searching for a suitable henchman to help him realize his diabolical plan. The Undertaker was searching for information that would help him preserve his nipple collection. One thing had led to another, and soon the two had agreed that theirs was a match made in hell.

"Do you know why a mummy's heart was protected by a scarab?" asked the Undertaker. As he posed the question to the Director, the hired killer plucked Sleeping Beauty's heart scarab from the counter and held it up to the light. The dark green beetle was carved out of serpentine and etched with an inscription from the Book of the Dead.

"The scarab is a dung beetle," the Director replied. "As Egyptians watched the beetle push a ball of dung around between its forelegs, they witnessed larvae emerging from the shit. Because they were unaware the larvae had hatched from eggs, they assumed the scarab was regenerating itself magically. Thus the scarab came to be associated with miraculous rebirth. Since the heart was the organ weighed by jackal-headed Anubis to decide whether the deceased could enter the afterlife, it required the most protection. So when the mummy was wrapped, a heart scarab was the amulet bound over the heart."

The Undertaker replaced the jewel among the severed nipples.

"Who's the most famous example of twentieth-century embalming?" the Director quizzed.

"Lenin," replied the killer.

"Have you seen him?"

"No."

"I have," said the Director. "In fact, that's where I got the idea for what we're doing here."

"How's that?"

"Lenin died in 1924, shortly after Tut's mummy was uncovered in Egypt. From Tutankhamen, the Soviets got the idea to mummify Lenin, so they could put the leader of the Russian Revolution on public display in a tomb in Red Square. The fluid used to embalm him was rumored to be based on an ancient Egyptian formula."

"Was it?"

"No. I paid a bribe to find out."

"So that's why you need Sleeping Beauty?"

"Yes," said the Director. "She's the *real* McCoy."

"You need her so you can sip from the Fountain of Youth. These gerontic tests the Doc plans to do on the progeric kid, I assume that's to see if the Egyptian formula used to preserve this mummy's flesh will provide the key to rejuvenating the aging freak? And once you have the means to make the old young again, you can sell the secret to the highest bidder among the huge drug companies, then live in style for the rest of your rejuvenated life off the profit you reap."

The Director grinned.

A satanic smirk.

"I already have more than enough money to live in style for the rest of my life."

"You aren't trying to conquer age?"

"Oh, but I am."

"I don't get it. Don't you think it's time you filled me in on what we're doing?"

So the Director told him.

One million dollars. That's what the Director had promised to pay the Undertaker as his half of their bargain, and for that sum, deposited in weekly increments to an offshore bank account where the bankers didn't give a rat's ass where the money came from as long as they got to use it, the hired killer had promised to snuff anyone and everyone the Director asked him to, and to assume all risks inherent in the hits.

"After you dump the body and before you snatch the kid, I have a third undertaking for you. The time has come to take Denning out."

"Why?" asked the killer.

"The Doctor is insatiable in his demands. When he was at work in L.A., before he came here, he let his predilection for torturing beautiful females loose like Mr. Hyde. The Picasso killer mutilated and murdered five women in Los Angeles a few years ago, and the LAPD is still on the hunt for him. The Doc was—and *is*—Picasso. The deal I struck with him is this: in exchange for his using his research talent to unlock the aging secrets of Sleeping Beauty and the progeric girl, I will supply him with both the flesh and the opportunity to turn his Hyde loose with no restraints whatsoever, and I will make sure that he's kept safe from arrest for the rest of his life. He too gets a million dollars deposited offshore, and I've guaranteed him a new identity to go with the money. To quench the Doc's appetite for movie stars, I've had Eternal Spring refer to the Panacea Clinic suitable Hollywood beauties traveling north incognito for plastic surgery under Denning's knife. Those are the bodies that you've been dumping after the Doc has finished playing with them."

"Five so far, and the sixth in the other room."

"The seventh is upstairs. We'll do her tonight. And tomorrow I'm off to Eternal Spring to lure in number eight."

"You're right. Insatiable. He's a sex fiend."

"The Doc's a driven man. It won't be long until the police identify those women. When they discover *all* were recent patients of Denning's, they'll have found the link that will lead them to the Panacea Clinic, and therefore to us. So tomorrow I want you to fly to Vancouver with me, and after I've seen the Doc's next victim at Eternal Spring, I want you to go in with a silenced gun. And when you take Denning out, also remove the eight files."

"Will that break the link?"

"Not entirely. But I have other plans to protect us. While you were snuffing Wolfe Capp at the porn king's Yaletown studio, Fletcher and I met privately at a nearby restaurant. In a booth tucked away in back so we could talk freely, I plumbed his fertile mind for new ideas on how to find the aging gene, then asked if he would be willing to do some *special* plastic surgery for me. He agreed.

"Fletcher's off to L.A. tomorrow morning. That fits perfectly with my protection plan. If the L.A. cops and the Mounties link the Picasso mutilations down there to the mutilated women you're dumping up here, Fletcher's L.A. connection and the rape allegations the LAPD have filed away on him will draw their suspicions toward him before they ever suspect us. That will give us enough warning to shut down things here on the island and move our operation somewhere safe."

Panacea was the Greek goddess of healing, so the Panacea Clinic was named after her. A panacea is a cure-all for disease, and the disease this clinic "cured" was gerontophobia. In an age of aging baby boomers and youth-conscious culture, gerontophobia—the fear of aging—was an angst of epidemic proportions. Baby boomers are a pampered generation, used to thinking they have a right to have it all *their* way, including the power to push back the relentless tide of time. Every year, in growing numbers, more and more choose to go under the plastic surgeon's knife or squander their assets on balms and potions thought to diminish age. They yearn for the chance to live their lives like *The Picture of Dorian Gray,* their outer skin frozen in youthful times, belying the damage free radicals continue to do to their inner canvas.

If beauty is only skin deep, so be it.

The Panacea Clinic, however, went a step beyond. It didn't deal with the consequences of free-radical damage, but instead engaged in battle with the enemy itself deep in the body's cells. The Panacea Clinic marshaled an army of antioxidants.

Prevention *is* the cure.

The only patient at the island clinic tonight was an incognito soap opera star up from Hollywood. Naked, she stood in front of a full-length mirror in her room on the upper floor of the mansion on the bluff. As the celebrity admired her rejuvenated assets, she hefted her uplifted breasts like Bette Midler does onstage.

"Mirror, mirror, on the wall, who has the knock-'em-deadest tits of all?"

She winked at herself.

"You do," the actress answered herself.

At thirty-eight, she was cresting the hump that would put her over the hill in Hollywood. Her looks provided her living, as well as her self-esteem, and she was under no illusion about the paramount importance of a woman's appearance in Tinseltown. Go to the movies and what did you see? Robert Redford, Sean Connery, Clint Eastwood fooling around with females young enough to be their granddaughters. Meanwhile, women over forty struggled to land roles, as the latest ingénues usurped their stars.

Appearance *does* make a difference. Everyone knows that.

Mothers are more loving toward good-looking babies. Her own had been with her, ignoring her plain sister. Grade-school teachers are more attentive to good-looking students. That's why she had qualified as a teacher's pet. As for teenage dating . . . Hey, come on! Is there any doubt about the blessing of good looks? Or for job procurement once you're out in the world? In any calling, but most of all in hers. There are lots of actresses with bland mugs, but how many do you see in big roles? You think Tom Cruise and Brad Pitt chase after them?

Simply *looking* old is a disadvantage to women.

As the philosopher Bertrand Russell observed: "On the whole, women tend to love men for their character while men tend to love women for their appearance."

If reinforcement was needed, that truth was driven home to her on the plane that flew her from Los Angeles to Vancouver. In first class, the seats were two abreast. A woman in her forties, then this actress, then a woman in her twenties sat beside the windows in three consecutive rows, each with an empty seat beside her. A handsome man in his fifties came aboard and stood for a moment at the front of the cabin. Then he walked past the oldest woman, continued on past the actress on the cusp of forty and took the seat (not his assigned seat) beside the sweet young thing.

"Hello," he said. "My name is Bill."

If seventy-four is the average human life expectancy, thirty-seven—work it out—is middle age. Middle age in onscreen women is over the hill, so as far as the overlooked actress was concerned, she couldn't land soon enough in Hollywood North.

Some women flaunt the fact that they've had "work done." For others, having gone under the knife is poison to their careers. In Tinseltown, the kiss of death is the *need* for such rejuvenation, for in an industry that packages youthful female flesh for fantasy consumption, plastic surgery equates with "damaged goods."

Enter Dr. Denning.

Eternal Spring was the name of Denning's surgery. There isn't an actress alive who doesn't need that. Transplanted from Hollywood South to Hollywood North, his operation offered those with money to burn not only Denning's dazzling skill with a scalpel and a laser, but also comfort in his guarantee that included within the price was an assurance that he was dependably discreet.

Most of Denning's patients were on the verge of forty. Secrecy was why they came to him, flying to Vancouver under the cover of sneaking away "on holiday" to escape from it all for a while. Because their desire was to be forgotten during that sojourn, most let it be known they'd be incommunicado for a month. After the plastic surgery and their recuperation, they were ready for the follow-up. Prevention, obviously, is the best cure, and because Denning, as he explained, didn't want them to become "plastic surgery addicts," he referred them to a private clinic on Ebbtide Island. There, with a day or two at the retreat by herself, each got the focused attention of the director and his staff, and each was instructed in how to use the panacea of antioxidants to thwart future damage to her body by free radicals.

That's why the actress was here.

To *defeat* age.

The woman turned around to gaze back at her reflection over one bare shoulder, then she grabbed her buttocks in both hands like studio execs used to do when auditioning on the casting couch.

"Mirror, mirror, on the wall, who has the tushiest ass of all?"

She winked.

"You do."

Watching her surreptitiously from the hidden side of the one-way mirror, the Doctor thought, And I want a piece of it.

ISLOMANIA

Orcas Island, Washington State

The wind had picked up after Nick Craven was out on open water, heaving him to and fro on a moonlit bounding main all the way south to Orcas Island. With him the sole sailor aboard, the RCMP launch passed under Lions Gate Bridge to leave Vancouver harbor for English Bay and the strait beyond. Rush-hour traffic hummed on the overhead span. The Point Atkinson lighthouse, near DeClercq's wooded home, swept the waves to the right, slipping astern as the boat rounded the cliff face of Point Grey above battered Wreck Beach. Nick heard the sea surging in to drown the shore. Waves were whipped into whitecaps as he bobbed down the wide, onyx, lunar-swathed strait, and by the time he crossed the border south of the mouth of the Fraser River, the crests and dips were undulating like a nautical roller coaster. Strung north to south along the inland shore of Vancouver Island were three of the Gulf Islands Nick policed: Galiano, Mayne and Saturna. The launch skirted them in reverse order to how the wolf-dog had island-hopped and continued on past clusters of lights on the mainland of Washington State, the split jurisdiction the result of a kink in the borderline. Ebbtide Island was the northernmost of the American San Juans, and farther ahead, beyond Boundary Pass and President Channel, rose the black hump of Mount Constitution, on Orcas Island. South along the inland arm of the inverted U that made up that largest island of the archipelago, the boat rode the seesaw waves like a bucking bronco. Finally, as Nick was on the verge of seasickness himself, the end of his voyage materialized in the moonlit breakers that rolled ashore near the southern tip.

The *Islomania* was moored to one side of a float that extended out into the cove from the waterfront farm. Nick approached to within a hundred feet of the other boat, then slowed the throttle so he could leave the wheel long enough to drop both rubber fenders over the rail. Ready to dock, he nosed in parallel to the vacant side of the float, and when the transom was even with its offshore end, he pulled the transmission lever back into reverse. Goosing the engine to halt the forward motion, the Mountie let the waves ease in the launch.

Nick leaped from the cockpit to secure the stern line to a float cleat. As he moved along the slippery planks toward the bow to grab the painter off the foredeck and lash it too, the lights of the farmhouse porch uphill flared in the night. The front door opened to release two silhouettes, one about half the height of the other. Flashlight beams dueled like swords as they came down the path, past the garden that was hibernating behind a deer fence, then across the slope of seaside lawn to the pebble cove. Having tied the spring line to moor his boat, Nick turned off both the ignition and the battery before raising the leg to protect it from low tide. Side by side, the boats heaved up and down like a teeter-totter.

Clomp, clomp, clomp . . .

The pint-sized silhouette came down the gangplank to the float first, arriving as Nick climbed out of the cockpit for the last time. With her arms extended like a tightrope walker's with a flashlight in one hand, the young girl approached him, one foot placed carefully in front of the other so she could keep her balance within a single plank.

"Who goes there?"

"Me," said the six-year-old.

"Who's 'me'?" Nick demanded. "Identify yourself, or you'll walk the plank."

"I *am* walking the plank."

"Avast, ye hearty. So you *are.*"

"It's *me,*" said Becky, swinging the flashlight up to illuminate her impish face. By the glow of the beam Nick saw her unruly russet hair and the sly, mischievous eyes of a practical joker.

Just like her father, Jenna had told him.

"So it *is!*" Nick confirmed. "I never would have guessed. You're lucky I'm not a pirate who kidnaps little girls."

Becky shook her head. "*You're* lucky you're not a pirate, Captain Hook."

"Oh? Why's that?"

"'Cause the moment you put a hand on me, I'd squash your balls like grapes."

So sudden was her kick that Nick had no time to react, no time to avoid a boot that would have bounced his testicles off his chin had the child not pulled her assault at the last instant. An inch or two more and he wouldn't be doing what he hoped to be doing with her mom later that night.

Becky's grounded foot slipped on the sea-splashed plank. She did a pratfall onto her butt. Nick reached down and grabbed her coat to pull the miniature Bruce Lee to her feet as the taller silhouette descended the gangplank to the float.

"Are you molesting my kid?"

"This lethal weapon?" said Nick. "Give me a break, Jenna. She's molesting *me!*"

"Choke! Gouge! Smash!" Becky exclaimed, bunching her fists to pummel the air between her and him. "Want to see how ya break bones, Captain Hook?"

"Not *mine!*" Nick said, holding her at arm's length. He glanced at Becky's mom. "What's going on?" he asked.

"*Krav maga,*" Jenna Bond replied.

"I doubted you were coming."

"At times, so did I. The sea turned rough after I was under way. It got dicey with some of those waves."

"You should have called."

"Then you'd have warned me off. I'd have taken your advice, and I wouldn't be here."

"I'd rather have you alive."

"Aren't you flattered that a novice sailor like me would brave the high seas to gaze upon your face?"

"How gallant," she said, clasping the flashlight to her breast and batting her eyes.

"Call me Ulysses, entranced by your siren call."

"I don't hear a siren," Becky said from below, one hand cupped to her eavesdropping ear.

"A siren is a sea nymph," Jenna explained to her, "who lures men ashore with her beautiful song."

"He hasn't heard you sing, has he, Mom?"

"Shhhh," said Jenna.

Becky grimaced up at Nick. "She sings along with Shania Twain. Mom's a pain in the ear."

"Actually, Becs, it's *you* I came to see."

"Fibber," said the six-year-old. "You only came to be with my mom."

"You did, didn't you? Shame on you," Jenna chastised.

Nick stared at his shoes.

"Take him away, Smee."

"Come on, Captain Hook."

Becky took the marauding pirate by his artificial hand and led him up the dark path toward the beckoning warmth of the farmhouse perched above the strait. Along the way, Nick glanced back to find Jenna smiling at him, her grin that of a co-conspirator of the hanky-panky kind. With her cobalt eyes in an angular face devoid of makeup, sand-colored hair cut short and a figure that was athletically trim, she reminded Nick of a beached mermaid from Atlantis. No better description of Jenna could be found than this passage from Lawrence Durrell, which Nick had discovered pasted inside the captain's log of the *Islomania,* moored in the cove below. The opening lines of *Reflections on a Marine Venus:*

> Somewhere among the notebooks of Gideon I once found a list of diseases as yet unclassified by medical science, and among these there occurred the word *Islomania,* which was described as a rare but by no means unknown affliction of spirit. There are people, Gideon used to say, by way of explanation, who find islands somehow irresistible. The mere knowledge that they are on an island, a little world surrounded by the sea, fills them with an indescribable intoxication. These born "islomanes," he used to add, are the direct descendants of the Atlanteans, and it is towards the lost Atlantis that their subconscious yearns throughout their island life.

Islomania had brought Nick and Jenna together. An affliction that struck in varying degrees, it had first drawn Jenna back to Orcas Island from Seattle. Like many rural kids, she had found the Rock too small in her teens. After attending college on the mainland, she had opted for city life as a special agent with the FBI, and there she had met her husband, Don, who worked for the DEA.

Colombian machismo had destroyed any hope that the two would live happily ever after. A run-of-the-mill drug bust had gone horribly awry, and coked-up enforcers for the Bogota cartel had kidnapped Don and cut him apart piece by piece in revenge. Though his body was never found, a recording of the grisly torture session was sent to the Drug Enforcement Administration.

Enjoy this, gringos.

A week later, Jenna had learned she was pregnant. She was faced with the option of working and raising the child alone, as a single mom mired in urban grunge, or going home to help her own widowed mother maintain the island farm. A no-brainer that, she had returned to the tranquil vistas, salt air and breathing space of her childhood memories, forsaking the Bureau to become a hick cop like her dearly departed dad. Sheriff Hank Bond had been a no-nonsense cop. Twelve times in a row, the good folks of San Juan County had elected him to protect their islands. Felled by a stroke while sitting at his office desk, Jenna's dad had died with his boots on in the best Wild West tradition. Now in plainclothes, she was *the* detective for the San Juan County sheriff.

Her wounds had been healing . . .

Until Mephisto.

Nick's islomania was a fantasy. Having lived in the city all of his life, Nick had an idyllic illusion of Gulf Island living. Arguably the most beautiful part of North America, the islands off the West Coast north and south of the border were in the running to become a World Heritage Site. Eagles by the dozen circled above, and pods of killer whales made the straits and channels home. "Love thy neighbor" was the social code—or so Nick thought in his dreamy state—as carefree kids played with puppies and kittens among the towering Douglas firs and the psychedelic arbutuses. So when Gill Macbeth had broken Nick's heart by ending their ill-fated love affair, the corporal had abandoned the elite ranks of Special X and followed his fantasy rainbow to its island pot of gold.

Poof! had gone his illusions.

Reality bites.

For what he had encountered in the Gulf Islands was the same shit a cop scrapes from his shoe in the city. "Love thy neighbor?" *Ha!* "Spite thy neighbor" was more like it. Island politics was a war zone fought by those on the right wing, who wished to blacktop the land from beach to beach, and those on the left wing, who freaked out at the sight of a bent blade of grass. Community meetings were free-for-alls in which the goal was to see who could do the most trampling on opponents' democratic rights. Arranging a barbecue took the same skill as navigating a minefield, for who refused to speak to whom changed by the moment. Illicit liaisons, interbreeding, wife-swapping and other scandals kept the grapevine humming . . . or so it had seemed to Nick as he surveyed that tarnished paradise from amid the shattered shards of his rose-tinted glasses.

Policing petty squabbles . . .

Until Mephisto.

A psycho whose islomania was of the madder-than-a-shithouse-rat kind.

Based on Shipwreck Island in America's San Juans, Mephisto had embarked on a madcap scheme to find a treasure trove. Why did he want it? No one really knew. But nothing gets in the way of an obsessive-compulsive megalomaniac whose fixation has locked on something he needs. So when Mephisto failed to find the hoard himself, he kidnapped Nick as a means to force DeClercq to find it for him. By the time that ordeal was over, Nick had lost a hand and an ear and Jenna had been gang-raped by Mephisto's thugs.

Now they had each other.

To heal each other's wounds.

Imi Lichtenfeld was born in Budapest in 1910. He was the son of a circus strongman turned cop who also ran the Hercules gym. Raised in Bratislava, Slovakia, Imi was a natural athlete at boxing, wrestling and gymnastics. And he was Jewish.

The 1930s saw the Nazis on the rise. Fascist hooligans roamed the streets of Europe's Jewish areas, and the best protection their Bratislava prey had was Imi Lichtenfeld. He quickly learned the difference between sport and street fighting, for when you are up against anti-Semitic goons whose not-so-secret agenda is to fashion your skin into lampshades and your body fat into soap, you don't fight back according to the Queensberry Rules.

In such a confrontation, *anything* goes.

What Imi created was *krav maga*. A Hebrew term, it translates as "contact combat." Adopting defenses from aikido, karate, boxing, judo, ju-jitsu and lesser-known martial arts, Imi distinguished his system from older ones by incorporating no rules. If it's illegal in boxing, it's okay in *krav maga*.

The underlying theory is as basic as can be: when you are fighting for your life, you must be as fast and as fierce as a wild animal. Because the *only* goal is to save yourself, groin kicks, elbow jabs, head butts, hair pulling, eye gouging and biting are acceptable. And—if it's necessary to do the job—these are the vulnerable points where a well-placed blow will kill your adversary.

Krav maga is brutally effective.

Hitler's conquest of Europe forced Imi to flee his homeland on the last emigrant ship to escape from the Nazis' clutches. His odyssey began on an old riverboat called the *Pentcho* and finally ended when he set foot in Palestine, where he joined the Haganah, an underground force dedicated to founding the state of Israel.

To accomplish that, *krav maga* helped.

The state of Israel was born in 1948. It was on the defensive from the get-go, so Imi was assigned the task of instructing the Israeli defense forces in how to use *krav maga* to maintain that independence. So good was his self-defense system at subduing attackers that it remained a state secret until 1964.

"There's an old man on Orcas," Jenna explained as the three made their way up the path toward the inviting farmhouse, "who learned *krav maga* in the Mossad."

"A spook?"

The detective nodded. "Israeli intelligence deployed him to kidnap Adolf Eichmann from Argentina."

"He must be good."

"He is. He was a friend of my dad's. I knew him as a girl, but not about *krav maga*."

"Leo's showing us how to protect ourselves," said Becky.

"History *won't* repeat itself," Jenna added. "Not for me. And not for my daughter."

"How does *krav maga* work?"

"The emphasis is on instinctive movements. Unlike classic martial arts, there are no *katas*—specific sequences—that must be followed. The technique builds on a person's natural 'fight or flight' reactions, teaching her how to channel them into a lethal response."

"I'm a warrior spirit," Becky declared.

"I'll bet you are," replied Nick.

"You swiftly build up a repertoire of simple but effective defenses to headlocks, throat chokes, bear hugs, shirt holds and arm grabs," Jenna continued. "You learn how to punch from boxing and how to kick from Asia, then after that it's no holds barred. The key to fending off attack is your ability to adapt to new threats through improvisation. Use whatever you've got and whatever's at hand. All the body's natural defenses and any object you can convert into a weapon. Low kicks to the knee and to the groin are encouraged."

"So I learned," Nick said, scowling down at Becky.

That not-so-innocent face beamed up at him in the moonlight.

"Want to see how I do the spinning ball-buster, Captain Hook?"

"Not right now, honey."

"Later?" Becky asked.

"It's geared toward *molesters,*" Jenna added slyly.

Nick flashed her a V-fingered peace sign. *"Shalom!"* he said.

The smell of smoke from the wood-burning stove grew stronger as they approached the farmhouse. Up the stone steps to the pillared porch they climbed, angling left along the veranda of the white-and-yellow two-story, past bay windows beneath gabled dormers in the shake roof overhead. Footwear is always removed at a farmhouse door, so they slipped out of their muddy boots on this side of the threshold and entered the rustic interior in stockinged feet.

Nick stepped back in time.

The heart of a farmhouse in spring is the wood-burning stove. The blaze behind the glass portal seemed to pulse, beating out a bronze glow in waves of warmth. They shucked their jackets at the door and hung them on hooks, then crossed to the rocking chairs waiting by the fire. Could a home be cozier than this? Rockwell prints hung on the knotty pine walls. Ruffled curtains cinched back with bows flanked the window seats. Braided rugs created plush oval islands on the blond fir floor. Wild West weapons—a Colt Peacemaker .45, a Buntline Special, a LeMat revolver—were mounted here and there. Jenna's mom sat in what was once Hank Bond's comfy reading chair, a cup of tea beside her on a trunk branded by the irons of ranches around Washington State. In granny glasses, she was reading *Harrowsmith Country Life.*

Nick had bought her a subscription to the magazine.

The Mountie sniffed the air. "What's cooking?" he asked.

"Country meatloaf," said Jenna's mom. "With mushroom gravy.

And apple pie."

Yes, thought the bachelor. I could get *used* to this.

A cook, he was not.

"Let's have some music," Jenna suggested, veering away from the rocking chairs toward the stereo. A functional dresser, she preferred the haberdashery of men—panted business suits for work and flannel shirts with overalls to groom the farm—instead of the frills and frippery loved by fashion addicts. When she was expecting Nick, however, she always wore a dress, and he found its clinging, down-home simplicity as sexy as could be.

But hey, Jenna would look good in a gunny sack.

The country queen punched a button on the CD player.

"Let's go, girls," Shania Twain beckoned from the speakers, as an intro to what Becky called her "hiccup song."

"Uh-oh," said Becky. "Mom's gonna sing!"

Some women sing with their voices. Some women sing with their bodies. And what you lose on the swings, you make up on the merry-go-round.

They made love in the brass bed in which Jenna was born, upstairs in the gabled room in which she had entered life. The passion they both put into the act was fueled by Mephisto's cruelty, for in carving a hand and an ear from Nick, the sadist had reduced him to less than a man, and in sicking the Druids on Jenna, he had crippled her comfort and confidence in her sexuality. Each was out to prove to the other that he or she had the courage to overcome the psychic damage that psychopath had done, and at the same time to let his or her partner know that he or she was in no way diminished in the eyes of his or her lover.

Sex as release.

Sex as therapy.

For the only natural defense the human body has to remembering the traumas done to it in the past is that exquisite moment of forgetfulness that comes with orgasm.

Exhausted, they fell asleep in each other's embrace.

The dream came to Nick in the darkest depths of the night.

"Hello, lover. Remember me?"

Donella's silhouette is framed by the flickering flames of torches burning in brackets across the underground passage behind her. Wind along the tunnel keens like bagpipes from the grave, animating her wild hair into Medusa snakes and plastering the folds of her tartan to the curves of her stripper's body. The light seems to follow the Devil Woman into the dungeon. There, he blinks against its blinding glare before it creeps across the front of her as she turns toward his cowering shadow chained to the wall. Her face is dyed blue. One breast is bare. Tattoos whirl out and back from its nipple. Her other breast is hidden by pleats draped over one shoulder and gathered at her waist to fashion a Highland kilt. As short as a miniskirt, the kilt ends high on the thigh, below which her long legs straddle him like the Colossus of Rhodes.

"I need a piece of you."

Another voice at the door.

And suddenly the torchlight burns brighter in his cell.

Amid a clink of chains from the ties that lash him spread-eagled to the angle of wall and floor, he turns to see the passage beyond ablaze with flames from hell, and standing in the midst of the fire and brimstone looms the Devil himself.

Mephisto!

The sadist who uses other sadists to get his kinky kicks.

His black hair is slicked back from a widow's peak that matches the satyr's V of his Vandyke beard. The flickering light dancing across his inverted pyramid of a face sinks his dark eyes deep in their orbs like the fathomless pits of a skull. Not a flaw of fat mars the perfection of his physique, draped in the tartan of the Campbell clan. Gripped in one fist beside his kilt is a keen-edged dirk, and he enters the dungeon to pass it to his statuesque Highland queen.

"Do it!" Mephisto orders.

Donella slips the pleats from her shoulder so they can fall to her waist, then she unclasps the silver pin in her kilt and casts aside the tartan. One long leg, then the next, steps into the wide V formed by lashing his ankles to distant rings. Squatting, the sadist uses the dagger to cut away his pants, clenching the dirk in her teeth like a pirate as she grabs his cock and balls. One hand yanks his manhood taut like a rubber band while the other retrieves the blade from her mouth to begin the slow . . . rhythmic. . . sawing . . . back . . . and . . . forth . . .

Nick jerked awake in Jenna's brass bed.

It took him a moment to catch his fugitive breath. When he heard the word *no* fill the absolute silence of the room, he thought it was an echo from his fading nightmare, until he realized that it wasn't *his* cry of distress.

"No!" Jenna gasped again in her sleep . . .

She is Little Red Riding Hood and the woods are full of wolves. Is she on her way to Granny's house like in Becky's storybook? No, not unless Granny's house is a lighthouse on Madrona Island. A lighthouse she can no longer see because ocean fog is creeping in to smother her like a shroud.

Now it is pitch black as premature night falls, the only light that of the beacon that sweeps through the skeletal trees of the forest. And each time the beam catches the eyes of the wolves, the pack has closed in tighter.

Shewwww! *goes the beam.*

Pitch black again.

The eyes of the wolves begin to fade from the spaces between the trees.

Then . . .

"Get her!" orders a disembodied voice.

Now they are upon her in the dead black night, the foul breath of each wolf breathing down her neck as they shove her face into the dirt and strip her below the waist.

"No!" she cries.

But crying is no use.

Boots, socks, jeans and underwear are thrown aside.

Shewwww! *comes the beam, which freezes on her, and she finds herself staring down a hole that sinks to hell, and climbing up the hole is a demon of a man—Svengali, Casanova and Don Juan fused in one—who would be devilishly handsome if it weren't for the utter perversion in his glare.*

He reaches up . . .

And grabs her cheeks in a vise-like grip . . .

And says to her, "Keep staring at me while they fuck the ass off you."

"No!" she cries again.

"Jenna, wake up."

"No . . ."

"Jenna!" Nick coaxed, shaking her from sleep.

Her eyes flew open to discover it was dawn, and Jenna snapped to consciousness to find herself gazing up from her pillow at Nick Craven's face.

"Mephisto," she whispered.

"Me too, Jen."

"He's *alive,* Nick."

The Mountie shook his head. "Only in our nightmares."

They were still in bed when the phone rang. The caller identified by number display was the sheriff, ringing from home. Reaching for the receiver, Jenna answered it, "Bond."

After she hung up, the San Juan County detective told the Mountie she had to go. A corpse had been found on Lopez Island. "This one's bizarre, Nick."

"Bizarre in what way?"

It had been a while since they had last talked shop. As a rule, they both preferred to leave the office behind. So Jenna had not heard about the corpse he'd found on Galiano. After Nick had heard the details relayed in the sheriff's call, he said to her, "If you don't mind, I think I'll tag along."

Cruising up Rosario Strait on his way back to Ebbtide Island from his pre-dawn undertaking for the Director, the Undertaker slowed the throttle as he passed Jenna Bond's farm. From inside the wheelhouse, he could see cast-off activity on the float jutting out into the cove. Focusing his binoculars on the *Islomania,* the killer was able to spy on the woman as she scaled the cabin ladder to the command bridge. Like Superman, with X-ray vision supplied by his rabid imagination, the Undertaker ogled her breasts beneath the waterproof jacket, yearning to add her nipples to his growing collection.

So as not to arouse suspicion, he continued on, but before the boat passed out of eyeshot of the sleepy farm, the Director's henchman swept the lenses uphill to the farmhouse dormers.

There's our guinea pig, he thought.

BED OF NAILS

Vancouver

The Plains Cree didn't know quite what to make of his new-found friends. Ghost Keeper had been forced to deal with thousands of racists like Mad Dog Rabidowski in his life, for what African Americans were to the backwoods mentality of the South, Native Canadians were to the North. If his people had been conquered like Indians were in the States, then at least they'd be in the same position as the French in Quebec. But what made it worse was the fact that their plight had resulted not from defeat in battle, but instead from negotiating treaties in good faith with whites whom they considered to be friends.

Whites in red tunics.

In exchange for the thousand miles of prairie that the Cree had held in sacred trust for future generations for at least ten thousand years, they got in return the demeaning misery of compact reservations, on one of which Ghost Keeper was born in a one-room shack. An Indian reservation is a depressing place. Cut off from the resources that had sustained their ancestors since the ice age and denied self-government by patronizing whites, the Cree were forced to eke out an existence any way they could, and that meant relying on aboriginal hunting rights, which brought them into conflict with backwoods whites.

Whites like Rabidowski.

The son of a Yukon trapper raised in the North, the Mad Dog had heard it all from his old man. "Reserves don't pay taxes, so Indians get a free ride. Handouts from the government are squandered by their chiefs. Most of the adults are drunks, and most of their kids sniff gas. And when the red niggers do get off their asses to do something, what they do is poach game that belongs to us. They use their supposed 'hunting rights' to steal money from *our* pockets."

But not Ghost Keeper.

Insp. Bob George was anything but that stereotype. True, the Cree had grown up on a troubled, ground-down reserve, but he wasn't part of the problem, he became part of the cure. Raised by his mom in accordance with the tradition of his people, he had ventured out alone as a boy to survive on his wits in the threatening northern woods, and there he had found the supernatural spirit that would guide him through life and beyond. His skill at spotting and tracking animal spoor to bring down his next meal had laid the groundwork for him to become the best forensic detective in all of Canada.

Canadian women got the right to vote in 1918. As incredible as it seems today, Natives didn't get that right until 1960. Instead, they were governed by the Department of Indian Affairs, which decreed that a Native couldn't remain a Native if he was college-educated, became a clergyman or a lawyer, or got the right to vote. An Indian with the right to vote would be a full-fledged citizen of Canada, which meant he would be deemed to be civilized, and consequently he could not be an Indian.

How's that for bullshit?

1960!

And those who enforced that draconian law were *white* mounted policemen.

When the "special constable" program was introduced on reservations—a program for Native quasi-cops to police their own people—Ghost Keeper was the first to sign up, if only because he wanted to give the Natives some long overdue racial respect. So adept was the Cree at tracking down wrongdoers that it was inevitable he would be headhunted by DeClercq, for the chief was a military tactician who staffed Special X with the *best* of the best in every expertise.

Including the Mad Dog.

Mad Dog Rabidowski was a diamond in the rough. A sexist and a racist, he lived to kill: hunting grizzly bears at Kakwa River, wolf packs near Tweedsmuir Park, elk on Pink Mountain and armed punks on the mean streets of the big bad city. He had joined the Mounted to be in the thick of the action, and the left sleeve cuff of his red-serge tunic boasted badges for distinguished marksmanship: a crown atop crossed revolvers above a crown atop crossed rifles. So long as the Mad Dog repressed his biases and didn't compromise Special X, DeClercq was willing to overlook his boorishness in order to have the benefit of his unique talent. When there's a malignant cancer to remove, you use the sharpest knife.

So that's how Ghost Keeper and the Mad Dog met.

Both made Special X.

The tribes to the east of the Rockies were fucked over by treaties, but at least there were pieces of paper legalizing the fraud. The tribes to the west of the Rockies fared even worse. Since they were denigrated as savages with no concept of deeds to property, their ancestral realms were hijacked without the bother of treaties. To this day that loot has not been returned, a fact that recently prompted some "terrorists" to seize back what had been stolen from them, which brought in the Mounties to retrieve it for the "lawful" owner, which in turn prompted an armed standoff that pitted Ghost Keeper against Native renegades entrenched in a sacred sun dance circle in the snowy woods up north. During a raging gun battle with the Mounted's emergency response team, the Mad Dog would have died if not for a deadeye covering shot by the Cree.

The upshot of which was that Rabidowski faced a moral dilemma.

He owed his life to the aim of a "red nigger."

Rabidowski saw himself as a man's man. He was a "Hemingway hero" in his view of the world, though others interpreted that phrase as being synonymous with an "overgrown Boy Scout." We all admire role models of one sort or another, and the Mad Dog's holy triumvirate was Charles Bronson, Harvey Keitel and Arnold Schwarzenegger. In need of spiritual guidance to resolve his ethical conundrum, the Mad Dog took to heart a media comment made by Big Arnie. When he was asked about his work to raise funds for Simon Wiesenthal's Holocaust Studies Center in Vienna, the Austrian-born actor had responded, "I had to fight through my own prejudice, because I came over here with prejudice, and by getting involved in those issues I got rid of it. Even if you have it, you can get rid of it. You can change."

Hey, if it works, it works . . .

And the Mad Dog was ready for an epiphany.

There was a time when most recruits were like Rabidowski. Back when the myth of the Mounted was forged, those who donned red serge were hard-knuckled, sharp-shooting action men, sent out alone to brave the harshest climate on earth as pioneers dispatched to police the last frontier. In an age when modern Mounties were recruited from universities, the Mad Dog thought he was the last of a dying breed until he was forced to work with the Cree.

Here was a man whose survival skills were honed as sharp as his, and who loved the awesome wilds of the Great White North as much as he did.

The Lone Ranger had found his Tonto.

And to make sure everyone knew what a truly repentant sinner he was, the Mad Dog had asked the Cree to be the best man at his wedding to Brittany Starr.

It was enough to make you feel warm and fuzzy all over.

"Inspector George," Ghost Keeper said, grabbing the ringing phone as he was about to leave Special X for the day.

"Hi. It's Brittany."

"You caught me going out the door."

"Dinner date?"

"I wish. Nothing like that. I'm off to my sweat lodge to wash the grime of this job away."

"By yourself?"

"Afraid so."

"I hear I was almost a widow."

"Who told you that?"

"Ed says a rabid wolf-dog would have torn out his throat if not for your backwoods aim."

"Ed exaggerates."

"I doubt that, Bob. I never know what to call you. Which do you prefer?"

"Whatever makes you comfortable. Doesn't matter to me."

"From now on, it'll be Ghost Keeper. That's out of the ordinary. It suits you."

The inspector was thinking Brittany Starr was out of the ordinary too. His mind's eye saw her as he had seen her that first time at the Red Serge Ball: with hair bleached blonde and a scoop-necked gown clinging to every dip and curve; with no panty line to spoil the sheath that was slit to her waist; with lips and nails painted the same hue as the Mad Dog's scarlet tunic. Trust Rabidowski to bring a hooker to the foremost formal of the force's social season.

"Thank you, G.K."

"Think nothing of it."

"Sleeping alone for the rest of my life means more than nothing to me."

It was hard to imagine Brittany sleeping alone.

"Ed says you have this place up the mountain where you go to get away from it all. He says you have a teepee and a sweat lodge and stuff like that. If you're going to the sweat lodge, will your dinner be a lonely weenie roast around a fire?"

"Sort of," he said, laughing.

"Instead, why don't you come home with Ed for a feast?"

"There's no need for that."

"It's the least I can do."

"I'm sure Ed would rather have a quiet dinner with you."

"If not for *you,* G.K., Eddy would *be* dinner for squirmy things in a grave. Besides, it won't hurt him to go without it once after work. He'll appreciate me even more tomorrow night."

Ghost Keeper stared at the phone.

You dirty dog, he thought.

Five minutes later, the Mad Dog rapped his knuckles on the door to the Cree's office. The sergeant was a brawny hulk who almost filled the doorframe, with muscles on his muscles like a steroid junky. His hair was jet black, as were his eyebrows and his droopy mustache, out of which glared the piercing stare of gun-barrel blue eyes. Spot him coming toward you on a deserted street at night and anyone with common sense would cross to the other side.

"I hope you're hungry. Brit's become quite the cook. It should be a meal you'll remember," said Rabidowski.

"I'm honored."

"Naw. The honor's mine."

As they were descending the staircase from the second floor of the Tudor building that housed Special X, a special-delivery courier came flying through the front door to hand a parcel to the security commissionaire. "Sir," said the elderly man as the inspector and the sergeant reached the foot of the stairs. "This just arrived from the FBI in Houston, Texas. It's for you or Inspector Chandler."

Ghost Keeper accepted the parcel and tore off the access strip.

A video cassette wrapped in a letter fell out into his hand.

"You can use my VCR," the Mad Dog said.

The letter from the FBI advised the pair of inspectors who jointly ran Operations at Special X that a search of the TV studio of the Texas televangelist who had commissioned the made-to-order video titled *Meat Grinder* from Snuff Lib had turned up this hellish treasure from a hidey-hole beneath the floor.

The cassette was stamped Copy.

Ghost Keeper turned it sideways to read the label on the spine.

Skull Fucker, it read.

North Vancouver

A white picket fence enclosed the front yard of Rabidowski's new home. The small bungalow painted sage green exuded the good taste of Martha Stewart's show. Dressed like a hostess with the mostest, Brittany greeted them in the front hall with a tray of drinks and tasty hors d'oeuvres. In decor, the interior was as far from a whorehouse as could be. On the mantel above the welcoming blaze behind a filigreed screen was the eagle feather Ghost Keeper had given the newlyweds at their reception. The curtains, the pillows scattered about for comfort and relaxation, the rich fabrics draped over hard surfaces to add warmth and ambiance: wherever Ghost Keeper looked, there were homey touches sewn by hand.

"I'm still working on it," Brittany said as her guest wandered about. And when he stopped at a bookshelf lined with a minimal collection of books, she added, "I'm making up for the education I never had. Each year I'm going to read the shortlist for the Booker Prize."

The Cree got the picture.

Brittany Starr had quit school at fifteen to turn Lolita tricks. She'd met the Mad Dog when he pulled her over for suspected drunk driving, only to find she was late for work stripping in a bar and was trying to change into her G-string as she drove. The Mad Dog was no Richard Gere and Brit was no Julia Roberts, but theirs was a Cinderella story akin to *Pretty Woman.* She had never been to a formal dance, and he was looking for a date who would cause a stir, so off they went on a shopping spree to buy an eye-popping dress, and . . .well, the rest, as they say, was who'da-thunk-it history.

Brit had retired from hooking to devote all of her sexual repertoire to plastering a perpetual smirk onto the Mad Dog's face. All the males at Special X feared his sex life was an exquisite wet dream compared with theirs, and that gave Rabidowski an envied status. Meanwhile, Brit spent each day indulging in whatever whims caught her fancy, learning how to cook like a gourmet and how to turn her home into a haven of domestic bliss. With no demands on her time, she felt as if she were living the life of pampered royalty, and this feeling was enhanced by the fact that the Mad Dog treated her like a queen. In the process, the diamond in the rough was being polished, so when all the factors were added up in this improbable marriage, it was hard to fathom who got the best part of the deal.

A Hollywood ending, with not a dry eye in the house.

The meal, as the Mad Dog had predicted, was one the Cree would remember. They sat around the multi-course feast like Hawkeye and Chingachgook, relating tales of hair-raising adventures in the wilds as Brit provided oohs and aahs to egg them on. Soon they were plotting a joint venture armed with bows and arrows into the Headless Valley of the Nahanni next summer, and as Brit prepared dessert and coffee in the kitchen, they carried that discussion on to the TV room so Rabidowski could feed the videotape sent from Texas into the VCR.

Skull Fucker.

The tape lived up to its horrific title.

Literally.

As a hooker, Brittany Starr thought she knew every sexual act, but so shocked was she by Woody Bone's perverted antics onscreen that as she came into the TV room with a serving tray, she gasped and sent the china crashing to the floor.

The Mad Dog jabbed the clicker.

The screen condensed to black.

And while the sergeant helped his wife gather up the mess, Ghost Keeper punched Zinc Chandler's number into his cellphone.

Ring . . .

Ring . . .

Ring . . .

Ring . . .

Zinc's machine answered.

Vancouver

Tortured by the pain in his head and his heart, Zinc Chandler was in the TV room of his home, contemplating his gun while in the grip of the curse of *The Mummy,* when the phone rang. In no condition to deal with a frivolous conversation, he let his answering machine advise the caller to record a message.

"Zinc, it's urgent. Pick up if you're there."

The voice was Ghost Keeper's. Chandler reached for the phone. "What's up?" he asked, putting down his gun.

"That porn king the Bureau thinks is behind Snuff Lib."

"Wolfe Capp?"

"Yeah."

"The Texas allegation?"

"It's no allegation. Snuff Lib's the *real* thing. They tossed the TV studio of that Houston televangelist who cracked, the one who confessed to ordering a made-to-measure snuff by Woody Bone. What the Bureau turned up was a video called *Skull Fucker*. It probably inspired the nut to order one of his own. The Suits shipped us a copy by courier. Ed and I just watched it. What a horror show. I tell you, Zinc, it's the sickest thing I've ever seen."

"What's got you worried?"

"The cutbacks affecting O. How many Watchers did O put on the Wolfe's lair?"

"A single team eyeing the street door to see who comes and goes."

"And the back door?"

"It's hidden. We don't know where it is. O's trying to free up some Watchers to find and cover it."

"You've seen the team reports?"

"Yes."

"Anything suspicious?"

"A U/M named Fletcher. ViCLAS is checking him."

"What about a girl?"

"Porn queens are in and out of the Wolfe's lair constantly. Wolfe Capp operates the Internet Spider's Web."

"I mean a young girl."

"There was one yesterday. About sixteen. She was seen arriving and was photographed as she left. O says she was too flat-chested to make it in the biz."

"*Skull Fucker* proves Snuff Lib exists. The Suits suspect it's more than just linked to the Spider's Web. They think that the Spider's Web fronts Snuff Lib, and that both operate out of the Yaletown building owned by Wolfe Capp. The Houston televangelist says he ordered a video of a teen being snuffed. If the Suits are right that Wolfe Capp shoots the Snuff Lib orders in Yaletown, what if the girl seen by O returned by the *back* door and the porn king snuffed her while we were watching him?"

"You want to take him down?"

"Yes. Tonight. I'll get the telewarrant from a judge. The Mad Dog and I will meet you outside."

So that's why the near suicide now found himself racking his gun again, only this time in the company of the Mad Dog and the Cree, as the three Mounties readied themselves to cross the street to the front door of the Wolfe's lair. After dark, Yaletown transformed into a hookers' stroll, where painted ladies of the night climbed in and out of prowling cars. By dawn, however, all were tucked away in various beds, so the cops had a deserted backdrop for their raid.

As senior inspector, Zinc was in command.

He was going in.

With the specialists.

The thirty-inch-long cylinder weighed thirty-five pounds. When it was swung in a roundhouse arc by semiflex grips, the Ram-It hit the lock with a kinetic smash of fourteen thousand pounds, with extra "pop" added by Ghost Keeper's follow-through. The single-man battering ram was too heavy a hitter for the wooden door, which burst open in a spray of splinters. Not for nothing is a Ram-It called the key to the city.

The Mounties were in.

"Police! Police! Search warrant!" bellowed Rabidowski, the first cop through the fractured frame. His words got lost in the insistent clang of an alarm that preceded him along a hollow hall inside to alert any bad guys ahead that a raid was under way. The primary weapon slung around the Mad Dog's neck was a Heckler & Koch MP5 submachine gun. With thirty rounds in the mag in front of the trigger guard, it could mow down any armed resistance mounted against the attack.

The Mad Dog was outfitted entirely in black. The Mounted's emergency response team had recently switched to black from blue for urban assaults. On his head, he wore a balaclava rolled up into a cap instead of pulled down like a terrorist's mask. His underlying uniform was a combat jacket over a turtleneck and combat pants with cargo pockets tucked into heavy-duty army boots. The tactical armored vest he wore over that was known to ERT cops as "the beast." POLICE RCMP blared white letters on a pull-down flap; this flap was surrounded by Velcro pockets that could be repositioned according to the firepower required. The pockets held tear gas, pepper spray, extra clips and stun grenades. The secondary weapon holstered at the Mad Dog's hip was a SIG/Sauer P226 nine-millimeter pistol.

Flanking him for backup were a pair of Smith nines in the fists of Ghost Keeper and Zinc Chandler, both of whom were hot on the Mad Dog's heels. Night-vision goggles aren't strapped on unless the assault team controls all lights, for everyone could be blinded by a bad guy suddenly switching one on. To see as they rushed forward along the dark hall, the cops pressed pressure plates on their weapons to activate the Surefire bulbs affixed beneath the barrels. Sharp beams swept through the pitch black to guide them.

The Wolfe's lair was wired for such an assault. Not only had the break-in set off the alarm, but shorting the circuit had also automatically secured every door between the cops' point of entry and the porn king's office. The hall that led to Capp's inner sanctum was a maze with almost as many twists and turns as the garden maze at Hampton Court, the royal palace upriver from the Thames estate from which Sleeping Beauty had been heisted. It took as much effort to breach each internal barrier as it did to pound in the front door, and by the time the Ram-It popped the lock on the business office from which the ex-lawyer spun the Spider's Web—and allegedly operated Snuff Lib—anyone in the building who had heard the alarm go off could have fled to California and been enjoying the rides at Disneyland.

"Police! Search warrant! Freeze!" the Mad Dog hollered again as he stormed into darkness lit by a bright curtained window that looked in on an adjacent, fully illuminated room with an empty cage in the center of the floor.

Here, there, everywhere, the three Surefire beams darted around in the gloom, until one of them spotted the corpse lying face down in a pool of blood beneath the curtained window.

"We got a stiff."

"I see him."

"Here comes the light."

Instantly, the murky office came to life as Chandler hit the switch on the wall beside the busted door.

"Anything?"

"Nothing."

"Check the cage room."

The door through the windowed wall was in the far corner, behind a TV and a VCR on a wheeled table. The meat-grinder cover from *Hustler* was framed beside the jamb. With the H&K gripped waist-high and ready to spit if need be, and with the Cree at his back for covering fire, the Mad Dog wrenched the door and blitzkrieged in.

Chandler sidestepped the corpse in the pool and watched through the blood-spattered window. On completing his search of the room, the Mad Dog turned to face the one-way glass and shrugged. He looked like a soldier geared up to fight, but one who had somehow missed the battle.

"Capp?" Ghost Keeper asked, joining Zinc over the body.

"Yeah," replied Chandler. "Probably iced with that." He indicated a stiletto lying in the sticky pool.

"When?"

"A while ago. The stiff's cold and rigor has set in."

"Must have spiked an artery," said the Cree. From a distance, his index finger traced the blood patterns on the glass. They criss-crossed the window like a grisly Jackson Pollock painting.

"I'd say he was gazing through the window when the killer stuck him from behind."

"Someone he knew."

"A good bet. The glass would catch their reflections."

"All there is to see in the adjoining room is an empty cage."

"It wasn't empty," the Mad Dog piped in, returning to the office from the room in question. "There's a puddle of piss on the floor beneath the bars."

"An animal?" Chandler suggested.

"Could be. Or a kid. The cage is too cramped to imprison an adult of average size."

"Whatever it was, the captive's gone. I wonder if that cage is why Capp was killed."

Ghost Keeper squatted beside the body and seemed to concentrate on the head and hands. "Notice anything?" he asked, looking quizzically at Rabidowski.

"The number of jabs in the back of the neck, it looks like he tried to sleep on a bed of nails."

"Recognize him?"

"No."

"You've seen him before. Study his features, imagine him naked, then paint a skeleton on his body."

"The guy in the snuff film! The Suits' report. What'd the preacher in Texas call him?"

"Woody Bone."

In storming the room, the Mounties had contaminated any forensic traces left by the killer of Wolfe Capp and Woody Bone. Normally, they would have withdrawn until Ident arrived, to avoid further milling around in the midst of a murder scene. The empty cage, however, worried them. What if the prisoner had been a child, and what if the killer had taken the child with him, and what if the child had been kidnapped to quench the killer's perversion? In that case, there was a tough dilemma here. Did they waste time that might usefully be spent picking up the trail before it got even colder, or did they wait to see if forensic clues would point them in the direction of their quarry?

"He could still be in the building," Rabidowski said. "With the kid, if it was a kid in the cage."

"What makes you say that?" Chandler asked.

"There's gotta be a studio hidden someplace if the snuff stuff was shot here."

"He's right," said Ghost Keeper. "And where's the back door?"

"There's something else."

"What's that, Ed?"

The Mad Dog returned to the hall door they had rammed in. "This slide bolt was engaged manually from in here. We tore it off the jam by waxing the door. The other room also has a door to the hall. And its slide bolt was locked from inside too."

"A secret passage?"

"Unless you believe in ghosts. If both doors were locked from the inside and Capp's still here, how did the killer and whatever was in the cage get out?"

"The longer we stand here twiddling our thumbs, the longer he has to escape," said the Cree.

Chandler nodded.

"Let's find it," he said.

The porn king's desk was command central. It was cluttered with all the usual electronics of today: computer, fax, phone system, intercom and closed-circuit TV. A remote control to activate the TV and the VCR on the wheeled table lay beside two movie guides open at pages that had one film in common: Tod Browning's *Freaks*. The stench of stale cigar smoke lingered around an ashtray where a stubbed stogie lay waiting to be relit. Porn queens by the dozen populated a photo album displayed on the leather surface, and under it were before-and-after Polaroids of a teenage girl with pneumatic breasts.

"Jesus!" exclaimed the Mad Dog. "Her tits are *twice* as big as my wife's."

"The tape in the VCR might give us a line on who we're looking for. The remote might have fingerprints," Chandler warned. "Play it manually, Ed."

Zinc moved around behind the porn king's desk. The Cree and the Mad Dog faced him from the other side. The sergeant turned and stepped away several paces, leaving Ghost Keeper standing alone with both feet on the trap door the cops knew nothing about. If someone pushed the wrong button on Wolfe Capp's desk, the unsuspecting inspector would drop to an ugly death by impalement on the spikes hidden below.

"It isn't *Freaks,*" the Mad Dog said. "That tape's lying on top of the tube."

While the sergeant busied himself with generating images off the tape in the VCR, Chandler was careful not to disturb any latent prints on the closed-circuit TV monitor as he switched it on. The screen filled with a bird's-eye view caught by an external camera covering a ramp that led to an underground parking lot.

"Hey," said Rabidowski, "get a look at this."

"It seems we've found the back door," Chandler said, ignoring the sergeant's summons for a moment while he reached for the button beside the monitor.

Ghost Keeper watched him push it with a paper clip . . .

And got the surprise of his life . . .

As the floor beneath his feet dropped away like the trap door on a gallows scaffold . . .

Yawning wide above the spikes of a bed of nails.

MONSTER MAKER

Lopez Island, Washington State
March 22

These waterways were some of the last in the world to be explored by Europeans in the Age of Discovery. A Greek captain sailing under the flag of Spain was the first to pass this way in 1592, but he was too intent on finding the fabled Northwest Passage to the Orient to bother poking his bow into the strait that runs between what is now Vancouver Island in Canada and the Olympic Peninsula in the States. The Greek captain's name was Apostolos Valerianos, but what the Spaniards called him was Juan de Fuca.

Two hundred years would pass before the first ship sailed into the Strait of Juan de Fuca. Under the command of the Spaniard Francisco Eliza, it explored the San Juan Islands hidden within. Of the three large islands that form an inverted pyramid pointing south toward Puget Sound, the top two—San Juan and Orcas (as well as the archipelago itself)—were named for the fifty-third viceroy of New Spain (now Mexico), Don *Juan* Vincente de Guemes Pacheco de Padilla H*orcas*itees y Aguayo, Conde Revilla de Gigedo.

Hopefully, he let his friends call him Don.

Of humbler origin was a sailor on that first ship, Gonzales Lopez de Haro. In "Upstairs, Downstairs" fashion, the lowest island was named Lopez Island.

Jenna and Nick sat side by side up on the open command bridge of the *Islomania.* Skipping over the troubled waters like a stone thrown side-hand to make it bounce, the boat hit the caps of wave after wave with a *bomph-bomph-bomph.* A wet wind spat sea spray in their faces and whipped away the wayward locks tufting out of the hoods of their waterproof jackets. Nick would have preferred the protection of the cabin below, but he was riding with Marine Venus, so that was that.

"Fun, huh?" Jenna shouted above the whine of the wind.

"Never had a better time," Nick shouted back, giving her a thumbs-up with his drenched hand, the hand they'd have to amputate if frostbite set in.

"Want more?"

"More of what?"

Jenna shoved the throttle forward to give the cruiser more oomph, and as the *Islomania* transmogrified into a plane, the Mountie gritted his teeth. The way they were tossing about, Nick hoped he wouldn't belie his joy by tossing his cookies.

"Yahoo!" wailed the detective.

"Ride 'em, cowgirl," Nick muttered.

If the British had got their way, this strait to the east of the San Juans would currently mark the border between Canada and the States, and the butt of the *Islomania* would be flapping the red Maple Leaf, not the Stars and Stripes. A year after the Spaniards, in 1792, Captain Vancouver had charted these waters, sailing the *Discovery* down the sound that harbors Seattle today, then up Rosario Strait, in the opposite direction to the *Islomania*'s present course, to confront the Spanish off Wreck Beach, where Vancouver—the city—is now.

Flutter, flutter . . .

Up went the Union Jack.

American "squatters" didn't arrive until the 1850s. The reaction of the British was summed up like this:

> The mode in which the far [American] West is prepared for civilization is familiar to all readers of [James Fenimore] Cooper's novels, which, although overdrawn, afford some idea

of it. How the hardy squatter penetrates, rifle and axe on shoulder, into the recesses of the forests, how he builds his bark huts, and makes the little clearing in which he plants a few potatoes and sows a little Indian maize; how, when civilization presses upon him, he sells his hut and clearing, and disappears again into the forest. . . . Men of this stamp would appear to be eminently unfitted for life in a respectable and civilized colony, and might be most unpleasant neighbours.

Push eventually came to shove over a San Juan pig, a *British* pig that raided the potato patch of such an *American* squatter, prompting the Yank to bring home the bacon, you might say, which riled the limeys enough to want to try him for the crime, inducing the U.S. army to land troops on the island to protect one of their own. This in turn goaded the British navy into aiming the guns of its warships at Uncle Sam's invaders, causing the great-grandsons of Revolutionaries to itch for the opportunity to have a go at John Bull too, which is how the Pig War might have played out if a cooler head had not suggested arbitration.

The arbitrator agreed upon was the German emperor. That should have put the fix in for the British, one would think, what with the incest among European monarchies and all. But as two subsequent world wars would establish, the relations between those two countries weren't *that* close, and in the end, the U.S. won. The border became Haro Strait to the west of the San Juans, which was also named after that humble sailor, Gonzales Lopez de Haro, on the first Spanish ship.

Flutter, flutter . . .

Down came the Union Jack.

After all that kerfuffle, thought a queasy Nick, you'd think there'd be smooth sailing in Rosario Strait.

"Lopez," Jenna shouted, pointing ahead.

"I know," the seasick Canadian shouted back.

"Oh? Really? A landlubber like you?"

"I'll have you know that both my good and my bad ears hide gills."

"So I see. And such a nice *green* around them too."

"Ha! Ha!" groused Nick.

"All I ask," Jenna implored, "is that you don't puke into the wind."

They were speeding down the eastern shore of Lopez, closing on rugged Chadwick Hill, above Watmough Head at the southern tip. It was another fine spring day of sunshine warming a cloudless china-blue sky, with only the wind on the choppy water to remind them of winter's chill. In pioneer times, Lopez had been an inhospitable island, with timber crowding the beaches so densely that it was hard to penetrate inland. Once the spars were cut, farmers tilled the gaps, so if you want to see today what it was like back then, you sail across Haro Strait to Canada. What distinguishes the Gulf Islands from the San Juans is that south of the line, there's a No Trespassing sign in every cove.

Too many people, thought Nick.

"Lopezians," Jenna said, easing the throttle back so she could be heard, "used to say their climate was so damn good that they had to kill a man to start a cemetery."

"Lopezians? That sounds like *Gulliver's Travels*."

"You know, you might have solved a case in our cold file: this guy we found tied down on a beach by lots of little ropes."

"Did *he* begin the cemetery?"

"No, that was a Swede named Anderson, who had the farm beside the farm of a Norwegian named Kay."

"Near here?" Nick asked.

"Over there," said Jenna, pointing west to Sperry Peninsula. "The early 1880s."

"What happened?"

"The Swede's cow broke through a fence and ate the Norwegian's grass, so the Norwegian shooed the critter into his own corral, prompting the Swede to see red."

Nick shook his head. "If it ain't pigs, it's cows."

"Island crime," Jenna said, sighing. "The Swede pounded on the Norwegian's door with his blood at full boil. Different Scandinavians don't hitch well, I'm told. What began with fists turned to beard pulling and ended when Kay shot Anderson at such close range that powder exploding from his pistol set the Swede's shirt on fire. The Norwegian's hysterical Native wife doused the flames with a pan of water."

"What'd Kay get?"

"Ten years of hard labor at the McNeil Island jail."

Rounding Watmough Head to venture west toward Iceberg Point, the *Islomania* slowed to navigate closer to shore. Beyond the point was the channel between Lopez and San Juan Island, with its two-thousand-resident metropolis of Friday Harbor.

"Over there," said Jenna, pointing toward Richardson, "is the site of another Lopez shooting."

"When was that?"

"Shortly after the first."

The Mountie raised an eyebrow. "In a century and a half, there's never been a murder on my island, Pender."

"Well, there you have it."

"Have what?" Nick asked.

"The reason we Americans find your country so boring. You don't kill enough people."

Spring fever seemed to be epidemic around Lopez, for the wildlife of the archipelago was cavorting this morning. A pair of bald eagles, the female larger than the male, descended like Stuka dive-bombers with talons spread wide to pluck unwary fish from the deep blue sea. The sea itself was alive with the fiercest predators that prey in the Pacific, a resident pod of twenty-five-foot killer whales. One of the orcas breached for them.

"Know what a shivaree is?" Jenna asked.

"Yeah, the chill that's making my teeth chatter."

"You're a disappointment."

"I am?" said Nick.

"I thought you Mounties were hardy, stalwart and resolute."

"They relaxed the rules when they let women in."

"A shivaree is a time-honored tradition on Lopez. After a newlywed couple retire to their matrimonial bed, the members of the groom's stag gather outside the window to serenade them with noisemakers like cowbells, dishpans, horns and such."

"That could put the poor guy off his stroke."

"Which happened to Martin Phillips when the caterwauling went on and on and on . . ."

"This was the second killing?"

"*Two* killings, actually. Back in 1889 or thereabouts. The story is that Martin got pissed off at the boys for ruining his nuptials, so he burst out of his homestead with a double-barreled shotgun and ended the shivaree by pulling both triggers. When he saw the result, Phillips, aghast, cried, 'My God, boys! What have I done?' To which one of the survivors replied, 'You've just killed two of your best friends.'"

"I'll bet he got off."

"It took the jury less than five minutes."

"Every man can empathize with a ruined piece of tail."

"Island crime," said Jenna.

"Island crime," the Mountie agreed.

And then they spotted something that didn't look like an island crime at all.

A police boat from Friday Harbor was already at the scene. It was anchored in the cove with no one aboard. The crest displayed on its hull was gray and black: the bewigged head of George Washington, ringed by the words "The Seal of the State of Washington, 1889," with "Sheriff Dept., San Juan Co." encircling that and a seven-point star spiking from the rim. "A clean, no-nonsense crest," Hank Bond used to say, "unlike all that folderol on the Horsemen's badge, with its hoity-toity crown and cheesy buffalo head, and all those flowery maple leaves around a motto in some language I don't understand." Dep. Irv Coutts had rowed the dinghy ashore, where he guarded the corpse positioned on the tidal rock to preserve any forensics at the crime scene. To show authority, he rested his hand on his gun.

Dead slow, the *Islomania* putted into the cove. Jenna slipped the transmission handle into neutral, then into reverse for fifteen seconds to bring them to a stop, then into neutral again.

"Irv?" she called on the police radio.

"Roger," squawked a voice from the speaker.

"Fill me in," said the detective. As she spoke, Jenna passed a pair of binoculars to Nick. He busied himself with adjusting their focus to his eyes.

"A local took his dog for a walk at dawn," said Coutts. "The mutt began to bark as they combed this beach, and he drew his master's attention to the rock offshore. The stiff shocked the hell out of him, so he rushed home and summoned us. When I saw it, I called the sheriff. He phoned you and the Suits in Seattle."

"Speak of the devil," Jenna said.

They could hear the *whup-whup-whup* of a chopper approaching from the mainland. Nick assumed that Special X had sent out an APB on the Galiano and Wreck Beach crimes in Canada, and because this body also fit the M.O., the cross-border aspect gave the FBI jurisdiction over the San Juan case.

"From this distance," Jenna said, "the vic looks like that statue in Copenhagen." She was alluding to the *Little Mermaid,* based on the story by Hans Christian Andersen, which had sat on a rock in the harbor of the Danish capital since 1913. With her bare breasts and fishtail, the maid had become the symbol of that city.

Nick had never been to Copenhagen. Nor had he fantasized that he was the heroine of that classic fairytale—as Jenna had as a young islomane. Instead, his point of reference was a notorious ripoff in Vancouver harbor, where since 1972 the *Girl in a Wetsuit* had sat on a similar offshore rock. Her fishtail was a pair of flippers; her modesty hid beneath a body sheath.

"Jesus Christ!" swore Nick.

The binoculars had focused on the corpse.

Like those statues, it too was perched on a rock near the shore. Stark fear was etched into the woman's face, which was cyanotic blue from strangulation. Blood had gushed from her mouth to cake the skin below; the top half of her body wore no wetsuit to hide her modesty, while the bottom half had no fishtail for public decency. What grabbed Nick's attention, however, was her breasts: the enhanced two resulting from puberty and the *additional* two grafted below to her torso skin. The stitching was as thick and black as that which, according to Hollywood, bound Dr. Frankenstein's monster together.

In his gut, the Mountie knew that he had found the pair of breasts severed from the rotting Galiano remains.

FantasyLand

Los Angeles

The former Dr. Ryland Fletcher was off in fantasyland.

It is the middle of the night and she is fast asleep, a conclusion he draws from noting that the windows of her home are dark, and from his knowledge that her line of work demands she get her beauty sleep. In the business of fuck fantasies, a porn queen must look fuckable, so the weight of baggy eyes could pull her down off her throne. Besides, it takes energy to pump your pussy all day.

He is a lurker among the shadows that skulk around her home. As he steals toward her door like the night stalker he is, moonlight shines on a doorknob with a keyhole in its center the same way a spotlight hits her shaved vulva when close-ups are shot at work. In his hand, he holds the key to his *and* her satisfaction, copied from the wax impression he made of the key he removed from her purse while she was undressing in his surgery last year.

Slipping the key into the lock jerks his penis erect.

It is a heady cocktail of emotions that he feels as he slowly twists the knob: excitement, anxiety, anticipated pleasure and fear. Fear rises to the top as the door eases open, for this is the moment when he could set off a security alarm.

Nothing.

Home free.

Here I come, ready or not.

In he slips and closes the door, and creeps toward her bedroom.

In fantasyland, the woman of his wet dreams is always asleep. He stands at the threshold to her boudoir and watches her dream on, then the stud of her fantasies—though she doesn't know it—tiptoes in to awaken the *real* woman inside, as she will discover when he bestows the fuck of a lifetime on her.

How many times will she come?

The sky's the limit, lover.

Stealthily, he closes in on her bed, looming above her supine form as he strips off his clothes, getting harder and harder by the moment as he watches the breasts that he enhanced rise and fall with her shallow breathing. The image he has of the male physique that emerges from the cocoon of his clothes is Michelangelo's *David,* arguably the most perfect hunk there is. Bending over this porn queen like Prince Charming, he plants a quick kiss on her lips as they part to draw another breath, and when her eyes snap wide open from that thrill, the first thing she glimpses is the gleaming scalpel in his hand.

"I made you with this," he tells her, the opening line of his fantasy script.

She stifles a cry of surprise.

"Now I'll make you with *this,*" he says, posing erect so she can admire his manly cock.

She gasps with awe at the virility of it.

The scalpel isn't to scare her. That would make this rape. Instead, it is to teach her that he is her *god.* The fact that she is a sex kitten worthy of the camera adoration of a Brigitte Bardot is directly due to the ministrations of *his* stainless steel.

And God Created Woman.

That's me and you, lover.

She may think she doesn't want it, but that's to be expected. After all, she spends her working life getting fucked around on set by woodsmen and porn producers in order to titillate the voyeuristic fantasies of video-viewers like . . . well, like *him.* But he doesn't devour fuck films for some prurient jack-off like a puerile wanker. He absorbs them because only a porn queen capable of igniting the fantasies of those with overblown sex drives is worthy of his cock. That's why he has trouble getting it up with the camera-shy females average guys screw. They're just too *ordinary* to stoke his fire.

This, however, is a two-way street. She may resist his advances at first, playing hard to get to add to the chime-ringing orgasm of being conquered, but they both know what she craves deep down inside. Hell, what kind of woman fucks on film except one who yearns for the perfect white knight to scratch her itch? She flaunts her wares onscreen in the hope of attracting Prince Charming.

"Wake up, Sleeping Beauty. Sir Lance-a-lot is here."

A lot of lance jousts majestically at her.

"No. Please," she says.

Which, of course, means yes.

Even porn queens feel the need to hide coquettishness.

You want to be taken?

Okay, I'll take you.

"Take off your nightie. Don't play coy with me. Show me the tits I put my art into creating. Don't deflate me, or I may deflate you. That's better. Now how do you want it? Missionary position? Doggie style? Or do you have something else in mind?"

Getting her to take it takes some effort. But once he sticks the key in the lock that guards her itch, she cannot—in spite of herself—resist his prowess. She's a porn queen, the sexiest example of the female sex. But that means nothing once Sir Lance-a-lot teaches her the meaning of bowing down to God, and her ecstasy during this revelation is something to behold, as she crumples in orgasm again and again and again. "Ooahh, Doctor . . . what a rod . . . what length . . . what girth . . . and so fucking hard. . . . God, you're gutting me . . . but oh, you're good. . . . Ram it, Doctor . . . cram it, Doctor. . . . Jesus, you're the BEST. . . . More, more, I don't think I can bear any MORE . . . but oh, lover, don't STOP. . . . Here I come AGAIN. . . . I can't hold back . . . I'm yours . . . body and SOUL. . . . Just keep it in . . . and keep it hard . . . and pump . . . pump . . . MAAAASTER . . ."

"Ladies and gentlemen . . ."

Not now! Go away! he thought.

"This is the captain speaking . . ."

Oh, shit!

Poof.

Coitus interruptus.

"We have begun our descent into Los Angeles . . . "

No more porn queen.

No more fantasy.

"Fasten your seat belts, and thank you for flying with us."

The former Dr. Ryland Fletcher came back from fantasyland to find he was on a real flight above the real world, with the real Fantasyland several miles below in Anaheim, and not the flight of fantasy that—interrupted at its climax—had aroused him during his trip south to the City of Angels.

Fortunately for the porn queen, unfortunately for him, Dr. Ryland Fletcher currently had no time to act out his fantasy in the real world by stalking the actress he had chosen from among the spreads in the stable album the porn king kept in his office. Fletcher had planned to surprise her after dark that night, using a key to her basement suite that Wolfe had copied on the sly, but that was before the recent e-mail he'd received through the Spider's Web just before yesterday's meeting with the director of the Panacea Clinic at Vancouver's hottest restaurant. The e-mail was from a former porn producer in L.A. who offered to slip the underground surgeon a wad of tax-free cash for a facial reconstruction—with no questions asked—ASAP.

So that's what saw Fletcher on this flight about to land in the City of Angels.

Hollywood North.

Hollywood South.

It was fateful how his life was playing out like a game of Snakes and Ladders. Up one moment, down the next, then up again. Near the top of his class in med school at UCLA, he had earned a plum research job at a biotechnology firm, and might have gone on to unravel the secret of why we age and been lauded as the scientist who actually found Ponce de León's elusive Fountain of Youth if not for that unfortunate vivisection scandal in the firm's lab. Not that he was to blame—that was someone else—but he had been willfully blind to what was going on, so when the ax fell, it chopped him too.

Animal-rights activists.

What a pain in the ass.

Thankfully, the cover-up by the company had saved his reputation as a doctor, so out into practice he had scurried, to swap the lure of research fame for the lucre of plastic surgery. He might have established a high-end clinic in ritzy Beverly Hills, catering to the beauty queens of Hollywood, if not for his obsession with the lower end, so to speak, of L.A.'s porn queens.

So he had opened his flesh pit downtown.

For years, the surgeon had enjoyed the best of both worlds. As Dr. Jekyll by day, he had made a lush living out of the porn trade, pumping luscious babes up to fantasy size while secretly indulging in fantasyland himself. Once they were anesthetized, he was free to explore, a skin mag in the flesh you might say; it was an experience akin to viewing the photo spreads in *Playboy, Penthouse* or *Hustler* in braille. Every now and then, the powerful potion of that aphrodisiac would turn the doctor into Mr. Hyde, and out he'd go into the night to turn his libido loose. At first, he went in masked, fucking his porn queens anonymously, but in his fantasy they *knew* who was the best stud they'd ever had—"Ram it, Doctor . . . cram it, Doctor. . . . Jesus, you're the BEST . . ."—so before long, he had been compelled to expose himself in more ways than one.

"Ooahh, *Doctor* . . . what a rod . . . what length . . . what girth . . . and so fucking hard . . ."

Fletcher had figured he was home safe. What porn queen would ruin her career by crying rape when the content of her work itself implied consent? Besides, doctors are common victims of false allegations by female patients who harbor sexual fantasies weaved around "saviors," and when their dreams are shattered by an ethical man who remains true to the Hippocratic oath . . . well, there is no wrath like a woman scorned.

Especially a woman who pumps her pussy for all to see.

Who'd believe her?

Unfortunately, the stigma of age applies to porn queens too. When an actress reaches the hump year that puts her over the hill—say twenty-five in the porn industry—she has little to lose. The work dries up and her reputation is blown, so she must start looking for another cow to milk, and that applied to one of the porn queens forced to entertain Sir Lance-a-lot in the middle of the night.

"I want money, Doctor."

"For what, Phoebe?"

"*Not* blowing the whistle."

"Blow away."

And damn if the bitch didn't run to the police, prompting a second porn queen to follow suit. That brought medical authorities down on him like the foot of an elephant, and then he was waylaid at his car by a thug with a scarred face.

"Here's how it is, Doc. You're going down. 'Cause what you don't know is that you were caught on tape boning my girl. Reality TV is big right now. Interactive crap. On the Web too. So what we're putting together is a site where you can watch my girl going about her life. In the shower. On the can. Doing herself in bed. Twenty-four hours a day. Just log on. And if you find those goings-on thump your stump, you can order these videos that made her a queen. Get the picture? It made *you* a star. 'Cause we were recording a dry run the night you slipped in, and that tape'll be Exhibit A unless we make a deal."

"What sort of deal?"

"One that wipes you out. But at least it will keep your virginal ass and delicate mouth out of jail."

And damn if they didn't know what he was worth, having hacked into his accountant's files. In exchange for both the tape and the dropping of all charges—the thug had made a side deal with the other porn queen—he had escaped the ignominy of prison and the albatross of a criminal record. However, in a move that insured he would never prey on another porn queen, they also forced him not to contest the lifting of his license to practice medicine.

He was out on the street.

With Hollywood South a bust, Fletcher had cast his eyes north. So weak was the Canadian dollar compared with America's that moviemakers by the hundreds had abandoned L.A. for Vancouver. That was where the Spider's Web was spun by Wolfe Capp, from whom the plastic surgeon had ordered three videos tailored to his fantasy to tide him over between excursions by Mr. Hyde, the jousts by Sir Lance-a-lot. One of those videos had been paid for—but *not* shot—when the scarred thug representing the porn queens cleaned him out, so Fletcher, at loose ends and down on his luck, had e-mailed the Canadian porn king to ask if he could personally be the woodsman in the third fantasy he had ordered on the Spider's Web.

And damn if Wolfe Capp hadn't e-mailed back to invite the plastic surgeon to come to his Vancouver studio to discuss a quid pro quo offer.

Things were looking up.

So Fletcher had climbed the ladder.

As luck would have it, the porn king wasn't the only contact the destitute doctor had in Vancouver. A fellow plastic surgeon—Dr. David Denning—had relocated his lucrative Hollywood South medical practice to Hollywood North to accommodate the discretionary needs of his touchy patients, who knew the mere rumor of having had work done could cause their stock to plunge in the flesh markets of L.A.

For several days, Fletcher had surveilled Eternal Spring, watching the comings and goings of Denning's well-heeled clientele, and damn if he didn't catch sight of the two L.A. porn queens who had taken him to the cleaners down south and were now using *his* money to have touch-up vanity work done by the best. So angered had he been by that twist of fate that he had waylaid Denning and a lunch companion on the street as they exited from Eternal Spring.

"Ryland!"

"David."

"I hear you've had . . . a setback?"

"Yes, I was hoping you might help me out."

"Help? How?"

"I need work."

"That's a little difficult without a medical license."

"Who's this, David?"

A question from Denning's companion.

"Ryland Fletcher. A colleague from L.A. Ryland recently suffered a blow from sexual allegations by two patients, and he was forced to take a permanent sabbatical from plastic surgery."

"Yes," said Fletcher. "But that's not *all* I can do. You will recall my first job was in biotechnology."

"Research?" asked Denning's companion.

Fletcher nodded. "Into the effects of free radicals on human cells. We were searching for a way to slow human aging. I've kept up on the literature."

"How interesting," said the companion. "I too am in that line of work."

Denning glanced impatiently at his watch. "We'll be late," he said. "Nice to see you, Ryland."

"Perhaps we'll meet again," said Denning's companion, extending his hand to shake good-bye. When Fletcher gripped it, they weren't flesh to flesh, and as he disengaged, the other man palmed off a business card. The disgraced doctor waited until the two had moved on before he read the print:

Graham Worlock
Director of the Panacea Clinic

This morning, while on his way to the Vancouver airport to catch this flight, Fletcher had heard a news report about Wolfe Capp's murder. He wondered if the fifteen grand in cash that the porn king had paid him—the thirteen thousand agreed upon for pumping up the teen and the extra deuce as a retainer "for future work"—could be traced back to its source by police? Not that it mattered. He could afford to flush it away. The cash from this L.A. job was more than enough to replace it, and his deal with the Director would see him on easy street.

As he pondered that spin of the wheel of fate, Fletcher glanced out through the window of the descending plane and saw the giant fifty-foot letters of the Hollywood sign perched on the barren hillside near the summit of Mount Lee.

Fantasyland.

Hit List

Vancouver

"So there I was," Zinc Chandler said, sipping coffee as he planted a buttock on one of the library tables that made up DeClercq's horseshoe desk and filled the chief in on what had happened during the raid on Wolfe Capp's Yaletown studio, "standing behind the pornographer's desk in his business office, with Ghost Keeper facing me on the far side and the Mad Dog excited by what he'd found on the videotape. Ignoring Rabidowski for the moment, I reached down and pushed a button that I hoped would expose the rear door of the Wolfe's lair, and suddenly the floor beneath Ghost Keeper disappeared."

"I thought I was dead," said the Cree. "There I was, looking down as Zinc pushed the button, and what I saw was a trap door drop beneath my feet. With no time to react, I began to plummet toward a bed of nails spiking up in the pit below."

"Did you ever see *King of the Royal Mounted?*" Chandler asked.

"Of course," replied DeClercq. "No one could write 'em quite like Zane Grey. He was the most popular American author of his day. If my memory serves me well, I read somewhere that more than a hundred of his stories were filmed."

"Ah, those Saturday movie matinees!" mused Zinc. "When I was a farm boy in Saskatchewan, the weekend meant a drive into Rosetown with Mom. There, my brother Tom and I would spend the afternoon lost in our imaginations at the Hitching Post while she did the shopping for the following week. We'd run past the movie posters and the lobby cards, stock up with goodies at the concession stand, plop down in the fifth row back from the screen, with popcorn clutched in one hand and a Coke in the other, pockets stuffed with candy bars for after the main course, eagerly waiting for the screen to burst into life. Our anticipation wasn't for the double feature and the five cartoons, but so that the week of agony would finally be over, and the Rosetown Rustlers—what we Saturday afternoon moviegoers called ourselves—could see how the Mountie hero of the halftime serial shown a week before would escape from whatever cliffhanger imperiled him. The words *'To be continued . . .'* at the end of *King of the Royal Mounted* were the most excruciating I remember reading as a kid."

"I know how you felt," DeClercq sighed, with a wink at the Cree. "Your verbosity is having the same effect on me. Why don't you cut to the chase, to coin a phrase, and tell me why Ghost Keeper is sitting here *alive* in my office."

"The Mad Dog," said Zinc.

"I should have guessed."

"So excited was Rabidowski by what he had found on the videotape that he reached out and grabbed Ghost Keeper's arm to give him a will-you-take-a-look-at-this shake, and that was the moment when the floor dropped away."

"I fully expected to plunge to my death by impalement on those spikes," said the Cree, "but the Mad Dog had the reflexes, the bulk and the strength to react to my peril on raw instinct. So instead of ending up as a shish kebab on that bed of nails, I was yanked back just enough to keep my butt from plummeting into the pit."

"With a spine-jarring smack," Chandler said to script this real-life cliffhanger for the chief, "Ghost Keeper's backside struck the rim of the square hole. He would still have slipped off and been spiked to death had the Mad Dog not thrown his own weight away in counterbalance, hauling Bob with him like a sack of spuds."

"There I was," Ghost Keeper said, "sprawled on my back on the floor—"

"Ripped from the jaws of death to survive another episode," Zinc interjected.

"—with the Mad Dog gazing down at me. 'We're even,' I said to settle the score for what he thought he owed me for that kill shot at the wolf-dog two days ago. He shrugged it off and helped me up. 'I'm not going into the Headless Valley alone next summer, Tonto,' Ed replied, a reference to a hunting trip we have planned."

"To be continued . . ." said Zinc.

The chief smiled. "I too saw several of those Mountie serials that Hollywood churned out. *Perils of the Royal Mounted, Dangers of the Canadian Mounted,* and my favorite, *Canadian Mounties vs. Atomic Invaders.* As I recall, each had twelve episodes. That's more cliffhangers than the nine lives of a cat. There isn't a bookmaker alive who will give you those odds, so at one for the wolf-dog and two for the bed of nails, let's count ourselves lucky and leave it at that."

It's actually three, Zinc thought, adding how he had contemplated his loaded gun in the grip of the curse of *The Mummy.*

But he left it at that.

"Sleuthing time," said DeClercq. "What have we got?"

Space had been cleared on the Strategy Wall next to the collage of the mummy heist so the Mounties could develop an overview that linked the surgical mutilations to Snuff Lib. Flanked by his inspectors, the chief superintendent studied the morgue photos pinned to the corkboard while they briefed him.

"From the top," he said.

"Wolfe Capp was a pornographer," Zinc recapped, "who launched a site called the Spider's Web on the Internet. The Spider's Web served rich pervs around the globe who had the bucks to commission Wolfe to film their fantasies as personal porn. Whatever your kink, he would visualize it for a suitable price."

"Snuff too," Ghost Keeper added, picking up from Zinc. "Hidden behind the Spider's Web was Snuff Lib. It served the most *outré* of sick minds, homicidal misogynists who got their voyeuristic kicks by ordering videos of women killed in outlandish ways."

"Killed by Woody Bone."

"This high-camp ghoul. The Alice Cooper and Marilyn Manson of the snuff clique."

"The rumor is he was a naked guy made up like a skeleton who would perpetrate *any* perversion for Snuff Lib."

"Made-to-order women snuffed in made-to-order ways."

"It was like commissioning Jason of *Friday the 13th* or Freddy of *Nightmare on Elm Street* to do your bidding."

"Woody was *it* if you were into that sort of thing."

"Owning a Woody Bone is to snuff aficionados what owning a Rembrandt is to galleries."

"At least, that's the rumor."

"Which Interpol had picked up from snitches around the world."

"But there was never any proof to substantiate the gossip."

"Until the Bureau got a break in Texas," said Zinc.

"I thought the FBI's position, after exhaustive research, was that snuff films don't exist?" said DeClercq. "Never, in worldwide police searches, has a snuff film *ever* been found. Only crude enactments of murder, like that bogus film, *Snuff*, in the 1970s."

"The Bureau probably did that research with the same computer it used to keep track of files in the Oklahoma bombing. Somehow they lost a roomful, remember? In an era rife with sexism and the serial slaughter of women, it's naïve to think no one has filmed snuff to turn a buck. You can hire a contract killer for the price of a cap of junk, yet the Bureau maintains snuff films are taboo."

"They're whistling a different tune now," added the Cree. "What they found in Texas is the Holy Grail of snuff."

Ghost Keeper broke away from the group to feed the tape of *Skull Fucker* into the VCR of an audio-visual console angled into the corner to their right. He switched on the TV. Kids' cartoons. "Brace yourself," he warned DeClercq as he returned with the clicker.

"A televangelist in Houston cracked from guilt," said Zinc. "In a religious ramble, he confessed to ordering a video from Snuff Lib. The Bible-thumper got twisted up in a Lolita perversion, something about the Devil having used 'teenage titties' to lead him astray, so he paid Woody Bone with diverted ministry funds to videotape a 'big-boobed teenage harlot' being ground into mincemeat for him. Praise the Lord, he found God not a moment too soon and ran to the Suits to beg them to head off the murder the Devil had abetted in him."

"They thought he was nuts. But even nuts can kill," said Ghost Keeper, "so the Bureau traced the link the preacher said he used to commission Woody Bone to grind the buxom teen, and found that Snuff Lib was masked by Wolfe Capp's Spider's Web."

"The Suits asked us to check Wolfe out. We dubbed the operation 'the Wolfe's lair' and convinced Special O to put a team of Watchers on the front door."

From a pile of photos in his hand, Zinc selected a shot of a teenage girl exiting from a brick building and pinned it to the empty corkboard on the Strategy Wall.

"That was taken two days ago, shortly after O began surveillance. The girl was snapped leaving Wolfe's studio."

"She doesn't look big-boobed to me," said DeClercq.

"No," agreed Zinc. "So no cause for alarm."

He tacked another photo from the pile to the space beneath the photo of the girl. It showed a good-looking, trim man in a designer suit leaving the brick building by the same door.

"That was snapped later the same afternoon. Again, two days ago, on the twentieth. Yesterday, this same fellow returned at about the same time. O's door bug caught what he said to the intercom. 'It's Fletcher. The job is done.'"

Zinc pinned another photo of the same man to the space beside the earlier shot.

"That's Fletcher leaving the Wolfe's lair yesterday."

"Is this where I came in?" asked DeClercq.

The inspector nodded. "That's where the investigation stood when I went down to ViCLAS and found you talking with Chris at the end of the day. The Fletcher I asked her to try to get a line on is the fellow in these shots. Then I went home."

"Meanwhile," Ghost Keeper interjected, "the Suits had tossed the ministry of the Texas preacher. The search turned up a hidden videotape, and they couriered a copy to us. It arrived after Zinc had left. I watched it last night. This is what I saw."

The Cree punched Play on the remote control. Woody Bone and a screaming woman appeared on TV. "*Skull Fucker* is the title on the label."

It took a hell of a lot to surprise the chief these days, but the atrocity onscreen shocked the hell out of him. By the time it was over, DeClercq was emotionally drained.

"Grueling, huh?"

"That's an understatement."

"The way we figure it is this," said Zinc. "The Spider's Web is a network that passes tapes around, the same way pedophiles pass kids to one another. Part of it's like Napster, sharing old stuff. And part of it's made-to-order porn fantasies. The ghouls of Snuff Lib use that network too, and that's how the preacher got this tape. *Skull Fucker* is old stuff. It's an early snuff by Woody Bone, from back when he was starting out. The tape was made years ago, and somehow it worked its way into the limited public domain of snuff aficionados. A preacher needs a glimpse of hell to justify his commitment and something evil to save sinners from. *Skull Fucker*'s enough to drop *me* to my knees."

"You think it inspired the Texan to order a snuff film of his own?"

"And inspired us to smash in Wolfe's door."

"Where you found him dead."

"Him *and* Woody Bone. The porn king *was* the ghoul in that snuff video. And we found these on his desk."

Zinc pinned the last two photos in his hand to the Strategy Wall, beside O's shot of the teenage girl.

"Yikes!" exclaimed DeClercq. "*That's* breast enhancement. What did the preacher order? Science-fiction snuff?"

"Everything's bigger in Texas, so *big* he was going to get. The girl snapped leaving the building was normal size, and when we broke in, those before-and-after Polaroids were on Wolfe's desk. The porn king also had a tape of what happened in between."

Ghost Keeper returned to the VCR, where he switched the video cassette of *Skull Fucker* with the tape they had seized from the office machine, the tape the Mad Dog was viewing when he fortuitously reached out to grab the Cree's arm to give him that will-you-take-a-look-at-this lifesaving shake.

"Guess who?" Chandler said.

The new cassette played like one of those medical documentaries on The Learning Channel, except this was a one-man operation. The camera was stationary, no tracking around. It remained focused on the back of a plastic surgeon while he enhanced the breasts of the same teenage girl whose before-and-after pictures were pinned to the Strategy Wall. She was intubated, with dual tubes running from her mouth to an anesthetic machine, and every now and then her naked body twitched as it reacted to the shifting level of knockout drugs. An IV snaked from her arm like a serpent in a sterile anti-Eden.

With the operation finished, the surgeon turned toward the camera and removed his surgical mask.

"Fletcher," said DeClercq.

"The guy's a plastic surgeon. He must have done the tit job on the girl between the time she left on the twentieth and when he returned to Capp's yesterday." Zinc tapped the before-and-after photos. "Fletcher probably gave the porn king these."

"And the video?"

"That's doubtful," Ghost Keeper said. "The doc looks too relaxed to know he's being taped."

"Wolfe caught him on the sly?"

"That would explain why the tape was left in the machine."

"Think Fletcher killed Capp?"

"Possibly. According to the Watchers, he was the last person seen leaving before we smashed in."

"All doors covered?"

"That's the rub. We didn't find the back door until after the raid. It connected with a separate underground parking lot. With all the recent cutbacks, O could spare only one team of Watchers to cover the Wolfe's lair."

"The bloody solicitor general! I should have thrown him down the stairs when he was here. So the sad fact is that someone might have come and gone, unseen by O?"

"And probably did. The doors between Capp's office and the front entrance were hand-bolted from the inside. And pooled urine was found in an empty cage off the office."

"Human?"

"Most likely, yes. The specific gravity of animal urine is higher."

"The teenage girl?"

"Doubt it. The cage was the size of a child. And according to the lab, no estrogen was found in the urine test. If it was a girl, she had yet to reach puberty."

"That worries me," said DeClercq.

"Us too."

"What's your take on what's going on?"

The inspectors exchanged glances, then Zinc gave Ghost Keeper a nod.

"Snuff Lib is as bad as it comes," said the Cree. "The underground Web site satisfied the homicidal fantasies of the sickest misogynists in the world. Welcome to the potential of the Internet. What Snuff Lib offered was made-to-order females snuffed in made-to-order ways. We think Fletcher and Wolfe were partners. The plastic surgeon's job was to turn real-life females into made-to-order fantasy victims for the world's sickest minds. Wolfe Capp's job was to transform himself into Woody Bone. Before the Web, it was almost impossible for snuff producers and consumers to interconnect, but Fletcher and Wolfe solved that hurdle through the Spider's Web."

"Based here?" said DeClercq.

"Yes, in Hollywood North. And we think that explains a lot more than just the two videos you watched: the body found on Galiano Island with surgically removed breasts; the sucked-dry 'mummy' deposited on Wreck Beach, her skin perforated by surgical liposuction cuts; the stiff found at Cowichan with a surgically altered face. We think those women were operated on by Fletcher—the same way he operated on the teenage girl in the video you saw—to turn them into made-to-order victims for Wolfe as Woody Bone."

"For Snuff Lib?"

"Uh-huh. Then discarded."

As Ghost Keeper linked the surgical mutilations to Snuff Lib, the chief watched Zinc's finger jump from one previously pinned-up morgue shot to another. DeClercq sucked in a deep breath and slowly let it out as he assessed the earlier autopsy collage in light of the Snuff Lib overview taking shape in the empty space, until both sets of visuals on the corkboard bled into one.

"So what happened? They had a falling-out?"

"That's our theory," Chandler said. "We think Fletcher returned to the studio by the back door. He stabbed Wolfe to death while they gazed through a one-way window at whatever was in the cage in the adjoining room. Then he released the captive and left with whoever that was by the same route."

"Money?"

"Our guess. The root of all evil. They must have charged a fortune for those videos. With Wolfe snuffed, the ill-gotten gains fall to Fletcher. We think he'll capitalize on two more commissions by transforming into Woody Bone himself."

"The captive from the cage?"

"That's one. Why else go to the trouble of abducting whoever was in there?"

"And the 'big-boobed' teen?"

"Money in the bank. Assuming he doesn't know the preacher gave them up, why leave a witness alive who's already made to order for the meat-grinding snuff?"

"Any idea who she is?"

"No," Chandler replied. "Nor where to find her. But a good bet is that she's still alive. With all that swelling and bruising from her recent breast enhancement, I doubt she'll satisfy the televangelist's murderous Lolita fantasy for a while. We could wait to see if Fletcher contacts the Bible-thumper, but will he do that before she's snuffed?"

A knock on the door.

"Enter," called out the chief.

The door swung open like the lid of a sarcophagus. The threshold framed S/Sgt. Christine Wozney of ViCLAS.

"Am I party-crashing?"

"For you, we'll make an exception. Cheer us up, Chris. What did you find?"

"Two more bodies."

"Where?"

"Both in Washington State. I queried HITS in Seattle to search for links with a surgical signature. HITS turned up two ongoing cases that matched: a body dumped near Port Angeles, on the Olympic Peninsula, a week or so back, and another discovered a week before that just east of Lake Whatcom, near Bellingham."

"Women?"

"Yes."

"That's *five,*" said Zinc.

"There's more," Chris replied. "I just got a call from Nick Craven. He's currently at a crime scene in Washington State with a San Juan cop named Jenna Bond."

"I know her," DeClercq said. "She worked the American half of the manhunt for Mephisto."

"A female corpse with *four* breasts was dumped on Lopez Island. She could be the Bride of Frankenstein, according to Nick. He thinks the extra breasts are from the breastless Galiano remains, and he wanted me to query HITS for similar links."

"You fill him in?"

"Yes."

"What was Nick's reaction?"

"He and Bond are boating here now."

"That's six," said Zinc.

"There's more," Chris replied. "I also queried VICAP at Quantico and asked them to search wide for surgical signatures. VICAP uncovered a string of unsolved murders in Los Angeles several years ago, all attributed to a psycho called Picasso."

"Never heard of him."

"A sign of the times," said Chris, sighing. "A crazy can kill five women and mutilate them, and all his fifteen minutes of fame earns him is local infamy. The name Picasso evolved from the fact that he rearranged their flesh surgically to mimic the artist's work."

"That's eleven," said Zinc.

"I've come bearing a hit list."

"Don't tell me there's more?"

"Remember your query?" said Chris.

Zinc was beginning to wonder how cops solved cases before there were computers, crime-linkage systems and cyber sleuths. Probably the same way they *still* solve cases in most detective novels, he told himself.

"You asked me to try to get a line on someone named Fletcher," said Chris. "I did a search of every porn connection we have, figuring a porn king would associate with porn types. The name Fletcher scored a hit in L.A. And when I photo-faxed that picture the Watchers took of him, the LAPD confirmed the ID."

"He's a plastic surgeon?"

"Was," said Chris. "The U/M's a disgraced plastic surgeon named Ryland Fletcher. He had a thriving practice in downtown L.A., focused on the porn industry. He lost his license to operate after he was charged with rape. Two porn queens said he attacked them in their homes. Court charges died after Fletcher did a deal not to contest allegations of sexual impropriety with his patients. Porn queens and lack of consent are poor bed partners at trial. In a compromise, Fletcher was stripped of his license by the state."

"For malpractice?"

"Uh-huh."

"So he went underground?"

"There's been nothing concrete on Fletcher since. But there'd be plenty of call for a renegade plastic surgeon who can alter looks with no questions asked."

"Good work, Chris. Now if only we knew where to *find* him," said DeClercq.

"Easy," Wozney replied. "L.A. airport. An immigration check on him turned up another hit. The former Dr. Ryland Fletcher left Vancouver earlier today on a flight to Los Angeles. I asked the LAPD to tail him from the airport. I just got a call from them on the move. Right now, Fletcher's in a cab heading for Hollywood."

SKIN DEEP

Ebbtide Island

The weirdest museum in the world is probably the one you'll find at 7 avenue du Général de Gaulle in Maisons-Alfort, a bleak industrial town on the eastern outskirts of Paris. Honoré Fragonard (1732–1799) was France's answer to Dr. Frankenstein. An eighteenth-century anatomist who taught at the national veterinary school, he was a cousin to Jean-Honoré Fragonard, the French master famed for paintings of sunny landscapes and chubby cherubs that still grace the Louvre. Honoré, the black sheep, was a talented artist too, but his brushes were scalpels and his canvases were the bodies of men and beasts. The word "bizarre" does not begin to describe his art, which Fragonard displayed in a museum that he set up in 1766 at the school where he taught. So distressed were his employers by what they saw that they fired France's first Dada artist in 1771, even though his detractors were savvy enough to keep his specimens. Today, they are still on display in the Fragonard Museum, which is housed in three rooms reeking of formaldehyde at the fortress-like veterinary school downriver from the Charenton asylum for the insane, the place where many thought Fragonard belonged.

It was evident that the Doctor appreciated Fragonard's art, for photographs the plastic surgeon had shot at the Fragonard Museum were tacked to a bulletin board beside the remains of the

Hollywood actress who was stretched out in death on the operating table in the Plastic Surgery Room, deep down in the bowels of the bluff beneath the Panacea Clinic. The Undertaker's eyes jumped from shot to shot as he studied the *outré* technique of this long-forgotten genius, who sculpted with cadavers instead of clay. Here were the mummified bodies of three skinned babies, so removed from human form that they could have been little aliens from outer space. One was positioned as if dancing a jig, and another had its arm bent at the elbow as if smoking a missing cigarette. Another photo, *"L'Homme à la mandibule,"* showed a skinned man posed in an attitude of combat, an evocation of Samson decimating the Philistines with the jawbone of an ass. Except for his bulging glass eyes, which looked human, he was a full-size warrior turned inside out, so his guts were the raw material from which Fragonard had created a gruesome image that occupied the nether terrain between science and art.

The pièce de résistance, however, of the museum's collection was *"Le Cavalier de l'apocolypse."* A real flayed horseman mounted on a real flayed stallion, caught in time as if galloping toward doomsday, it stood as a mummified testament to Fragonard's grisly technique. According to the recipe scrawled in the Doctor's surprisingly legible handwriting on a sheet of paper pinned beside the photo, the artist had first preserved the cadavers—both man and beast—by soaking them in alcohol mixed with pepper and herbs. Next, after skinning them, he had injected the blood vessels and bronchial tubes with either dyed tallow or wax mixed with turpentine. Red for arteries, blue for veins. Then finally, he had arranged the bodies to his satisfaction on a drying frame and left them to mummify. The result was an *organic* equestrian statue from more than two hundred years ago, with glass eyes popping out like those of strangled victims and bulging muscles, tendons and ligaments still attached to both skeletons, exposing the internal landscape of flesh, blood and bone that had obsessed Fragonard and now mesmerized the Doctor.

There were photos of other *objets d'art* from scattered locations, for just as the mummies of Egypt had found homes as conversation pieces on the estates of hoity-toits like Lord Ridding in Britain, so had the anatomist's eerie art decorated the lavish parlors of France's powdered and wigged *crème de la crème,* those who would soon be cut short by the Reign of Terror, as one by one each climbed the scaffold steps for a fatal date with Mme. Guillotine.

But why dwell on photos when *here* was the real thing?

Last night, after the three psychos had strangled the woman with four breasts whose head was locked in the branks, the Doctor had climbed the stone steps that corkscrewed up from the underground charnel vault through the heart of the cliff to the clinic surmounting its bluff. Continuing on past the main floor, where the Director's office could be entered by way of a sliding panel that opened off a staircase hidden in the wall, the Doctor had climbed to the upper story, and there—like Peeping Tom ogling Lady Godiva—he had spied on the naked Hollywood actress through the one-way full-length mirror in her room.

Meanwhile, down in the charnel chamber off the Mummy Room, the Director and the Undertaker had prepared the plastic surgery theater for work on a *new* patient. Releasing the multi-breasted corpse from the branks and the garroting chair, they had lugged the body out of the room to the subterranean passage beyond, and along the tunnel that snaked like an intestine to the sea cave burrowed into the cliff face this side of a hull-gutting reef. The cave, the tunnel and the vaults had been used to store illegal booze back in the rum-running days, when America had Prohibition and Canada didn't. Moored within that hidden cavern was the boat by which the Undertaker had smuggled Sleeping Beauty into the States from the Fraser River dock off which he had submerged the hearse and the two customs inspectors.

Once the four-breasted body was stowed onboard the launch, the hired killer had also climbed the stone stairs up through the cliff to the mansion above.

As always, the Doctor had encountered trouble with his victim, so the Undertaker had been summoned to subdue her. Earlier, the Panacea Clinic staff had left for the day by helicopter, *whup-whup-whupping* off to the mainland from the helipad out front of the imposing stone manor. There had been just the four of them on the deserted island, so no one had caught her shrieks echoing through the clinic as they trundled her, flailing and kicking, like a reluctant Alice though the now open looking-glass and down the secret staircase to the wonderland below, where the marvels of human anatomy were laid bare.

Beauty's only skin deep?

Not to the Doctor.

Oh, how the Hollywood actress had shrieked and gasped and cried and gibbered long into the wee hours of last night as the plastic surgeon had meticulously skinned her alive. Even the Undertaker, who was no slouch when it came to "preparing" the female body, had marveled at the Doc's vivisection skill. Using no anesthetic—that would have spoiled the erotic thrill—he had slit her skin with his surgeon's scalpel and peeled it away to expose the wonders of what glistened within. Spread-eagled and lashed to the autopsy table in the Plastic Surgery Room, the naked woman had thrashed and bucked and twitched and begged for forgiveness while her undisputed master had taunted several times, "Comfy? Satisfied? I'll bet you wish you could take back the words that brought you to this. You're ugly. Look at you, Ms. Hollywood Has-been. No man in his right mind would find you attractive. As far as I'm concerned, you're fit to be a mummy, and a mummy is what you'll be. Serves you right for what you did to *me*."

Oh, those shrieks!

What music to their ears.

The Doctor, the Director and the Undertaker.

As with the remains of the breastless woman the Undertaker had dumped by the woodland path on Galiano Island, and the desiccated "mummy" he had left on Wreck Beach, and the deformed castaway he had beached at Cowichan, and the other two human monsters he had discarded in Washington State, and the four-breasted corpse they had loaded onto the boat in the cave that night, the new victim was also a travesty of medical art.

In her case, the technique adapted by the spurned Doctor was known in body-beautiful circles as a peel, dermabrasion, skin resurfacing or sub-epidermal remodeling. In all those variations, the skin on the surface was removed to reveal the new, undamaged skin beneath. In the Doc's perversion, the skin beneath went too, and for excruciating hours long into last night, he had stripped the Hollywood actress down to the beauty *deeper* than skin deep.

Unfortunately, there had been more work for the Undertaker to do. So after he had watched the woman die from surgical shock, the hired killer had once again ventured out into the nautical night to dump another body where the Director had directed, this time the four-breasted woman on the rock off Lopez Island. The sun was rising by the time he had guided the cruiser back into the sea cave through the shipwreck reef that guarded the mouth of the cavern, the reef for which the island had been named before the recent change. On docking, the killer had returned to the Plastic Surgery Room to see what the Doctor had fashioned out of human flesh while he was gone.

It was some sort of mummy.

And what a *ghastly* creation!

For while the necrophile had been off on his pre-dawn undertaking, the Doc had begun to Fragonize the flayed Hollywood actress. As if to satisfy the Undertaker's lifelong breast fixation, the plastic surgeon, after flushing the flesh of blood and soaking it in a preservative, had set to work injecting colored wax into her bountiful tits, which unlike those of so many phony actresses these days were her own.

Suddenly, a compulsion seized the Undertaker.

An irresistible impulse had him in its grip.

The Doctor had preserved the nipples tipping both breasts. He had peeled the skin back from the areolas to bare the vessels and milk ducts in the flesh beneath. Using red and blue and white, he had created art out of functional tubes. Because six dump sites were enough to activate the Director's smokescreen to fool the Mounted Police, this creation was a keeper. Knowing that it too might last as long as Fragonard's art, the Doctor had gone about mummifying the actress as a perfectionist would. So beautiful was the esthetic of the surgeon's Fragonized masterpiece that the Undertaker found himself as stiff as steel in his pants.

Bending forward like that prince over Sleeping Beauty, he sucked satisfaction from her chemical-tasting nipples.

Different strokes for different folks.

Earlier that day, after he had Fragonized the night away, the Doctor had left Ebbtide Island by private helicopter for the helipad at Vancouver International Airport. Now, shortly after noon, the time had come for the Director and the Undertaker to follow him.

The two had work to do in the city at Eternal Spring.

The Director was off to meet Gill Macbeth.

The Undertaker was off to take out David Denning.

WHAT? WHY? WHO?

Vancouver

"Okay, folks. Time for the test. You didn't know there'd be a test? Read the fine print."

That's how S/Sgt. Rusty Lewis, the psychological profiler at Special X, kicked off his guest lecture this morning to the students in Det. Insp. Kim Rossmo's class on forensic behavioral science at the downtown campus of BCIT, the British Columbia Institute of Technology. It wasn't a test of the turn-your-bowels-to-water kind—no one was going to pass or fail because of this quiz—but the mention of the word "test" to these student cyber cops grabbed their attention. The hook was in. Now to land the catch.

"How much do you *really* know about sex? You look like a class that's versed in the wicked ways of the world, but we all know looks can be deceiving. So your knowledge of sex *is* the test. Shall we separate the men from the boys, the women from the girls?"

Faces leaned forward intently. Gonads were on the line. Flunk this test and each would be exposed—to him- or herself, if not to others—as a naïve priss. Psych profilers *understand* psychology.

True to his name, Rusty Lewis was a freckled redhead in his forties with the sleepy eyes of the actor Robert Mitchum. In fact, he was sleepy this morning, having been up late last night in Kamloops writing a profile on a bizarre case involving a weirdo who dressed black dogs in women's underwear before hanging them by ropes looped around their front paws and nailed to the branch of a tree so he could have anal intercourse with them through a hole torn in the panties as he strangled them to death. Committed to giving this lecture, Lewis had caught the red-eye flight at dawn.

"You might have read about the discovery of two naked female bodies this week: a woman with her breasts removed who was left to rot in the woods on Galiano Island, and a woman whose body was sucked dry to skin and bones before her remains were dumped on Wreck Beach. What this test about sex will determine is whether you have the knowledge to profile the type of killer involved. In other words, do you have what it takes to join Special X? Are you ready?"

Eager heads nodded.

"Okay," said Rusty Lewis, "let's do some groundwork before you take the test, to make sure we're all on the same playing field. First, what is human sexuality? It's 10 percent biological, 20 percent physiological and, most important, 70 percent psychological. That means the dominant sex organ in our body is our brain. And that's why sex so often gets psychologically fucked up."

A good play on words.

The class was listening and learning.

Sex and violence: *that's* what this was about.

"Human sexuality is a sensory act. The primary sexual sense is *not* the same for both sexes. Sight is the primary sense for the male, so that's why pornography, strip bars, men's magazines and lingerie outlets make billions a year. Hearing is the secondary sense for the male, both what he says and what is said to him. 'Tell me I'm the best you've ever had.' For the female, the primary sense is touch."

As if to prove the point, a sly male near the back of the room was surreptitiously ogling the breasts of unaware females as they listened to Lewis. Subconsciously, one woman folded her arms across her chest and cupped her breasts.

Body language.

"Every person in this class has sexual fantasies. Each fantasy is a brainchild of our personal psychosexuality, and as such, it influences how we act out sexually in the real world. The complex fantasies we develop at puberty trigger what arouses us and culminates in orgasm. Paraphilia is a mental disorder in which a person's sexual arousal and gratification depend on obsessively fantasizing about, and engaging in, sexual behavior that is unusual and extreme. A paraphilia can revolve around a particular object or a particular act. So preoccupying can the obsession be that *only* by depending on the object or the act can the deviant overcome sexual dysfunctions—erectile insufficiency or premature, retarded or conditional ejaculation. In layman's terms, he can't get it up, he shoots in his pants or he can't get his rocks off without his fantasy crutch.

"Without paraphilia, I'd be out of a job, because paraphilia is what psychological profilers hunt."

At this point in the lecture, Lewis connected his laptop to the class projector and doused the lights. What appeared onscreen initially was the cyber cops' new crest. It depicted a human skull pieced together like a jigsaw puzzle and overlaid with a street map. Scrolled below the bony jaw was the ribbon of a polygraph chart marked with squiggly lines. Looking into the hollow eye sockets was like gazing into a fish tank. Inset in the left orb was the tail of a shark. Inset in the right orb were its grisly jaws. The shark represented the predator hidden in the psycho's mind. On the left side of the skull was the ViCLAS symbol. On the right side of the skull was the RCMP badge. The overall image was set in a circle on a black background. On top, in English, were the words "Behavioral Sciences Branch." At the bottom, in French, was *"S.-dir des sciences du comportement."* Seen from a distance, it was not unlike the crest of a motorcycle gang.

Lewis punched a key, and a list appeared onscreen in the front of the class.

"Okay," the staff sergeant said, "time for that test. How versed are you in the wicked ways of the world? Are you one of those who likes his or her sex served with white gloves, or do you have sufficient grounding in reality to hunt the hunters?"

That threw down the gauntlet.

No goody two-shoes here.

The criminology class was ready to tackle the list.

"These paraphilias are in the top twenty. Each is defined as sexual arousal from some object or unusual and extreme act. What turns these deviants on?"

Fetishism
Partialism
Transvestism
Voyeurism
Exhibitionism
Frotteurism
Sadism
Masochism
Pedophilia
Zoophilia
Scatology
Apotemnophilia
Coprophilia
Urophilia
Klismaphilia
Cordophilia
Hypoxyphilia
Necrophilia

"If it exists," Lewis explained, "it turns *somebody* on. Type the word 'sex' into any search engine on the Internet and you'll be amazed by what you find. Diapers, of course. Clean *and* dirty. But what I found the other day were sites dedicated exclusively to smoke and balloons. Pictures of sexy women smoking or holding balloons.

"Both are examples of fetishism, the first kink on our list, defined as a deviant fixation on an object not primarily sexual in nature. A fetishist has the compulsive need to incorporate the object that turns him or her on into sexual activity in order to obtain sexual gratification. A fetishist invariably collects the object of his favor, and might go to great lengths to acquire the 'right' addition for his collection. Including murder.

"Common fetishes," Lewis went on, "are women's underwear,

spiked heels or specific materials like rubber, leather, silk or fur. In the case of the Headhunter a few years back, the killer's compulsion was to collect shrunken human heads.

"Technically, a shrunken head belongs in partialism. Fetishism is fixation on *inanimate* objects. Partialism is fixation on a particular body part: feet, hair, legs. Those are the common ones."

"Make it breasts," someone called out, "and every straight male in this room is a partialist."

"Uh-uh," replied Lewis. "*Non*-sexual body parts. The reason those shrunken heads defy classification is that they were a stand-in for the killer's mother's genitals, and they were shrunken to deform them into an inanimate object unconnected to sex."

"Weird," said someone else.

"We're in the realm of the weird. Weird is what psych profiling is all about."

The interesting thing about this class was the fidget level. Assess any group of students and you will find several bored out of their skulls and constantly checking their watches, shifting from buttock to buttock until the hour is up and they can get out of there. But not this class. And why would that be? Because what Lewis was outlining was paraphilia escalating to murder, and every person with a normal range of sexual experience had encountered someone who hinted at deviant symptoms.

Sex and violence.

It's everywhere, folks.

Closing in around you.

Whether you know it or not.

"Transvestism," Lewis continued, "like *Psycho*'s Norman Bates. Dressing up in the other sex's clothes for arousal and release."

"Drag queens," someone said.

"No," the profiler replied. "The paraphilia of transvestism applies to heterosexuals. Voyeurism: watching other people undress or have sex without their knowledge or consent. Exhibitionism: the compulsive act of exposing one's genitals to strangers. Here the desire is to evoke shock or fear, and the pleasure is derived from the reaction of the victim. React the wrong way, and that might lead to rape. Frotteurism: sexual arousal from rubbing one's genitals against the body of a fully dressed person in a crowded place."

"Rush hour on a crowded bus," a student suggested.

"Dry-humping commuters."

The class was really getting into the lecture.

"My dog does that to my legs. I think I'll rename him Frotteur."

"Sadism," Lewis emphasized, "the deadliest deviation. The sadist intentionally inflicts pain on another person, or threatens to do so, for the arousal and satisfaction he gets from the suffering of the victim. Torture, rape and mutilation are means to that end, and often culminate in the death of the tormented.

"Masochism: arousal from being subjected to pain or the threat of pain. Being whipped, trampled or semi-strangled are extreme thrills. The same with self-mutilation. 'Torture me,' begs the masochist. 'No,' the sadist grins.

"Pedophilia, there's a common one. Sexual satisfaction from acts with prepubescent children. Two subtypes: the preferential molester and the situational stalker. The preferential pedophile goes after kids because they turn him on. The situational stalker is hunting for an easy victim. It could just as easily be an eighty-year-old woman. If his preference was the elderly, his kink would be gerontophilia.

"Zoophilia: arousal by animals. We're not talking about the horny farmer who does it with sheep because his wife left him—unless she left him because he *preferred* to do it with sheep. That's bestiality, and often involves curiosity, a desire for novelty or the urge for sexual release when a partner isn't around. Zoophilia results when *that's* your fantasy, and it might involve sadistic acts that harm the beast."

The profiler tapped a key on his laptop to complete the paraphilia list onscreen:

Scatology	Obscene phone calls
Apotemnophilia	Amputations
Coprophilia	Feces
Urophilia	Urine

Klismaphilia	Enemas
Cordophilia	Bondage ropes
Hypoxyphilia	Oxygen deprivation
Necrophilia	Corpses

"Anyone see themselves? Someone they know?"

The class laughed.

"Yeah, Ben," a student called out, pointing to the fellow seated in front of him.

Ben flipped a finger in the air by way of reply.

"Such paraphilias could seem foreign to you, and you might find yourself wondering how *anybody* could find that object or act arousing, until you consider them in their milder versions," Lewis said. "It is not uncommon to have a partner who likes to 'talk dirty.' Or one who bites, scratches, spanks or enjoys role-playing. Ever had a hickey? Do you like to watch someone strip? Or be watched as you undress? And who do you think keeps all the adult video stores in business by renting tapes of strangers having sex?"

"Ben," the wag called out again.

"Unless you're a prude, those acts will seem innocuous. And they are . . . unless the arousal becomes magnified to the point of psychological dependence. If you find one paraphilia, there is a very strong probability that there is at least one more. What causes them to develop is unclear. The deviant might be repeating or reverting to a sexual habit that spawned early in life. Or paraphilia might begin through a process of conditioning, like Pavlov's dog. Because a bell rang each time the dog ate, the ringing of the bell soon caused the dog to salivate, whether food was present or not. Likewise, non-sexual objects may become sexually arousing if they are associated with pleasurable sex activity. And perhaps because sight is the primary sense for the male, paraphilias are far more common in men.

"The crux of the matter, however, is that *there is no cure.* Once a paraphilia develops, it takes hold forever. The focus of that kink remains specific and unchanging, and sex activity outside the bounds of whatever the kink is will lose its arousal or satisfaction potential unless the deviant fantasizes about the paraphilia at the same time. Paraphiliacs rarely seek treatment because the kink results in such immense sexual pleasure that giving it up is unthinkable. Consequently, the fantasy and its paraphilias will be incorporated into any acted-out crimes, and they will be left behind to be seen in the crime scene.

"That's where *we* come in, me and you budding profilers. For profiling deals mainly with sexually motivated crimes. What I'm about to say is very important if you want to have the tools to solve a psycho's serial crimes. Remember, the crimes *always* reflect what's going on inside his head, so if you want to know *who,* work back from *what* and *why.*

"Profiling is an art, not a science. It's like medicine, which though based on scientific knowledge is a subjective endeavor. A profiler starts by observing the crime scene to gather the facts, then he or she uses logic to work back to a primary and a secondary conclusion. Every profiler *is* Sherlock Holmes, and psych profiling is a police procedure because it relies on the experience a cop learns at crime scenes. To become a profiler in Canada, you must first have fifteen years on the job, with at least five in serious crime investigation.

"Okay," said Lewis, "let's consider the two naked female bodies I mentioned earlier: the woman with her breasts removed who was left to rot in the woods on Galiano Island, and the woman whose body was sucked dry to skin and bones before her remains were dumped on Wreck Beach. From the list onscreen, you now know enough about paraphilias to profile the type of killer involved. So imagine you're me, and Special X has called you to both murder scenes. How do you go about working up a psych profile?

"Basically, it all boils down to three questions: What happened? Why did it happen? Who would do those things for those reasons?

"*What* to *why* to *who.* And don't go to *who* too quickly. Ideally, a profiler doesn't want to know about suspects. That's like reading the last page of a whodunit, then looking for the clues. Except a suspect is just a suspect, so the clues may be red herrings.

"Okay," said Lewis. "What happened? This first step involves reconstructing events by examining in detail the crime scene, backed by autopsy findings, forensic lab results, witness statements and such. You have two primary objectives: to know each and every single thing that occurred, and to know the sequence in which they occurred. Only after the question 'What happened?' is answered as fully as possible do you address why it happened.

"In this second step of analysis, issues of motivation are assessed. You determine all the *possible* reasons why the offender might have done what he did, then draw a conclusion about the most probable reason. At this stage, you separate *necessary* from *unnecessary* behavior, which is determined from your point of view.

"Necessary behavior is that part of the killer's M.O. needed to: one, insure success of the crime; two, protect identity; or three, facilitate escape. Anything else that doesn't accomplish one of those three ends is unnecessary behavior. Where there is unnecessary behavior from *your* point of view, that is what you focus on, because that behavior is necessary to the psycho for his psycho-sexual gratification. Unnecessary behavior is psychologically motivated. In a sex crime, we treat *every* sex act as unnecessary behavior. Ritual. Signature. Fantasy. They make up the psycho.

"What you seek to do is develop the pattern. The verbal activity. The physical activity. The various sex acts. Ask yourself, Is he doing that deliberately, for a certain effect? What is he seeing? What is he hearing? What fantasy is he trying to set up?

"Remember, the fantasy developed to complement his motivation. The motivation for sexual violence is threefold: power, anger, sex, or a combination thereof. The complexity of the crime will be directly proportional to the intelligence of the offender.

"Only after the why is answered do you address the next question: *Who would do those things for those reasons?* Once the most probable reasons are determined for each event in the crime, the psychological motives can be deduced. Once the psychological motives are understood, then the primary characteristics and traits of the offender can be fathomed.

"Now you are ready to create a profile of your psycho, including a description of his behavioral kinks, which could be recognized by someone who knows him, and a description of his probable behavior immediately following the crime, which might have been observed by those who know him."

To illustrate how a profiler must look beyond what he thinks he is seeing to understand what is really going on in the psycho's mind, Rusty could have described the dog-hanging crime scene that took him north to Kamloops yesterday. The limb of the tree from which the dog hung had ten more nails pounded into the branch, each dangling a short strand of cut rope. The black dog was dressed in a red bra, red panties and a red garter belt. The panties, torn in the anal area, were stained with semen. The dog had been strangled with a chain, which was still buried in the fur of its neck. A number of black dogs had gone missing over the past few months, and they were found buried in a pet cemetery next to the hanging tree. Each grave was marked with a tombstone bearing a girl's name.

At first glance, it looked like a case of zoophilia. But if the weirdo was sexually aroused by animals, why dress them up? The crucial facts were the *black* dogs and the women's underwear. The profile Lewis had worked up was of a psycho far more dangerous than he seemed. What Rusty saw in the crime scene was a serial sex killer in the making, a man acting out his fantasy at the rehearsal stage. The black dogs were merely surrogate stand-ins for those he wanted to rape and strangle, and judging from the uniform color of the animals, that was black women.

From experience, Rusty knew the importance of complaints to the police by frightened wives and girlfriends. Last year, he had been called in to help the Chilliwack detachment hunt a necrophile who was digging up fresh graves and raping the corpses. When they caught the guy, it turned out his necrophilia had begun with a dry-run phase evident in a fantasy re-enactment at home. He had his wife take a cold bath and lie perfectly still in bed because that's the only way he could achieve orgasm during sex.

His profile on the dog strangler finished, Rusty—who had created the ViCLAS prototype—had queried that system's database late last night with the words "black victim." What ViCLAS had found was a recent complaint to the Penticton RCMP by the former girlfriend of a known white supremacist. He had forced her to put on blackface before they had sex, then he had strangled her to the point where she had passed out. When she was asked where her racist boyfriend was living now, his former girlfriend had replied, "Up Kamloops way."

That case was a good example of how psych profiling is done, but it was sensitive because the Kamloops Mounties were currently hunting the would-be sex killer before he tried the real thing, so Lewis was focusing on the Galiano Island and Wreck Beach crime scenes instead. It didn't really matter which case Rusty put to the BCIT class, for he knew the same three questions would profile the psychological motivation driving the killer of the mutilated women.

What?

Why?

Who?

While S/Sgt. Rusty Lewis delivered his guest lecture to the students in Det. Insp. Kim Rossmo's class on forensic behavioral science, Rossmo sat at the back of the room and worked on a geographic profile for the South African police. Though they were on different forces—Kim was a cyber cop with the Vancouver city police, not the federal Mounties—both officers had similar jobs. You could say they were brothers-in-law.

When Rossmo's cellphone jangled, he stepped out of the room to take the call. The phone call was from Chief Superintendent DeClercq at Special X; he wondered if the two cyber cops would do him the honor of bringing their combined psycho-hunting skills uptown to the Strategy Wall in his office at RCMP HQ.

IN THE EYE OF THE BEHOLDER

Vancouver

"Gill Macbeth," said Dr. David Denning, "meet Graham Worlock. Graham, Gill's the best pathologist in town. Gill, Graham's the director of the Panacea Clinic. The anti-aging treatments at his clinic provide the best post-operative defense available to slow the ongoing damage caused to human body cells by the ravages of free radicals. The Panacea Clinic has been open for less than a month, but already I have referred several of my patients to Graham's care. Because the kinks of starting up are still being ironed out, the Panacea Clinic offers post-operative referrals from Eternal Spring a special introductory rate. Graham is the fellow I told you about in the morgue yesterday."

"Mr. Worlock," Gill said, offering her hand.

"Dr. Macbeth," he acknowledged, with a disarming bow of his head. "My pleasure."

Gill would not have been surprised if instead of shaking her hand, the director had bent down and kissed it. His accent was American, but there was something about this handsome charmer with the sorcerer's last name that could be the cultured sophistication of a European aristocrat. His was the aura of a Continental dealer in classical works of art, a buyer and seller who would feel at home in the high-stakes auction salons of Christie's or Sotheby's. Not an ounce of fat marred his buffed, lean physique, and his scalp was shaved as smooth as his clean-cut jaws. Impeccably dressed in a charcoal suit from Savile Row, a conservative white shirt and a burgundy tie, Worlock could grace the cover of *GQ*. His most riveting feature, however, was his dark, hypnotic eyes, so seductive that they seemed to combine Casanova, Don Juan and Svengali in one man. Feeling their tug, Gill wondered how many women this rake had drawn into bed.

A hundred?

A *thousand?*

Possibly.

"End of the week," Denning said, uncorking a bottle of wine. "We were discussing beauty, and nothing complements that subject quite like Beaujolais."

"Or a woman like you," said Worlock, causing Gill to blush as red as the juice of the grape.

"You flatter me."

"That's not flattery. It's the truth."

Three long-stemmed wine glasses sat on a silver tray on the plastic surgeon's walnut desk. Denning's private office at Eternal Spring was as tastefully appointed as money can buy, thanks to the largesse of his wealthy Hollywood patients. The painting behind his desk was modern art, befitting an artist whose surgical technique was as cutting-edge as the latest medical journals. The only anachronism that Gill could see was a glass-fronted bookcase shelved with anatomy texts from as early as the 1700s. But those would have cost a pretty penny, so they too fit in.

Denning poured the Beaujolais and passed around the glasses.

Worlock raised his in a toast to Gill: "Her beauty made / the bright world dim, and everything beside / seemed like the fleeting image of a shade."

"Shelley," said Macbeth.

"You know your stuff."

"So do you."

"It's my line of work."

"Graham picks up where I leave off," interjected Denning. "That's why I thought you should meet him, Gill."

From the jacket of her tailored business suit, Macbeth withdrew a slim cellphone and placed it on the desk. "It irks me to hear these things go off when people are relaxing. I'm waiting for confirmation of sketchy weekend plans, so I hope you won't mind the interruption of just such an irksome call."

"Romance?" queried Denning.

"Thanks to your rejuvenating skill."

"I'm sure you required no help from David," Worlock said.

"It never hurts to shed a decade or two," Macbeth replied. "Please continue the discussion that my arrival interrupted."

"We were discussing beauty."

"So David said."

"And I was making the point that beauty is at the heart of natural selection. Regardless of the time in history, the location in the world or even the species of plant or animal, attractive traits have been seen—and are *still* seen—as conducive to successful mating. The glorious colors of flowers aid pollination. The plumage of birds, the antlers of elk, the strut of peacocks in full display help mating rituals. In fact, it was *specifically* the dazzling variety of plants and animals on the Galápagos Islands that made Darwin realize all of that was linked to reproductive biology and evolution."

"Beauty as instinct?"

"Exactly," said the Director. "Visual communication travels at the speed of light. At 186,000 miles per second. It's not only rapid, but also works at a distance. And because sight is the sense involved, *appearance* is the message it communicates. In a visual world, attractiveness is what draws attention, so beautiful traits lead to evolutionary success."

"Survival of the fittest?"

Worlock nodded. "We see it all around: in movies, in magazines, on TV. Beautiful traits in women—smooth skin, small noses, full lips, high cheekbones, slim necks, bountiful breasts, tight waists, curvy hips, shapely legs—all are perceived as sexually desirable, so they are thought to be a boon to successful mating, which makes them *instinctively* desirable from an evolutionary standpoint for natural selection."

"Beauty as function?"

"That's why we manipulate it to get what we want. Thanks to the evolution of man's remarkable brain, we have learned to reconstruct our appearance to enhance our instinctive needs. A bushman ties foliage to his body so prey will think him a tree. A TV news anchor sports a power suit to convey authority. We adorn ourselves with feathers and furs, etch our skins with tattoos and pierce them with jewels, fund a megabillion-dollar-a-year cosmetics industry and transform our flesh through plastic surgery to increase our attractiveness. Even Marilyn Monroe—who was idolized for her *natural* beauty—had two touch-ups: a rhinoplasty and a chin augmentation in 1949."

"That's one patient I wish had been mine," said Denning.

"What's your theory, David?" Gill asked the plastic surgeon.

"Looks are important for self-esteem. Appearance is so integral to our personality that one cannot be separated from the other. If memory serves me correctly, the Latin word for mask is *persona.* That means our very person is the mask we wear—namely, our appearance."

"Well put," said Worlock. "I agree."

"Me too," said Gill. "Because we intuitively evaluate others on the way they look, we assume that others also evaluate us on our appearance. I'm happier and more confident when I look my best. I think that's because my sense of self depends upon my constantly assessing my own appearance and comparing it—often subconsciously—with that of others in society at large."

"You want to fit in?" said Worlock.

"I want to stand out. But I want to stand out attractively, because I know from experience that good-looking individuals are given credit for more intelligence than their less attractive equals, and are accepted as more desirable friends, and are thought to be more honest, trustworthy and romantic than their plainer peers. When you look good, life becomes a self-fulfilling prophesy."

"You not only want to *be* the fittest," Worlock said, "but you also want to be *seen* as the fittest?"

"It sure makes life easier."

"Beauty rules," said Denning. "And that's why intelligent people spend large sums of money and subject themselves to discomfort so they can alter—or merely maintain—their visual image. The baby boomers pushed into their fifties a few years ago. The stampede for nips and tucks and major overhauls is under way. Last year, the number of patients who had work done jumped 25 percent. Boomers are coming out of the vanity closet in droves to sign up for an extended warranty on youth and attractiveness. The demographics used to be 90 percent women, 10 percent men. But men are discovering that youth counts in the cutthroat jungle of business, and they hope facial rejuvenation will keep them in the race. Everyone—no matter what age—is influenced by this worldwide frenzy to grab hold of perpetual youth. We live in an age that's obsessed with smoother, tighter, bigger. More than two hundred thousand American women had their breasts redone last year."

"And me," added Gill.

"So the question is," Denning said, "where do you go from here? Now that you've had a sip from the Fountain of Youth, will those results draw you back for more plastic surgery, feeding a growing addiction to going under the knife until you end up like one of those aging has-beens on TV, with skin stretched so tight it looks like a hurricane is blowing in your face."

"I hope not," said Gill.

"So that's where Graham comes in."

The plastic surgeon raised his glass in a toast to the Director.

"I run a clinic," Worlock said, "that's top secret. For most patients, the stigma of plastic surgery is inconsequential. They feel comfortable baring and sharing all. But that doesn't apply to Hollywood celebrities."

"Who make up most of my patients," Denning said.

"To them, if the secret gets out of the bag, that's the kiss of death to their careers."

The trilling of the cellphone on the desk interrupted the Director.

"Sorry," said Gill, "that's my call."

She punched on the phone.

"Hello," she answered.

"Hi, Gill. It's Robert. Something's come up. It appears the LAPD has the killer who surgically mutilated those women up here cornered in Los Angeles. It's likely there were previous murders in California. I'm flying down there early tomorrow, and there's a lot to do before then, so I'm afraid I have to beg off from our weekend plans. How 'bout a rain check?"

"You bet. Good to know the Northwest is safe again. I'll see you when you get back. As for this weekend, I have a stack of books a mile high to read."

Gill rang off and switched off the phone.

"Uh-oh," said Worlock. "A broken heart?"

Gill grinned. "A broken date. Much less serious. You were saying, before the interruption?"

"For obvious reasons, the clinic I operate is hush-hush," Worlock continued. "After David has turned back the hands of time, what I do is slow down the aging clock. The Panacea Clinic is a pampering oasis for metabolic therapy. A spoonful of sugar to help the medicine go down, you might say."

"Inner wellness to outer beauty?"

"I hate that word, don't you?"

Gill laughed. "'Wellness'? On that, we see eye to eye. That word is the sort of sop thrown around by smoothies who call themselves Dr. Bob or Nurse Cindy."

"You're poking fun at me?"

"I'm smoking you out."

"For complimenting you on your beauty?"

"I guess."

"I won't do that again. Besides, a woman of your beauty—"

Another laugh from Macbeth.

"—probably thinks she has no use for what I have to offer."

"And what's that?"

"The *real* Fountain of Youth."

"Ponce de León?"

"At your service, ma'am."

Gill glanced at Denning and arched her eyebrow.

"I can treat the symptoms, but I don't have the cure. You made the decision to go under the knife, so what do you have to lose by taking the war against aging to the culprit in your cells? What Graham does, among other things, is counter the nasty effect of free radicals with antioxidants that work at the cellular level. Besides, your weekend plans fell through. Escape the ordinary."

"Sold," said Gill. "Where am I going?"

"Shhhh," said Worlock, a finger bisecting the smile that curled his lips. "That's a secret."

From his vantage point across the street, the Undertaker watched Denning's nurse leave Eternal Spring for the day. Half an hour after she came out, the Director and Gill Macbeth exited from the clinic. Pausing on the sidewalk for a look at the sky, the Director flashed the killer a signal that now was the time to act. The Undertaker dawdled until those two were clear of the scene before crossing the road to enter Eternal Spring.

The time has come, the Director had said, to take Denning out. It won't be long until the police identify the mutilated women you've been dumping around the islands. When they discover *all* were recent patients of Denning's, because we've been poaching from his patients to satisfy the Doctor's insatiable sexual demands under the terms of the deal that I struck with him, the cops will have found the link that will lead them to the Panacea Clinic, and therefore to us. So tomorrow, I want you to fly to Vancouver with me, and after I've seen the Doc's next victim at the clinic, I want you to enter Eternal Spring with a silenced gun and do what's necessary to take Denning out. After you remove the eight files from his office, there's a trap I want you to set in a hidey-hole, so if the cops who investigate what you've done at Eternal Spring find what you're going to hide there and spring the trap, it will send a warning signal to Ebbtide Island.

To that end, the Undertaker now entered the clinic and locked the door behind him. Denning was still in his private office when the killer walked in unannounced. It was Friday afternoon, so the clinic was closed for the weekend. They were the only two people in Eternal Spring when the Undertaker fired his pistol. It wouldn't have mattered if the waiting room was full of patients. The silencer on the end of the barrel muffled the sound of the shot.

HUNTING THE HUNTERS

Vancouver

If it was up to the Ottawa bureaucrats who organize the RCMP, Chris Wozney's ViCLAS section would still work out of the Annex next door, and Rusty Lewis's profiling unit would be housed four blocks up Heather Street, in the Operations building. You'd think the guiding principle of those federal mandarins was "divide and conquer," which—in this era of the last gasp of the old guard, who were suspicious of computers and baffled by cyberspace—perhaps it was.

In DeClercq, however, the Mounted Police had "the right man in the right place at the right time," for he had not only the insight to grasp how the pieces fit together, but also two close friends in Comm. François Chartrand, the top cop of the force, and Dep. Comm. Eric Chan, head of all the Mounted Police units in B.C. and the Yukon. If you want to get something done, it pays to have powerful friends in high places, and the chief had a clear idea of what to do with Special X.

When it came to being a cop, DeClercq was, above all else, a military tactician. The way he saw it, what was going on out there was a guerrilla war, and the fort of civilized behavior was in danger of being overrun by barbarians. The RCMP was the last vestige of the British colonial army—thus the scarlet tunic—and when that army was under attack, it closed ranks, for the best offense was always fought from a strong defensive position.

Consolidate.

That was his primary tactic.

And the origin of the Strategy Wall.

The first step in psycho-hunting is to consolidate the pieces. You must gather his crimes together to know a serial killer is on the loose, and the tool the Mounties created as a result of the Olson case was the best crime-linkage system around. So DeClercq's first move on the chessboard of the hunting ground was to shift ViCLAS across the parking lot, from the Annex to the new cyber-cop cellar at Special X.

"Six murders," Chris Wozney said to the seven cops facing the photos on the Strategy Wall in DeClercq's office: the chief, Zinc Chandler, Ghost Keeper, Rusty Lewis, Kim Rossmo, Nick Craven and Jenna Bond. "Three here in British Columbia and three in Washington State." The photos of the six were pinned to a large map of the Pacific Northwest.

"What's the signature?" Rossmo asked.

"Surgical wounds," Wozney replied. "That's the query ViCLAS and HITS used to link the six cases. Each victim was mutilated in a cruel parody of a plastic surgery technique."

"On Galiano, the breasts were cut off," Craven said. "On Lopez, the cut-off breasts were sewn on."

"Breast reduction and breast enhancement," Wozney reiterated. "The victim on Wreck Beach was liposuctioned to death. The Cowichan woman had her eyelids, ears and nose removed instead of sculpted. The body found near Port Angeles was bloated and deformed from microfat and collagen injections. The facelift on the Bellingham woman was so severe that her skin was almost stretched flat."

"The Lopez victim was strangled," offered Bond.

"So were three of the others," Wozney added. "The remaining two died during their mutilations."

"There are no murder scenes?" asked Lewis.

"No," said Wozney, "only dump sites."

"So all I have to work with to build a psych profile is what was done to the bodies before they were dumped?"

"Afraid so."

"Were the women mutilated while they were alive?"

"The Lopez victim was," Bond answered. "There's bruising of the tissues around the surgical cuts."

"The others too," Wozney said, "near as we can tell. Some are in a state of decomposition."

"Were they raped?" Lewis asked.

"No semen was found."

"He might have used a condom," Bond suggested, "so we wouldn't recover his DNA."

"What troubles me most," Wozney stated, "is that none of the six have been identified. If they're missing persons, Rapid ID should have made a link by now."

"How far back do the dumpings go?"

"A couple of weeks."

"So odds are the six women themselves didn't want to be traced," Chandler piped in.

"Why?" asked Rossmo.

"That's the question," said DeClercq.

"One more thing," Wozney contributed, "and it might be our best lead: VICAP linked our signature to a serial killer operating in L.A. a few years ago. Five women were disfigured by a psycho dubbed Picasso. Not only was that killer never caught, but the prime suspect for these mutilations in the Pacific Northwest just flew down to L.A."

DeClercq turned to Lewis. "Rusty, you're up to bat."

Step two in psycho-hunting is to profile the behavior that left the signature gleaned from each of the consolidated crimes. In Rusty Lewis, DeClercq had not only a psychological profiler versed in the latest insights pioneered by the FBI, but also the man who programmed such mind-reading techniques into the questions of the ViCLAS system. So the chief's second move on the chessboard of the hunting ground was to shift Lewis four blocks down Heather

Street, from the Operations building to the cyber-cop cellar at Special X.

"What we're looking at," Lewis said, his finger jumping from one photo to another on the Strategy Wall, "is a series of mutilations focused on the female sexuality of the victims. Two important points. First, these mutilations were done while the women were alive. And second, as Chris put it, each victim was mutilated in a cruel parody of a plastic surgery technique.

"Why would someone do that? In order to have complete mastery and control over the sexuality of each victim. So much so that he can transform his victims from women into mutant monsters and enjoy watching them suffer under his cruelty. For him, hatred and control are eroticized. He finds the intentional maltreatment of each victim intensely gratifying. He is sexually aroused by a highly ritualistic fantasy in which he is master and a captive female is slave. When he acts out his fantasy in the real world, he sexually transforms his anger and power into cruel aggression.

"Who would do that? A sexual sadist."

Lewis had carried his profiler's bible up from the cellar with him. He flipped through the pages until he found a quote.

"This," he said, "was written by someone who knows. The author was a sexual sadist who kidnapped and held captive, then raped, tortured and killed, a number of victims in several American states over a period of twenty years. The emphasis is his:

> *Sadism:* The wish to inflict pain on others is not the essence of sadism. One essential impulse: *to have complete mastery over another person,* to make her a helpless object of our will, to become the absolute ruler over her, to become her God, to do with her as one pleases. To humiliate her, to enslave her, *are means to this end,* and the most important radical aim is to make her *suffer,* since *there is no greater power over another person than that of inflicting pain on her* to force her to undergo suffering without her being able to defend herself. The pleasure in the complete domination over another person is the very essence of the sadistic drive.

"That," said Lewis, "is who we're looking for."

"Captivity is important?" asked Bond.

"It's crucial," Lewis responded. "The definition of captivity *is* complete control. Sadists will lure or transport their victims from the initial contact scene to a preselected prison, where they can torture at will."

"Thus the dumpings?" said Craven.

Lewis nodded. "Far from the murder scenes. The torture is often done with instruments. Some commercially obtained, some homemade. Torture by instruments is guaranteed to reduce the victim to depths of fear impossible to imagine."

"Like a surgeon's scalpel?" Ghost Keeper offered.

"That would do the trick. Imagine being conscious and seeing a scalpel cut into you."

"And the strangulations?" asked Bond.

"That's the preferred means of finishing off. In a third of the cases studied, ligature strangulation was the cause of death. Manual throttling made up another quarter."

Chandler asked Lewis, "What about demeanor?"

"He'll be a details man. His attacks will be planned with the utmost care. His fantasy will have been rehearsed many times. His brutal level of force will seem at odds with his outward manner. He'll be calm, unemotional and detached during the attack. He'll be very attuned to the visual and audio aspects. He'll likely script his victim in what to say and do. He may remain relatively uninvolved sexually with her. He's likely to record the torture in some way. And as trophies, he'll probably collect a personal item from each victim."

"Why stay sexually uninvolved?" asked Bond.

"Because he's superior to them," Lewis replied. "Emotion equals weakness in his eyes."

"He gets a *mental* kick?" Craven said.

"Right. The torture and the killing provide his pleasure. 'Better than an orgasm,' as one guy put it."

"We have a suspect," Chandler said. "A renegade plastic surgeon. And we have video of him surgically deforming the breasts of a teenage victim."

"Sounds good," Lewis said. "What do we know about him?"
"Not much," Wozney said. "The file is down in L.A."

Step three in psycho-hunting is to profile the geography mapped out by the consolidated crimes. The cutting edge of psycho-hunting was supposed to remain in Quantico, Virginia. The FBI developed VICAP and psychological profiling. When the Mounties one-upped the Bureau with the mind-reading capacity of ViCLAS, it was easy to grab back the lead by retooling VICAP along similar lines. But while it's all very well to have mastered the formula what = why = who, for that equation to *really* pay off, you must factor in the where. The Suits got close, but in the end it was no cigar, for that missing element was resolved in the redcoats' realm.

Not by the Mounties themselves.

But near enough.

When it came to cyber cops, Det. Insp. Kim Rossmo of the Vancouver Police Department—a municipal force independent of the Mounties—was in a different league.

Like Zinc Chandler, Rossmo was a Prairie boy from Saskatchewan. A math whiz during high school in Saskatoon, he wrote his grade twelve final exam in algebra after only one week of classes and got a perfect score. Chasing bad guys on the streets seemed more thrilling than doing mathematics, so Rossmo took a break from university to try his hand at being a private eye. When he went back, it was to switch to criminology, and that brought him to Vancouver, which had the best course of study for graduate work in his area of interest, under Profs. Paul and Patricia Brantingham.

To earn a living, Kim joined the Vancouver police. Only by going without sleep could he cover both tasks, so Rossmo would walk his skid-row beat until 2 a.m., then work on his master's and eventually Ph.D. theses at the university until dawn, then drive to court and read research journals until he was called to give evidence against those he had busted, all before catching a few winks at home and starting again.

As luck would have it, skid row became his lab.

For what Rossmo began to fathom as he patrolled that low-life beat was that petty criminals behave like everybody else. We are all lazy. We take the shortest route. If we need a quart of milk, we drive to the corner store. If we go to the gym, we use the local fitness center. In geographic terms, this is known as the nearness, or "least effort," principle. So if we were to plot those destinations on a map, there would be a cluster of dots around our home and place of work. The farther afield we venture from our "anchor points," the fewer stops we make, so the fewer the dots on the map.

Each time a serial killer meets, attacks, kills or dumps a victim, he leaves a point on a map. Like everyone else, he relies on a geographic template in his head, an inner logic that guides his predatory movements. Because his hunting ground overlaps the "awareness space" in which he lives from day to day—an image of the city founded on his non-criminal experience and knowledge—his crime sites are linked by predictable behavior to his anchor points: the serial killer's home or his place of work.

That which is predictable can be mathematically quantified, for by definition the laws of probability apply. So as a mathematician walking a grid of crime, Constable Rossmo asked himself, If you knew where a series of crimes occurred, could you use the nearness principle and the laws of probability and logic to develop a formula that would accurately predict where the criminal responsible for those crimes most likely lived or worked?

The search for the answer to that question would consume Kim for six years.

All on minimal sleep.

In the end, what he created was geographic profiling. First came the formula, which was based on research into typical journeys to crime sites. Then came the computer program, which Kim wrote himself, to perform up to a million calculations to analyze any case. Analysis is done by plotting a predator's crime sites on a screen map. The system draws a box around his hunting ground and divides it into a grid of thousands of pixels. Then, using Kim's formula, the computer calculates the probability of each point on the grid being the anchor point from which the killer began. Finally, points of equal probability are linked together and color-coded according to a scale, so what results is a geographic profile of the hunting ground that shows the likelihood of an area being the killer's home or place of work.

The accuracy of what Rossmo invented was easy to prove. When he applied geographic profiling to the cases of known serial killers, the results were astounding. By computing back from their crime sites, he was able to narrow the anchor points of serial killers such as Clifford Olson, the Son of Sam and the Yorkshire Ripper to less than 5 percent of their respective hunting grounds. What that meant was instantly clear to DeClercq: not only had Rossmo solved step three in psycho-hunting—by adding the where that was previously missing from the what = why = who equation—but he had solved step four as well. For once psycho-hunters knew where to look for their prey, they could focus on applying the psychological profile developed in step two to the narrowed-down list of psycho possibilities within that neighborhood.

Consequently, when Rossmo came searching for support and backing to perfect his prototype, DeClercq greeted him with open arms, and Kim was made an honorary member of Special X. It wasn't long before he paid them back a hundredfold by profiling exactly where Mephisto could be found, which was instrumental in saving Nick Craven's life.

Step one.

Step two.

Step three.

Step four.

That's how it's done.

And that, Virginia, is why it's said that the Mounties always get their man.

Rossmo approached the Strategy Wall to take over the "bounce session" from Rusty Lewis. Shorter and stockier than the psych profiler, Kim was a physically fit man somewhere in his forties who sported the mustache common to the Vancouver police. Meticulous in his work, he was known for dotting every *i* and crossing every *t*. On a flight to Ottawa several years ago to sell the Mounted's brass on investing in geographic profiling, Kim had listened to DeClercq describe his moonlight trek with Katt up the side of the Great Pyramid of Cheops. "It's said," the Mountie told the mathematician, "that pi is built into the dimensions of the Great Pyramid. If so, that means the Egyptians knew the ratio of the circumference of a circle to its diameter a thousand years before the Greeks supposedly discovered it." In Ottawa, Kim purchased a book on that pyramid. He spent the four-hour flight back to Vancouver filling sheets of paper with calculations. "You're right," he said to DeClercq as they landed. "Pi to four decimal places. All four sides of the pyramid are equal to pi x 2. So the ratio of the length of one side to its height is pi over 2."

Yes, indeed. A different kind of cop.

"The configuration of these dump sites is out of line," commented Kim. He referred the cops facing him to the map of the West Coast to which the six crime-scene photos were pinned.

"How so?" asked DeClercq.

"They're too in line."

"I see what you mean," said Bond. "They look like the pattern of six dots on a die. A boxcar. The three sites north of the border are strung in a row, and so are the three sites south of the border, parallel directly under them."

"The odds of that configuration occurring are too high if someone dumped these bodies randomly."

"The pattern was *planned?*" Ghost Keeper said.

"Probably."

"Like the cross left by Jack the Ripper?" said DeClercq.

"What cross?" Bond asked.

"The victim pattern," DeClercq explained. "If you had a bird's-eye view of the East End of London in 1888, you would see that the first four prostitutes knifed by the Ripper form a perfect inverted cross on a street map of his hunting ground."

"Why?"

"Too long a story," replied the chief. "Remind me sometime to tell you the tale of *our* Ripper case."

"If the victim pattern here was planned," Craven said, "that would solve what's bugging me. The Galiano remains found near the public footpath were in a state of decomposition. The logical explanation for why no one smelled them rotting is that the body was dumped there recently. So why would someone move a decaying body to a place where it was sure to be found, unless *that's* the reason why it was moved?"

"This killer goes to great pains," Wozney said, "to make sure each corpse is dumped conspicuously."

"For whatever reason the pattern developed," Rossmo explained, "it developed *after* the Galiano corpse was initially dumped. Unless the first dump site wasn't conspicuous enough."

"The bottom line is that you can't help us," Chandler said. "Since the dump sites are patterned, they don't geographically profile?"

"Up here," Rossmo agreed. "But that's not the end of the matter. Did I not hear Chris say that she linked these murders to an earlier series of deaths in L.A.?"

"You did," Wozney said. "The killer dubbed Picasso."

"Then if the *same* killer is behind *both* series of murders, and if he developed this dumping pattern only recently, perhaps a profile of the L.A. killings will lead us to him."

"Tomorrow morning, early, we're going to take a trip," DeClercq announced. "I'll requisition the Super King Air from Air Services. Who wants to go to Disneyland?"

GUINEA PIG

Orcas Island

"Hello. This is Becky Bond speaking."

"Hello, Pumpkin. It's your ma."

"Where are you, Mom? You missed dinner. Gram made spaghetti and meatballs. It was yummy."

"Pasta Pete. That's my girl."

"Pete's not a girl's name."

"Okay, Pasta Paula."

"My name's not Paula."

"Okay, Broccoli Becky."

"I *hate* broccoli. And we didn't have it."

"That can be arranged."

"Don't do that, Mom."

"It's either Broccoli Becky or Pasta Pete. What's it going to be?"

"Pasta Pete."

"Isn't that what I said? 'Pasta Pete. That's my girl.'"

The six-year-old laughed, a joyous laugh that filled her end of the conversation, and for at least the zillionth time in her single motherhood, Jenna thanked heaven for how blessed she was.

"We have *krav maga* tomorrow."

"I'll try to be back. If not, we'll have to skip a week, Becs."

"Maybe Gram can take me?"

This time Jenna laughed. "Can you see your grandmother, with a bout of arthritis, throwing Leo around?"

"I guess not."

"Pass the phone to Gram."

As always, on a cold night when her joints were acting up, Jenna's mom sat back in the overstuffed comfort of what was once Hank Bond's reading chair, a cup of tea beside her on the branded trunk that still held the .357 Magnum Python that her husband had packed on his hip for the twelve terms he had served as the San Juan County sheriff. For her, there was as much comfort in the fact that he had sat here as there was in the contours and padding of the chair.

She took the phone.

"Jenna?"

"Hi, Mom. I'm still in Vancouver. Nick and I are off to California early in the morning. Don't worry, I'm not eloping."

"Eloping, my dear, is what I *wish* you'd do. You are not going to meet a better man than him."

"My mother, the matchmaker."

"Someone has to hitch you up. You can't be a detective, and work the farm, and raise Becky, and take care of me all by yourself forever. I don't want to see you burn out."

"Gee, that sounds like a *lot* of work. Maybe I'll go to Disneyland, build a cabin on Tom Sawyer's Island, live like a hermit and never come back."

"Why California?"

"The Horsemen have a lead that affects a San Juan murder, and by sticking with them, I can do an end run around the Bureau."

"When will you be back?"

"I hope by tomorrow night."

"Take care."

"I will. For Becky's bedtime story, I think we're into chapter 3 of *Wind in the Willows.*"

Jenna's mom punched off the portable phone and peered over the top of her reading glasses at her precious granddaughter. On the floor in front of the wood-burning stove and accompanied by her cat, Becky was beading a necklace.

"Bedtime," said Gram. "Ready for your story?"

"Sure am," Becky said. "Mom's reading me that book she used to get ideas from for Hallowe'en."

"Wind in the Willows?"

"Dracula!" the imp said with a straight face.

The opalescence of the moon dappled the onyx waters of Rosario Strait. The sea was calm tonight compared with the wild roller-coaster ride that Nick Craven had braved the night before. So as not to make a sound as he crept in, the Undertaker had anchored his boat to a buoy a distance upshore that served the deserted getaway of some summer people, then he had switched to a canoe to paddle silently down to the docking float out front of Jenna Bond's farm. Plainly visible among the canopy of stars were the three studs of Orion's belt, fitting since the hunter below was closing in on the guinea pig.

Dip, dip, dip went the paddle as the killer approached the jutting finger of the float. The rubber buffer between the berth and the ramp up to the rocky beach squeaked as the creaking planks rose and fell with the pulse of the tide. No voices, no motors, no stereos, nothing disturbed the tranquility of nature at rest except the slapping of waves against the log pontoons of the float as the Undertaker sidled the canoe in to dock. Slap turned to lap as he stepped up onto the planks to secure the line, the water echoing hollowly in the cavern between the surface of the sea and the flat boards under his feet. The float rocked and rolled a little as he walked the plank that angled up to the sloping shore.

Squeak, squeak . . .

Creak, creak . . .

Slap, slap . . .

Lap, lap . . .

The Undertaker stepped onto the rocky beach.

A quick glance over his shoulder confirmed that his escape route was secure. The ghoul's stealthy stalking had gone unobserved. That was to be expected in the hours before dawn, which was why he was undertaking this snatch now. The float was vacant, the *Islomania* gone, so that meant the San Juan County cop was off somewhere, no doubt investigating the death of the four-breasted woman whom the Undertaker had dumped on Lopez Island. The Mountie's boat was gone too, so her boyfriend wasn't around.

The kid and her granny.

A walk in the park.

Smudges of light on the horizon of the hunched black mainland across the strait betrayed the location of population clusters inland. If the continent was a castle, the strait would be its moat, fortressing those who cowered in the urban beehives over there from the dangers that lurked in the wilderness of the outland over here.

Dangers like him.

He skulked toward the house.

This beach could be the moonscape shining above, for the rugged rocks glistened with an iridescent glaze. Stones crunched under his feet as he abandoned the barren shore for the path that wormed up the hillside to his quarry's bed. As always, the Undertaker's garb was black—a black leather jacket against the cold snap that chilled the dead of night, a rolled-up black watch cap that tugged down into a face-hiding balaclava if need be, black jeans, black boots, black gloves and a black heart. The trees up the right side of the path shadowed it from the moon, so, black on black, the killer was swallowed up.

The Undertaker paused a moment to unzip his jacket. Reaching in, he withdrew an automatic pistol from the shoulder holster beneath his armpit. From one pocket, he fetched the threaded silencer and screwed it onto the muzzle, then—a quiet killer with a hushed means of murder—the death dealer snaked up the garden path.

You'd think the sky above would be dark and the moonlit ground light, but actually the reverse was true. The overhead dome was blue from lunar and cosmic glow, while the terrestrial woods were stark sentinels casting gloom. Climbing the path was like moving along a deep trench. Only where the trees were cleared did light patch the ground: the garden to the left that thrived on summer sun, with its pond catching the glare of the moon as a streak of parallel lines surrounded by the fireflies of reflected stars; and the greenhouse in another open spot, so moonbeams shone through its glass skin to expose its skeletal frame like X-rayed bones.

The Undertaker reached the steps and crept up to the porch.

As he snuck along the veranda to the front door, the ghoul skirted the bow window and peered into the parlor. It was a common practice in the country not to draw the drapes, so leering in like a Peeping Tom, the killer cased the interior of the house by the flicker of dying firelight from the wood-burning stove. The coziness of the warmth within did nothing to thaw his heart, for out here it was the icy white sheen on Death's door that made him feel welcome.

The lockpicks he fished from his pocket made quick work of the deadbolt. The moist air of winter had swollen the wood, so he had to force the door to push it open. Noise from that shove and the squeak of hinges not yet oiled during spring cleaning seemed to shriek a warning to those asleep upstairs, but as he listened for an excuse to use the silenced pistol, all he could hear was the scurrying of a mouse in one of the kitchen cupboards.

Easing the door shut against drafts, he left it slightly ajar.

The floorboards creaked under the psycho's feet. As he tiptoed toward the tunnel staircase that climbed to the upper story, the contracting metal of the damped-down stove pinged like a cooling auto motor. The smell of smoke that had escaped from the stove when the last log was fed in before bed, mixed with the tangy aroma of Italian cuisine, still scented the air in the room. Guided by orange embers, a single blue flame struggling to ignite into a cheery blaze and a rectangle of moonlight spilled on the floor by a side window, the Undertaker crossed to the stairs that would take him up to the snoozing guinea pig.

Creak . . .

Creak . . .

Creak . . .

Gun first, up he went.

"Gram?" a sleepy voice mumbled from the open door off the crest of the stairs. It was a question asked from the far-off land of nod, and not one from consciousness here and now. Looking in, he could see the child tucked into bed, kissed by moonglow streaming in through a skylight like the beneficence of God. The cat curled up beside her opened one eye, warily watching the killer as he approached the girl.

"Mom?"

Again, a question from never-never land.

Russet hair radiated out across the feather pillow from the face of the experimental guinea pig. Looming over her like the shadow of death, the Undertaker eased the protective comforter down from her chin to her waist with the same loving care he'd use to strip a female cadaver. The arm exposed was hammerlocked around her teddy bear, and as the caress of the invading chill goosebumped her skin, this sleeping beauty curled up in a fetal ball.

From another pocket, the creeper pulled the hypodermic prepared by the Doctor and, clamping the pistol under one armpit, tugged off the plastic cap protecting the needle.

The girl's pajamas bore a print of E. H. Shepard's illustrations of *Winnie-the-Pooh.* The Undertaker jabbed the spike through the image of Eeyore as if pinning the lost tail back on the donkey. The eyes of the child shot wide open in startled response, but the psycho clamped his hand over her mouth to stifle any cry. Slowly, her lids began to fall as the drug took hold, then, like Wynken, Blynken and Nod, who sailed off in a wooden shoe, the girl drifted on a river of crystal light into a sea of dew.

Her body went limp.

The Undertaker let go.

Her cat hissed at him.

So he shot it through the head.

The clap of the silenced pistol echoed out the door and along the hall.

"Becky?"

A groggy voice from another room.

My, what big ears you have, Granny, he thought.

Gun in hand, the Undertaker stalked down the hall to deal with the old lady.

PICASSO

Los Angeles
March 23

The thin red line met the thin blue line in a squad room on the third floor of the Parker Center. The downtown headquarters of the Los Angeles Police Department was a rectangular glass-and-steel structure of the kind that has blighted urban landscapes since the 1950s. The historic core in which it rose, at 150 N. Los Angeles Street, between Temple and First, also housed El Pueblo de Los Angeles, the site where the city was founded by a Spanish garrison sent from Mexico in 1781, as well as Union Station, City Hall, the Los Angeles Times building, Chinatown and Little Tokyo. Dubbed "the Glass House" and made famous on the "Dragnet" TV show, the eight-story building was named for William Parker, the LAPD's most famous chief. The meeting of the two police forces took place in the squad room of the Homicide Special Section of the Robbery-Homicide Division.

The thin red line. The thin blue line.

The point man for the red was Chief Superintendent DeClercq. His backup on slide show was Rusty Lewis. Nick Craven, as near as Jenna Bond could tell, was here to flaunt the colors, like one of those lancers in the nineteenth-century paintings on the walls of Special X, the redcoats who stood guard while their officers powwowed with the Natives.

DeClercq had begun this powwow with an overview of the

Pacific Northwest murder victims. Like one of those visual montages shown at the Academy Awards—a gathering of the artistic oeuvre of the recipient of a special lifetime-achievement Oscar—the work of the grisly killer who surgically mutilated the six women had flashed onscreen as Lewis repeatedly punched a key on his laptop computer. With the crimes reviewed, the chief had moved on to brief the Los Angeles cops on the link between Wolfe Capp's Spider's Web, fronting Snuff Lib, and their prime suspect in the surgical murders, the former Dr. Ryland Fletcher of L.A.

"And that," DeClercq finished up, "is why we're here."

The Mountie relinquished the podium to the captain in command of the Robbery-Homicide Division. An Oscar ceremony requires an MC—a Bob Hope, a Billy Crystal, a Steve Martin—and the captain was it. In stature, he was a short man who seemed ten feet tall, ramrod erect in his posture to add that extra inch. His voice left no doubt that if you crossed him, he'd tear you another asshole, which reminded Jenna of George C. Scott as the famous general in *Patton.*

The detective called to the podium by his captain had answered a casting call for a typical Hollywood cop. His broad shoulders and tight musculature were those of a man who knew his way around a football field, and his large knuckles warned he could take care of himself on the street. His nine was in a shoulder holster cinched to his powerful pecs, butt forward as if mooning all takers. He had the good but tough looks of a clean-cut American male, though this impression was undercut by the chance he had been in that gauntlet around Rodney King or was one of the dicks who had traipsed through the crime scene in the O. J. Simpson fiasco. Pity the LAPD for having to police a real-life studio lot, where every citizen not writing a screenplay was practicing with a camcorder to make it as an up-and-coming director of photography.

The cop's name was Kev Harding.

"The media dubbed him 'Picasso,'" the L.A. detective kicked off. "A fitting name, we thought here in the RHD. You'll see why, once you get a look at his artwork."

Not to be outdone by the slide show Rusty Lewis had given from the ViCLAS photos stored in his laptop, Harding trotted out his own

HITMAN screening. HITMAN is an acronym for Homicide Information Tracking Management Automated Network, the computer database that stores every L.A. homicide. The glance the Mounties exchanged was one that Jenna could read. They were thinking that the LAPD had made the same mistake as the Bureau. How do you hunt a sex killer with a database that doesn't track sex crimes? But being Canadians, they were far too polite to voice that concern.

A map of Los Angeles appeared onscreen.

"Five killings," Harding said, "in as many years. This map charts where the mutilated bodies were dumped. We don't know where Picasso met, deformed and killed the women."

"Deformed, *then* killed?" Lewis asked.

"Yeah, the vics were alive while it was done. This monster maker is a monster too."

"A sadist," said Rusty.

"As sick as they come."

One after another, five morgue montages flashed onscreen, photos of the corpses stretched out naked on autopsy tables, with close-up shots of their rearranged faces. Jenna saw immediately why this perp had been dubbed Picasso. The features of each face had been removed from their usual locations, then the killer had stitched the eyes, ears and noses back on to create Frankenstein's monsters.

Like the monster with four breasts that she and Nick had found on the Lopez beach.

Through with the chamber of horrors, Harding lightened the slide show with a tour of an art gallery. As each Picasso print was projected onscreen, he gave it a title.

"Dora Maar Seated."

The nose was split and parted.

"Woman in an Armchair."

The ear was next to the eye.

"Sleeping Woman before Green Shutters."

The mouth and nose were side by side beneath the eyes.

"The Red Armchair."

The eyes were off-kilter, the nose on the side of the head.

"Woman Dressing Her Hair."

The lids of one eye were twisted sideways, the nose in profile on the cheek and the mouth on the side of the jaw.

"The cuts that removed the features were sliced with the precision of a razor. The stitches that sewed them back on, however, were crudely crafted for shock effect."

"Cut with a scalpel?" asked Lewis.

"Possibly."

"That's how it's entered on VICAP. The phrase 'surgical cuts' is what linked your cases to ours."

"It's entered under a lot of things that might score hits."

"You checked out plastic surgeons?"

"We checked out doctors of *every* kind. Have you any idea how many cosmetic wizards live in this city? And not just medical types. We have artists, sculptors, model makers, canvas cutters, makeup magicians, anatomists, prosthesis designers and monster makers by the thousands who work in the movies. To hide his needle in a haystack, Picasso chose the right farm."

"When was the last killing?"

"Two years ago."

"Think Picasso moved on?"

"Or topped himself."

"What about Fletcher?"

"We checked him out. But there was nothing untoward on him at that time. Since you gave us the heads up, we've been gathering more. The info's in those files." Harding pointed to folders on a table. "And we've got the doc staked out in Hollywood."

Now the captain was back as MC. Moving to the podium, he stood beside his detective and addressed DeClercq. "You've got the lever to use on Fletcher. We don't. Pry him with Wolfe Capp's murder and he might open up. If he spills his guts, it might all tumble out. What's your thinking?"

"You know what Al Jolson said?"

"No, what's that?"

"'Hollywood, here I come.'"

It was actually "California." But the captain was far too polite to correct him.

FOUNTAIN OF YOUTH

Ebbtide Island

Yet another glorious spring morning greeted Gill Macbeth as she stepped down from the chopper on the helipad out front of the Panacea Clinic. Nowhere on earth is spring more glorious than it is in the islands off the West Coast. Eagles, owls, herons, kingfishers and hummingbirds soar in the sky. Killer whales, sea lions, harbor seals and salmon swim in the sea. Deer, beaver, mink, muskrats and frogs walk the land. Towering Douglas firs and shedding arbutus trees—called madronas down here in Washington State—blend with a ground cover of ferns, salal, orchids, lilies and violets for an otherworldly feel. As Gill basked in the smog-free sunshine and drew in deep breaths of the clean, salty air, she reveled in spring as it *should* be enjoyed.

As Mother Nature intended.

The Panacea Clinic had the beauty of spring on Ebbtide Island all to itself. The only man-made structure was a Victorian-style mansion that crowned the bluff like a German castle overlooking the Rhine, except in this location the deep green sea was its surrounding moat. A greenhouse was built into the southern slant of the roof on the uppermost floor, and sunbeams glinted off it like deflected arrows. Once the rotor noise of the chopper had died away, the only sounds were the *swoop-swoop* of wings overhead and the *wash-wash* of whitecap waves lapping the surrounding shore.

If she closed her eyes, Gill could imagine herself the only person on earth.

As instructed by the Director, she had left her cellphone behind at home. "A getaway should be a getaway," he had said, "and where you're going is the best-kept secret in Hollywood. Once the camera stops loving you, baby, it's time to check in, and our goal is to make you feel like the most pampered movie star."

"I can live with that," Gill had said, laughing.

Fatal words.

The staff of the Panacea Clinic—perhaps the three *blondest* people on the globe—met them on the steps outside the front door. The Director introduced the three as Olaf, Ingrid and Tidi: a Norwegian, a Swede and a Finn. They wore loose tunics of pastel shades.

"Olaf will be your masseur," the Director said.

Gill looked the god-like Norwegian over from head to foot. That I can live with too, she thought, and with an inaudible sigh, she wondered how *complete* a massage he gave.

"Tidi. Ingrid. What's on tap for Gill?"

At this oasis of comfort for body and soul, her stay would begin with a coconut-milk massage, followed by a lemon ginger scrub. The pair would use soft loofahs to exfoliate her skin of dead cells—"It will feel like the lick of a cat's tongue," Tidi teased—to rejuvenate her flesh to silky smoothness. Then Gill would slip into the Moor Mud Bath, filled with rare mud from Austria. "The mud isn't as thick as you'd expect," Ingrid soothed. "It's a rich, warm, chocolate-colored milkshake, and you're the straw that stirs through its detoxifying mineral soak." Purified, Gill would then choose between the ozonated pool or the eucalyptus steam room, followed by an invigorating splash in the Vichy Shower, with its ten strategically placed heads.

"Of course, there'll be spa cuisine with each treatment," added the Director.

"Of course," said Gill, grinning in return.

"Pampering is the spoonful of sugar that makes the medicine go down. That medicine is metabolic therapy. Vitamin A to repair skin damage. Vitamins C and E and carotenoids to thwart aging by free radicals. The vitamins, proteins and enzymes that you will encounter here will work at the cellular level to reverse age and promote longevity. We emphasize preventive medicine, with yoga and meditation for holistic well-being. Diet, exercise, supplements, stress management and mind/body relaxation. With those keys, you can turn back the hands of time."

"Plus," said Tidi, "I do the best pedicure you'll ever have."

"Shall we?" said the Director.

The staff stood aside so Gill could enter the mansion. On walking in, she found herself engulfed by a magnificent vault of an entrance hall, with dark hardwood walls and a sweeping marble staircase, stained-glass windows and chandeliers, an elegant mural on the ceiling and a mosaic floor. At the foot of the stairs spewed a Florentine fountain out of the Renaissance, the catch basin of which glittered with several silver coins.

"The Fountain of Youth," said the Director, holding a silver dollar out to Gill. "Make a wish."

Approaching the fountain, she read the inscription engraved on the pedestal: "Youth is wasted on the young."

Amen, she thought.

And tossed in the coin.

TINSELTOWN

Los Angeles

HOLLYWOOD.

The most famous sign in the world said it all, perched up there on the steep slopes near the summit of Mount Lee, the steel letters so large that they could be seen for miles, and so magnetic that they drew wannabe stars in from around the world. Daeida Wilcox, the wife of the fellow who registered the subdivision in 1887, named the area after the Chicago summer home of a woman she met on a train. The sign, which then read HOLLYWOODLAND, was constructed in 1923 to advertise a five-hundred-acre residential development on the slopes below. A fading starlet named Peg Entwistle made the landmark infamous on September 18, 1932. Born in London and a hit on Broadway, she had moved west to become a movie star. Her first film—RKO's *Thirteen Women* with Myrna Loy—bombed, and Peg was unable to land another role. So, defeated in that attempt to claw her way to the top, she had clambered up by an alternative route. The thirteen letters in the sign were Peg's bad luck, and having scrambled up the slopes at night, she left behind her coat and purse and a note—"I'm afraid I'm a coward. I'm sorry for everything"—then scaled the ladder a workman had forgotten until she stood on top of the fifty-foot-high *H*. From there, the glittering lights of Tinseltown were at her feet, including those of RKO, the studio that had slammed the door in her face. Death's door, as it turned out, for in desperation Peg threw herself off the sign in what became Hollywood's most celebrated death leap.

But wait!

There's a kicker.

The perfect Hollywood ending.

In a stroke of irony worthy of any tearjerker, at the moment of Peg's jump off the hillside sign, a letter was in the mail to her from the Beverly Hills Community Players, offering her a plum role in their next production—that of a woman who commits suicide at the end of the third act.

Shattered dreams.

But hey, that's Hollywood.

If the camera doesn't love you, baby, it's time to check out.

As the unmarked police car drove northwest from Parker Center to Hollywood, DeClercq sat back in the passenger's seat and contemplated the sign. Though it might have been, it wasn't Peg Entwistle who tugged at his mind. It was Elizabeth Short, another woman who moved west to find fame and fortune, but instead fell victim to the flesh factory. In the chief's pantheon of most intriguing unsolved murders, Jack the Ripper was number one, Zodiac was number two, and the number-three puzzle was the Black Dahlia.

Elizabeth Short grew up in Hyde Park, Massachusetts, then made her way to Hollywood, and there she had met her death at the hands of a Mr. Hyde. With black hair, blue eyes and a rose tattoo on her left thigh, she derived the catchy name the Black Dahlia from her invariable habit of wearing black clothes and black underwear. Unfortunately—like Peg—she didn't catch on. A bit part as an extra was as high as she could climb, and when her dream of breaking into the movies failed to materialize, the Black Dahlia drifted off into prostitution. The last person to see her in one piece was the doorman of the Biltmore Hotel in downtown L.A., when, at 10 p.m. on the night of January 10, 1947, he noticed her, decked out in black, walking south on Olive Street.

Five days later, on the fifteenth, at 7:30 on a sunny morning, a mother escorting her little girl to school was walking past an empty lot at South Norton Avenue and 39th Street, in the Crenshaw area of southwest L.A. Suddenly, the child pointed toward what seemed to be a broken mannequin in the long grass.

It wasn't a dummy.

It was Elizabeth Short.

Her naked body had been bisected at the waist, sundering her above the hips and below the rib cage. Her legs were spread as if in open invitation, and her arms were crooked about her head as if to flaunt her breasts. Her mouth had been slashed at the corners to create a ghastly leer, and blows to her face had bashed it almost beyond recognition. In addition to other mutilations, her breasts had been sliced and were pockmarked with cigarette burns, and the rose tattoo had been chunked from the flesh of her thigh. It was found later during the autopsy, secreted deep within her anatomy. Rope burns on her wrists and ankles indicated she had been trussed, and according to the coroner's report filed after the postmortem, Elizabeth Short had, during a torture session that lasted three days, been suspended upside down by her feet and was alive throughout the methodical vivisection. At some point, the initials B.D.—for Black Dahlia—had been carved into her thigh.

After Short's death, the killer had primped and fussed over the remains to enhance his art for public showing. The body was drained of blood, then washed clean. The hair was shampooed, hennaed and carefully set so that when the Black Dahlia was found, she'd be a redhead. And finally, in the shroud of night, he had transported both naked halves to Norton and 39th, where he had worked diligently under the threat of discovery to lay out his *Grand Guignol* tableau.

Two hundred and fifty L.A. cops took part in the dragnet to catch the Black Dahlia's killer. It was the largest manhunt in the city's history. A local newspaper received from the killer a note fashioned from cut-out and pasted words: "Here is Dahlia's belongings. Letter to follow." And enclosed with the message were Elizabeth

Short's birth certificate, social security card and address book, with one page missing. But the weirdest aspect of the murder was the number of false confessions. Twenty-seven men immediately claimed to be the killer, and over years that climbed to many more. Several women—mostly "bull-dykes"—followed suit, and a slew of copycat killings plagued the City of Angels. Which goes to show that in Tinseltown, *everyone* has a fantasy to act out.

The Black Dahlia murder remains unsolved.

Now, as the cop car ventured into that twilight zone between the hard reality and the soft-focus fantasy of Hollywood, DeClercq wondered if that's what they had here in the former Dr. Ryland Fletcher. Was he another predator like the Dahlia's shadowy Mr. Hyde, who—as Picasso—had preyed on wannabe starlets in Tinseltown? Had he followed that with a stint of six mutilations in the Pacific Northwest? And had he now returned home to Fantasyland to pick up where he had left off?

Sunset Boulevard cuts like a knife across the throat of Hollywood beneath the multi-chinned hills to the north. You pass from Hollywood central, where ever since Norma Talmadge stepped by accident into the original concrete of the forecourt, fading stars have pushed their hand- and footprints into wet cement out front of Mann's Chinese Theatre, to West Hollywood and the legendary Sunset Strip, where Errol Flynn, Clark Gable and Rita Hayworth used to party the night away in flashy clubs like Ciro's and Mocambo. The same strip where John Belushi OD'd, River Phoenix dropped dead in front of Johnny Depp's Viper Room and Led Zeppelin allegedly indulged in wild orgies. Then you moved into the lush, plush, green of Beverly Hills, where Mary Pickford and Douglas Fairbanks were the first to begin a trend by setting up home in a hunting lodge they called Pickfair, and soon everyone who was anyone among the shooting stars was doing the same. So many rumors came out of these fabled pockets tucked away in time. Of how Clara Bow, the "It Girl," certainly enjoyed "it," entertaining not only Gary Cooper and Bela Lugosi in her Beverly Hills love nest, but also the entire eleven-player starting lineup of the USC football team, including the tackle Marion Morrison, who later changed his name to John Wayne. And of William Randolph Hearst and Marion Davies, who met at the Follies and fell in love when she was twenty and he was fifty-four. The newspaper tycoon's pet name for the "love bump" between her legs was Rosebud, and Hollywood being Hollywood, word got around, so when he became the role model for Orson Welles's *Citizen Kane,* the last word from the dying Daddy Warbucks in the movie was a reference to . . . well, to his childhood sled.

And then there were the murders. And the suicides.

No wonder sex and violence are Hollywood staples.

Fantasy and reality.

Which breeds which?

The unmarked police car angled off Sunset Boulevard and headed up into an outlandish time warp. With castles and cottages, with Spanish haciendas and Moorish temples, with winding tree-lined streets and high chaparral, an exotic smorgasbord of architectural styles was hidden away for those who took the Yellow Brick Road. This was the realm of *Sunset Boulevard,* the Hollywood classic of 1950 about what happens to actresses who age, in which pathetic Norma Desmond, once a silent film queen whose stardom has faded, utters the immortal line, "All right, Mr. DeMille, I'm ready for my close-up."

Yeah, sure, baby.

In your dreams.

Four of them had ventured out from Parker Center: the chief, Nick Craven, Jenna Bond and the L.A. detective. As he drove along the shady street, with its eclectic mix of soaring palms and spreading fig trees fighting for space with unkempt flowering shrubs that splashed color randomly, Kev Harding filled the northern contingent in on what to expect.

"Fletcher's holed up in a house that once belonged to a vet. They say the vet did work in the fifties on Lassie, Trigger, Silver, Rin Tin Tin. That's before my time."

"Not mine," said DeClercq.

"The vet flipped out after he retired. He converted the surgery in his home into a taxidermy center, and the vacant lot beside it became a pet cemetery. If Fido the dog or Foo Foo the cat croaked on you, the corpse could either be stuffed so you could keep it in your living room or be buried in the boneyard so you could lay flowers on Sunday."

"Bet he had a booming business," Jenna said dryly from the back seat.

"You'd be surprised. This is Hollywood. Some stars buy their pets diamond collars on Rodeo Drive."

"Does the vet still own it?" Nick asked. He was in the back seat with Jenna.

"Nope, he died a few years back. They say he was cremated so his ashes could be spread over his former patients."

"In the cemetery?"

"If you believe what they say."

"Who owns the place now?" asked DeClercq.

"It's held in trust for the vet's estate. The trust rents out the house to cover costs."

"Fletcher rent it?"

"Dunno. The trustee's away in Europe."

The cops on stakeout were both black. Their names were Otis Temple and Ty Higgs. Higgs was chewing a toothpick, and every so often he reversed it with the tip of his tongue. Both were packing in belt holsters under tailored jackets.

The vantage point from which they watched was well chosen. The house across from the residence-surgery overlooked both it and the cemetery from a hill. The hill was high enough that they could cover both the front and the back. There were shadow cars waiting along the street to follow their quarry if he ventured out.

"What's happening, Otis?"

"Nada, Kev."

Harding introduced Bond and both Mounties to the stakeout cops. Hands were gripped.

"Is Fletcher the only one home?"

"Close as we can tell," Higgs replied to DeClercq. "We tailed him here from the airport when he flew in. We didn't see him enter, but since then there have been two deliveries: groceries, and then some medical supplies. Both were intercepted down the street so we could take them up to the door and check things out. The drapes are drawn. You can't see inside. For both deliveries, Fletcher alone answered the door. No sign of anyone else."

"Medical supplies?" said Nick.

"He's going on the hunt," said Jenna.

The stakeout cops were squirreled away in a copse of trees beyond the swimming pool. A telescope and a camera with a telephoto lens were mounted on tripods in the thick of their camouflaged hideout. Jenna and both Mounties took turns as spies.

The house resembled the Tudor home of Special X.

The half-timbers of the upper story were California redwoods. The rounded rocks bricking the lower level were arroyo stones, smoothed by river water that once ran over the gathering place. The chalet roof curled up at the eaves for a tinge of Oriental influence. A miniature replica of the big house was attached to its front wall, and no doubt contained the surgery-cum-taxidermy shop. The vegetation surrounding the place had gone to seed, including that growing wild in the pet cemetery. Kitschiest of all were the cemetery headstones: cuddly hounds and felines chipped from marble. Seen through the camera eye of the telescope, it seemed as if Special X had been reconstructed in Fantasyland, and waited on a back lot for Hansel and Gretel to drop by.

"It's a remake of the setup in Vancouver," said DeClercq.

"How so?" asked Harding.

"We seized a video of Fletcher performing breast enhancement on a teenage girl. According to a plastic surgeon who assessed the tape, the operation was done in a vet's facility. When you think about it, a vet's is the perfect front. It's an operating theater that isn't known as such. So if you're an underground surgeon who wants to masquerade illegal work, what better location?"

"That's where Picasso cut 'em up?"

"*If* Fletcher is Picasso. But if I were Picasso, that's what I would do."

The sun sat high in the sky, and it seemed hot to the pale-skinned cops from the Pacific Northwest. The glare distorted sunlit patches like overexposed film, bleaching color out of them with a shimmering mirage of white. By contrast, the blinding effect darkened shadows to black, and each of the three kicked him- or herself for leaving his or her sunglasses at home.

"Want an assault team?" Temple asked.

"Does Fletcher merit that?" replied DeClercq.

"The doc looks like a pussy. He's a pretty boy. Might be good-looking if his skin weren't so pale."

The black cops shared a glance and a grin.

"I find that offensive," Jenna huffed in mock umbrage.

"Calling him pale?"

"Calling him a pussy."

"Bite my tongue," Otis said with a smile.

Enough kibitzing. The ice was broken. Sexual banter, like gallows humor, was stock-in-trade to cops. Jenna fit right in. The L.A. bulls liked her. The jury was still out on the Horsemen.

"Who's calling the shots?" Temple asked.

"You put us onto Fletcher. What do you want to do?" Harding asked DeClercq.

"If I were home, I'd walk up to the door and flash my badge. Then I'd ask myself in and gauge his response. I'd tell him we're investigating the death of Wolfe Capp and have reason to believe they met just before the porn king was snuffed. Then I'd warn him and ask if Fletcher would help us with our inquiries. At the moment, that's all we have on him. If he balks, we've got enough to take him downtown for questioning."

"Okay, let's do it."

"Pause a moment. The real question," said the Mountie, "is what do *you* want to do? We're fish out of water in your jurisdiction, so you call the shots."

Harding glanced at Temple. "Otis?" he said.

"The doc's a pushover."

Harding nodded. "The bottom line is that he'll know we're watching and won't go hunting."

So down the hill in two groups they walked from the lookout site. Temple and Higgs broke off to cover the rear and lurk in the shadows as backup in case it was needed. The walkway to the front door was hedged in by overgrowth, requiring Harding, Craven, DeClercq and Bond to approach in pairs. The surgery theater was built onto the house to the right of the front entrance, with its own door opening into the elbow angle. On both sides of the path stood transplanted trees, eucalyptus from Australia and gray-green olives from the Mediterranean, so the cops moved from glare to shadow to glare again. The northerners squinted their eyes to slits as they struggled to adjust, with one hand across each brow as a visor. The path widened near the right-angled doors, so Jenna moved up to join the vanguard of Harding and Craven. That's when the front door burst open and out rushed the coke freak.

"Bugs!" he screamed, as if commenting on pests in the overgrown garden. But what he was really commenting on were the phantom bugs crawling beneath his skin, as evidenced by the ice-pick wounds bleeding up and down both bare legs. He had stripped to his undershorts to get at the little buggers.

Bwam! Bwam! Bwam! The coke freak lost in the nightmare realm of cocaine psychosis opened up on the approaching cops with the pistol he gripped in one fist, and he drew the gun slung in a shoulder holster under his armpit with the other hand. The first shot was aimed directly at Jenna's heart, and the force of the nine-millimeter slug slamming into her chest blew the San Juan County detective back off her feet. The double punch of the next two shots dropped Nick Craven in his tracks. Then—*Bwam!*—the coke freak fired again, and blood and brains exploded around Robert DeClercq's head.

CYBER SLEUTHS

Los Angeles

"I don't like him," Rusty Lewis said.

Sitting across a table spread with files and photos in the Robbery-Homicide Division of the LAPD at Parker Center, Kim Rossmo glanced up from his laptop computer, on which he was geographically profiling the dump sites of Picasso, the L.A. monster maker, to respond, "I never met a rapist I liked either."

"I mean I don't like him as our killer."

"Fletcher?"

"Uh-huh. He doesn't fit the profile. Whoever mutilated the women down here in L.A. and up north in our neck of the woods has all the earmarks of a sexual sadist. He's an Anger Excitation Rapist who's crossed the line to serial killer. This guy Fletcher lurks at the *least* violent end of the spectrum. He's a classic Power Reassurance Rapist, if ever there was one."

The FBI has profiled the behavioral characteristics of four types of rapists.

The Anger Excitation Rapist is the most dangerous kind. Physical and emotional pain and suffering motivates his fantasy, because that's what arouses him sexually. This rapist will strike night or day. He is usually controlled and doesn't reveal his temper unless something revs up the anger seething deep inside.

He is the sexual sadist.

The Anger Retaliatory Rapist is next on the danger scale. Angry at women in general, or at specific women in his past whom he feels have used and abused him, he is motivated by a compulsive need to punish the female sex. Rape is his way both to retaliate and to gain control over his troubled past.

The Power Assertive Rapist has a different motivation. Typically, his are macho fantasies. He believes women are commodities to be used for sex. He figures he is *entitled* to have sex with any woman. Usually a date rapist, he tends to attack at night.

The Power Reassurance Rapist is the least violent. Motivated by an insecure need to reassure himself about his manhood or masculinity, he fantasizes about exercising power over desirable women by having *consensual* sex with them. Because he lacks confidence in his ability to seduce and perform—his sexual dysfunction is often one of impotence or premature ejaculation—he can prove himself to himself only through forced sexual encounters. Though it's the end result of every rape, he has no intent to punish, degrade or traumatize his victims. He equates hurt with *physical* harm, not the emotional and psychological damage he causes. Typically a night stalker, this despoiler is known by an oxymoron: the gentleman rapist.

Kim punched a key to activate his screensaver. Using the moment for a coffee break, he picked up his mug in one hand and reached for his vice—chocolate chip cookies—with the other. "You have my undivided attention," he said.

"That's your third."

"Third what? My third *cookie?*"

"Yes," said Rusty.

"You're actually keeping count?"

"They're fattening."

"I know. That's why they're my *vice.* I thought this was Robbery-Homicide, not the Vice Squad."

"It's your funeral, Kim."

"How touching," Rossmo said. "I might not live as long as you vegetarians, but I'll enjoy life more. Make sure I get 'Amazing Grace' on the bagpipes, eh."

The VPD detective munched his cookie with relish.

"The Power Reassurance Rapist is highly ritualistic," Rusty continued. "He has a strong relational fantasy, typically centered around a mutually consenting sexual encounter. In other words, he and his victim are *lovers* in his fantasyland."

An irresistible impulse seized the psych profiler. As compulsively as those driven to act out their fantasies in the real world, he snatched a chocolate chip cookie before Kim could protect the plate.

"Stop! Thief!" the geographic profiler cried.

The LAPD cops working nearby turned to zoom in on the scene of the crime. Assessing what they saw going on at the cyber sleuths' table, they shrugged, rolled their eyes and went back to their donuts.

"Canadians," one explained.

"Aaah," said another, nodding.

What more was there to say?

"The typical masturbatory fantasy of a Power Reassurance Rapist is this," Lewis picked up. "His is a saga of sexual conquest, in which a reluctant woman initially spurns his sexual advances. Overpowering her, he achieves penetration. In spite of herself, the woman cannot resist his sexual prowess. Aroused to fever pitch, she abandons herself to his masculine dominance and revels in her conquest by a superman."

"That's Fletcher's fantasy?"

"Got to be. It goes hand in glove with the rape allegations in these files." He swept his hand across the papers culled from the investigations into the porn queens' complaints that ultimately cost the doctor his license to practice. "Fletcher is the classic gentleman rapist. He pre-selected both victims from among his patients. Porn queens make perfect targets for this type of rapist's M.O. Striking between midnight and 5 a.m., Fletcher surprised each victim in her own home, thereby extending his sense of power and control as he reduced hers. He flashed a weapon—a scalpel—but didn't cut her, so a minimal amount of physical force was used. During the assault, he was verbally and sexually unselfish. He didn't rip off her clothing. He asked her to remove it. Instead of creating terror, he assured each woman that he wouldn't hurt her. And as for the act itself, he let each choose how they were going to do it. When he left her, there wasn't a mark on her body. That's about as far from the sexual sadist as rapists come."

"Did they search his home?" asked Rossmo.

"Yes, and they found what I'd expect: a vast pornography collection featuring non-violent erotica, including photos and videos of the women he allegedly raped."

"Allegedly?"

"Nothing stuck. A porn queen without a mark on her body is hard to sell to a jury. They must have had second thoughts about going ahead with a trial. The charges were dropped. That's the problem with a gentleman rapist. He doesn't fit the public's and the media's concept of a violent predator. It's the same problem I have with our case. All rapists are violent by definition, but the profile of our killer places him at the top of the violence spectrum, while the profile of Fletcher's crimes relegates him to the lowest level."

"Houston, we have a problem."

"How's your profile, Kim?"

While Rusty Lewis had been hunched over his laptop computer on that side of the table, psychologically profiling the former Dr. Ryland Fletcher, Det. Insp. Kim Rossmo had (between chocolate chip cookies) been mathematically processing the geography of the dump sites left by Picasso, the L.A. monster maker. First, he had copied an ArcView GIS (geographic information system) street file of Los Angeles onto his laptop. Then he had digitalized the five crime-scene locations onto the computerized street map. A click of the mouse had seen Rigel—the powerful software program Rossmo had created and named after one of the stars in the constellation of Orion the Hunter—produce a map marred by five pockmarks on Picasso's crimespace. A second click of the mouse on the GeoProfile button, and within a few moments, Rigel had processed hundreds of thousands of calculations based on human nature to determine the probability of each of the forty thousand cells making up the screen being the anchor point of the serial killer. By connecting and color-coding those cells with equal probability, Rigel had superimposed over the L.A. street map what seemed to be a rainbow amoeba akin to that gelatinous creeper out of *The Blob.*

"So what have you got?" Rusty asked, moving around to this side of the table to stare over Kim's shoulder.

The geographic profiler clicked the mouse a third time to convert the amoeba into a "jeopardy surface," a 3-D overlay that resembled a mountain range. The peaks rose above those cells on the computer map with the highest probability of being the killer's anchor point.

"The pinnacle of pinnacles. Is that where I think it juts up?" Lewis asked.

"If you're thinking Hollywood."

"Houston, we have another problem."

"How bad?" Kim asked.

"Fletcher's surgery was here, *downtown.* And his home was miles away from Hollywood."

"Not even close."

"It sure doesn't look like Fletcher is Picasso. His psych profile and his geoprofile are way out of whack. It's a wild goose chase."

Rossmo stared long and hard at the map.

"I have an idea," he said.

COKE FIENDS

Los Angeles

Cocaine psychosis is shocking to behold, especially if formication is a symptom. (No, Charlie, that's not a typo. It's for*m*ication, with an *m,* not an *n.*)

Too much blow up your nose or pumped into your veins can drive you insane. Psychosis is defined as a break with reality, and formication is the false sensation or hallucination that imaginary bugs are burrowing under or crawling on your skin. DeClercq had seen cokeheads claw flesh from their faces to get at the phantom bugs, and during an interview, one had really bugged out, grabbing his pen and stabbing it repeatedly into the flesh of his own forearm, shrieking, "Gotcha! Gotcha! Gotcha!" with each spurt of blood.

So when the psycho with coke powder caked around his nose and puncture marks down both legs had suddenly burst out of the staked-out Hollywood house with a pistol gripped in one hand to shriek "Bugs!" at them, it took DeClercq less than a split second to grasp the situation. For all he knew, the description "Bugs!" might refer to *them,* for a cokehead hallucinating under the effect of that insidious drug was like the wretch in Kafka's *Metamorphosis* who wakes up to discover that he has turned into a bug overnight.

Then—*Bwam! Bwam! Bwam!*—cops were going down. This was followed by another *Bwam!* that spewed blood and brains back around the chief's head.

DeClercq hit the ground.

The huge difference between the States and Canada is the attitude toward guns. It's not that Canada doesn't have them—guns are around, although strictly controlled—it's that Canada doesn't have a history of the *cult* of the gun.

In other words, guns aren't worshiped.

This difference in attitude goes back to the American Revolution. Down south, the right to bear arms equates with the nation's resolve to protect hard-won freedoms. The Stars and Stripes and the cult of the gun were born of the same mother. Packing a piece harks back to holding the line against armed Redcoats. North of the border, however, there is no history of revolution. The head of state—the queen—represents laws that have been in continuous effect since the Norman Conquest of 1066, and perhaps before. The guardians of those laws are the Royal Canadian Mounted Police, direct descendants of the British colonial army, so in Canada today, guns remain where they used to be in America: firmly in the hands of the redcoats.

This historical schism plays out in many ways. In America, a gun is viewed as an "equalizer." If a kid feels bullied at school or a laid-off employee feels unfairly treated, then a gun makes a good equalizer to get even with those responsible (and perhaps take out a dozen innocents for good measure). In Canada, those packing guns don't carry them to level the playing field. They carry them to enforce the unequal power given to them by law. Yes, there's a *limited* right to bear arms—a right that says if you're packing, you're a cop.

The cops from Canada weren't packing today, for they didn't have the right to bear arms in this country. But like all Canadians, they had been conditioned by the barrage of U.S. shootings that seemed to pepper the daily news to see America as a dangerous place, where if you found yourself in the wrong place at the wrong time, when some nut armed to the teeth decided to "equalize," the odds on the roulette wheel of life were such that you could get shot. So while they didn't pack their pistols with their underwear, they did pack their Kevlar vests.

As the mother of a six-year-old who had already lost her father, and as a cop who had served with the FBI in the big bad city before she had returned to the San Juans, Jenna Bond wore a vest every day she worked, even if it was the safest of tasks on one of the islands. So when the slug slammed into her heart and blew her back off her feet, it didn't pierce the bulletproof shield of her Kevlar vest, and it didn't blow her protected heart to smithereens.

It just laid her flat.

The double punch of the next two shots dropped Nick Craven in his tracks. Conditioned to see L.A. as a throwback to the Wild West—hell, some guy had recently strolled out of a botched bank robbery to open up on the LAPD with an assault rifle, all of which was caught on tape for the nightly news—he too had a Kevlar condom sheathing his torso. The double punch dropped him in his tracks, but it didn't punch out his lights.

Then . . .

Bwam!

The gunman pulled off another shot.

Det. Kev Harding was also wearing a vest, but unfortunately the bullet caught him between the eyes. Luckily, DeClercq followed him a step to the side, so while the Mountie was spattered with gore from the headshot, the bullet that ripped through Harding's brain missed him by an inch when it blew out the back of his skull.

The dead detective crumpled on top of his shoulder-holstered gun, weighing down the weapon with dead weight.

DeClercq hit the ground at his feet.

Nobody lays on a Wild West shootout quite like Hollywood. What the cops didn't know—but were learning fast—was that this house with an attached vet's surgical theater wasn't the L.A. hideout of Dr. Ryland Fletcher. Instead, it was the Alamo of one of his previous clients, a porn producer who used to send wannabe starlets to the plastic surgeon for tit jobs back when he was still in practice downtown. Since then, the porn producer had moved on to trafficking, though he and his gang of three addicted Venice Beach surfers snorted as much as they sold. The paranoia that comes with coke psychosis had jitterbugged the gang, and as a direct consequence, the porn king turned drug kingpin turned coke fiend had shot a meddlesome cop. Now he was afraid the LAPD was out to settle that score by summarily executing him under the bogus cover of a drug-raid shootout, so using the far-flung network of the Spider's Web, he had contacted the former Dr. Ryland Fletcher—currently down on his luck—to ask the renegade plastic surgeon to perform an underground operation to alter his looks.

The disgraced doctor was looking for work wherever he could get it—from Wolfe Capp, from the director of the Panacea Clinic, from this former client—so he had told the cop killer to rent a tucked-away vet's surgery room somewhere in L.A., and then to lay low until he could fly down to California. Since then, the gang had been holed up in this Tudor house, snorting coke until they were so claustrophobic (but also afraid to go out) that their coke psychosis had ratcheted up to the let-me-outta-here screaming pitch of full-blown cabin fever. The gang members were in no shape to stand guard while their boss had his face rearranged by Fletcher to fool the phantom hit squad of vengeful L.A. cops. Bugs had already degenerated to self-mutilation—and the other two coke freaks were eyeing each other suspiciously, as if fearful of falling prey to one of those killer pods from *Invasion of the Body Snatchers*—when he had felt the sudden need to take a piss, and as he was limping to the john, he happened to peek outside.

Cops . . .

Bugs . . .

Whatever he saw, Bugs freaked out and—pistol in one hand as he wrenched open the door and drew the second gun—he burst out of the house like a madman in a TV ad for the bug-killing spray Raid.

The gunman shrieked again as two more jitterbugged men waving automatic weapons came charging out of the woodwork. Together, they looked like surfers who had caught the wrong wave, body-beautiful types with sun-bleached hair and studs in their lobes, sporting melanoma tans from Venice Beach and Malibu. Their eyes were so freaked from the snow they had snorted up their snouts that their pupils didn't know whether to pin, dilate or spin like those in cartoons.

The three cops on the ground were unarmed. Jenna was out of breath from the blow to her heart. Nick was reaching for a rock to use as a weapon. Bugs swung both pistols down to let Bond and Craven have it again, this time aiming for their heads to get the same bang for his buck that he had with Kev Harding.

Thank God—from DeClercq's point of view—the cult of the gun was embraced by American cops. The dead detective lay sprawled on the ground in front of the Mountie. Harding's pant leg had ridden up when he crumpled from that headshot, so DeClercq could see the holster strapped to his lower leg. An ankle gun. A *backup* piece. Insurance the detective had hidden away for dire straits like these.

In a spring holster, no less.

The gun was in the chief's hand before Bugs could fire. It bucked as DeClercq pulled off a shot from this awkward angle on the ground, and another, and yet another to make sure he hit the mark, which was the underside of the looming cokehead's chin. The fountain that sprayed up from the top of his skull was every bit as horrifying as the one that had come out of Harding. So fast and furious were the shots that the mechanism of the gun jammed just as the other surfers came down the pipeline to wipe out the sprawled cops.

These two had machine guns.

They say your life passes before your eyes when you know you're going to die. That's bullshit. DeClercq was in Hollywood, so his would be a Hollywood ending. On the screen in his mind, all he saw was Porky Pig saying, "That's all, folks!"

The Horsemen, however, weren't the only cavalry in town. Riding to the rescue came Otis Temple and Ty Higgs. The cult of the gun has an upside: it produces crack shots. The detectives came around the corner with their pieces gripped in both hands to lay down a line of fire the moment they had a target. Otis took out the cokehead on the left while Ty brought down the other surfer with a single shot. Not content to leave it at that, both LAPD bulls went for the door, and when they found no one home in the Tudor house, they came out and kicked in the door to the surgery theater.

There were two spiders in the taxidermy parlor. The cop killer was out of it on the operating table. Anesthetized, he was having his cut-up face remolded by a plastic surgeon, who had stopped mid-slice because of the commotion. When he saw the black detectives come bursting in gun-first, the former Dr. Ryland Fletcher dropped his scalpel and threw his blood-covered gloves up in surrender.

Caught red-handed.

PEEPING TOM

Ebbtide Island

It was a double fantasy, but Gill Macbeth didn't know it.

Her favorite Hitchcock actress was Grace Kelly and her favorite Hitchcock movie was *Rear Window*. As a leading lady, Grace had it all. Hers was a cool, blonde, elegant beauty, with hints of sexual passion and flashes of sparkling wit. Dressed to the nines by the wardrobe queen Edith Head, she wore a gown like a princess, which she later became when she deserted Hitch to marry the prince of Monaco. Now, standing before this full-length mirror in her room on the upper floor of the Panacea Clinic, Gill Macbeth indulged in a sexual fantasy of her own.

Rear Window was a film about a man confined to a chair. Injured in an accident resulting from his job, the photographer played by Jimmy Stewart (who was Gill's favorite film star) sat immobilized by a hip-to-toe plaster cast and passed the time by spying on his neighbors with a telescopic lens aimed out through the rear window of his apartment. One of those he watches and admires is a woman who unknowingly models a dress and a nightgown for him. One of Hitch's many kinks was scopophilia, sexual gratification through gazing. *Rear Window* was a fantasy motivated by that paraphilia in its director. Jimmy's chair was the director's chair. Jimmy's lens was the camera lens. And Jimmy's kinky kicks, seen through each rectangular window, were the images Hitch put up on the screen to make his viewers squirm in their seats.

Peeping Al.

It was Hitchcock who made Grace Kelly's career, and Grace—like Gill—was no prude beneath that cool exterior. As the story goes, she paid back the director with a secret performance intended solely for him.

It was a sultry night in Laurel Canyon. Grace was in her bedroom with the lights on bright. The curtains were open. The blinds were up. As if she had just returned from a night on the town, the actress removed her hat and slipped off her gloves. Slowly, like ecdysiasts did on the strip, she slid the straps of her evening gown from her graceful shoulders, then let the caressing crepe de Chine drop around her high heels. A flick of her sensuous fingers unsnapped her bountiful bra, which fell away from what no other viewer would *ever* see onscreen. There was a pause—and what a delicious, excruciating interval that was—before she removed her French lace panties and snuffed the lights.

Just one performance.

No more than five minutes long.

But it would feed forever the sexual fantasy of the solitary peeper seated a mile across Laurel Canyon, where, his eye glued to a powerful telescope mounted on a tripod and aimed out through his window, Hitch watched Grace Kelly strip for him.

In *her* fantasy, here alone in this bedroom on the upper floor of the Panacea Clinic, Gill imagined this full-length mirror was *her* window on the canyon, and way over there, a mile or so away, enraptured by her beauty as a rejuvenated woman, DeClercq sat with his connoisseur's eye glued to a peeping lens.

Uhhhh.

It made her shiver.

Me and Grace, she thought.

What a pair of exhibitionistic tramps.

Now, as she slinkily slipped the clothes off her revamped figure, Gill thought she was stripping in front of a mirror. But enjoying this strip as much as peeping Al had Grace's, the Doctor stood at the top of the stone steps hidden in the wall, steps that led down to the Mummy Room and the Plastic Surgery Room in the charnel chambers below, buried deep in the bowels of the Panacea Clinic. So close to Gill did he lurk that if it weren't for the sheet of one-way glass between them, he could have reached out and stripped her to the skin, and then—if he had had his scalpel—stripped her even further.

BINGO

Los Angeles

Det. Insp. Kim Rossmo was drawing a crowd as he sat at the table in the Robbery-Homicide Division of the LAPD and inserted another CD-ROM into his computer. It was no longer just S/Sgt. Rusty Lewis hovering over the geographic profiler's shoulder.

What intrigued the L.A. homicide cops was the opportunity to see this new Canadian dragnet tool in action. To that end, they had supplied the nets that Rossmo was dragging, one by one, through Hollywood. The nets were CD-ROMs. Computerized telephone books. Their hunting ability was in their SICs.

Most cops—like most of us—still let their fingers do the walking through the White and Yellow Pages of a paper telephone book to find a number or a corresponding address, or to locate a business to serve their needs. However, we live in the computer age, so all of that information can also be found on disk. As you'd expect, if you're conversant with the enhanced capabilities of DVDs, the digital versions of phone books also offer users cyber bells and whistles.

Like SICs.

Not only are CD-ROM phone books programmed to be able to search for an individual or business alphabetically, but they can also gather businesses *by type*. For integrated into a CD-ROM—unlike a normal phone book—is a series of SIC codes. SIC stands for standard industrial classification, a system utilized by census bureaus.

For example, the American SIC code for plastic surgeons is 8011-01. Enter that number as a search parameter into a computerized phone book of Los Angeles, as Det. Insp. Kim Rossmo did now, and the SIC will gather together all the plastic surgeons in L.A. Name, address, zip code and phone number for every doctor's office. Once you have that information . . .

"You copy it to a clipboard," Rossmo explained to the cops looking over his shoulder, "and import it directly into Rigel, the software created for geographic profiling. Now you can treat those plastic surgeons as a series of suspects."

"It's all done in one computer?" someone asked.

The cyber sleuth nodded. "The CD-ROM goes in here, as you can see, and Rigel is already on the laptop. It's written in Java, so it works with everything, and the laptop is so powerful that it performs a million calculations in less than ten seconds. It's all I need to do a case anywhere in the world."

"Drag the net," another said.

"Okay," said Rossmo. "What you see onscreen is a digital street map of Los Angeles. The multicolored mountain range sitting on top is a jeopardy surface. The highest peaks mark the most probable locations on this map for Picasso's anchor point: his home or his office. You'll note that the highest peak is over Hollywood. What Rigel will do"—he hit a button—"is locate every plastic surgeon's office on this map, so we can see who's closest to the peak. The closer the surgeon is, the higher he is as a 'hit' on the geoprofile. What Rigel is doing is prioritizing all of your plastic surgeons as a list of prime suspects."

"You're looking for Fletcher?"

"Hopefully. The surgery we have for him was downtown. His home was hell and gone. I'm checking to see if he had a branch office for a while, or assumed someone else's practice while he or she was off somewhere, or did anything else that put him near the peak."

"Why the different disks?"

"I'm working back in time." Rossmo hit a button to create another suspect list. "Each CD-ROM phone book covers different years. He may be in one and not the—"

"Bingo!" shouted Lewis, so loud that Kim almost jumped.

"You found Fletcher?" asked a cop near the back.

"No," said the cyber sleuth. "We found someone else. The second name on the list is a doctor we both know."

"Here in L.A?"

"No, in Vancouver."

The second name on the suspect list was Dr. David Denning.

THE PEAR

Ebbtide Island

The most fiendish misogynistic device ever invented by man—not the species, but the male sex—was the pear. The pear that hung on one wall of the Mummy Room, next to the key to the cages that confined the pair of six-year-old girls, had been ordered from Snuff Lib through the Internet Spider's Web. It had arrived with the branks, the scold's bridle the Doctor had used to cage the head of his next-to-last victim. The pear hung here for use tonight on Gill Macbeth if she balked at giving him the best blow job of her life.

Which she would.

They *always* did, the cunts.

The pear was a torture device shaped like the pear you eat. Made of metal, it was narrow at the top and plumped out at the bottom. Like a sliced pear yet to be divided, cut lines running lengthwise from the stem to the nub marked its abutting segments. In use, the Doctor would insert the plump end deep into Gill's vagina, then twist the flattened stem like a key to crank the screw inside, which would ratchet open the bottom of the segmented pear within her womb. At maximum aperture, the force of the widened metal lengths would rupture the sensitive membranes of Gill's female cavity while the pointed prongs of the pear's expanded nub tore into her cervix, ripping it apart.

In witch-hunting days, the pear was used on women found guilty of having had sex with the Devil or his familiars.

"I'm scared."

Sobbing, from the adjacent cell.

But not the sobbing of a six-year-old like Becky.

Instead, the sobbing of a raspy old woman.

"I'm scared too. But we'll get out. My mom will save both me and you," said Jenna Bond's daughter.

It didn't help.

The sobbing grew louder.

The wall between the two cells was a sheet of metal and the barred doors that opened into the Mummy Room were side by side, so except for a brief holding of hands earlier to quell a spell of hysteria in the child next door, neither girl had seen the other's face. The hand that had poked out through the bars to curl around the dividing wall to interlock with Becky's had given her a shock. One night, while Becky was sleeping over at a friend's on Orcas Island, the two had surreptitiously turned on the TV in the guest room where they were put to sleep, and had watched an ancient movie called *The Mummy* on Shock Theater. In that film, a grasping old mummy hand had reached out from a coffin, scaring the sleepover pair half to death. Seeing the wrinkled hand curling around from the adjacent cell had been just as shocking, but Becky was proud of herself for taking it in hers anyway.

She was Jenna's offspring.

Like mother, like daughter.

"Rebecca," her mom had once said (not a good sign—she always called her Rebecca if it was serious stuff), "I wish I could shield you from the evil in the world. But for your own protection, I can't do that. Sometimes, bad things happen to us, and we have to cope with them as best we can. Because girls don't grow up as big and as strong as most boys, we females have to rely on this"—her mom had tapped her on the head—"to *think* our way out of danger.

"Now, as your mom, I'll see that you're trained in how to protect yourself. But if you get into a jam and I'm not around, promise me that you'll stay calm and think, think, *think.*"

"I promise."

"Good girl. Nothing is likely to happen to you. But *if* you do run into someone bad who means you harm, here's what you must do to get away. You think, you watch, you look for an opening, and when it comes, you *act.*"

Never had Becky been as frightened as she was now, but the girl in the cage next to hers was even more terrified, so that made her *feel* as if she was brave . . . even if she wasn't.

The girl's name was Anna.

"Anna, give me your hand."

She waited . . .

And waited . . .

Then around the dividing wall the wrinkled hand curled, and when she took it in her own, to comfort herself as much as to soothe the sobbing wretch next door, Becky was afraid it might crumble to dust, the bones felt so brittle.

It puzzled her that the bad men had called the body on the table in the center of the room a mummy. Why did the hand of the girl next door look like the hand in *The Mummy,* yet "the mummy" on the table looked like Sleeping Beauty in the bedtime story Mom and Gram had both read to her? Except Sleeping Beauty wore clothes.

As she held the hand of the living mummy poking through the bars of the cage next to hers, the six-year-old silently mouthed the mantra that Jenna had drummed into her.

Think.

Watch.

Look for an opening.

And when it comes, *act.*

As she repeated it over and over again, her eyes stared through the bars on this side of the room and over the mummy stretched out on the table in the middle to gaze at the pair of hooks just left of the door in the far wall through which the bad men came and went.

From one hook hung the pear the Doctor planned to use on Gill Macbeth tonight if she rebuffed him.

But Becky's attention locked on the other hook.

The hook with the key to the doors of both cells.

HYDE AND SEEK

Los Angeles

So there they were, face to face, in the Hollywood surgery room, with a cop killer under the knife on the operating table and a dead cop on the ground outside with three dead surfers. Fletcher's bloody gloves reached for the sky as Temple and Higgs aimed their nines at the doc's pounding heart, itching for a reason to gun him down to even the score for Kev Harding. Still spattered with blood from the shootout in the yard, DeClercq gave the renegade plastic surgeon the necessary extraterritorial warning under the Canadian Charter of Rights, then followed that caution with: "Ryland Fletcher, you're under arrest for the murder of Wolfe Capp."

"What?" said Fletcher.

"And for the murders of six women in the Pacific Northwest."

"What?" Fletcher gasped.

Otis Temple gave him the Miranda warning before snarling, "And for the murders of five women here in L.A."

"What!" Fletcher exclaimed.

"And for the murder of Det. Kev Harding," Ty Higgs added.

"Jesus!" Fletcher cursed.

"I doubt he'll help," said Temple.

"I didn't do it! None of it!"

"No?" said DeClercq. "Then who did?"

And that was the beginning of yet another Hollywood deal.

The agent who put it together was an attorney named Ben Mason, known to his friends as Perry. The Canadians thought his combined practice a strange mix: half contract negotiations for Hollywood talent and the other half criminal law. But that's because in their country many cases still went to trial, while down here most charges were wheeled and dealed away. Criminal law was more about negotiating skills than courtroom techniques, so a contract lawyer was even more useful than a hired gun.

"Here's the deal," Mason said matter-of-factly. "My client didn't perpetrate these murders. The worst he's guilty of is practicing medicine without a license. Accept it now or accept it later, the verdict will be the same. Meanwhile, you have a serial killer on the prowl, and you'll look like Keystone Kops if he kills another woman while you're pursuing the wrong man . . . *and were warned of the fact.*"

The lawyer paused dramatically to let his words sink in.

"In exchange for your dropping *all* charges against him, my client will tell you the name *and* the motive of the probable serial killer. As for Wolfe Capp, my client has no idea. There must be dozens of suspects in the underworld."

The lawyer stood up.

"Take it or leave it," he said.

In the end, they took it.

The final contract had some fine print—wiggle-room provisions to protect the cops if overwhelming evidence against Fletcher should come to light—but if all they had was what they had now, then the deal would remain as solid as boilerplate. The cops didn't like it, but what else could they do? Their strongest case against Fletcher was for the snuffing of the porn king, but all they really had there was opportunity, and any number of others—underworld denizens all—could have come and gone by the unwatched rear door. As for the mutilated women, the case consisted of an operation on a consenting teen (she had been tracked down by Special X). And instead of indicating that the doctor was a viable suspect, Rusty Lewis's psychological profile now suggested that Fletcher's motivating fantasy didn't fit those crimes.

And there was something else.

Another name caught by the dragnet, enmeshed by Kim Rossmo's geographic profile of the California mutilations.

In exchange for a Get Out of Jail Free card, Fletcher—through Mason—offered them "the name *and* the motive of the probable serial killer" of those mutilated women.

The cops wanted that name. The cops wanted that motive.

"Take it or leave it."

So in the end, they took it.

"Dr. David Denning," said the former Dr. Ryland Fletcher. "He's the man you want."

No sooner had the name escaped from the plastic surgeon's lips—the very same name as that caught by the geoprofile—than DeClercq called for a brief pause so he could make a phone call. Stepping out of the interview room at Parker Center, the chief speed-dialed the number of a cellphone in Vancouver.

"Chandler," the call was answered.

"Zinc, it's Robert DeClercq. Our prime suspect for the mutilation murders has switched to David Denning."

"Denning?"

"I know. He seemed to be one of the good guys. That's because he did work on both Nick and Gill. Gill called him in for a second opinion on the surgical wounds suffered by the Galiano Island and Wreck Beach victims. Denning was supposedly helping us solve the mutilation killings that he himself had committed."

"What makes you think it's him?"

"He's been fingered by Fletcher and was caught by Kim's profile of the Picasso killings down here. Get a warrant to search his office and home. Leave no stone unturned. Concentrate on his foreign patients. It could be that their desire to hide their having work done is why we haven't ID'd the victims."

"Got it."

"Call me if anything turns up. I'll be interviewing Fletcher to nail down Denning's motive."

"It all began," Fletcher said, "with our common interest in Internet porn."

"When was that?" the captain in charge of the Robbery-Homicide Division asked. His name was James Butler Hickok, in honor of that American icon, Wild Bill Hickok, of frontier fame. Flanked by Temple and Higgs, Hickok acted as a powerful voice in the interview room, and with one of his men cooling on ice in the L.A. morgue, he was after just the facts, and he wanted them fucking fast.

Fletcher turned to Mason and whispered in his ear. This interview was being recorded not only by the police, but also by the lawyer. Again, he reiterated the deal concerning no charges, then added, "On that basis, I advise my client to answer."

"Eight years ago. David Denning and I went through med school together. We were a year apart at UCLA. Los Angeles is a city obsessed with age. There is no crime with a harsher penalty than growing old. To be one of the beautiful people, you have to remain forever young. That crap about internal beauty is for lesser souls who don't live at the center of the known world."

"Cut the crap," said the captain. "Get to Denning."

"David Denning and I both specialized in plastic surgery, but our studies delved deeper than other students' into the reason *why* humans age. David was a year ahead of me, and on qualifying as a surgeon, he was recruited by a biotech lab that was in the vanguard of research into rejuvenation. When I qualified a year later, I was recruited too."

"You worked together in a lab?"

"Yes," said Fletcher. "There, we had state-of-the-art audio-visual equipment. After-hours, I downloaded porn off the Internet to watch on a huge screen. David found out, and soon he was doing it too. Sometimes we'd download together and then go out to strip bars to see if we could spot porn queens from our collection. Several times, David tried to make it with the strippers, but they just laughed at him. Shortly after that, there was trouble at the lab."

"What sort of trouble?" asked Hickok.

"Mutilations."

"Of whom?" asked DeClercq.

"Female animals. Have you met David Denning?" Fletcher aimed the question at the Mountie.

"No," replied DeClercq.

"He's an odd-looking fellow. A little dork with simian features. If you saw him, you'd think he should be eating a banana and rubbing the crown of his head with his knuckles. He's one of those pathetic, horny, compulsive masturbators who spend their lives lusting after out-of-reach babes. Try though he might to seduce a beautiful woman, his chances of getting laid are on the far side of zero. Does that make him give up? Not on your life. Rejection makes David try harder, and each time he strikes out, the anger buried deep inside ratchets up a notch. How does he vent that anger? I found out in the lab. He takes a defenseless female creature and tortures it to death."

"How?" asked Hickok.

"Any number of ways. Skinning them alive was a favorite torture. Another was to amputate parts by vivisection, then stitch the mutilated creature back together in bizarre ways."

"Like Picasso's paintings."

"And Fragonard's sculptures. David was particularly fond of his work."

"Who's Fragonard?"

Fletcher smirked slyly. "Look him up on the Internet."

"Those mutilations. You saw Denning do it?"

"I saw the results. The lab ran afoul of animal-rights activists.

Our boss decided to clear the computer of incriminating tests in case a hacker got into our database. That's how she came across our joint porn collection—David's and mine—and the downloads that he'd been doing on the sly."

"Fem-jep?" asked Hickok.

"His, not ours. David's taste ran to the hardest of hard core. S&M. And blood on the floor. Not only had he downloaded images of brutality to captive women, but he had also scanned in photos of what he'd done to the animals in the lab. The juxtaposition of those atrocities spoke volumes. His fantasy was to do to females who rejected him what he had done to their animal stand-ins."

"The upshot?" asked DeClercq.

"David and I were fired. The biotech firm covered up the incident to shield itself against the animal activists' claims of sadistic vivisection, and we were given hush money—'severance packages'—for promising never to mention what happened in the lab."

"Then what?"

"We used the money to set up practices. Mine downtown. And his in Hollywood."

"Did you remain friends?"

"We never really were to begin with. David and I went through med school together, landed our first jobs in the same biotech lab, shared a mutual interest in porn downloaded off the Internet, then went our separate ways."

"You knew he was Picasso, didn't you?" Hickok said.

"Don't answer that," snapped Mason.

"Why didn't you tell us? Five women died here and six up north. Their blood is on your hands."

"That's out of line," said Mason.

"I *know* why," snarled Hickok, venom in his voice. "Because you were already involved in a frolic of your own, raping those porn queens who caught your fancy as their plastic surgeon. The *last* thing you'd do was focus our attention on you."

"Let's take a break," the lawyer suggested, "till the captain cools down."

"Sorry," said Hickok. "I lost it in there."

He and DeClercq were sipping coffee in the captain's office.

"Nothing I haven't done myself, Jim," replied the chief. "You lost a man today. I almost punched a lawyer once for trying to railroad Nick. And that was just a trial."

"So what's your take on Denning?"

"I think he's our killer."

"So do I."

"And here's how I see it. What we have on our hands is a real-life Dr. Jekyll and Mr. Hyde. I think Denning went from torturing animals in the lab as stand-ins for those women who rejected him to torturing actual women in L.A. as stand-ins for the out-of-reach movie stars who became his Hollywood patients."

"That's his thinking? I made you beautiful, so you should want me?"

"By becoming a Hollywood plastic surgeon, Denning was able to *create* his sexual fantasies. They were the goddesses he would want to bed, but I think he was still afraid to take his sexual anger out on the source of his perceived rejection. So Picasso deformed women without a connection to him."

"You rejected me, so I'll make you ugly?"

"Denning relocated his practice to Hollywood North so he'd have the freedom to act out his sadistic fantasies with the women who actually rejected him. By removing himself from Hollywood South, he presented them with a sanctuary to sneak away to, a surgery they could keep secret from prying minds. The ones who came incognito made perfect victims. First, he would perform the surgery they had requested. Then, he would demand they satisfy him as thanks. And if they balked, which they undoubtedly did, he would exact his sadistic revenge by mutilating them into grotesque travesties of the surgical procedure used to rejuvenate and beautify them."

"He made them into monsters?"

"Like *The Bride of Frankenstein.*"

"Think Fletcher was in on it?" asked Hickok. "You know, like the Hillside Strangler case here? It turned out that the Strangler was two cousins, Buono and Bianchi. We were hunting the Hillside *Stranglers* and didn't know it."

"It's tempting," said DeClercq. "But I doubt it. The psych profile of Fletcher isn't that of a sadist. I don't see him committing atrocities of this level of depravity."

"A mighty big coincidence, his going to Vancouver."

"In days of old perhaps. But not any more. We live in the era of the World Wide Web. Wolfe Capp worked out of Vancouver, and both men were into Internet porn. Given his penchant for sex with porn queens, is it not consistent that Fletcher would seek underground work from Capp, which he did? Perhaps he also approached Denning in order to land work. Who knows what connections there were—and are—between predators who lurk on the Spider's Web."

"Denning's still out there," Hickok said. "Let's hope that sadistic spider doesn't have his eye on another unsuspecting fly among his pretty patients."

MENTAL MAP

Vancouver

The Charnel House was the name of the painting that hung on the wall behind Denning's desk in his private office, off his surgery at his Eternal Spring clinic in Vancouver. A charnel house was a repository for the remains of the dead—the anteroom just beyond Death's door, you might say—and the painting was a modernist expression of a slaughterhouse littered with deformed corpses jumbled on the floor. It was only a copy, of course—the original was worth millions—for the name of the artist etched beneath the title of his work on the brass plaque affixed to the frame was Pablo Picasso. And because it was a Picasso, the theme of the painting would pass over most people's heads. Patients wouldn't see the fate facing them. It could just as easily be a painting of a picnic.

The balls of this guy, thought Chandler.

The arrogant psychopath.

Dr. Jekyll had flaunted Mr. Hyde in the aging faces of his patients doomed to *his* charnel house.

So where was Denning?

And what in hell was going on?

While the techs from Ident took this place apart, Zinc sat down in the doc's chair and punched in the number for the chief's cellphone in Los Angeles.

"DeClercq."

"It's Zinc. I'm in Denning's office. Something strange is going on here."

"How so?"

"When we arrived with the warrant, we found the door to the outside jimmied and the office ransacked. It looks as if a junky burglar tore the place apart, searching for drugs. Denning's nurse arrived to catch up on some paperwork over the weekend, and she assumed, with no help from me, that the police were on the scene because of a break-in call. On her own, she checked the office to see if anything was missing, and what she found was that a number of patients' files were gone from the filing cabinet."

"How many?"

"She's out in the reception room, trying to figure that out with the computer as we speak."

"Where are you?"

"In Denning's private office."

"Do you think he's on the run and has destroyed the files?"

"Don't know. Like I say, something strange is going on. There's a pool of blood on the carpet beside his desk, and we just found a bullet hole in the wall."

"But no body?"

"Nope. It looks like a kidnapping."

"That doesn't make sense," said DeClercq. "Why abduct Denning and steal some of his files, but leave his computer records behind and his nurse alive? When did she last see Denning?"

"Late yesterday afternoon. The doc was in his private office—the office I'm in now—consulting with his final patient of the week and a fellow the nurse knows only as the director. He's a business associate of Denning's. It's all very hush-hush. The nurse works on a need-to-know basis. But then that's the nature of Eternal Spring. The doc's patients, by and large, are Hollywood types who don't want anyone knowing they're at Denning's office, or wherever he refers them for post-operative care and rejuvenation."

"Interesting," said DeClercq. "That might explain why none of his victims have been identified."

"The last the nurse saw of the doc when she left yesterday, he was still in his office with those two. Do you think the director abducted the plastic surgeon once the nurse was gone?"

"I don't know. None of it makes sense. The only way it makes sense is if it's not supposed to. You know, like Lord Lucan in Britain. The peer who vanished forever when the nanny was found dead. Or Jimmy Hoffa and D. B. Cooper in the States. Remember Cooper?"

"The guy who pulled a skyjacking, then parachuted out of a plane over the Cascades."

"They're all open-ended cases that may never be solved. Could be that Denning's disappearance is set up that way."

"It's a ruse," said Chandler.

"That's my gut reaction. Denning is our serial killer, and now he's on the run. What you're seeing there is the endgame of his scheme. It's only a matter of time until those stars get reported missing and one or more is linked to Denning. What we have is his preemptive strike. He's taken himself out of the picture as if he's a victim too. What we're supposed to think is that someone like Dr. Ryland Fletcher poached his victims from among Denning's patients and then, for some psychotic reason, decided to take out the surgeon and his telltale files too."

While Chandler and DeClercq were conversing, an Ident team was working its way around Denning's office, searching for forensic clues or hiding places, or anything else that might clue them in to what was going on. One of the techs had dusted a locked bookcase for fingerprints, and having lifted them, he had pried open the glass front. The medical texts that lined the shelves inside were hundreds of years old. The head of the team was leafing through the volumes one by one when he interrupted Zinc's cellphone conversation with a cursed "Oh, shit!"

The inspector glanced at him.

"Found something, Zinc."

"Hold on, chief," Chandler said. "Something's up."

The anatomy text from the 1700s had been sacrificed to convert it into a hidey-hole. The pages had been glued together so it would dry into a solid block, then a square chunk had been carved out of the paper guts to provide a secret stash for purloined letters and such. Hidden within the hidey-hole was a single sheet of paper and a gadget designed to trigger a digital warning signal if the cover of the text was opened to reveal the buried treasure.

The "Oh, shit!" meant that the tech had tripped the trigger.

Launching the signal into cyberspace.

The tech held the book out for Chandler to see.

"Chief," Zinc said into his cellphone, "we've found a map hidden in a booby-trapped text. Finding it set off an electronic warning of some sort."

"A map of what?" asked DeClercq.

"The Gulf Islands, the San Juans and the land masses around."

"Just a map?"

"No. A map with six *X*'s."

"Find Denning's fax machine and fax it here *fast.*"

Los Angeles

The cops stood around the fax machine in the Robbery-Homicide Division on the third floor of the Parker Center in downtown L.A. as the transmission came in from Zinc at Denning's office. DeClercq grabbed the sheet of paper before it hit the in-tray and rushed it across to the table where Det. Insp. Kim Rossmo sat waiting at his laptop. From the memory bank of the high-end computer, he pulled up a map of the same area encompassed by the fax, programmed in when the geographic profiler had helped Special X locate Mephisto in the Burnt Bones case. After scanning in a map of the West Coast, from Vancouver south to Seattle, Kim had directly digitalized those ten crime sites onto that "crime space." Using his Rigel software to interpret the "mental map" left by that megalomaniac's mind on the geography of his hunting ground, the cyber cop had produced a jeopardy surface—first, the two-dimensional blob of the multi-colored amoeba linking the pixels of the computer screen with the same mathematical probability of their being that predator's "anchor point," then the three-dimensional mountain range of the jeopardy itself—that showed the most likely spot for Mephisto's hideout was Shipwreck Island.

Which it had been.

That jeopardy surface was still superimposed on the scanned-in map, so Kim instructed Rigel to strip it of the original geoprofile so he would have a "clean" landscape on which to digitalize the six new crime sites from Zinc's fax. With the chief staring over one shoulder and Lewis looming behind the other, the cyber cop entered the new locations onto the scanned-in map and clicked the mouse so Rigel could perform a multitude of calculations.

First, the GeoProfile button created the amoeba.

"I'll be damned," said Rossmo.

"Is there a glitch?" asked Lewis.

"No, the shape is different. It's the hot spot that's the same."

Kim clicked the mouse on the Jeopardy button, instructing Rigel to raise the mountain range.

"It's the *same island,*" said DeClercq.

"In fact, but not in name. After the notoriety of the Mephisto case, the state of Washington legally changed the name of Shipwreck Island to Ebbtide Island."

"That bastard Mephisto is still alive," said DeClercq.

"Heaven help us," Rossmo said.

"Hell on earth's more like it."

Robert's cellphone trilled as he stared in disbelief at the jeopardy surface on the laptop screen.

"DeClercq," he answered.

"Chief, it's Zinc. Denning's nurse recovered on the office computer the names of eight files that are missing from the filing cabinet. Like you said, I recognize most of those names as fading Hollywood stars. Seven of the eight were up here from L.A. The last name is that of the patient who was in the office with Denning and the director when the nurse left Eternal Spring yesterday. It's a *real* concern."

Robert's heart skipped a beat.

"The eighth name," Zinc said, "is Gillian Macbeth."

MEPHISTO

Los Angeles

"He is the Napoleon of crime, Watson," said Sherlock Holmes in reference to the most deep-dyed of all the villains with whom the great detective had ever matched wits.

Moriarty.

His arch-nemesis.

Crime was definitely the professor's forte. All he did was plan; his henchmen did the rest. The henchmen might be caught, but not Moriarty, whose profits from forgery, robbery and murder filled six bank accounts. The professor pervaded London, yet nobody knew he was even there until the criminal mastermind was flushed out by Sherlock Holmes. In the same way that slight tremors at the edge of a web tell you that a spider lurks at its center, so Holmes sensed the presence of Professor James Moriarty's malignant mind.

And so it was with DeClercq and *his* Moriarty.

The psychopath self-named Mephisto.

The arch-nemesis of Special X.

Those who don't believe in the supernatural are naïve. The supernatural lives in madmen's minds, and because they act out their otherworldly fantasies in the real world, ipso facto, the supernatural also exists in reality. It matters not whether *you* believe in talking dogs, a talking dog turned the Son of Sam into New York City's .44-Caliber Killer, and the dead in the morgue were dead enough despite your disbelief. The same goes with astrology. It matters not whether *you* accept the power in the alignment of the stars, that's what inspired the Zodiac Killer to kill flesh-and-blood sacrifices in San Francisco. And as for rock-and-roll being the Devil's music, *you* can believe what you want, but Sharon Tate and the rest were butchered because the Manson family took orders from Satan conveyed to them by means of the song "Helter Skelter" by the Beatles.

And so it was with Mephisto.

The Devil hungers for human souls, according to Christian myth. Every soul he can steal from God is a triumph in the war he has waged since he was expelled from heaven by the Almighty Himself. In the form of Mephistopheles—from the Greek for "he who does not like light"—the Devil has much to offer wayward souls who will sell themselves into eternal damnation for a barter here and now. Knowledge, power, money, sex . . . name your price. Buy now, pay later, and you too can satisfy your darkest desire.

Faust sought to know everything there was to know, so he sold his soul to Mephistopheles in exchange for ultimate wisdom and a sorcerer's power. Twenty-four years later, the Devil came at midnight for his due. A fearsome wind shrieked around the house, whistling and hissing like a legion of snakes. "Help! Murder!" Faust was heard to wail, but no one dared rush to his rescue. Come dawn, his mutilated corpse was found on the dung heap in the yard, while inside the house, his bedroom was swimming in blood, brains and teeth, and his eyeballs were stuck to one wall. That legend inspired Marlowe and Goethe, giants of literature, and Berlioz and Liszt, titans of music.

Now that legend had inspired this psycho self-named Mephisto, a madman who fantasized he was the Devil incarnate, a puppet master who preyed through killers as sadistic as he was, henchmen who sold their souls to him to turn their own Hydes loose.

The Devil in disguise.

Sherlock Holmes had the benefit of knowing his nemesis. He had met the professor face to face. Moriarty was tall and thin, with rounded shoulders. His gray hair crowned a domed forehead. His eyes, puckered and blinking, were sunk deep in his pale white head, a head that protruded forward and oscillated from side to side like a reptile's.

Reptilian was a description that fit Mephisto too, but unfortunately for Special X, the reptile he personified was a chameleon. A chameleon changes color to match his background, and that's what Mephisto did for each infernal scheme. Physically, he was an amorphous entity, a megalomaniac shape-shifter who saw himself as a supernatural being, a Mephistophelean representative of hell on earth. Like a parasite hunting for a suitable host, his psychopathy floated free of human form until he was ready to assume whatever carnal shape was dictated by the background of his scheme.

For the Burnt Bones case, Mephisto had become a Scot from the Campbell clan. His quest had been to find the stolen Highland Hoard, so he'd wrapped himself in tartan from the Scottish Highlands to seduce the necessary henchmen for that odyssey. Donella Grant, his sexy Highland queen, had hacked a hand and an ear from Nick Craven. A cult of Druids, the ideal goons for that scheme, had gang-raped Jenna Bond as a perk of the job. All—for whatever reasons—had sold their souls to Mephisto, and each had paid the same deadly price as Faust.

Well, now the Devil was back with another hellish scheme.

And *new* sadistic henchmen to help him pull it off.

Henchmen like Dr. Denning—the Picasso killer of L.A.—who, in exchange for the complete freedom to turn his Hyde loose on the beautiful women who rebuffed his advances after he made them young again, and for being taken out of the life he no longer desired, had agreed to carry out Mephisto's plan, whatever it was. In the realm of reptiles, Denning was a snake shedding his old skin.

And then there was the ghoulish Man in Black, the creepy hitman likened by those who had encountered him to an undertaker. What role did he play in Mephisto's nefarious scheme? And for what price had he sold his soul?

Whatever the scheme was this time, it was somehow linked to the hijacked Egyptian mummy. Only two concrete facts were known about Mephisto. One, he was American, or else he was so good at mimicking a Yankee accent that he could fool discerning Americans.

And two, he was an antiquarian obsessed with the past.

Thus the Highland Hoard.

Thus Sleeping Beauty.

A few years ago, a Japanese businessman paid somewhere around $40 million for Vincent Van Gogh's painting *Sunflowers.* It was rumored that when he died, the collector planned to have the canvas cremated with his corpse. You can't take it with you, the saying goes, so if he couldn't enjoy *Sunflowers* after death, why should others enjoy it in life, even though that masterpiece is one of history's treasures. Some folks, you see, see themselves as the center of it all.

Folks with too much money fall into two groups: philanthropists, who give the excess away, and egoists, who indulge their own self-centered fantasies.

Suppose a priceless piece of art is stolen from the Louvre or a Swiss bank wants to capitalize on Nazi loot before Holocaust survivors can win court access to its secret vaults. How do you slip something like that into the proper hands, the hands of well-heeled collectors obsessed with the thingishness of things, collectors who will swallow any price to squirrel away something priceless so they alone can enjoy it?

You commission Mephisto.

In his other identity—whatever that was—he knew the players and when to approach them. Those players paid him handsomely to sate their compulsive obsessions, and that's how Mephisto financed the devilish schemes that hatched out of his own megalomaniacal obsessions with the past.

So *what* was he up to now?

That was the question.

Megalomania: a mental illness marked by delusions of greatness and an obsession with doing extravagant things.

In Hitler's view of history, the Aryans—non-Jewish Caucasians—were the master race, and those who didn't measure up were subhuman *Untermenschen.* In Mephisto's view of history, that theory was much too inclusive. The way *he* saw the world, or so DeClercq suspected from what was known about this superpsycho, Mephisto was a master race of one, and the rest of us were *Untermenschen.*

What a megalomaniac craves to feed his overblown superego is a worthy adversary to defeat. A Napoleon needs his Nelson or Wellington. A Hitler needs his Churchill or Roosevelt. A Moriarty needs his Sherlock Holmes. A Mephisto needs his DeClercq.

The *last* thing DeClercq needed was a macho pissing contest with a nutcase like Mephisto. But that, his cop's gut told him, was what was happening here. Like it or not, they were squaring off for a second round in a winner-take-all grudge match made in hell.

Why me? thought the Mountie.

Which, of course, was the answer.

"The Mounties always get their man."

Unless he's Mephisto.

Was it chance or fate that brought this pair together? In the beginning, there was the Highland Hoard, which, thanks to the Highland clearances after the defeat of the Scottish clans by England at the Battle of Culloden in 1746, had been spirited away from Glencoe to the Pacific Northwest by Campbell emigrants. To obtain that treasure, the puppet master Mephisto had pulled a few strings by abducting a local Mountie to cut apart, one piece each day, unless the redcoats en masse became his unwilling henchmen.

By chance or fate, however, that scheme had straddled the border between Canada and the United States, consequently involving DeClercq and Special X. By chance or fate, Special X had developed the foremost one-two-three psycho-hunting punch in the world, and thanks to three—Kim Rossmo's geographic-profiling technique—DeClercq had thwarted the megalomaniac's diabolical scheme.

Well, now he was back.

Intent on sadistic revenge.

For if there's one thing history has taught us about megalomaniac madness, it's that superpsychos *never* give up until they're forced to face their Waterloo.

In short, they're relentless.

Lightning, they say, never strikes the same place twice. Not unless that lightning is Mephisto. How like him to return to his former hideout on Shipwreck—now Ebbtide—Island, gambling that the police would never expect him to be so bold. Since geographic profiling thwarted him last time, this time *he* would thwart that twenty-first-century technique by having Dr. Denning choose dump sites for his first six victims, using Ebbtide Island as his anchor point. The map found hidden in Denning's office exposed the doctor's "mental map" to Rossmo's profiling. To prevent that from happening until the time was right, Mephisto had the bodies dumped in the artificial boxcar pattern, two rows of three, one row on each side of the border. Did the ruse of using a smokescreen come to him *after* the first body was already rotting? Is that why no one smelled the corpse decomposing beside the footpath through the Galiano woods? Because it didn't rot there originally, but was moved there later to thwart Rossmo's ingenuity?

It all fit.

But what thrill was revenge unless Mephisto could rub DeClercq's nose in it? You fool, I used the *same* hideout I used before, and I kept your geoprofiler from homing in on me until I was ready for your arrival. That's why, after I had Denning taken out, I had the map of what *should* have been the dump sites hidden in the book, and that book was booby-trapped so I'd know when to expect you. If you hadn't found the map, or if your geoprofile turned out to be a dud, I'd eventually have had to *tell* you to search Shipwreck—Ebbtide—Island.

Yes, thought DeClercq.

That's his game.

The game of a sadistic spider playing with flies.

That one of those flies was Gill Macbeth, the Mountie was certain. Not only was Denning her plastic surgeon, and not only was hers one of the eight files taken from Denning's office when the deadly doctor shed his old skin, but Denning's nurse had also told Zinc that the final patient seen by the doctor with the mysterious "director" was Gill Macbeth. This time, DeClercq's gut told him, the Devil in disguise was that director, and by now the odds were that Gill was caught in his web.

Unless . . .

There was a slim chance that Mephisto wasn't ready to strike. He might still be in the planning stages, and could have been surprised by the Mounties' preemptive luck in tracing Dr. Ryland Fletcher through Wolfe Capp's Spider's Web. That might have put them on to Dr. David Denning before Mephisto's earliest expectation, in which case there might still be time to keep him from getting to Gill, whose horrible death was no doubt to be his revenge on DeClercq.

Unless . . .

FOUNTAIN OF AGE

Ebbtide Island

Humanity disgusted him. The mass of humanity. Overpopulation. All those bottom-feeders.

There was a time when nature, war and social Darwinism weeded out countless lowlife parasites. Life expectancy was short because there were no common cures for rampant diseases. Sterilization was nonexistent in makeshift operating sheds because no one knew about germs, and there were no antibiotics to save the infected. Those nature didn't kill off were left to die in endless wars that now fill history books, or to be worked to death as slaves by waves of foreign conquerors, or to be ground down in squalor by the aristocrats of local economies.

It took a million years for humankind to populate the earth with a billion people. That mark was reached around 1800. By the 1930s, there were two billion. That increased to three billion in 1960, four billion in 1975, five billion in 1987, six billion before the turn of this millennium, and that number will *double* within fifty years.

This planet can comfortably support between one and two billion humans. To sustain the current population at the standard of living of an average Joe in the United States, it would take a minimum of two more Mother Earths. Signs of stress fatigue are all around. Too much demand fed by too little supply. Water sources are failing. Waste is piling up. America, with a mere 275 million people, doesn't have the juice to run itself. Blackouts have begun, and the nation has been reduced to drilling in ecological reserves in the Arctic. Cancerous corporate elites think globalization is the answer. We want what you've got, so give it to us. Already the riots have started. The revolts of the bottom-feeders. We want the standard of living that you enjoy, and we're going to take it. Soon there will be billions of parasites infesting this shrinking earth with poverty, starvation and vandalism—marauding hordes of young, ill-educated cretins schooled in nihilistic fanaticism and fit to be nothing but cannon fodder.

Too many people.

And most were *sub*humans.

What the world required was a major culling. Something virulent enough to destroy at least three-quarters of the current population. We all see the problem: we've bred ourselves into crisis, but no one has the balls to do what must be done.

Except *me,* thought Mephisto.

Instead of a culling, what the world was facing was the rejuvenation of its overpopulation. People were living longer, and they thought that was their right. So instead of enjoying spring in their youth—the way nature intended—then accepting their evolutionary fate to waste away from old age, these arrogant King Canutes of the new millennium demanded that they be allowed to command the tide of time to reverse direction. In this quest for perpetual youth, they were trying every panacea from plastic surgery and chemical interventions, to hormone replacement, human growth injections, vitamin therapy and mind/body medicine—all aimed at prolonging youth, health and vitality. So desperate were women for anti-aging treatments that one of the latest rages was botox. Minute quantities of botulism toxin—a purified strain of the *same* toxin that causes food poisoning—were used to temporarily halt the activity of frown muscles. The toxin affected patients' motor nerve terminals to prevent the release of acetycholine, which causes muscle contractions. The treatment required repeating every four months, so basically they were poisoning themselves to remove a line from their brows.

Cheating the slag heap.

To look like Sleeping Beauty.

Mephisto's latest doomsday plan had hatched as a result of the discovery of the perfectly preserved Egyptian mummy at Lord Ridding's ancestral estate. As an antiquarian, the megalomaniac had been obsessed with ancient Egypt ever since he was a boy. The moment he read about the discovery on the Internet, the psycho knew he had to possess Sleeping Beauty. Possess it as a one-of-a-kind Egyptian artifact, and possess it because if it did hold the secret of youth in whatever the embalmers had used to thwart decay of the flesh, he didn't want all those New Age geriatrics to get their shriveled, liver-spotted hands on it. The only modern Methuselah who would—who *should*—be rejuvenated by the secret extracted from Sleeping Beauty's perfectly preserved flesh would be *him*. So at first, Mephisto's plan had been nothing more than a desire to hoard the one-of-a-kind treasure for himself, and to be the only human on earth to sip from the Fountain of Youth.

But then he got to thinking.

What the bottom-feeders required wasn't the Fountain of Youth, but the Fountain of Age. If a way could be found to speed up our internal clocks, aging kids so they're sterile *before* puberty, then we'd be killing off humans before they could be replaced, and down would spiral the overpopulation of the earth.

Could that be done?

Mephisto was going to find out.

What his scheme required was a suitable doctor, one with the necessary training in biotechnology and no ethics whatsoever. To find such a doctor, he had gone hunting on the Internet, and there he had hooked up with Wolfe Capp's Spider's Web and, through those connections, had joined Snuff Lib, where he had become the major patron of Woody Bone. Eventually, he had plumbed the cesspool of that sick fuck's mind to find a lead to a doctor even more warped than Woody himself.

If you search far and deep enough, there's *nothing* you can't find on the World Wide Web.

Enter the Doctor.

At first, their communications had been anonymous. Wolfe Capp, for an astronomical fee, had set up a private chat room for the psychos to feel each other out. What began as a swapping of personal fantasies had soon degenerated into a mutated hybrid of mutual psychopathy, and out of that had spawned this Faust's pact with the Devil. Eventually, the psychos had met face to face, and the events taking place here and now in the charnel vault buried deep in the rock beneath the Panacea Clinic had resulted from that encounter.

To cure the overpopulation of the earth genetically, Denning had told Mephisto at that meeting of warped minds, the gene you want to see expressed in the general population is the one that causes progeria, an accelerated aging condition. Everything in a body cell is about balance. Normal cell metabolism produces damaging free radicals known as reactive oxygen species, or ROS. The damage done by free radicals is why we age. To inhibit that damage and restore balance, healthy cells produce antioxidant enzymes that attack free radicals. Children with progeria have a deficient gene that restricts production of these antioxidants. For instance, the activity level of the enzyme catalase is 50 percent lower than normal. The level of glutathione peroxidase is 70 percent lower. The lack of those two enzymes makes it impossible for the cells to effectively remove toxic peroxides produced during metabolism, and that deficiency ages a child at such an accelerated rate that the average life expectancy is reduced to age twelve.

I want that gene, Mephisto had said. Can it be found?

Of course. And from it I can engineer a Franken-gene that will shut down production of antioxidant enzymes in human body cells so the free radicals now held in check can run amok and—instead of killing us off on average at age seventy-four—will kill most of humanity off by twelve.

How do we get it into the general populace?

Piece of cake, Denning had said. Transgenic mutations can enter through numerous doors. How did AIDS jump species from monkeys to us? How did mad cow disease transfer from cross-species animal feed to cattle and then on to us? Viruses. The same vehicles that can be used for adenovirus gene transfers. Genetic piggybacks. What we do is attach the Franken-gene to a disabled common cold virus, then give it to people so the virus takes the gene to their cells. Or we sneak it in through modified foods. Fish genes have been added to cereal crops, germ genes have been stitched into vegetables and our genes have been engineered into animals. There is no requirement to alert the public, so soon we'll all be swallowing fruit, vegetables, meat and drugs created in Petri dishes. Is it a new kind of cannibalism to eat a genetically modified food containing a human gene?

I like it.

I thought you would. Bring me a kid with progeria and a normal six-year-old to use as a test subject. I'll practice on the guinea pig to find a way of dissemination. First, I'll use a gene gun to shoot the Franken-gene prototypes into her. Then, once I find that something works to make her age prematurely, I'll engineer a suitable genetic vehicle to plague the general populace with progeria.

A depopulation implosion.

The *key* to Death's door.

Devolution.

Mephisto smiled.

So now the megalomaniac stood in the Mummy Room, surveying the various tools he'd assembled for his diabolical scheme. The secret of what keeps us young was hidden in the Egyptian mummy. If he could unlock that ancient secret, he would be the only person alive to drink from the Fountain of Youth. The secret of what makes us old was hidden in the genetic freak. If he could unlock that deadly secret, he could poison the gene pool of all those bottom-feeders from the Fountain of Age. In Denning, he had a gene jockey with no constraining ethics. In the guinea pig, he had his means to wreak revenge on Jenna Bond for her part in undermining his last scheme. And in Gill—if the rumor of romance between her and Robert DeClercq heard by the Doctor in surgical circles in Vancouver was true—the psycho had a bloody sacrifice that would get him even with the meddling Mountie. Given sufficient time to piece the jigsaw puzzle together—if necessary, Mephisto would send him a helpful clue—DeClercq would make his way to Ebbtide Island, only to find it abandoned by his adversary. Gone would be the Egyptian mummy and the pair of kids, moved to another hideout that Mephisto had secured in the States. What DeClercq would recover was the corpse of Macbeth, torn apart internally by the pear and stripped of her rejuvenated skin à la Fragonard. Beauty is only skin deep, they say. Would the Mountie still think the woman stretched out on the table in the Mummy Room was beautiful when all he had to look at was the flayed flesh beneath the external mask humans wear to face the world?

The effect of that monster on Jenna Bond would also be profound. She would not recover her daughter from the island, for there was delicious play to be had in making her fret for weeks, or months, or maybe years over what grisly torture had happened, was happening or would happen to her beloved child. Once Bond had been broken down sufficiently and teetered on the verge of insanity, Mephisto would bring her face to face with the Doctor's handiwork, and that mother could live out her golden years with a dying child who was twice as old as she was.

Nobody fucks with me, Mephisto thought.

I have no equal.

You're all bottom-feeders.

My final solution is as final as can be, and when I set my mind to something, there's nobody out there who can—

Buzzz . . . buzzz . . . buzzz . . .

The alarm went off.

So startled was Mephisto that he winced from the sound.

DeClercq had found the map.

So soon? the psycho thought.

Tick-tock . . . tick-tock . . .

His timetable lurched ahead.

He had underestimated the player on the other side.

Tick-tock . . . tick-tock . . .

The endgame was prematurely in play.

PSYCHO'S PSYCHO

Ebbtide Island

The sun was down and the moon was on the rise, its pockmarked fat face peeping in through the slant of the greenhouse that had been built into the roof of the clinic. Like a voyeur lurking outside an exhibitionist's window, it ogled Gill as she dressed for dinner with the aid of the full-length mirror in her room. Never had she felt as pampered as she did this evening, for she had spent the day being treated like Cleopatra. The staff of the Panacea Clinic might as well have been her personal slaves, their attentiveness to her was that profound. Olaf had massaged her in a candlelit loft scented with aromatherapy. The floor surrounding the table was strewn with fragrant flower blossoms. Then he had led Gill down to the cradle of Mother Earth, where black basalt stones selected for their ability to retain heat were positioned on the ground in a hand-hewn rock vault beside a similar configuration of white marble mounds. Olaf had stretched Gill out face up on the warm stones so they hit pressure points on her back, and the consequent relaxation from the pull of gravity made her feel as if she were a pat of melting butter. In contrast, the marble was icy cold against her skin, invigorating Gill immediately. Mixing fire with ice was holistic in its effect, the warm stones drawing toxins to the surface of her skin while the cold stones drove blood back to her heart to speed up filtering circulation.

Body, mind and soul, Macbeth had felt purified.

And so it had gone for the entire day. But now the staff had left in the chopper for the mainland, and Gill was left alone—*she thought*—on the island with the Director. They were to enjoy a dinner he would cook himself—"I trained as a chef at Cordon Bleu," he had informed her, "so I would never have to eat a poor meal"—and then, once the after-dinner chitchat was exhausted, it would be early to bed for a good night's sleep after all that exotic relaxation.

She was back where she had started on the first day of spring, face to face with the New Her in an adoring mirror. Like Narcissus staring at his handsome reflection in a pool, Gill admired her rejuvenated beauty in the glass. If she recalled her Psychology 100 course correctly, narcissism was a paraphilia that involved erotic gratification from the admiration of one's own physical attributes. To make matters worse, pride *was* one of the seven deadly sins.

And then there was the feminist's conundrum. The argument that cosmetic surgery was the latest manifestation of a large-scale conspiracy to subjugate women through enslavement to the worship of unattainable ideals. Who was behind the conspiracy? Probably the guy who invented girdles, high-heeled shoes and bikini waxing. The weakness in that argument was that it ignored biological forces of attractiveness—the points made by Graham Worlock yesterday at Eternal Spring—and the signals that cause us to feel allurement or revulsion. Gill was a feminist—she had breached the barricades for those who followed—but like every adult in these plastic times who had watched glamor win out over hairy armpits and charred bras, she was subject to cultural biases and indoctrination. So like many of her sisters-in-arms, those who were unable to reconcile a feminist ideology with the desire to beautify themselves and stay the inevitable process of aging, she had gone to Dr. David Denning to recapture and revel in all those aspects of being a beautiful woman that she had sacrificed to the cause.

Like seducing men.

With this classy body.

Men like Robert DeClercq.

Men like Graham Worlock.

So, narcissistic or not, Gill winked at the beauty in the mirror and raised her hand in a make-believe toast to the god who created *this* woman. "David Denning, you're the best!"

Gill blinked.

Her eyes were playing tricks.

Was the mirror opening?

Or had she so dehydrated herself from all those eucalyptus steams, ozonated whirl pools, mineral soaks and hydrotherapy tubs that she was light-headed?

"Hello, Gill."

"David? What are you doing here?"

"You called for me. Your wish is my command."

The full-length mirror had opened like a door into Gill's bedroom. Just inside the threshold stood Dr. David Denning, dressed in a tuxedo as if he were James Bond, with a long-stemmed red rose in one hand and a bottle of Dom Perignon and two champagne glasses in the other. James Bond, however, he certainly was not, this odd-looking man with the short physique that was the antithesis of a Greek god's. What made him even more bizarre was the freaky look in his eyes tonight, and the incongruity of such a non-attractive man wearing such classy clothes. Denning in his tux gave new meaning to the expression "monkey suit."

"For you," he said, handing Gill the rose.

She didn't know what to say in reply, she was that nonplused.

"Do you know how the size of a champagne glass originated?" the Doctor asked, setting the bottle of Dom down on a small table beside the open mirror. Holding the glasses by their bases, he aimed the two basins at Gill's breasts like a pair of headlights. "King Louis XVI of France had each glass made just large enough to hold one of Marie Antoinette's bare tits."

"David," Gill said softly, "what's going on?"

"I heard you, Gill. From behind the mirror. Don't be coy. We both know what you said."

His eyes were glittering with insane lust. They were still locked on the rejuvenated breasts that filled out the bodice of the cocktail dress Gill had donned for her dinner with Graham Worlock, the director of the clinic.

His degenerate eyes slid up to give her his sexiest slow burn. "'David Denning,'" he mimicked, "'you're the best!'"

Oh my God, thought Gill.

What a fantasy!

He thinks I want to fuck him!

How ludicrous!

And the thought of that, on reflex, made Gill make the mistake of her life.

She laughed.

The change that came over Denning was as dramatic as that in Robert Louis Stevenson's classic tale. The glitter in his eyes snuffed as dark as black holes. His nostrils flared as wide as those of a raging bull about to gore a picador. Blood suffused his face until it was as red as the Devil's in cartoons. His lips pulled back in a snarl from teeth so crooked that an orthodontist would throw his hands up in defeat, and as the two champagne glasses tumbled to shatter on the floor, he screamed at her in a spatter of spittle, "You ungrateful *cunt!*"

His hand reached out for the neck of the champagne bottle, and he gripped it with such ferocity that you'd have thought he was a starving man wringing the neck of the last chicken on earth. Denning swung it in a roundhouse arc worthy of a barroom brawl, and though Gill got her arm up in time to absorb most of the blow, the bottle of bubbly broke through her defense to clip her skull.

Down she went for the count.

Stunned, she seemed to hear his rant from the bottom of the sea. A fury of words muffled by a fathom of water on her brain screamed down at her from a shadow looming over the surface of consciousness above. "You fucking bitch! You're just like all the rest! Who do you think you are, twat, to treat *me* like shit! You'd twitch your cunt for any pretty boy who comes along! But me, who *made* you what you are, you think you can *laugh* in my face! *I'm* the reason those assholes want to spread your legs. There's lots of pussy out there younger than you! You're a middle-aged cow living a fantasy because

I took your sagging, wrinkled flesh and turned you into something you're not! *I* made you beautiful! *I* gave you a second spring! You owe *me,* bitch! Now give me some cunt, you *cunt!*"

The glitter was back.

But this time in Denning's hand, not his eyes.

And the shape of it was so terrifying to the pathologist who knew only too well the havoc it could wreak on human flesh that one glimpse of the scalpel was enough to bring Gill around. Down slashed the razor-sharp blade to bite into her upper arm, slicing open a thin red line as bloody as the red divider between *North by Northwest* and *Psycho* in her collection of Hitchcock videos back home. Image upon image flashed through her mind's eye. Janet Leigh ripped to ribbons in the *Psycho* shower scene. Tippi Hedren pecked to pieces in *The Birds.* Barbara Leigh-Hunt lovingly throttled in *Frenzy.* And looming in the background stood Hitch himself: the tubby man with the ugly, chinless mug, forever denied consummation with the blonde sex goddesses that *his* genius created and his leading men enjoyed, until his repressed lust exploded in a visual rampage of sadistic revenge against beautiful women for rejecting him.

The Hitchcock Syndrome.

That was Denning's disease.

This madman was acting out his rampage of sadistic revenge against the beautiful women who rejected him. The Doctor loomed above her, the bloody scalpel in one hand, the champagne bottle gripped like a club in the other, and Gill knew she was a moment away from being slashed and bludgeoned to death. So, seizing that moment of life to defend herself, she sprang up off the floor like a wildcat going for the kill and clawed her nails as deep as she could across the maniac's ugly, twisted face.

"Cunt!" screamed Denning—his obsessive refrain—as he recoiled from Gill's acrylics to protect his eyes.

Like a barber's pole, his skin was diagonally striped with deep red gashes. He almost slashed himself with the scalpel when his hands rose to his mangled face to assess the damage. Seeing an opening, Gill whirled 180 degrees to dash for the bedroom door, but someone outside was wrenching the knob to get in, and probably possessed a key to the engaged lock. So instead, she did a side run around Denning and, like Alice in *Through the Looking Glass,* fled across the threshold hidden by the full-length mirror to face whatever horrors lurked beyond.

The mirror swung shut behind her.

The deadbolt locked.

Her heart was pounding in her throat as she started down the stone steps secreted in the wall.

Gill was on the far side of Death's door.

The fantasy invariably played out like this. Come time for the Doc to enjoy his half of the deal he made with the Director, he would dress up as if he was off to meet the queen, then climb the secret stairs to the bedroom of his fantasy fuck. While the Undertaker stood guard in the hall outside the boudoir door (in case the woman lured to the island tried to bolt), the Doc would make his move on her within, and when he struck out—as he was sure to do, being such an ugly lover—the ghoul would enter the bedroom to help him subdue her. Together, they'd haul her, fighting and pleading, down the stone steps to the subterranean charnel house in the bowels of the bluff, where the rejected suitor would exact his revenge.

And so it was tonight with Dr. Gill Macbeth.

Who must have spurned the Doc like all his other fantasy fucks, to hear the shrieks of rage that echoed from the room.

The Undertaker wrenched the knob to find that the door was locked, so he fished in his pocket for the key.

"Cunt!" the Doc screamed through the wood.

He was *really* pissed.

And she would pay the ultimate price.

There is nothing more terrifying on earth than male sexuality gone berserk. The annals of crime are replete with ghastly case histories of the gruesome atrocities that bear witness to that truth. Gill Macbeth had seen her share on the autopsy table in the VGH morgue, and she knew she was going to end up like that if Dr. David Denning got his hands on her. So down, down, down the stone steps she fled, guided by an occasional dim bulb on the wall. It took all of Gill's control to hold in check the urge to take the steps three at a time, but if she tripped and twisted an ankle, she'd be as good as dead.

Smash!

Crash!

Tinkle!

The sounds of breaking glass echoed down the stairwell tunnel at her heels. Denning was using the champagne bottle to batter through the mirror, and now he would be sticking his hand in the hole to twist back the deadbolt. Yes, there was the clatter of tumbling glass as the frame swung open, and there was the clomp of feet starting down the stone steps, and if there was any doubt, Denning laid the matter to rest by yelling down at her, "Are you ready for *the pear,* cunt?"

The pear was no longer on the hook beside the mouth at the lower end of the stairwell that sank from the clinic above to the Mummy Room down below. The psychos had removed Sleeping Beauty from the table in the center of the underground chamber, and the Doctor had adapted it for Gill Macbeth. Handcuffs would secure both wrists to the corners flanking her head, gynecologist's stirrups fitted with restraining straps would spread-eagle her legs to the bottom corners, and she'd be prepped for the misogynist's revenge.

The pear lay on the table.

Between the stirrups.

"Mommy?" Becky Bond prayed. "Is that you?"

She knew the footfalls of the men by heart by now: the flat-footed thump of the Doctor, the athletic spring of the Director, the stealthy stalk of the Undertaker. The footfalls coming down the steps belonged to none of them. They were like the light-footed tread of her mom.

The woman who burst into the room wasn't Jenna Bond. That she was on Becky's side, however, was obvious from her terror. The intruder was fleeing so fast that she slammed into the central table. The hard edge caught her at the waist to double her forward across the surface in front of Becky's cage. As she pushed back to continue her flight, the horrified woman locked eyes with the imprisoned girl.

"Where's the key?"

"There," said Becky, pointing to the hooks on the wall.

Whirling, the woman dashed back to the mouth of the stairwell to grab the key, then rounded the central table to squat in front of the door to the cage. With more haste than speed, she dropped the key on the floor. It took time she didn't have to retrieve it, but after the fumble she managed to get the key into the lock and, twisting it sharply to the left, was able to spring the door.

"Let's go," she said, reaching in to yank Becky out.

"What about Anna?" asked the girl, pointing.

What Gill glimpsed in the other cage made her gasp. At first, she thought the child was being starved to death, for the little person behind the bars was nothing but thin skin and brittle bones. But then she grasped that the captive was afflicted with progeria, and she knew they'd never escape with a burden like that to weigh them down.

Cranking the key, she sprung the lock and told the old child, "Find a place to hide. I'll come back for you."

"The *fuck* you will!" snarled a livid voice behind Gill's shoulder. She craned around to see David Denning seize Becky by the hair, jerking back her head, ready to slit her throat from ear to ear.

Unmasking the Phantom of the Opera was no more shocking than this. Like Lon Chaney in the classic silent film, the Doctor was duded up in a handsome tux, but his face, no scream in hell to behold at the best of times, would be best described as a scream in hell now. As if lashed by a cat-o'-five-tails, the furrows clawed across it were dripping blood. One of Gill's nails had also slashed his eye, so ocular fluid ran down that cheek.

"Strip," he ordered, "or the kid is dead."

Denning held the scalpel high in the air, poised to sweep down in a powerful arc that would cut Becky's throat back to her vertebrae. What Gill saw in his glare chilled her to the bone, for the man she thought she knew was as warm-blooded as a *Tyrannosaurus rex.*

"Skinner" is the prison term for a sex offender. That Denning was a skinner, there was no doubt. A man named Imi Lichtenfeld had known skinners too, though his adversaries were of the lampshade-making kind. Sexual predator or Nazi sadist, it mattered not when it came to the *effect* of *krav maga.* The irony of this situation was lost on everyone trapped in the Mummy Room, for if Mephisto hadn't sicked those Druid henchmen on Jenna Bond, her daughter wouldn't be armed for "contact combat" by the age of six.

The wheel comes around.

The Doctor, standing to Becky's right, had a grip on her hair at the back of her head. On her right foot, the girl spun counterclockwise into him, slapping her right hand onto his ass to provide the anchor, then—fist bunched the way Leo had trained her—Becky drove the piston of her left hand into Denning's testicles as hard as she could.

Pop! Pop!

Jenna's kid burst both his balloons.

They don't call it the "spinning ball-buster" for nothing.

The shriek wrenched from Denning's throat tore his vocal cords. So violent was the contraction of both hands toward his balls that the scalpel went flipping like a pinwheel over the mummy table to skitter across the floor toward the mouth of the stairwell tunnel. With the table between her and the razor-sharp weapon, Gill had to make do with what was at hand, so she seized the pear by the skinny neck, and as Denning doubled over in pain from the bunching of the muscles linked to his groin, she let him have it with the bulbous end.

It might have been Becky's spinning ball-buster that inspired Gill's swing, but more likely it was her Scottish family's tradition of attending the Highland Games in her formative years, when little Macbeth used to watch those bare-chested and kilted Highland hulks perform the hammer throw, spinning 360 degrees like Gill was doing now to build up g-force to let it fly.

The pear slammed Denning so hard along the side of his head that his crooked teeth tumbled across the Mummy Room like multiple pairs of gamblers' dice. His shattered skull caved in, stabbing splinters by the hundreds into his gray matter. So wicked was the blow that it stretched the Doc out on the floor, where he thrashed, twitched and convulsed in the grisly grip of death throes.

Gill's peripheral vision caught sight of a shadow in the mouth of the stairwell tunnel. She turned from Denning to see a figure crouching to retrieve the bloody scalpel off the floor, though why he desired it was a mystery to Gill, since the ghoul was packing a pistol in a shoulder holster.

"Run!" she yelled at Becky.

And Gill ran too.

Armed with the scalpel, the Undertaker followed.

Macbeth had a nice rack.

There were nipples to harvest.

INVADERS

Los Angeles

It is one of the anomalies of twenty-first-century policing that the FBI has yet to embrace geographic profiling. How ironic that those responsible for sharpening the cutting edge of psycho hunting on the dual whetstones of homegrown crime-linkage analysis and psychological profiling should let their blade rust dull because, for whatever reason—was it narcissistic pride?—they refused to import a foreign technique that other police forces around the world found easy to adopt. So that's why DeClercq found himself on the phone with a skeptical bureaucratic honcho in the Bureau's upper echelons in Seattle, embroiled in a time-wasting verbal tug-of-war over whether a forensic advancement developed by—in the chief's opinion—a near mathematical genius working with laws of probability provided sufficient reasonable and probable grounds for the FBI to get a warrant to invade Shipwreck/Ebbtide Island to search for Gill Macbeth. The special agent in charge of Seattle was on vacation in Europe, and while the usual SAC was away, Tug's primary concern was to cover his own ass.

"The British use it," DeClercq said.

"Yeah?" replied the skeptic. He was not impressed.

"It located the Mardi Gras Bomber, who terrorized Greater London. And it was instrumental in Operation Lynx, the largest police manhunt in Britain since the Yorkshire Ripper murders. The

Leeds serial rapist got eight life terms."

"Really?" said Agent Tug-of-War, still not impressed. "Because it works in Britain doesn't mean it works here."

"Scotland Yard has two geoprofilers. The National Crime Faculty has one as well."

"Figures," said the jingoist. "You being a colony."

"An *ex*-colony," corrected DeClercq.

"Yeah, then how come you still kowtow to the queen?"

The Mountie held the phone out at arm's length and glared at it. Was this blockhead for real? His blood pressure was rising.

"The BKA uses it. The Bundeskriminalamt. The Federal Criminal Police," Robert added, to make sure Tug understood.

"Germans," Tug snorted. "Sounds like something we whupped in *two* wars."

"Is the ATF more to your liking? You *have* heard of them, *haven't* you? The Bureau of Alcohol, Tobacco and Firearms? *They* use Rossmo's system. And so does the National Law Enforcement and Corrections Technology Center in South Carolina. What do I have to do? Start citing cases? There have been hundreds."

"You need to follow appropriate channels, Superintendent."

"*Chief* Superintendent," said DeClercq, with edge.

"Have you gone through Interpol? Did you check with the State Department?"

"I'm checking with *you*."

"You should follow protocol. And by the way, fella, don't lay that tone on me. If we're to gang-bust this island you're so hot about, there has to be a *legitimate* basis to get a search warrant. So let's cut the crap, shall we, you and me? If your voodoo system is that fucking good, how come the Bureau doesn't use it?"

DeClercq sucked in a deep breath and slowly let it out. "Are you or are you not going to help us?"

"I'll get back to you."

And the line went dead.

No sooner was DeClercq off his cellphone than the cellphone in Bond's pocket trilled. The contingent of cops who had flown down from the Pacific Northwest had crowded around the chief while he placed that important call to the Bureau in Seattle. Caller ID told Jenna this call was from the farmhouse on Orcas Island, so she moved away from the others for privacy. As she walked, she punched the Talk button to take the call, and before she could say the word hello, her mother's hysterical voice stopped her in her tracks.

"Jenna! Becky's been kidnapped! He grabbed her last night! I was tied up and gagged! I just got free! My arthritis . . . I couldn't . . . I couldn't untie the rope! Oh God, Jenna! I'm sorry—"

"Calm down, Mom!" Her stomach lurched.

"I'm sorry! I'm sorry! He took me by surprise! He said he wanted to kill me but had to let me live so I could deliver this message from his boss to you! He said to warn you it's payback time. And when we next see Becky, we won't *recognize* her!"

The gasp wrenched from Jenna's heart filled the squad room with palpable tension. Though she tried to hold them back, tears gushed down her cheeks.

"Describe him, Mom!" she demanded, her voice choking on the question while the cops who had crowded around DeClercq a short time before now crowded around her.

"Dressed in black. Pasty skin. With a lot of stubble. He looked like . . . he looked like—"

"An undertaker, Mom?"

Her mother sobbed so hard that she couldn't answer the question. Jenna held the phone against the jackhammer of her heart and turned to face DeClercq and Craven. "Mephisto has Becky. He says it's payback time. You know what he did to me. What will he do to *her?*"

A shudder shook Nick. He couldn't suppress it. Memories of his trip to hell flooded back.

"She's dead," muttered Jenna.

"We don't know that," comforted Nick, wrapping his arm around her. "Chief"—his eyes locked with DeClercq's—"where's Zinc?"

"He should be in a chopper approaching Ebbtide Island."

"And his orders?"

"To look for any signs of life on the island from the air and watch the sea around it for boats approaching or leaving until we can convince the FBI to go in."

"So we wait for hell to freeze over?"

"The island *is* in the States."

Jenna looked up sharply. "I could deputize him."

Behind her, for DeClercq to see, Craven held up his artificial hand and touched his prosthetic ear.

DeClercq thought of Gill.

And of Becky.

And if it was Katt who had been kidnapped.

He didn't need convincing.

Maintiens le Droit.

Maintain the Right. The RCMP motto.

He'd resolve things later, *after* the fact. When the U.S. Feds got their knickers in a twist—and knowing the U.S. Feds, they *would*—he'd tell them to pretend the island was China.

So as the others listened, he flipped open his phone and punched in the number that would send a call from Los Angeles to Air Services in Vancouver, and when the corporal on duty answered, he had him patch it through to the airborne chopper.

"Inspector," he said when Zinc Chandler came on the line, "this is Chief Superintendent DeClercq."

Zinc knew exactly what the formality meant.

"I have reasonable and probable grounds to believe that a mentally ill fugitive known as Mephisto, who is wanted for murders in both Canada and the United States, is holding two hostages—Dr. Gillian Macbeth and a six-year-old girl named Rebecca Bond—on Ebbtide Island. Time is of the essence, so consider yourself in hot pursuit. You have been deputized by the San Juan County Sheriff's Department to deal with an emergency. Who's with you?"

"The pilot, Ghost Keeper and the Mad Dog."

"Good. Land on the island and *take* that fucker."

Over Boundary Pass, British Columbia and Washington State

Zinc Chandler twisted around in the co-pilot's seat of the Bell 206 LongRanger and spoke into his headset microphone over the *whup-whup-whup* of the rotors, "Break out the arsenal, Mad Dog. We're gonna take the island."

"Whoa," said the pilot. "I'm captain of this aircraft. It's *my* ass on the line. And you expect me to invade the United States?" He pointed down at Boundary Pass, glittering with moonlight and starshine beneath the belly of the chopper. "The border's down there. Bisecting the channel."

Ghost Keeper leaned forward in the seat behind the pilot. "That's the trouble with you white men. You don't think broad enough. You see a border, and your people have been here for only two hundred years. My people have been here for at least ten thousand years, and when I look down on water, all I see is *water*."

That was little comfort. So the pilot had another go at Zinc to make him see reality.

"There's the *border,*" he insisted.

"Fuck it," said Chandler. "That's an order."

He was going in.

With the specialists.

CLIFFHANGER

Ebbtide Island

From the horror of the Doctor's convulsive demise in the Mummy Room, Gill and Becky ran next door to be confronted by the horror of the actress flayed à la Fragonard in the Plastic Surgery Room. The glass eyes of the skinned victim seemed to follow the pair as they passed through, and so frightening was the human monster to the six-year-old—what with all the multicolored blood vessels, milk ducts and bronchial tubes worming amid the bulging muscles, tendons and ligaments clinging to the exposed skeletal frame—that Becky froze in her tracks. Gill literally had to yank her off her feet to keep her going.

The Mummy Room and the Plastic Surgery Room were new additions to the old smugglers' vault, added since Nick Craven was held prisoner down there during the Burnt Bones case. Having entered the surgery room by its door to the Mummy Room, the fugitives exited by crashing through an alarmed door opposite. They found themselves in a tunnel bored into the rock during Prohibition times, a tunnel that hadn't changed an iota since rumrunners used it to smuggle booze from Canada into the States. Disarmed so the psychos could move Sleeping Beauty out of the Mummy Room, the alarm didn't go off when the pair breached that defense.

The tunnel was lit along one flank by torches in brackets, their smoky flames flickering from wind whining in off the sea. The mournful keening reminded Gill of a funeral dirge, and the funeral was going to be theirs if this tunnel was barred by an iron grate.

"This way," Gill said, leading Becky into the teeth of the wind.

Their shadows rose and shrank as they ran the gauntlet of torches toward the unseen sea. Their footfalls echoed in the clammy tunnel like a stampede. Where the tunnel met the smugglers' cavern, which was eroded into the cliff by eons of ocean waves wearing away its rocky face, the wormhole *was* barred by a cross-hatched grate to prevent trespassers from sneaking in by sea. However, a gate in the grate was unlocked and ajar, so the two were able to get through to the deep-water cave, where a motor launch was moored.

Let there be a key in the ignition, Gill prayed.

Her prayer was answered, but that was little help because someone onboard had already cranked the key and fired up the engine before the fleeing pair could reach the launch. Like a desert mirage that never moves closer to a thirsty wretch crawling across the sand, the boat stayed equidistant from them as the fugitives ran toward it.

Their last hope of escape was putting out to sea.

Mephisto had underestimated DeClercq. The premature activation of the tripwire hidden in the hollowed-out text in Denning's office had caught him by surprise. Chances were it would still be days before the Mountie homed in on Ebbtide Island—assuming last time's luck with Rossmo's geoprofile wasn't a fluke—but the psycho wasn't going to make that mistake again. Brinkmanship was okay, but don't get suicidal.

The shank of the day had been spent preparing to abandon Ebbtide Island. As always, the megalomaniac had a backup hideaway, so he and his two henchmen had carried Sleeping Beauty from the Mummy Room to the getaway boat while Gill Macbeth was being attended to upstairs in the clinic by its pampering staff. With the setting of the sun, the staff had left the island for the mainland in the chopper. With the mummy secure in the hold of the boat, it was time to play out the endgame, so while Mephisto prepared the pair of backup cages onboard to receive the two girls, the Doctor had scaled the stone steps to Gill's bedroom, where she would be dressing for dinner with the Director.

By now, Macbeth would have rejected Denning's advances. So he would have called on the Undertaker to help him force her downstairs to the Mummy Room, where they would have Gill strapped down naked to the central table. As soon as Mephisto joined them, Denning would use the pear to tear Macbeth apart inside. Then they would drag the progeric girl and Becky Bond to the boat and sail away from the island, leaving a bloody mess behind for DeClercq.

Wait a minute!

Hold the phone!

Something was wrong.

For as Mephisto stepped out on deck to go and watch Gill die, who did he see coming out of the tunnel with one of the caged kids but the same woman who should have been strapped to the table. She was carrying the pear as if it were a club, and hot on her tail in the distance was the Undertaker. The one thing Mephisto couldn't risk was losing Sleeping Beauty, so for that reason alone, he'd decided to set out to sea to weather this sudden storm. The sadist in him had a motive too, for how Gill's heart would sink to see her only chance of survival slip away. So with a grin on his devious face, Mephisto cast off the mooring lines and returned to the wheelhouse to crank the ignition.

Bon voyage, Gill, he thought.

See you in hell.

By the time Gill and Becky emerged into the chilly night, the escaping boat was a fading memory. With its depth sounder on, it had navigated the treacherous reef that once gave Shipwreck Island its menacing name. Having safely cleared the only channel that bisected the hull-tearing rocks, the boat had vanished around the side of this cliff the same way the moon lurked behind the overhead bluff. The sound of its engine was swallowed by the whine of the wind that whistled into the cavern and the breaking of black waves on black rocks that hardened the black shore.

"Climb," said Gill, pointing up the cliff.

Like Jonah coming out of the whale, the Undertaker emerged from the cave to find the shore deserted. His head craned right and left to search the cliff above, and there the two females were, struggling up its vertical face. The route they had selected was a zigzag crevice in the sheer drop, with handholds and footholds on both sides. However, the Undertaker knew an easier path that connected with the one now daunting the fugitives by means of a horizontal ridge across the slab of rock.

The scalpel clenched in his teeth like a cutthroat buccaneer, the man in black began to climb.

Gill Macbeth was ill-prepared for this survival ordeal. To scale the cliff, she was forced to throw the pear aside. What she wouldn't give for a cellphone now. Instead, weaponless, all she had was *her,* and she was next to useless in this mountain-climbing gear. A cocktail dress! Catchy and clingy in all the wrong places if you had a psycho killer hot on your ass. And speaking of psycho killers, *she* ought to hire one and have him take out whoever designs women's shoes. Sensible shoes, that's what she was in desperate need of now, not these goddamn, fucking spaghetti-strapped death traps on her feet, which at first she'd had no time to kick off, and which she later had to keep on to cope with rough terrain, shoes of any type being better than bare feet.

"Ooww!" cried Gill.

She had twisted her ankle, spraining it as she scrambled up out of the vertical zigzag crevice to cross the horizontal ridge wrinkling the cliff face.

The crippled leg crumpled.

Ending her climb.

Easy pickings.

Nipples was down.

Harvest time, thought the Undertaker.

The easy path had taken him up the cliff face quickly, eliminating the head start the fugitives had on him. The killer was inching over to the junction of the vertical zigzag crevice and the horizontal ridge, aiming to cut the females off at the proverbial pass. He was twenty feet away when Becky gained the ridge, hauling herself up out of the crevice like the little rock climber she was. First one hand, then two, and Nipples came into view, clambering up onto the horizontal ledge to join the kid. That's when she saw him, and winced away in fear, and twisted her dainty foot in those ridiculous shoes.

Whup-whup-whup . . .

In the distance.

Almost too faint to hear.

Scalpel in hand, the Undertaker closed in for the kill.

The Mad Dog was arming up.

In the early days, as you'd expect, the British armed the Mounted. The Adams and Enfield six-shot revolvers were habitually carried in reverse, on the left side, and were drawn across the body. The force, however, was the British army playing white hats vs. black hats, and cowboys and Indians in the Wild West, so it wasn't long before they switched to a more suitable gun.

No one manufactures a better sidearm than American armories, so from 1905 to 1954, the Colt New Service six-shot, .455 and .45 Long, attached to the new Sam Browne belt, was worn on the right side by the Mounties for a quick draw. Since 1954, the gunsmiths by appointment to Her Majesty the Queen have been Messieurs Smith and Wesson. First, they armed her Horsemen with the .38 Special six-shot revolver, and recently they converted that to the greater firepower of the nine-millimeter S&W Series 5946, fifteen rounds staggered zigzag in a double-stack mag with one in the spout.

That's what Zinc and Ghost Keeper were packing.

The first to pack semi-auto nines were the ERT squads, back when those in harness still wore the .38. Delusions of Bondian grandeur afflict kick-the-door-in supercops assigned to the force's emergency response team. To prove to the rank and file that they truly were a law unto themselves, they went European. So that's why the Mad Dog, maverick that he was, packed the Swiss-made SIG/Sauer P 226 nine-mill, its fifteen-round magazine "short loaded" by one to take pressure off the spring to ensure it wouldn't jam.

Tricks of the trade.

For long arms, however, America still won out. That was true back in the early days, when the rifle that was carried in a sling attached to the pommel of the California stock saddle on a Mountie's mount was the Winchester model 1876. That held just as true today, for the rifle the Mad Dog had pulled from the carryall that served as his portable armory was the Remington 700. He was feeding it .308 Winchester cartridges when Zinc turned around in the co-pilot's seat and barked into his headset microphone above the noise of the rotor blades whirling overhead, "See 'em, Ed? Three of them? About thirty feet up on the face of the cliff?"

"Climb!" Gill shouted.

"I'm scared! Don't leave me!"

"I'm hurt," Gill said. "I can't go on. But *you* can get away. Save yourself. Climb!"

From where she lay crippled on the rocky ledge, a little more than thirty feet up from the wave-washed shore, Macbeth pointed up the cliff where the zigzagging crevice climbed all the way to the bluff. To her right, the Undertaker was closing in fast, the still-bloody blade that had slashed her earlier gripped in his fist.

"Climb!" Gill ordered with anger in her voice, which frightened Becky into a burst of tears, but . . .

Whup-whup-whup . . .

Closing in from the sea . . .

And . . .

Crunch . . .

Six feet . . .

Crunch . . .

Five feet . . .

Closing in from the right . . .

That scared the kid enough to galvanize her into continuing her climb.

Becky vanished into the upper crevice.

Four feet short of Gill, the Undertaker swiveled ninety degrees to face the threat from the sea. Seen front on as it approached from Canada, the Bell 206 LongRanger looked like Huey, Louie or Dewey Duck: big-eyed cockpit windows with a small bill. As it neared the cliff at the same level as the horizontal ledge, the pilot brought the chopper around to hover out of ground effect above the seething brine. His back to the cliff, the killer faced the livery markings along the port side. Red and yellow stripes up near the rotor, a thick swath of blue the length of the fuselage and, displayed on the white belly under that, the bison-head crest of the RCMP.

The crest low down on the rear door began to move.

Feet spread wide in a shooter's stance and aiming out to sea, the Undertaker drew the pistol from his shoulder holster and, scalpel back in his teeth to give both hands to the gun, opened fire.

"I've got him," yelled the Mad Dog, kneeling on the floor of the chopper behind Zinc's seat, the weight of his body against the rear door to wedge it open so he could aim the rifle through the gap between it and the doorjamb. The Remington was hard against his shoulder and his eye was to the scope.

The pilot sat to the right of Zinc, his left hand on the collective-pitch lever to control the height of the chopper, his right hand on the cyclic-pitch stick to govern direction, his feet on the anti-torque pedals to work the tail rotor to neutralize the effect of spin from the main airfoils. The nose was into the wind to keep them up. The attitude, or tilt, of the fuselage was level to hover effectively. The tail was angled toward the cliff to give Ed a shot.

It was a balancing act.

On a high wire without a net.

His head craned back to witness the result of the Mad Dog's shot, Zinc Chandler felt his imagination shoot back to those Saturday movie matinees with the Rosetown Rustlers at the Hitching Post in the Saskatchewan of his farm-boy youth. This was a cliffhanger if ever there was one. There was a cliff and a damsel in distress, and here in the nick of time to pick the bad guy off came thundering in the cavalry of the Royal Canadian Mounted Police.

King of the Royal Mounted.

Zane Grey would have been proud.

That thought, however, barely had time to gel in his mind when—*Thud! Thud! Thud!*—the fusillade from the bad guy's gun peppered the chopper with lead. One of the slugs zipped in through the wedged-open door, missing the Mad Dog's neck by an inch as his finger closed around the trigger. But the bullet hit the pilot's neck dead-on as it bored diagonally through the cockpit, blowing a wash of arterial blood onto the exploding windshield.

You might get nine lives in fantasy.

But not in real life.

From Ghost Keeper's point of view in the cabin behind the pilot, the effect of the incoming shot was dramatic. The pilot's death threw his body forward onto the cyclic-pitch stick, which flopped that control over hard to the front right, which caused the rotor disk above to pitch in the same direction, which whipped the chopper around in a downward spiral, the centrifugal force of which hurled the Mad Dog out through the open door as he took the shot.

The shot went wild.

The Remington flew from his hands.

And the airborne Mountie plummeted toward the waiting sea.

The force of the violent jerk to the right also caught Zinc Chandler by surprise. With no time to brace himself against the sudden whiplash, he smashed his skull hard against the fuselage wall, knocking himself unconscious.

Down the chopper plunged into the rock-strewn sea, its reaction to the wrenched controls so precipitous that the turbine screamed in protest and the rotors were bent, buckled or torn off by striking the waves. One blade slashed down through the shattered window to hack off the head of the pilot and bowl it caroming about the cabin.

Within a minute, the Bell sank like a stone.

The Undertaker ejected the spent clip from the butt of the nine and slammed in a new mag armed with body-armor-piercing steel bullets, but before he could pull off another round, the chopper had corkscrewed out of the sky into the sea.

Four feet to his right, Gill lay face up on the ledge, which was a ten-foot-wide shelf at this point. Her jaw was clenched with pain from her sprained ankle and her eyes were aghast with concern over who was in the downed chopper. She was breathing hard from exertion, fright and agony, and that made her chest heave up and down. The flimsy bodice of her dress provided no protection against the chilly wind, her nipples ripe for the plucking.

Three feet . . .

Two feet . . .

One foot . . .

The killer stood over her.

Gill gasped from pain when he stepped on her injured ankle. Then his other foot stepped on her other ankle to pin her legs down, ensuring the impossibility of a kick to his groin. Bending forward from his waist toward her supine head, the crown of which extended over the edge of the cliff so her hair hung down like Rapunzel's, he pressed the muzzle of the gun to the hollow above the bridge of her nose between her eyes. Then, with a deft clutch of his other hand, he tore the bodice of the dress away to expose her breasts.

The moon peeked over the crest of the bluff above. As lunar light caught the stark fear etched in Gill's eyes, the lunatic reached up to fetch the scalpel clamped between his teeth. Four fingers snaked around the steel so his opposable thumb could meet the blade, then his hand began to lower toward one of her nipples.

"Blink and I'll blow your brains out."

So obsessed was the Undertaker with nipping Gill's nips in the bud that he made a big mistake.

The *same* mistake as Denning.

He overlooked the kid.

By now, Becky Bond could have been halfway up the crevice to the bluff. However, the sharp rebuke by the pretty lady when she'd balked at doing what was good for her had reminded the precocious imp of previous stern words from her mom, and that had triggered a memory of their little chat about what she should do if she ever ran into a bad man who meant her harm.

"If you get into a jam and I'm not around, promise me that you'll stay calm and think, think, *think*. You think, you watch, you look for an opening, and when it comes, you *act*."

So instead of being halfway up the crevice to the bluff, Becky was *in* the crevice behind this boulder, watching the drama come to a head on the ledge in front of her and looking for an opening so she could *act*. Like the opening she saw now.

For while Gill was staring up in fear at the moon playing peeping Tom over the lunatic's shoulder, Becky's eyes were locked on a moon of a lower kind—namely, the jutting ass of the Undertaker as he bent over the injured woman. And seeing that opening, she knew it was time to act, so using all the strength in her short legs, Becky burst—hands outstretched—from the crevice and shot across the narrow ledge to give the bad man a Mighty Mouse push, which propelled him into the empty air above the rocky beach—and her along with him.

As if touched by an angel, Gill watched the ghoulish gunman take flight, catapulting over her head and over the edge of the ledge, a shock that wrenched a

Y
A
A
A
A
A
A
!

from him all the way down.

Then she was shocked to see Becky follow him into outer space, the kid passing weightlessly over her like an astronaut leaving the shuttle for a space walk. On reflex, Gill caught a leg as it went by and was able to clamp a lifeline around Becky's ankle. The jerk that reeled the kid back from almost certain death nearly tore Macbeth's arm from its socket. It took all her strength, all her weight and the anchor of her other hand grasping hold of an outcrop on the ledge, but Gill held on for dear life.

It was a cliffhanger.

Literally.

Becky banged into the rock and dangled upside down by one leg against the sheer drop of the cliff face.

Nothing bleeds like a head wound.

The Undertaker lay broken and bloody among the rocks where the sea met the shore. His legs were shattered from his landing feet first to break his fall, and bones stuck out through mangled flesh. The gash across his forehead gushed blood into his eyes so copiously that he could barely wipe them clean enough to see before a red refill topped them up once more. You'd think the pain was so severe that he would pass out, but the Undertaker was driven by a compulsion for revenge, and he used that vendetta to focus his psychopathy on the kid.

There she hung, from the cliff above the rocky beach, and here he lay, among the surf-sprayed rocks with the nine-millimeter armed with steel slugs still gripped in his hand.

All that kept him from picking off the guinea pig was this wound gushing blood in his eyes.

Bam!

Bam!

Bam!

The Mad Dog had made a choice that was no choice at all. Hurled from the helicopter into the offshore fathoms, he had luckily missed the submerged rocks. His eyes had broken the surface to find two calamities under way: the chopper was down in the sea and sinking fast, and a child was hanging upside down from the ledge above the shore. Brother cops might drown if he didn't swim to their rescue, assuming those trapped inside had survived, and the child was in imminent peril of plummeting headfirst onto the rock-strewn beach if the shooter he couldn't locate didn't plug her first.

What to do?

There was a time before this era of the paper-pusher when RCMP recruits came straight off the farm or out of the woods with the light of Jesus in their eyes and a sense of sacred duty embedded in their Canadian hearts. Well, them days are gone, Gertie, for all but a dwindling few, and the Mad Dog—the son of a Yukon trapper raised in the arctic woods—was one of the last throwbacks to that time.

His duty wasn't to brother cops.

They knew the risk.

His duty was to the kid hanging from the cliff.

So, coming out of the sea like a Second World War marine in the South Pacific, Ed Rabidowski hit the beach for this suicide run. With the SIG sweeping the waves in case he spotted the shooter and his other arm thrown wide for support from the eroded cliff to keep him from slipping on the wet rocks, the Mad Dog took off in a desperate dash that would take him across the shooting gallery.

With no backup.

Gill's grip on Becky was slipping. The arm that held her hanging down the sheer drop of the cliff was the arm that Denning had wounded with the scalpel. The stress of the girl's weight was tearing open the slash, and blood seeped down Gill's arm to her hand. The jagged edge of the ledge cutting into her armpit was putting her arm to sleep, so pins and needles ran up and down Becky's lifeline. The slightest shift in Gill's vise-like grip on the child's ankle let slippery blood—my, how it slipped!—trickle into her tired grasp.

The kid was about to fall.

The Undertaker was perfectly positioned for the kill. As he wiped another wash of blood from his eyes to fire shot four at the dangling girl, he caught sight of the Mad Dog struggling along the slippery shore from the right to try to catch the guinea pig if she took a head dive.

The rock to the Undertaker's right was higher than the rock to his left, so it shielded him from any shots by the cop. The cop was a moving target, with no protection from the nestled killer he couldn't see.

The Undertaker had him.

He took a shot.

Bam!

The Mad Dog slipped on slime and fell to his knees.

Pingggg! A slug ricocheted off the cliff face beside him, chipping the stone where he'd have been except for the slip.

As he scrambled to his feet, his head jerked up.

This was it.

The kid was in free fall.

He dropped the SIG.

And ran for Death's door.

"No!" Gill cried as Becky slipped away.

From the ledge, she watched the girl plunge headfirst toward the rocks.

The kid was coming down.

The cop was coming in.

They were both on a collision course with a *third* trajectory.

With his left arm across his brow to staunch the blinding blood and his arm with the nine extended to line up the shot, the Undertaker had a bead on the collision point.

He couldn't miss.

The chopper had crashed into the deep-water channel through the shipwrecking reef. As it sank into the stygian depths, Ghost Keeper, shaken but still stirring, had popped his seat belt and crawled on his hands and knees to unbuckle the unconscious Zinc Chandler. The now headless pilot had modified the LongRanger from its original design by removing the panel that kept the cockpit separate from the rear compartment, just in case of an emergency like this. With his foot, Ghost Keeper had stomped the Plexiglas window out of that side. Then, with one hand plugging Zinc's mouth and nose, he had hauled the concussed inspector out of the sinking chopper and up to the surface of the sea.

Bam!

Bam!

Bam!

That's when he heard the shots.

On either side of the deep-water channel were reefs with jutting rocks. Swimming toward the action, the Cree found a foothold and stood up waist-deep in the ocean. His right arm was hooked around Chandler, who hung slumped like a rag doll, and with his other hand, Ghost Keeper drew the Smith.

An intriguing theory about right-brain–left-brain thinking: the two hemispheres of the cerebral cortex see the world differently. The right is creative, imaginative, perceptive and spiritual. It grasps whole things and overall patterns. The left is logical, analytic, deductive and scientific. It gets down to nuts and bolts. The theory is that Natives think primarily with the right side of the brain and whites think predominantly with the left. That's why the two cultures were doomed to clash.

When Native people rode into battle, back when this land was theirs, warriors used to shout, "It's a good day to die." What Ghost Keeper saw for the Mad Dog was a good death, for he was stumbling along the shore in a desperate bid to catch the cliff-hanging kid while someone unseen took a shot at him. These two Mounties, however, were locked in a contest of one-upmanship, so the Mad Dog had backup he didn't know he had. The good death was fine, on Ed's *own* time, but it wasn't going to happen on Ghost Keeper's watch.

Whites may have conceived the Smith.

But the Cree knew how to *use* it.

The steel bullet ricocheting off the rock created a spark. That spark in the dark, where the cliff's overhang prevented the moonlight from masking it, registered in the right hemisphere of the Cree's brain. He was hunting on instinct, as he had learned on his spirit quest in the woods as a boy, and that spark gave him the outer end of the bullet's trajectory.

Yes, there it was.

The muzzle flash.

Against the black background of that rock in the surf, which would protect the shooter from any return shot the Mad Dog took but left him open on this side.

The Cree extended his left arm and turned the Smith sideways. He lined the gun sights up with the point of the ricochet spark and followed the straight line of the slug's trajectory back to the muzzle flash. Adding two feet for the gunman's outstretched arm and jigging the Smith a bit to line up with the phantom head, the Cree knew instinctively where the shooter was, for though he couldn't see him, his right brain had grasped the overall pattern.

In the world of fantasy, the shooter thought *he* had the Mad Dog.

But in reality, the Cree had *him*.

Continuing the sweep of the Smith along that trajectory, Insp. Bob George pulled the trigger as fast as the ejection port could spit spent shells. He laid down a line of fire as withering as the deadly barrage of a machine gun, and he knew in his gut that it had cut across his target's head. The air above the offshore rock was suddenly filled with moonlit mist like that blown from the blowholes of the pods of killer whales that make these waters their year-round home.

It wasn't the Fountain of Youth.

It wasn't the Fountain of Age.

It was the Fountain of Life.

Spewing dry.

He wasn't going to make it. The gap was too large. The falling kid would hit the rocks before he could run under her. But the Mad Dog had played enough football to know what you do in a crunch like this. If you can't run it, you try a dive. Launching himself off one of the rocks, the sergeant threw himself into a tackle, twisting his body face up as he flew under the plummeting girl and caught her with the shock absorbers of his muscular arms. As he buffered her with his torso and was slammed hard against the ground, the Mad Dog heard the ribs cracking down on both sides of his chest.

WASTE AWAY

Los Angeles
March 29

The Vancouver, Seattle and Los Angeles papers for the past week were spread across the desk in the front room of the mansion perched on the hills above Hollywood. The papers were full of stories elaborating on the aftermath of the Mounties' invasion of Shipwreck/Ebbtide Island. The U.S. Feds, as DeClercq had expected, took him to task for his "illegal" decision to breach their sovereign jurisdiction, but the chief had routed them with the support of an unexpected ally. Sheriff Hank Bond—reelected twelve times in a row by the good citizens of San Juan County—was a local legend. The rumor was that his daughter, Jenna, had her eye on the old man's job, and her stance before the media was that she had deputized the Mounted Police to deal with a law-enforcement crisis after the Feds—in the person of the Bureau honcho in Seattle—refused to act. The San Juan County sheriff was not about to be upstaged by a can-do amazon whom he might find himself running against, so he told the Feds outright—by way of the media pens and cameras—that sheriffs have *always* had the power to raise a *posse comitatus*—the posse of the county—to assist them in preserving the peace. He'd thank the Feds to keep their Eastern bullshit out of the West.

And what about our heroes?

Those kings of the Royal Mounted?

The force never misses a chance to pump its legend up LARGER THAN LIFE. If you want that Oscar for Best Police Myth, you must promote the colors. Not for nothing had the RCMP once signed a marketing deal with Disney. So there was Sergeant Preston—sorry, Rabidowski—of the Yukon in his hospital bed, his chest bare to show off his muscles and his multiple cracked ribs, informing the world that all he had done was his duty, and that on recovery, he was looking forward to a trek into the Headless Valley with his close friend Inspector Ghost Keeper—"a Plains Cree, you know,"—whom he was sure would teach him a thing or two about the wilds.

As for Insp. Zinc Chandler, who had led the charge, the blow to his head was worrisome because of a previous injury in the line of duty, so he had been told by his doctors to take a well-earned rest. He was going to recuperate in the South Pacific.

There would be no recuperation for the corporal who piloted the chopper. He would join that thin red line of Horsemen who had lost their lives in the line of duty, and for him the force would put on a red-serge funeral, the most colorful sendoff there is among cops, complete with a riderless horse for his "last ride," with jackboots placed backward in the stirrups, spurs to the front. In grandeur, that procession would rival *any* Hollywood spectacle, and remind those adrenaline junkies caught up in the straight-shooting fantasy that the scarlet of the red-serge tunic is the color of real-life blood.

And then there were the kids.

Becky and Anna.

The photo of Becky Bond in one Seattle paper showed her holding the hand of an elderly Jew named Leo, who had instructed her in the art of *krav maga.* It was a sad comment on this day and age, read the sidebar piece, that our children must be taught how to protect themselves.

The most poignant reunion, however, was that of the progeric girl, Anna, with her mom. The child was wasting away so quickly from that cruel aging disease that every minute they had together was as precious to them as a day was to most families.

The savior who had delivered Anna into the arms of her mom was Dr. Gillian Macbeth. When she was asked if she had anything to say about how the ordeal she had survived might change her outlook on life, her cryptic reply was, "Beauty *isn't* skin deep, and I think it a crime that Hollywood brainwashes women into thinking it is. I bought into the fantasy, and now I'm ashamed of myself, which is ironic—don't you think?—since the reason I fell for the cure-all panacea of going under the knife was so I *wouldn't* be ashamed of the *real* me."

That was a bit of a downer, seeing as how she looked so damn good. Even though Gill was forty, with T&A like hers, she might get lead work in the movies for another year or so.

Ah, well.

Time to call it a wrap.

All in all, the case had an almost-perfect Hollywood ending.

None of that, however, was of interest to Mephisto. His attention was focused on the photo of DeClercq. Snapped a few years ago during the red-serge funeral of Insp. Jack MacDougall, it had captured him as the commander of the coffin-bearers. Resplendent in his scarlet tunic and world-renowned Stetson, with his service medals on display, the chief, as officer in command, wore a sword slung from a frog supported by a strap over his right shoulder. He might as well have been the Iron Duke facing Napoleon at Waterloo.

Mephisto nodded.

A worthy adversary, thought the megalomaniac.

You've not seen the last of me, chief.

And when we meet again, it will be at Death's door.

From the desk, Mephisto crossed the room and exited through the French doors to the open-air terrace and azure blue swimming pool that overlooked Hollywood. With his back to the mansion and his arms crossed on top of the balcony's rail, the psycho's guest leaned over the precipitous drop to watch the sun set on the beautiful people who rushed hither and yon, up and down Sunset Boulevard.

"Well?"

"Tell me again. What's my half of the bargain?"

"You'll change how I look," Mephisto said, "with plastic surgery. And you'll complete the research you began years ago."

"What about the nasty stuff?"

"I'll take care of that."

"Really? Any woman I want?"

"Pick and choose."

This was the third time these two had met. Their first meeting had occurred by chance outside Dr. David Denning's Eternal Spring clinic in Vancouver, at which time the Director—always on the lookout for useful henchmen—had slipped the former Dr. Ryland Fletcher his business card. Their second meeting had also taken place in Vancouver, at that city's priciest restaurant while the Undertaker was taking care of the porn king, Wolfe Capp, in his Yaletown studio. The Director had told the renegade doctor that the Panacea Clinic could use a specialist with training similar to that of Dr. David Denning: a plastic surgeon with a biotechnical background aimed at discovering why we age. Would Dr. Fletcher be interested in that kind of work?

Yes, Fletcher had told the Director, he certainly would. Currently down on his luck as a result of those allegations made against him in Los Angeles by two scheming porn queens, he was looking for work—with no questions asked—wherever he could find it. A job for an old client meant he had to fly down to L.A. the next day, but perhaps as soon as he returned they could meet again.

Mephisto's original plan had been to use Fletcher in several ways. If the LAPD connected the Picasso murders there a few years back with the new mutilation murders in the Pacific Northwest, it wouldn't hurt to have a handy lightning rod around to attract their initial suspicion—a disgraced plastic surgeon from L.A. with a penchant for raping porn queens, who might now be moving up the Hollywood victim ladder—and that would alert Mephisto to the fact that the police were closing in. Alternatively, two heads, as they say, are better than one. After their initial meeting outside Eternal Spring, Denning had filled Mephisto in on Fletcher's background. Just as Denning and Fletcher had once worked together in that L.A. biotech lab at trying to solve the puzzle of what causes human aging, Mephisto realized it might advance his doomsday scheme to team them up again. If something happened to either one, he would have a spare doc to carry on researching.

And then there was the question of how to satisfy Mephisto's half of the deal with Denning. In return for the Doctor's creating and releasing the Franken-gene, the Director had to deposit one million dollars in an offshore bank account, *and* provide Denning with the opportunity and means to wreak carnage on the put-down queens he lusted after from among his patients. And finally, when Denning's lack of restraint brought danger from the police, Mephisto had to take the Doctor out of his everyday life.

How would he do that?

He'd change the Doc's ugly looks.

And since Denning couldn't operate on himself, Mephisto had to find a renegade plastic surgeon who—no questions asked—would do the job.

Thus his second meeting with Fletcher at the restaurant.

Much of that plan, as things had turned out, was now frustrated and in disarray.

The consequence?

Time for Plan B.

Late that afternoon, the former Dr. Ryland Fletcher had been drowning his sorrows in a beer by himself in a strip club on Sunset Strip, fantasizing about a night visit to the naked lovely onstage, when a voice behind his left shoulder—the shoulder on which, in cartoons, that little devil lurks to wage his whispering tug-of-war with the moral angel on the right—had whispered in his ear, "The tits and ass in this town could make a grown man cry."

Startled, Fletcher turned.

The chameleon behind him was already starting to metamorphose. Dark hair was sprouting in a widow's peak and stubble had been shaved to form a Vandyke beard. By the time he was hirsute, the Director would resemble Mephistopheles.

"I still want you to work for me," Mephisto said, taking the chair across from Fletcher in the dingy club. "In exchange, you won't believe what I'll do for you."

"Oh? What's that?"

"Drink up. Let's take a drive."

The car in which they took a spin was a red Ferrari. As it wound up into the hills overlooking Hollywood, Fletcher listened as Mephisto outlined their prospective deal. "Denning told me all about your lust for porn queens. I'll supply them, if that's what you want, but I think it's time you moved uptown. This city attracts the finest women from around the world, the best of the best who hope to make it in Hollywood. What would you like to do to them if you could?"

"Anything?"

"Anything. Sink as deep as you desire."

Every man has his price, and Mephisto had found Fletcher's. That deal-closer for which a Faust will sell his soul to the Devil. Now, gazing down from the terrace of the hilltop mansion at Hollywood cowering submissively at his feet, the plastic surgeon was itching to go on his first shopping spree on Rodeo Drive. Eenie, meenie, miney, moe, who'll be my first collected ho?

"I'll do it."

"This calls for a toast," said Mephisto.

The "Nile style" of the twenties had gripped Hollywood. It began with Rudolph Valentino's dark, sensual bedroom eyes in *The Sheik*, an erotic image so potent that it turned women into rapists, compelling the most brazen to storm Falcon Lair, his Benedict Canyon home, where not even a surrounding wall could make them take no for an answer. Just one hour of lovemaking with their idol would be enough to carry them through an entire lifetime, they told the security guards who caught them scaling the wall or prowling through the mansion. Finally, Valentino had to resort to dogs—three Great Danes, two Italian mastiffs and one Spanish greyhound—to keep them back. The Sheik was a stud who got all the female tail he wanted, and not only did that inspire Sheik condoms, which are still going strong, but it also motivated the silent-era Hollywood mogul who commissioned this mansion to design a bedroom called the Harem.

"Here's where you'll do it," Mephisto said, leading his lusty Faust through the fantasyland of this wet-dream palace in Hollywood Babylon to a decadent Roaring Twenties boudoir that could be a brothel at a desert oasis. The mirrors were strategically placed to capture the action on the sheik-size bed, as were the cages built to hold the collected harem. They were fitted with an assortment of disciplinary devices to keep those who watched willing to perform. On a pedestal table at the foot of the bed sat an Egyptian perfume lamp that would fill the boudoir with fragrance if it was switched on.

"Abracadabra," said Mephisto, withdrawing a remote control from his pocket and aiming it at one of the mirrors. "Open sesame," he commanded as the mirror swung back to reveal an antechamber to the afterlife.

The secret hideaway dated from the decade when Tut's tomb was discovered in Egypt's Valley of the Kings, so its kitsch harked back to the mythical Land of the Pharaohs. The murals on the walls depicted the court of Osiris, king of the dead, where spirits passing through Death's door into the afterlife had to justify their deeds on earth if they were to loll forever in the Field of Reeds. Here was Anubis, the jackal-headed god, weighing the heart of the mummified deceased against a feather. Here was Thoth, the ibis-headed god, with his scroll to record the result. And here was Ammit, Eater of the Dead, hungry for the hearts of those who flunked the feather test.

Who knows what hijinks went on in this mansion in Hollywood's early days, for the Egyptian throne in the center of the antechamber was positioned so the mogul could ogle the action in the Harem through his one-way mirrors. But whatever hanky-panky had gone on in the past, it was nothing compared with what Mephisto schemed for the future, for if there was a lesson to learn in Hollywood, it was that every hit production deserves a sequel.

That's why Sleeping Beauty lay naked in the stone sarcophagus to one side of the throne, in place of the fake Egyptian mummy that was originally used to decorate this pharaonic fantasy.

That's why Dr. David Denning's research notes into the Fountain of Age were piled on an authentic Egyptian embalming table, waiting for Ryland Fletcher to complete his work.

And that's why there were side-by-side cages in the darkest corner of this charnel house. Tacked above one cage was a movie poster of little Shirley Temple in *Susannah of the Mounties,* surrounded by Hollywood horsemen in red serge. Above the other cage—Mephisto's private joke—was pinned a computer-generated version of the same poster, with the innocent face of the classic child star transformed into that of a crumbling old crone.

"Here," said Mephisto, handing Fletcher a glass. "There's Scot in my background," he added, holding out a bottle of whisky and splashing in single malt.

As the men locked arms to down the drams, Fletcher caught sight of the fires of hell burning deep in the brimstone pits of this madman's hypnotic eyes. He suddenly knew that there was much more to this deal than he had bargained for, and that Mephisto had a brand-new plan hidden up his sleeve. But in far too deep to turn back now, he sold his soul to the Devil and wondered what hell on earth would come out of this conspiracy. As Fletcher snapped back the dram, Mephisto winked at the aged Susannah of the Mounties on the wall.

"To youth," he said. "May it *waste* on the young."

AUTHOR'S NOTE

This is a work of fiction. The plot and characters are a product of the author's imagination. Where real persons, places or institutions are incorporated to create the illusion of authenticity, they are used fictitiously. Inspiration was drawn from the following non-fiction sources:

Airey, Douglas, and Duncan Hazeldene. *Great British Pubs.* Bordon, Hampshire: John Hine, 1988.

Anger, Kenneth. *Hollywood Babylon II.* New York: Dutton, 1984.

Blatner, David. *The Joy of Pi.* London: Penguin, 1997.

Cannon, Lou. *Official Negligence: How Rodney King and the Riots Changed Los Angeles and the LAPD.* New York: Times Books, 1997.

Casson, Lionel. *Ancient Egypt.* New York, Time-Life, 1965.

Coleman, William P., III, C. William Hanke, William R. Cook Jr. and Rhoda S. Narins. *Body Contouring: The New Art of Liposculpture.* Carmel, IN: Cooper, 1997.

Collins, Peter I., Gregory F. Johnson, Alberto Choy, Keith T. Davidson and Ronald E. MacKay. "Advances in Violent Crime Analysis and Law Enforcement: The Canadian Violent Crime Linkage Analysis System." *Journal of Government Information* 25 (1998).

Cox, Bill G., et al. *Crimes of the 20th Century: A Chronology.* Lincolnwood: Publications International, 1991.

Davidson, Keith. *Criminal Behavior Analysis.* RCMP, unpublished.
Davis, Richard, ed. *The Encyclopedia of Horror.* London: Octopus, 1981.
The Editors of Consumer Guide. *The Best, Worst, and Most Unusual: Horror Films.* New York: Beekman House, 1983.
Edwards, I.E.S. *Tutankhamun: His Tomb and its Treasures.* New York: The Metropolitan Museum of Art and Knopf, 1976.
El Mahdy, Christine. *Mummies, Myth and Magic in Ancient Egypt.* London: Thames and Hudson, 1989.
Finley, John M. *Considering Plastic Surgery?* Gretna, LA: Pelican, 1991.
Gates, Daryl F., and Diane K. Shah. *Chief: My Life in the LAPD.* New York: Bantam, 1992.
Gaute, J.H.H., and Robin Odell. *Murder "Whatdunit": An Illustrated Account of the Methods of Murder.* London: Pan, 1982.
Gelfant, Benjamin. *Cosmetic Plastic Surgery: A Patient's Guide.* Vancouver: Flapartz Press, 1997.
Gibson, Pamela Church, and Roma Gibson, eds. *Dirty Looks: Women, Pornography, Power.* London: British Film Institute, 1993.
Greene, Gerald, and Caroline Greene. *S-M: The Last Taboo.* New York: Grove, 1974.
Groth, Nicholas A. *Men Who Rape: The Psychology of the Offender.* New York: Plenum Press, 1979.
Hazelwood, Robert R., and Ann Wolbert Burgess, eds. *Practical Aspects of Rape Investigation: A Multidisciplinary Approach.* Boca Raton: CRC Press, 2001.
Horrall, S.W. *The Pictorial History of the Royal Canadian Mounted Police.* Toronto: McGraw-Hill, 1973.
Kimmel, Michael S., ed. *Men Confront Pornography.* New York: Meridian, 1991.
Lockwood, Charles. *Dream Palaces: Hollywood At Home.* New York: Viking, 1981.
McGrew, Patrick, and Robert Julian. *Landmarks of Los Angeles.* New York: Abrams, 1994.
Minneapolis City Council. *Pornography and Sexual Violence: Evidence of the Links.* London: Everywoman, 1988.

Murphy, Danielle. "Top R&R Spas." *Vancouver Lifestyles Magazine* vol. 7, issue 6 (2000).

Newman, Peter C. *Titans: How the New Canadian Establishment Seized Power.* Toronto: Penguin, 1998.

Northorp, Bruce, and Les Holmes. *Where Shadows Linger.* Vancouver: Heritage House, 2000.

O'Toole, Laurence. *Pornocopia: Porn, Sex, Technology and Desire.* London: Serpent's Tail, 1998.

Pringle, Heather. *The Mummy Congress: Science, Obsession, and the Everlasting Dead.* Toronto: Penguin, 2001.

Reader's Digest. *Quest for the Past.* New York, Reader's Digest, 1984.

Richardson, David. *Pig War Islands: The San Juans of Northwest Washington.* Eastsound: Orcas, 1990.

Roberts, Paul William. *River in the Desert: Modern Travels in Ancient Egypt.* New York: Random House, 1993.

Rosenfield, Paul. *The Club Rules: Power, Money, Sex, and Fear—How It Works in Hollywood.* New York: Warner, 1992.

Rossmo, D. Kim. *Geographic Profiling.* Boca Raton: CRC Press, 2000.

Rubin, William, ed. *Pablo Picasso: A Retrospective.* New York: Museum of Modern Art, 1980.

Russell, Diana E. H. *Dangerous Relationships: Pornography, Misogyny, and Rape.* Thousand Oaks: CA, 1998.

Sde-Or (Lichtenfeld), Imi, and Eyal Yanilov. *Krav Maga: How to Defend Yourself Against Armed Assault.* Berkeley: Frog, 2000.

Simpson, Keith. *Police: The Investigation of Violence.* Estover: Macdonald and Evans, 1978.

Spoto, Donald. *The Dark Side of Genius: The Life of Alfred Hitchcock.* New York: Little, Brown, 1983.

Stenson, Fred. *RCMP: The March West.* Nepean, ON: GAPC Entertainment, 1999.

Sullivan, Jack, ed. *The Penguin Encyclopedia of Horror and the Supernatural.* New York: Viking, 1986.

Suzuki, David, and Peter Knudtson. *Genethics: The Ethics of Engineering Life.* Toronto: Stoddart, 1988.

Tompkins, Peter. *Secrets of the Great Pyramid.* New York: Harper & Row, 1971.

Tyldesley, Joyce. *The Mummy: Unwrap the Ancient Secrets of the Mummies' Tombs.* London: Carlton, 1999.

ViCLAS. *Crime Analysis Report.* Ottawa: RCMP, 1998.

——— *Field Investigator's Guide for Completion of the ViCLAS Booklet.* Ottawa: RCMP, 1999.

Weigall, Arthur. *Tutankhamen and Other Essays.* London: Thornton, 1924.

Wilson, Larry. *Violent Crime Linkage Analysis System (ViCLAS).* Ottawa: www.rcmp-grc.gc.ca, 1998.

Wolf, Leonard. *Horror: A Connoisseur's Guide to Literature and Film.* New York: Facts On File, 1989.

My thanks to the cyber cops of the real "Special X," who showed me how they hunt a serial killer in the twenty-first century. Especially to Staff Sergeant Christine Wozney of the Mounted Police and to Detective Inspector Kim Rossmo of the Vancouver Police, who allowed me to fictionalize them so shamelessly in Slade's parallel universe. They're DeClercq's kind of cop.

Slade
Vancouver, B.C.